GHOULS DON'T SCAMPER
BOOK 6 OF THE VALKYRIE BESTIARY SERIES

KIM MCDOUGALL

Hardcover ISBN: 978-1-990570-12-4
Paperback ISBN: 978-1-990570-11-7
eBook ISBN: 978-1-990570-10-0

Version 2

FICTION / Fantasy / Urban
FICTION / Fantasy / Paranormal

ABOUT THIS BOOK

CRITTER WRANGLER RULE #17: EVEN THE SMALLEST CREATURE CAN BE BIG IN MAGIC.

Kyra Greene never thought she'd return to Asgard. Not after she burned the only bridge home. Now she has no choice. With her unborn child's life at stake, she must find a new route to the old world, or die trying.

Asgard will bring up ghosts of her past and Kyra will have to atone for her crimes, but none of that is as important as saving the life of her child—until a ghoul infestation threatens the very fabric of Asgard itself.

Can Kyra find the source of the ghouls before Asgard becomes the next Terra and falls into a war of magic and demons?

Ghouls Don't Scamper is Book 6 of the Valkyrie Bestiary Series. With over 2000 five-star reviews, readers say Valkyrie Bestiary is "very funny," "a sweeping adventure," "a slow-burn romance," and more than one reader has said, "I want to be a supernatural pest controller too!"

ALSO BY KIM MCDOUGALL

Valkyrie Bestiary Novels
Dragons Don't Eat Meat
Dervishes Don't Dance
Hell Hounds Don't Heel
Grimalkins Don't Purr
Kelpies Don't Fly
Ghouls Don't Scamper

Valkyrie Bestiary Novellas
The Last Door to Underhill
The Girl Who Cried Banshee
Three Half Goats Gruff
Oh, Come All Ye Dragons

Hidden Coven Series
Inborn Magic
Soothed by Magic
Trigger Magic
Bellwether Magic
Gone Magic
Hidden Coven: The Complete Series

Shifted Dreams Series(Writing as Eliza Crowe)
Pick Your Monster
Lost Rogues

CHAPTER

1

It was a perfect day, one of those warm October days that make you believe winter will never come. I sipped my allowance of coffee from my favorite snail mug. The current coffee shortages—due to a failed crop in Montreal's protected greenhouses—made limiting my caffeine intake easy. I enjoyed it on the patio overlooking the barn and the vegetable garden. I'd been fussing over the garden all summer. Now it was yellow and brown and in no need of my attention. There was something satisfying in that.

Gleeful squeals floated up from the car park. The goblits, Tums and Tad, were teaching my new ward, Raven, how to play soccer. From the barn, where my many rescued critters were now comfortably housed, came the faint wail of a banshee. Gita was doing her morning chores. Far from being unsettling, the wail was as comforting as a lullaby.

Beside my table, our two feline roommates were napping on the warm paving stones, not exactly cuddled together, but not disdaining each other either. Willow was finally accepting the new cat in our lives, and Grim seemed to enjoy imitating a simple house cat for Willow's sake.

I sipped my coffee. Such a perfect day.

My belly was full with a warm breakfast. My womb was full too. The baby was still no bigger than a kidney bean, but the magic of a new life tingled along my veins.

Mason stepped onto the patio and caught me patting my stomach.

"How's Little Bean this morning?" He swept my hair aside to kiss my neck.

"Busy growing arms and legs."

"Sounds exhausting." He sat at the table and poured himself coffee from the carafe. Every Sunday, Dutch baked for the week, so we had fresh muffins and scones this morning. Mason would choose a cheese scone and slather it with strawberry jam like he did every Sunday.

"How's the morning sickness?" he asked.

"Better. I think I might actually keep my breakfast down."

"Good." He reached for a scone, and I passed him the jam with a smile. He paused as he sliced the scone and grinned with one eyebrow quirked upward. "What's so funny?"

"Not funny. Just happy. I like this." I waved to the patio, the table, the house. "I like having breakfast with you and knowing that you'll bypass the muffins and go right for the scones."

"Hmmm." He frowned over a mouthful of scone. "I don't want to be predictable. Maybe I should change my diet."

He pulled me onto his lap and roared as he pretended to bite my neck. It was so fast, I didn't have time to squeal. One minute, I was sitting in my chair, the next I was wrapped in essence of Mason. His hands found my butt and gave it a good squeeze as he nipped and kissed his way down my throat. I was laughing too hard to protest. I squirmed on his lap and suddenly his kisses slowed and became more serious. I turned my head, meeting his lips with mine. And I opened to him.

Kissing Mason was like nothing I'd ever experienced. Every time. It didn't matter that we were now comfortable enough to share a bathroom or that I knew exactly what he wanted for breakfast. The feel of his lips on mine was like coming home and being shot to the moon at the same time.

His tongue teased mine, hands let go of my hips to tangle in the loose hair around my shoulders. He cupped the back of my head, drawing me closer. My fingers fumbled with his freshly buttoned shirt...

A wheezing noise stopped us. It escalated to masterful gagging, then a retching cough. Mason and I side-eyed the night sun jaguar masquerading as a Maine Coon who was trying to bring up a hairball not ten paces away. The retching crescendoed to a truly glorious hacking upchuck. Grim's ribs shuddered and he produced a trichobezoar the size of a golf ball. His green eyes gazed at us accusingly over his prize, then he flicked his tail and sauntered off.

Mason leaned his forehead against my chest. His shoulders shook with silent laughs.

"I think that's the cat equivalent of 'Get a room!'" I slid off his lap and found my own seat again.

"He's probably right. The patio is no place for what I want to do to you." Mason's grin was decidedly wolfish and sent a little thrill zinging through me. Then he sighed. "But I have to get going, I suppose."

It was Sunday, but that didn't matter to the new Prime Minister of the Alchemist Party.

"Big day ruling the world?" I asked.

"Oh, you know, busting heads and taking names."

He'd been Prime Minister for three weeks already. I was glad to see he hadn't lost his sense of humor among all the red tape.

His widget hummed. He glanced at it and frowned. "It's Ramona. I have to take this." He rose, already thumbing the screen. As he walked inside, I heard him say, "I'm on my way. What's up?" He disappeared down the hall to our bedroom, cutting off the conversation.

Ramona Becker was his new Deputy Minister. It seemed a trivial title for a woman who'd been in politics for nearly fifty years, and Mason had chosen her for that experience. She knew everyone in the biz, and he relied on her to help him navigate his first months in office. She also had an uncanny ability to disturb our peace at the worst possible moments.

The childish shouts coming from the front yard shifted from playful to outraged. I listened for a moment, hoping the boys would sort out the problem themselves. I started counting to ten but made it only to six before the arguing spiraled to yelps of pain and fear.

I shot from my seat and ran to the front of the house. Tums lay on the ground with a split lip. He was a gangly goblin with large pointed ears that poked through his curly hair. His twin, Tad was furiously defending him against Raven who had his head bowed and was pawing the ground like a bull ready to charge. Princess lay in the dust with her nose on her paws. She whined and licked her lips. Her three favorite people were in trouble, and she didn't know which one to protect.

"What's going on?" I demanded.

Tums pointed at Raven. "He hit me!"

"He said my wings were stunted." Raven's eyes were black fire.

"They are!" Tums said and Tad nodded vigorously. Raven loomed over the smaller boys. When he'd first arrived, he wasn't much bigger than the goblit twins, but in the weeks since, he'd sprouted at an unnatural rate. His thirteenth birthday was only few months away. He didn't look like a teenager yet, but at least he didn't have the physique of a six-year-old anymore. One white forelock stood out against the shaggy black hair that fell over his forehead and almost covered his glowering eyes.

I adopted my reasonable voice and turned to Tums and Tad. "Raven's wings are just fine." Tums scowled. I turned to Raven. "No matter what he said, that was no reason to hit him." Raven scowled. Back to the twins. "Now don't you two have lessons this morning?" The goblits nodded and slunk off.

Raven picked up the ball and stared forlornly after the boys.

I sighed. He was still withdrawn and cranky, and nothing I did changed that. I would be cranky too if I'd been pulled from the only world I'd ever known and forced to live with strangers. But still, I wished my attempts at trying to bond with him were more successful. Mason was better at reaching him. They spent hours together in the alchemy lab in our basement. When I asked Raven what they were working on, he only shrugged.

My hand strayed to Little Bean. I was so not ready to be a mother. So far my kid negotiations were like peace talks—no one ever got what they wanted.

Mason came out the front door, jacket on and widget still pressed to his ear. He disconnected the call and headed toward us.

"*Salut, mon homme,*" he said to Raven. "You and the twins playing ball?"

Raven's lip curled in true adolescent disdain. He threw the ball into the bushes and ran into the house.

"What's up with him?"

"Fight with the twins. We really need to make a decision about school. He's bored more than anything."

Mason frowned. "About that…" His tone told me I wasn't going to like what came next. "You're going to have to interview that second school on your own. My trip to Manhattan just got pushed up."

"What? When?"

"I leave tonight."

Damn and damn. Mason's first big diplomatic trip had been booked for the end of the month. I was still dithering about going with him. A trip to Manhattan Ward would be amazing, but Mason could use alone time with Kester Owens, our demon friend from Manhattan. He didn't need me around while Kester mentored him on mastering his new dark magic. Still, a trip to Manhattan...But now the choice was taken from me. I couldn't organize my schedule in time to leave tonight.

I didn't like being left behind. Mason and I were a team. But I had to console myself that he'd be fighting with words and diplomacy in Manhattan. Swords and bug traps were more my thing.

"What happened?" I asked.

"The trade union is putting pressure on the Senate to get the trains running full time by the new year." Until now, only soldiers and delegates like Mason used the one railroad that ran between Montreal and Manhattan.

He saw the look on my face and pulled me into his arms. "I'm sorry. I know it's short notice. But I'll only be gone a few days. When I get back, we'll make a decision about school for Raven. I promise." He leaned down and spoke to my belly in a stage whisper, "Take care of your mama, Little Bean."

He kissed me, held me tight for so long I thought, and hoped, he might never let go. Then he got into his car and drove off.

And just like that, my perfect day ended.

CHAPTER

2

OSCAR LEWIS, ALCHEMIST inventor and former Prime Minister of the Alchemist Party, lived in a swamp. I drove along a causeway between cedar groves steeped in black water. Late fall leaf litter mottled the water's surface. Even with my windows rolled up, the earthy stench of stagnation and rot filled the truck. I wouldn't have been surprised to find an ogre wading through the mire.

"Peee-eew!" Jacoby held his nose. My sentiments exactly.

The smell didn't deter my dervish apprentice for long. He plastered his nose against the passenger side window and peered into the gloom between trees. Every job was exciting to Jacoby. I wished I could recapture some of his novice enthusiasm, but morning sickness had stolen my passion. I drove with one hand on the wheel and the other pressed to my lips as if that could keep my breakfast from splattering all over the windshield.

I stopped the truck. The way ahead didn't look any different—dark, dismal and damp—but I keened a ward dissecting the road. Jacoby felt it too. He turned his gaze forward, his eyes wide and pupils dilated in the dim light.

"Angry magic." The furred fringe around his eyes bristled.

"Just a ward. Oscar warned me about it." I punched a quick message into my widget: *We're here.* A moment later, the angry magic popped and the ward disappeared.

We drove on.

The causeway ended, the trees opened up, and we left the swamp behind. Ahead, a gravel road ended at a house that looked like it had been plucked out of seventeenth century England. Great slabs of gray stone were dotted with arched windows and sweeping balustrades. I half expected a butler in livery to greet us when I parked by the grand front doors, but it was only Oscar who stepped out.

He wore jeans and a faded gray sweatshirt. White hair fluttered in a ring around about his mostly bald head. I'd never seen him in anything other than business attire, and he looked even more gnomish than usual. He waved as I got out of the truck. Jacoby jumped out too. Our feet crunched on gravel as we walked toward the door.

"Sorry to make you drive all this way," Oscar said by way of greeting. "But I thought it would be better to run these tests here rather than my lab in the city."

"I appreciate the discretion."

In exchange for Oscar's help breaking into the Grandill prison, I had promised he could run tests on my ward-breaking sword. I held the blade out to him now. It was eerily quiet in my hands, and had been so since my cousin used up all its magic to rid herself of a rare biological curse.

"You might find it hard to test though. It seems to be…dormant." I shied away from the word "dead." My sword couldn't be dead. That would be like carrying around a dead limb. My sword was an extension of me. I wasn't ready to give up on it yet.

"Let's give it a try anyway." Oscar rubbed his hands. A cool wind had blown up overnight, blustering away the warm weather. "If it doesn't work, I have Gunora's sword too."

That surprised me, but it shouldn't have. Hub had confiscated her sword when Gunora was arrested, but no one had Hub connections like Oscar. And without a Valkyrie to wield it, the blade would masquerade as an antique hunk of junk. If Oscar asked for it, Hub probably hadn't seen the need to turn him down.

I don't know what I expected of Oscar's house, maybe a foyer with an elegant staircase, a parlor done up in chintz and rosewood. This wasn't that. Inside, the place had been gutted to create one enormous space. Steel girders ran along the unadorned ceiling. At least a dozen separate work stations dotted the room. Cables hung above these in great snaking tangles. A staircase of iron and cement led up to a dark loft.

I stood in the open doorway, the wind whipping at my back, and stared in amazement.

"You live here?"

"Work mostly. There's an apartment up there if I need it." Oscar pointed to the loft. "Now let's see what that little knife of yours can do."

Oscar shut the door and we headed deeper into his lair. It really was a lair. I expected to find a lab-coated, hunch-backed Igor puttering around. We passed several work stations with unfinished projects laid out—robots in pieces, great glass distilleries, something that resembled a dune buggy with wings, and a raised bed of mushroom-like growths under a red lamp.

We stopped at a cast-iron contraption with a chimney. A glass pot filled with dark liquid rested on it.

"What's this?" I asked. "Some new magical compound?"

Oscar grinned. "Coffee. A rare treat these days. Want some?"

"No, thanks." I'd already had my one cup for the day. I stopped my fingers before they reached for my belly. Mason and I hadn't told anyone about Little Bean yet.

Jacoby had stopped by a hanging solar system display. The planets turned slowly around a glowing sun.

"Don't touch that!" I said as his multi-knuckled fingers reached for the shiny globes.

"Oh, he can't hurt it," Oscar said. He gulped down his coffee then waved me over to another work station.

"You'd be surprised," I mumbled. Jacoby had a knack for disaster. I grabbed the dervish by his shoulder and steered him to follow Oscar.

My teeth hummed as we neared a ping-pong table set up in an open space. Instead of a net, a small ward dissected it. The magic shield rose about six feet in the air and shimmered like oil on water.

"I've done some tests with Gunora's sword already." He waved to a vise bolted to the table that held Gunora's sword, poised to pierce the ward.

"That won't work."

"I know. Under my hand, the sword's inert. Call it a baseline. I want to see what you can do."

Memories tugged at me and I closed my eyes for a moment to dispel them. Another alchemist from Underhill had tried to break the secrets of the Valkyrie sword. He'd been willing to kill to do it. I wasn't sure I wanted to go down this road again.

When I opened my eyes, Oscar was watching me with concern.

"What exactly are you trying to prove with these tests?" I asked.

He frowned and considered me for a long moment, like he was deciding on how much truth to tell me.

"Does Mason talk to you about the current state of affairs in Montreal?"

"Not much. I know the godlings are still making noise about wanting their own party. And the trade union is being a pain. He left for Manhattan yesterday just to appease them."

"Hmmm. I'd heard that trip was moved up. How're you doing on your own?"

I shrugged. "I was alone a long time before Mason. I'll be fine."

Oscar's expression suggested he wasn't buying it. Then he swept a hand toward the mini ward. "What I want to do here is test the ward technology for weaknesses."

"Why? These are the only two Valkyries swords in Montreal. In the world, as far as I know. What harm could they do?"

"The opji are on the move agin." Oscar's eyebrows bunched together. "Hub scouts have been tracking their movements in the Inbetween. We're not really sure what it means."

"Nothing good." The opji vampires had been harassing Montreal since its inception. Once the ward was established, they turned to hunting outsiders and homesteaders. They captured humans and kept them as breeding stock. A year and a half ago, they had almost succeeded in breaking through our ward, thanks to a rebellious fae prince.

"Since that fiasco with Leighna's brother," continued Oscar, "they have a taste for sweet Montreal blood. And recent infrastructure analyses show that our defenses have some weaknesses. I hope that by understanding how your sword cuts through magic, I might detect these weaknesses and fix them before they become an issue."

It sounded like a long shot, but I was no alchemist. "Okay. Where do we start?" He pointed to Gunora's sword. "First, I want to see you cut through that ward. Then maybe we can figure out why your sword is dormant."

TWO HOURS LATER I'd cut through Oscar's mini ward dozens of times while he captured the results on a variety of scopes, thaumagauges and cameras.

He doused the ward in different powders and had me try again. Every time I sliced through it, he simply grunted and reset the test.

Jacoby and had long ago fallen asleep on his back under the model solar system.

"Again." Oscar waved to the ward without looking up from his thaumascanner.

I winced. I was exhausted. Gunora's sword was unfamiliar and its magic jangled incoherently inside me. But it was all in the name of science and saving my ward from vampires, so I raised the blade again. My hand shook. I pressed the blade's tip against the ward, and grating magic buzzed along the nerves of my arm, right into my skull. The edges of my vision clouded. My heart beat in that run-away horse-and-carriage manner that usually happened before I fell into a seizure.

"I can't." I lowered the blade. "I'm sorry. It's too much." I gasped and hiccuped, trying to regulate my breathing. "I've never had a magic overload since…" I stopped short.

Oscar raised one bushy eyebrow. "Since what?"

I sighed, laid the blade on the table and crossed my arms over my stomach. "I'm pregnant."

Oscar's eyebrows convulsed, conveying expressions that ran the gamut from surprise to joy to anger. "Why didn't you tell me?" He ran for a chair and shoved it against the back of my knees, so I collapsed into it.

He shoved a bottle of water at me, then grabbed it back.

"Juice! You should have juice!" He dashed over to a small fridge and came back with a bottle of apple juice and a tin of biscuits.

"Stop fussing," I said. "I'm fine. Just tired."

Oscar pushed the tin toward me anyway. I chuffed out a ragged laugh but took the food. Little Bean was hungry enough to gnaw through my backbone. I gobbled two biscuits and downed half the juice.

Oscar pulled up another chair and sat frowning. "You shouldn't have let me push you so hard in your condition."

"I didn't see the harm. I'm pregnant, not sick. It's only that sometimes too much magic sort of overloads my circuits."

"Right." Oscar slapped his hands on his knees. "No more tests for you."

"I'm sorry. I really do want to help."

"I know. And you will. When it's safe to do so. And here I thought your odd mood was just from missing Mason." His eyes went wide. "He does know, doesn't he?"

I smiled. "Yes. He knows."

"Good."

"I was supposed to go to Manhattan with him, but we decided against it."

"I agree. The train is a marvel, but travel through the Inbetween is still hazardous."

The sugar in the juice and cookies steadied my keening, but I still felt drained. Instinctively, I reached for my sword, but got no boost from it.

"I don't suppose you have any way to test this sword?" I handed it to Oscar. He ran a finger along the sheathed blade.

"How long has it been dormant?"

"Since Grandill. Gunora abused its store of magic and since then, it hasn't...um...spoken."

Oscar raised an eyebrow. "And it usually talks to you?"

"Yes. Not in words, of course. But I can always feel it, you know? Like the presence of another person in the room. And sometimes it hums. Only now I can't and it doesn't."

"I see." He gave me back the sword and turned off the mini ward with a flick of a switch on a nearby generator. "Well, you've given me some good data today. Maybe analyzing that will bring insight into this problem too."

I rose, feeling a little unsteady on my pegs. "Can I ask a favor? It's a big one."

Oscar paused as he was tidying the work station. "If it's in my power."

"When you're done with Gunora's sword, can I have it?"

His eyebrows shot up. I was asking him for confiscated Hub goods.

"I suppose I can tell Hub it's inert, magic-wise. That's true enough in anyone else's hands. Why?"

My hands strayed to Little Bean again.

"She'll need it one day."

"You're so sure it's a girl, then."

"I am." I smiled, suddenly sure. I was having a little Valkyrie.

he screen froze on Mason's frown. I had to hide a smile at the deep crease between his brows. Then the Ley-net caught up to our conversation and unfroze the screen.

"…you overdoing it. Oscar told me what happened yesterday. Kyra, promise me you'll take it easy."

"I am taking it easy. See this is me, feet up, resting in bed." I panned the camera across the bed with Jacoby snoring in a heap to prove it. In fact, I was tired, and I'd already asked Emil, my new office manager, to postpone all my bookings for a few days.

"And I'm going to talk to Oscar about being a tattle-tale," I said.

"He's just worried about you. So am I."

"Right back at you."

Mason was pale and haggard-looking.

"I hope you haven't been out partying with Kester," I said.

He smiled and shook his head. As a senator and head of the committee set up to oversee the railroad expansion, Kester would be an important part of the delegation that greeted Mason in Manhattan, but he wasn't much of a party animal.

"But seriously, have you been able to work with Kester…you know, on your *other* project?" I didn't want to announce Mason's demon issues over the Ley-net. The line probably wasn't tapped. Probably. But he was Prime Minister now, so I decided not to assume anything.

A hint of a smile flickered over Mason's face. "Yes, Kester has been very enlightening."

Good. In the Nether, Mason had been blessed by a demon masquerading as a god. The blessing turned out to be an ability to reanimate the dead, a useful talent but a dark one. Mason didn't want any surprises when he tried to tap into this new magic, and I couldn't blame him. I was glad Kester could help.

"I'm looking forward to going home," Mason said.

"One more day." The delegation would be heading back by train in the morning.

"One more day," he agreed. "Try to stay out of trouble until then."

"You too."

We signed off and I wandered down the hall to Raven's room. He was reading something on his widget by the last light coming through the window. I resisted the urge to tell him to turn on a lamp.

"I'm going to head down to the barn and help with the evening feeding. Want to come?"

"No."

I lingered in the doorway.

"Are you hungry? Want a snack before dinner?"

"No."

If I asked him if he had two eyes and ten fingers, he would probably say "no."

"Okay, supper will be in about an hour."

"Uh-huh."

"Maybe tomorrow you and I could do something together. Go into the city?"

"Sure." He didn't look up from his widget. I took another minute to study him. It seemed like he grew an inch every day. Even with my limited Mom experience, I knew that adolescents were prone to growth spurts, but this was something else. Mason and I theorized that the magic-dampening field on Grandill had stunted his growth. Now free of it, his body was quickly regrouping. It must be exhausting. After what he'd been through and with all the changes he was still experiencing, I could forgive the sullenness. For now.

I left him to his reading.

Muzzy and Tak, two of the older goblin children, didn't really need my help with the evening feeding, but I liked to spend time with my critters. I decided to make a pitstop in the kitchen first to feed the insatiable Little Bean.

A pot of savory pasta sauce boiled gently on the stove. An apron-bound

Dutch held a wooden spoon poised over the pot, but all his attention was on the small vid-screen above the counter.

A breaking news flash banner scrolled across the bottom of the screen.

"What's going on?" I asked.

"Not sure." Dutch pointed at the screen with the spoon. "Some kind of protest. It came over the Ley-net as an alert, but it's not from any regular news channel."

I leaned in to get a better look. Dozens of people were gathered by a wooden building in the dying light. Their faces were covered with brightly colored scarves.

"Who are they?" I asked.

"The Saivites," Dutch said. "Damned godlings are up to no good again."

"That's a railroad behind them! Where are they?"

"Somewhere south of Hedge," Dutch confirmed, naming the shanty town outside the South Gate.

"In the Inbetween? Is this live?"

"Seems so." Dutch had lost all pretense of cooking. We stood riveted to the drama unfolding onscreen.

Someone was filming as the mob's leader spoke. I turned up the volume to hear the tail end of his rant.

"We will no longer wait for the slow wheels of democracy to turn in our favor. No one is listening to our calls for action, but we demand to be heard!"

The man turned away and the camera zoomed into the scene behind him.

An explosion lit the twilight. The camera jerked and tilted. Someone off screen swore. Smoke filled the air. The cameraman's voice was ragged as he narrated.

"It's done! The rail line is broken!" He swiveled the camera again to the leader's face. Only deep brown eyes showed through his scarf.

"You will listen now! Your trade unions won't have access to the south. Come and fix your railroad and we'll derail trade in another way. We won't stop until all citizens of Montreal have a voice in Parliament!"

Screams echoed behind him. The cameraman was running now. Someone shouted "They're here!" The sounds of blasters crackled from nearby. The camera panned down, showing the ground racing by, then it went black.

Dutch and I stood in silent shock, staring at the blank screen. Then he quietly reached out and turned off the stove.

"I'll go see what the regular news channels are saying." He headed into the living room to turn on the bigger vid-screen behind the desk.

I found my widget on the side table under Grim's swishing tail.

"Something going on?" Grim asked.

"I'm not sure. It could be a hoax, but it looks like the godlings just blew up the railroad."

"Is that all?" Grim stretched and yawned, showing off his impressive fangs. He jumped down and went out the cat door to the back yard.

I called Gabe. It went straight to voicemail. Gabe had left his job as my office manager to return to his family's business—business that was tied closely with the Saivites. But surely he wouldn't be stupid enough to fall in with these terrorists?

I left a quick message. "I hope you're watching the news at home and not part of this madness going on outside Hedge." I disconnected, then called Mason. Again, I got voicemail, and again I left a message. I hung up and gripped my widget in two hands.

This was bad. Really bad. I could feel it, like the first rumblings of a distant storm.

Dutch and I watched the news reporters scramble to get information on the developing story. After the sun went down, Berto and another Guardian came over from the guardhouse to watch too.

I called Oscar. No answer.

On the screen a reporter outlined how a group of godlings had taken hostages at a railroad outpost about fifty kilometers south of Hedge. They'd blown up the generators that kept the ward line between Montreal and Manhattan running. And finally, they'd destroyed a section of railroad.

Luckily, Hub militia had been in the area, patrolling the farms that fed Montreal. When they arrived at the outpost, the guards had already tried to fight back against the godlings. Three guards were dead. Hub captured several "godling terrorists," as they were being called.

My widget buzzed in my hand. I looked down to see Gabe's message flash across the screen. "At home. Did not go to the party."

Hmmm. Gabe thought someone was watching his messages too. I sent him back a smiley face. His family was deeply involved in the godling uprising, but the Saivites were divided in their approach. Gabe's group were

19

trying to negotiate peacefully, but others were too impatient to wait for change. Tonight they had murdered to prove their point. There would be no going back now.

Raven wandered in, looking sleepy and rumpled. He watched the drama on the screen for a few minutes, then said, "Is there food?"

If only I could ignore people-made crises with the ease of a cat or a teenager.

I put a pot on to boil for the pasta. My widget was never far from my fingers as I waited for Mason to call. Twenty minutes later, I dumped a bowl of pasta and sauce on the table and gave everyone instructions to help themselves. I could only pick at my food.

Raven sat in the breakfast nook, watching the drama unfold in the news.

"What's all the fighting about?" he asked.

"A group of citizens wants power and they think this is the best way to get it," I said.

Raven nodded. "The kelpies blew up a barn once. That's how they got power. Blowing up stuff always works." He slurped his noodles.

"Not always." This wasn't a lesson I wanted him to learn. "Sometimes it just shows desperation."

"Papa said desperation was as good as anger for winning a fight."

I spared him a look of disbelief, but this wasn't the time to try and undo his father's misguided—if necessary—teachings.

The evening dragged into night. Mason still hadn't called. The reporters were short on information. The explosion had damaged one of the Apex stones that generated Montreal's ward, but alchemist leaders made assurances that the ward was in no danger of going down.

Two godlings were identified. Ishir Kadam and Dimitrios Dukas. And now the pundits were speculating that the Saivites and the Olympians had put their grudges aside to work together.

Near midnight a commotion outside had me jumping up from the couch. I'd fallen into a doze. On the video screen, the pundits were still trying to decipher what this new godling outburst would mean for the rest of Montreal.

Dutch stood by the patio door. He put a finger to his lips and made a "be still" gesture with his other hand. The only light in the room came from the video. Outside it was even darker, with no moon or stars to light the way.

Two figures—one burly, the other scrawny—stepped from the shadows beyond the patio.

I released my pent up breath. Angus dragged an irate Raven by the elbow with one hand and carried an assortment of weapons in the other.

Dutch opened the door and Angus shoved the boy inside.

"Caught this little blighter in the weapons locker, red-pawed and guilty as a feathered fox. Look at the goods he was 'bout to sequestrate."

Raven yanked his arm from Angus's grip. "What does any of that even mean, you freak!"

"Raven! Don't talk to Angus like that!" I was appalled by his rudeness, but my mind was like butter and couldn't come up with anything less confrontational.

Angus leaned in and poked Raven on his bony shoulder. "It means you have no business with our guns and knives."

Raven jerked away.

"Mason would have let me! He'd understand. I deserve to be armed too. What if those godlings show up here tonight? Besides, I've been playing with weapons since I was a kid."

I sighed. As if he were so grown up now.

"You don't need to be scared." I reached for him, but he pulled away.

"I'm not scared." Raven crossed his arms over his chest. In the low light, his eyes were near black.

"The wards around the house are excellent. And the Guardians will patrol all night." I took a knife from Angus and handed it to Raven. "Here. Put that under your pillow. Between that and the hell hound on the end of your bed, no one will mess with you."

"Fine." He shot a parting glare at Angus before heading down the hall to his bedroom.

"I'm sorry," I said to Angus. "His politeness muscle could use some exercising."

"Oh, och. E's just a wee pigeon flexing 'is wings. No harm done."

Angus might have seemed all right, but his accent always thickened when he was really worried.

I was about to question him about our defenses when my widget finally buzzed. I grabbed it, hoping to see Mason's face, but the screen was black. Only his voice came through, distant and tinny.

"I tried to call before, but the lines were down. Are you okay? Everyone is safe?"

"We're fine." Just hearing his voice filled me with relief, like being doused by a warm shower after a day in the cold rain.

"You should stay out of the city for a few days," he said. "There may be some backlash to all this. And I'm going to tell Angus to keep the Guardians close to home."

"Angus is right here. They already know. You don't have to worry about us. Just get home soon."

There was a long pause. "That's the thing. I don't know when I'll be home now."

I closed my eyes, trying to ward off the panic filling my lungs. I'd known this was coming. It would take a day or two to fix the railroad.

"When?" I whispered.

"I don't know. It's not just the road. They blew up a couple of generators. Those will take longer to fix."

"When?" I repeated.

"A week at least." I could hear voices in the background, then Mason said, "I love you. I'll be home as soon as I can."

"Love you too," I said, but he was already gone.

I stood by the patio door, with my forehead pressed against the cool glass. Outside, the wind had picked up, tossing red and yellow leaves around like confetti.

Most of the godlings had escaped Hub's soldiers. They'd be fleeing through the Inbetween now. Fifty kilometers of dense forest lay between us and the rail station. Surely, they would never make it this far, but I was glad to spot one of the Guardians flying over the trees behind the house. They would patrol all night long, and tomorrow, I would reinforce the wards around the house. I could do no more tonight other than go to bed, stare at the ceiling and worry until I finally slept.

I woke to complete darkness and knew immediately something was very wrong.

ight came from thin cracks around the window blinds. The wind had turned into bluster, and branches scraped against the bricks. I listened for noises other than the usual household creaks and groans. Something had woken me, but I had no idea what.

A spasm shivered down my spine, not a pain, exactly. More like a shifting of gears. Or like I was a violin strung too tightly, and someone had just twanged my strings. Fearing a miscarriage, my hand clutched my stomach, but the tiny life was still strong and humming with the pure joy of new existence. It was too early to feel her move, but something *had* moved me.

I'd been dreaming before my rude awakening and the murky images came back now. I'd been standing on that hill again—the one I'd seen in the instant after Gunora tried to infect me with her blood. Thousands of women gazing upward. Their stares were…voracious. They would devour me given the chance. Only their leader held them in check.

She was beautiful and terrifying. Primeval. She danced—no…prowled around me, and I had to pivot in a circle to keep her in my sights. Turning my back was not an option. Her long black braids, streaked in white ash, masked her expression but not her black eyes. They were like staring into the space between the stars.

Another shudder went through me from the roots of my hair to the nails on my toes. I gasped and clutched my throat until the spasms left me wilted and spent.

Suddenly too hot, I threw off the bed covers and groped for my glass of water on the bedside table. I gulped it all down. The empty glass slipped from my grasp and hit the carpet with a thud.

The dream of the thousand women led by one primitive and powerful queen had haunted me since Gunora's failed attempt to pass the Maid Mother Crone curse onto me. At first I'd assumed the spirit queen was Terra, guarding the gates to her realm. And the women? Were they Terra's disciples or her warriors?

Either way, I'd felt a solidarity with them, as if they were the silenced voices of all women, and when Gunora's spell failed, I assumed they protected me too. But as time went on and I saw their faces in my dreams, they felt less and less protective and more hostile. And had that even been Terra? How could I know?

I wrapped a blanket around my shoulders and huddled into it. The wind whipped against the window, slashing the house with bits of debris. A wail followed in its wake, long and low and mournful.

Gita was awake.

In recent weeks, she'd taken to prowling the dark and filling it with her cries. When I asked her what it meant, she couldn't tell me. Or wouldn't.

I shivered and dug deeper into my blankets, but sleep wouldn't come. My eyes kept popping open to watch the shadows of branches quivering outside my window.

And now I had to pee.

Might as well get used to it, I thought. Soon Little Bean would be getting me up every night.

I sighed and sat up again.

When Mason was away, Jacoby often slept on the end of the bed, but I found him sprawled on the rug across the bedroom doorway. Sweet. My dervish was guarding my door while I slept. I wasn't the only one on edge after this night's news.

I was too tired to find my slippers, so I padded barefoot to the adjoining bathroom wearing only my sleep shirt and panties. In my half-asleep state, I banged my thigh on the bedpost, jerked my leg up in response and whacked my knee too.

"By the one-eyed ghost!" I cursed in a whisper and limped on. My sense of balance was still asleep. I hobbled to the bathroom and stubbed my toe on the threshold. I cursed again and collapsed heavily onto the toilet seat.

Minutes later, while I washed my hands, I studied my haggard reflection in the mirror. I looked awful. Light from the high window threw ghastly shadows, and my eyes were lost in pockets of darkness. I wish I could say the same for my chin. Maybe it was just the shadows, but it seemed swollen.

I flicked on the switch. Nope, not just the shadows. In fact, I had two chins, one sagging below the first like a pouty little lip.

What the…what?

I stretched my neck, trying to smooth away the creases on it. No good. Then I examined my face. Lips full. Eyes large and bright. Round cheeks with a new dimple on the right one. I looked like I'd gained ten pounds since dinner. The effect was startling. I wasn't exactly fat. I looked solid. One might say hearty. Or matronly.

Oh, no.

No, no, no.

My hands went to my breasts and squeezed.

Ouch. They were full and tender, too much so for a first trimester pregnancy. My hips were wider too. That's what had thrown off my balance.

That's what had woken me.

My body had made its first Maid Mother Crone shift while I slept.

I sank to the cold tile floor. This couldn't be happening.

I'd been so sure that Gunora had failed in her attempt to pass on the curse. But why? Why hadn't I even considered the possibility that she'd succeeded?

Because that possibility was unthinkable. And now the unthinkable had happened. My boobs weren't sore because I was pregnant. They were sore because I'd suddenly turned into the archetypal Mother.

It had been weeks since Gunora's attack on Grandill Island. How long until the next shift? Days? Hours?

Pain shot through me.

The spasms cut like a garroting cord. I couldn't breathe. The face in the mirror melted and stretched. Hair sprouted white and wild. Wrinkles crackled around my eyes and lips.

The Crone.

And the shifts kept going.

Light burst from under my skin. Cheeks plumped and turned rosy. Crows feet retreated. My hair cascaded around my shoulders in a halo of shining auburn waves.

The Maid.

I felt eighteen again.

It didn't last.

The spasms wouldn't let go, and I shifted once more, regaining the curves and the sturdy matron looks.

Fear froze the marrow in my bones, and I clutched at my stomach, sending my keening deep like the sonar of an old-time submarine.

Silence.

Then a tiny sprout of magic pinged me back.

Little Bean was alive.

I sagged against the counter.

She'd survived the shifts, but only because they happened fast. She wouldn't survive long in the atrophied womb of a crone. And what if the shifts continued? I'd seen Gunora shift a dozen times in only a few minutes. The violence of the changes had been terrifying. Little Bean would never live through that.

I sank to the floor and drew my knees up to my chin. Every muscle in my body tensed as if I could hold off another shift by the sheer force of my will.

I spent the next hours vacillating between panic and rage. I didn't sleep. I didn't think I would ever rest again, not if my body might betray me while I slept.

Before the sun rose, I got up and dressed. I wanted to be away before anyone saw me. Jacoby opened a bleary eye, but I told him to go back to sleep, and he was snoring again before I left the bedroom. I could hear Dutch moving around upstairs. I had only minutes before he came down.

In the kitchen, I gulped down a glass of juice. My stomach rumbled with hunger, but I'd pick up something in the city.

From his perch on the table by the patio door, Grim watched me tiptoe through the living room.

"You look different," he said. "Kind of—"

"Don't say it." I tossed the words over my shoulder as I slipped on my shoes. I didn't need to hear about how I looked. I had enough worries. "Tell Dutch I had an early doctor's appointment. I should be back for lunch."

I pulled a baseball cap on over my braids and stepped into the chill morning. The sky was only a shade lighter to the east. The wind had died and mist swirled like lost ghosts between the trees.

A figure stepped off the porch from the gatehouse.

Damn. I'd hoped to avoid the Guardians too.

Angus waited beside my truck. I pulled the rim of the cap down, hoping it would shade my face.

"Shouldn't you be getting to bed soon?" I asked.

"And shouldn't you still be in bed?"

"Early appointment."

"I heard you tell Mason you'd be sticking around here."

"Yeah, I forgot about the doctor." I fumbled my keys and dropped them in the gravel.

"You okay?" Angus asked as he watched me stoop awkwardly and fish for them.

I waved him off. "I'm fine. I'll see you tonight." I got into the truck and backed out too quickly. Gravel spun out under my tires.

TWO HOURS LATER, I lay on a padded table, naked from the waist down and covered in a crinkly sheet. I'd been poked, prodded and ultrasounded by a very nice, but slightly condescending young doctor.

"There's nothing wrong, that I can see. No bleeding?" He typed into his tablet.

"No." I'd been holding my breath for so long, my lungs hurt.

"The baby seems perfectly fine," he said, still not looking at me.

I raised my hand to my jaw. I swear I could feel jowls forming even as I lay there. "But—"

"I know you feel like you gained some weight. That's normal. I'd be worried if you didn't."

"But—"

"Now just go home and take it easy for a bit. You'll feel better."

"But—"

"And you can call any time if you feel those pangs again. There's a nurse on duty twenty-four hours. But I'm sure it's nothing."

At least he stopped before declaring I had new-mother blues. He smiled briefly and swept out the door, leaving me alone with my doubts and my crinkly sheet.

I fought back unreasonable tears as I dressed and headed out to my truck. I sat in the front seat and watched the wind chase pedestrians across the intersection.

My thoughts felt frozen in time, like someone had hit the pause button in my brain. The doctor had me second guessing myself. Had I dreamed the whole terrible episode last night?

No. I knew something was wrong. It was my body. I just *knew* it. Something was out of whack, and my keening kept prodding it the way your tongue can't keep away from a sore tooth. It was there, that *something*. I just couldn't pinpoint exactly where.

"To hell with doctors." I pounded my fist on the steering wheel. "Right, Little Bean. We'll figure this out the old fashioned way. With witchcraft."

I pounded a message into my widget. My fingers felt pudgy and awkward. Then I threw the device into the passenger seat and leaned back against the head rest. I closed my eyes until I heard the widget vibrate with a response.

CHAPTER

5

bbott's Agora was in that lull between morning rush and early lunch. Fall leaves licked at my shoes along the winding path that led deep into the market. The Agora was a fey place with subtle magic. If you knew your destination well, your feet would eventually take you there, but if you'd never visited a particular shop, you wouldn't find it without directions because the path shifted on the whim of the market's magic.

I had to ask merchants twice before I found the faded tent with a hand-painted sign sewn into the fabric by the front door. It read:

Avalon Moodie
Tinctures
Herbs
Charms
Palms read
Healings

That last one seemed like an odd afterthought. I almost turned away, but I had nowhere else to go.

The tent was a good size and made of heavy canvas that looked reasonably permanent. Ms. Moodie wasn't a fly-by-nighter, according to my source.

A heavy tapestry of a goddess figure spewing flowers hung in the doorway. It was vaguely reminiscent of Botticelli's "The Birth of Venus" but with more clothing and forest animals. I pushed it aside and entered the tent.

A dozen different scents assailed my nose—spicy incense, sweet basil, the tang of growing mushrooms and others I couldn't identify. Shelves framed three tent walls and these were stocked with jars, bags and pots. A gust of wind followed me in and rattled a display of metal charms for luck, protection, courage or a dozen other attributes that could be nudged into alignment with just the right combination of magic and core elements.

A small round table draped in red cloth heavily embroidered with gold filled the tent's back portion. Two chairs sat by the table, but only one was occupied.

"Can I help you?" A young white woman with dark curls looked up and smiled. Her fingers worked deftly at some task but the one candle on the table did little to illuminate her.

"I'm looking for Avalon Moodie."

"You found her." Her smile deepened to reveal a dimple on one cheek. My eyes had adjusted to the gloom inside the tent, and I could see now that she was making charms. Her fingers deftly wound silver wire around a stick and attached several small copper disks.

I gazed around the shop. This was definitely the right place, but this young woman couldn't be Avalon Moodie. It took years of study and practice to become adept at magic. But the only hedge witch I knew, and the one I'd contacted for advice was Cece Moodie, a long-time supporter of my blog. She assured me that Avalon was the best witch in Montreal.

I cleared my throat.

"My friend Cece suggested I contact you."

The woman's face lit up with a grin. "Auntie Cece? How's she doing?"

"Um, fine I guess. We only chat by Ley-net. She said you'd be able to help me."

Avalon jumped from her seat and stuck a sign to the outside curtain that said, "Gone for lunch." Then she waved me over to the empty chair.

"Come in. Sit down." She swept aside the charm workings.

I hesitated.

"Don't worry." She grinned. "Witches don't bite. Much."

I sat and fiddled with the tabled cloth. "It's not that. It's just that Cece assured me you'd be able to help, but you're so…young."

"Oh, I get it. You were expecting some old hag with twigs tied in her hair. You know that stereotype is really hurtful."

"I'm sorry. But my condition is...unusual."

Avalon looked a little miffed. "My magic is as good as any. Just because I don't look the part, doesn't mean I'm not good." She crossed her arms over her chest.

I sighed. This is why I had no friends. I wasn't good at making small talk. Or big talk, for that matter.

"I'm sorry. I don't mean to be dismissive. I own a business in a traditionally male profession. I get that it isn't always easy to live up to expectations."

She nodded. "And what business is that?"

"Pest control."

Avalon raised an eyebrow.

"Humane pest control," I amended. "At least as humane as I can be. I deal mostly with fae and ubernatural creatures."

"Interesting. And is this why you've come?"

"No." I fidgeted in my seat. "I've been cursed. Or at least I've contracted a disease that is curse based. Have you ever heard of Maid Mother Crone?"

"The goddess archetype? It's not one of my favorites. Really, it was invented by a bunch of men trying to reduce women to their basic incarnations. No subtlety at all."

"Not the archetype. And not the goddesses. It's a disease." I fidgeted in my seat. "It comes from the Aesir and affects only young women. I was told a giant began it with a curse. My cousin had it, and she passed it on to me." I didn't want to get into the whole sacrifice-on-a-prison-island story with a total stranger.

"Interesting." Her big brown eyes assessed me and I felt like she saw right down to my molecular composition. "Give me your hands then."

Tentatively, I lifted my hands from my lap. Avalon gripped them in her own, resting the backs of her hands on the table. Her eyes were wide but unfocused. I keened magic in her touch. It wasn't aggressive, but it hummed and shifted like a blanket of bees over my skin.

Her grip tightened on my fingers until it hurt. Avalon's head whipped back. Black curls fell away from her face and her eyes rolled to white.

She sat frozen like that for a long moment. I tried to pull my hand away, but her grip held me firmly.

"Uh...Miss Avalon," I said when after several minutes she made no signs of moving.

31

Her mouth opened and closed several times, then she shouted in a raucous voice, "Beware the crone! Beware the mother! The undead will have your skin and the unborn will take your spirit!"

Her back arched painfully. Then she relaxed her grip. Her head fell forward, and she wiped drool from her chin.

"Well, that was fun. Please call me Avie." She smiled wanly.

"Uh, Avie, does that happen often?"

"Not often, thankfully. Only when the spirits are riled up. It gives me a real kink in the neck." She bent her head side to side and the bones cracked. "That's better. Now, let's put aside that message from beyond for the moment. Why didn't you tell me you're pregnant."

"I was getting to that. Does it make a difference?"

"Definitely. Some cures for curses can be…invasive."

A spark of hope lit in me and died.

"I'm not looking for a cure," I said. "Just a confirmation of the curse." Gunora had spent years looking for a cure. She had consulted with hedge witches, mages and mage-doctors, all to no avail.

"I see. And how can you be so sure that your cousin cursed you? Other than that message from the aether, of course." She waved a hand in the air, as if talking to the spirits was a minor thing.

I squirmed some more. "It's a long story."

"Then a pot of tea is in order. Come on."

She rose and beckoned me through a second flap at the back of the tent. The tent butted up against an old college dormitory. We walked right from the shop into an apartment. It was small—a kitchen and living area all in one with three doors that probably led to bedrooms and a bathroom. Dishes were piled over every surface in the kitchen. Toys and pillows covered the carpeted living room. A vid-screen on the wall played a loud cartoon. A horde of children ranging in age from toddler to pre-teen were lounging, jumping and squirming in the small space. One boy ran around naked, whistling like a train. Another bounced on the sofa. A girl and a boy wore pillows taped to their heads and sparred like boxers. I thought there were seven children in all, but they wouldn't stand still long enough to be counted.

Avie put her fingers to her mouth and whistled sharply. The noise and bustle stopped. All eyes turned to us.

"Bartie! Bronwyn!" Avie shouted.

A bedroom door opened and a skinny boy of about fourteen emerged. He wore only boxer shorts and his face was creased from sleeping on it.

"Where's your sister?" Avie asked.

Bartie shrugged. "Dunno."

After some searching, we found Bronwyn under a pile of pillows with earbuds in her ears. She looked enough like Bartie that I thought they might be twins.

"Did the cubs eat lunch?" Avie asked.

"Yes," Bronwyn said.

"Good. Take them to the park. It's a beautiful day. No more vids."

There was a chorus of "Aww, Mom!" as the older children lugged the younger ones into the bedroom

"And make sure to put clothes on!" Avie called after them, then mumbled, "I can't believe I have to say that." A few minutes later, the whole troop filed out wearing pants and jackets. Avie tucked in shirts and tied shoes as the children shuffled out the door.

"I suggest you stay out all afternoon," she shouted after them, "because when you come home, you'll all be doing the dishes!"

With the children gone, the apartment suddenly felt like the quiet after the passing of a tornado.

"They must keep you busy," I said.

Avie grunted, but she also grinned. "Nine of them. All twins, except for the triplets, Kirk, Keith and Gatsby."

I couldn't even imagine it. I was already bowled over by my one Little Bean.

Avie cleared away the debris from lunch and put a kettle on to boil.

"Please excuse the mess. They should be in school, but it's been closed for a week because of an infestation of leeches on the electrical wires."

"Oh. That's too bad." Guilt curdled in my stomach. I knew which school she was talking about. I'd been scheduled to clear the infestation. Because of my keening, electrical leeches were one of my specialties. But I'd canceled the job when my morning sickness had kept me in bed last week. For a normal pest controller, the leeches would be nearly impossible to remove.

Avie plunked the teapot on the table. She also brought out a tin of cookies that had been hidden on the pantry's top shelf. She opened the tin and pushed it toward me.

"My secret stash." She winked.

I took a cookie. It was crescent-shaped and pale like a shortbread, but when I bit into it, I got a burst of cinnamon on my tongue. I ate two before I'd realized it.

Avie smiled. "Those first weeks are brutal. I've been known to eat a whole tin in one sitting. Go on, have another."

Avie poured the tea. "So tell me about this curse."

I sipped tea and ate another cookie before I could find the words to even begin. Avie waited patiently.

"I know you're supposed to gain weight when you're pregnant, but not like this." I flapped a hand at my face. "Last night it happened all at once. I went to crone, maiden and then back to this in a minute." I paused with another cookie halfway to my mouth. "If it's true. I'll shift again and I'm worried..." I couldn't finish that thought.

Avie watched me with sharp, intelligent eyes.

"What did the doctor say?"

I snorted. "He was no help."

"And you're sure about these...shifts you had? Has it happened again?"

I shook my head and reached for another cookie.

Had I imagined the shifts? The more time and space that came between me and that moment, the more I wasn't sure of my own sanity.

"When my cousin tried to pass on her curse, I thought she'd failed. I thought some higher power intervened. But that's stupid right? The gods don't intervene."

My thoughts were manic and my words were muffled by cookie crumbs.

"Your cousin did this to you on purpose?" Avie asked.

I nodded.

She sighed and spoke like a mom trying to figure out who flooded the bathroom. "Just tell it from the beginning. What happened."

So I told her about Gunora showing up and the MMC disease, a biological curse that affects only Aesir women. I hesitated when I came to the part about breaking into Grandill, but then forged ahead. None of that would matter if I truly had the disease.

Avie listened with eyes growing steadily wider. I left out any mention of Mason and his demon blessing and finished with my dream of meeting Terra on the hillside.

"At least I thought it was Terra, and I'd hoped that she'd intervened on my behalf, but now that seems foolish. I mean, why would Terra care about me, one way or another. Right? Maybe what I saw was the curse's manifestation. The avatar of the maid, mother and crone. Or maybe it was just my brain lacking oxygen and firing random synapses." I popped another cookie in my mouth and sat back like a deflating balloon.

"Wow," Avie said.

"Yeah."

"So this all happened six weeks ago?"

"About that."

"And you felt the first change yesterday?"

I nodded. "Last night. It woke me up. I ran the full gamut of maid-mother-crone in seconds. After talking to the doctor, I thought maybe I'd dreamed the whole thing. I don't know…" I raised my eyes and met her gaze, willing her to understand how desperate I felt. "I know you don't know me, but I don't usually look this…motherly." I waved a hand at my face and body. "I gained ten pounds since yesterday. That's not normal."

"Maybe. Maybe not."

I scrolled through the images on my widget and paused at one of Mason, Raven and me, from only three weeks before. Dutch had taken it. We were sitting around the patio, celebrating Mason's win as the new Prime Minister. A small fire burned in my chest looking at those happy, carefree people.

I turned the widget to Avie. "This is what I looked like just yesterday. Tell me that this change is normal."

Avie studied the image and then me. She tapped a long, elegant finger against her lips as she thought.

"So, this MMC has three phases, is that right? It seems the real worry is the next change."

"Yes. I can only assume that last night's change happened too fast to affect the baby. But if I really do have the curse, it's only a matter of time before I shift to crone again.

"How much time?" Avie asked.

"I don't know. Normally, the curse takes years to develop, but I didn't get it the normal way. It could be years before I shift again. It could be days. And if that happens…" My knees clenched as if I could hold in all my worry.

"If that happens, you'll most likely miscarry."

I nodded again, not trusting my voice.

"And you want me to confirm that you have this bio-curse. Then what?"

I tried to answer but my throat felt thick with unshed tears. I cleared it and tried again. "Then I have to find a way home to Asgard."

Avie cocked her head. Her silence encouraged me to keep going.

"There's a tree there. An apple tree. It has golden apples and they keep the Aesir young."

"These apples will cure you?"

"No. But they will stave off the curse long enough for me to deliver. That's all I can hope for."

Avie could see the possibilities grinding at my heart. Her brown eyes softened. She squeezed my arm, and I had to fight back tears. Then she planted her palms flat on the table and pushed herself upright.

"Well, then. Let's run a few tests and see what we find."

CHAPTER

6

edge is less of a town and more of a collection of hovels, tents, and wagons clustered around a few solid establishments. One of those was The Dragon Pony Inn, a two-story building on the main road leading to the ward gate. Any traveler with a bit of money could get a room and a hot meal, though the meat in the stewpot was of dubious origin. Of course, most refugees traveling with all their possessions on their backs could never afford to stay at the inn, and so the tents and wagons.

The Dragon Pony was where the kidnappers had wanted to trade Gunora for Tums and Tad. The Guardians knew everyone in Hedge and had saved most of its regulars a time or two, so it hadn't taken long for Berto to shake loose information about the twins. Before Mason and I returned from Grandill, they'd found the goblits sleeping in a cottage on the outskirts of town. Their kidnappers had been nowhere in sight, but in the weeks since, Tums had regaled us all with tales of the giant who'd taken them. He made it sound like a trip with a favorite uncle. The giant had taught them to bet on dice. They'd eaten nothing but cookies and cake for three days. He'd even taken them on an outing to the old abandoned amusement park on the bits of Saint Helen's Island that survived the Flood Wars.

Gunora had mentioned a giant too, said he would take her through Jotunheim to Asgard, if only I'd help her escape conviction. I'd turned her down, of course, but the idea that there might be a way home had sprouted in me like an invasive vine. It crept through my dreams and curled into my thoughts at the oddest moments, so that in the middle of dinner, I might stop with the fork halfway to my mouth, imagining my feet taking those last steps through the gates of Asgard to find my mother and grandfather—a dream that was as thrilling as it was horrifying.

And now I was going to make it come true. I *had* to make it come true. Avie had confirmed the MMC curse in my aura. I had nowhere left to go but home. And no way to get there without this unnamed giant's help.

I stepped from the chilly street into the warm tap room. The Dragon Pony was quiet in the afternoon lull. Only three patrons sat at tables. Two nursed mugs of beer with uninviting expressions. The other was asleep with his head on the table. A fire burned low in the hearth along the wall by the kitchen. On the other side of that wall another hearth would be in full use. Smells of onions, garlic and roasting meat came from there. A leather flap across the kitchen doorway split and a man came out lugging a keg. He set it down and growled at a boy dozing on a stool beside the bar.

"Fetch clean mugs from the kitchen, boy. I don't pay you to sit around on your ass all day."

The boy scurried off to the kitchen and the barkeeper turned.

"What'll you have?"

He was a short, broad-chested guy with sallow, ash-tinted skin under a black beard.

"Got anything without alcohol?" I asked.

His eyes were almost lost in folds of skin as he squinted. "Tea."

"I'll have tea then."

He grunted, probably not pleased at having to boil water. Beer was much easier. A few minutes later he returned with an earthenware pot and a chipped mug. He plunked both down in front of me.

"Will you be eating? Supper's not ready, but there's stew left over from lunch."

"Depends on how long I'll be here. I'm waiting for someone." I placed a silver coin on the counter. It was ten times the worth of the tea.

He glanced at the coin, but made no move to pick it up. I added another coin and after a pause, a third.

"Who're you looking for."

"A giant. I don't know his name."

The barkeep scooped up the coins. "No giants in here."

"But there was, wasn't there?" I said before he could turn away. "Last month. Maybe six weeks ago."

"Don't keep track of every face that comes through here."

"But you'd remember a giant."

"Apparently not."

He turned his back to stow the keg under the counter.

I sighed and poured my tea, adding a drop from the bottle of tincture Avie had given me. It was mostly raspberry leaves and valerian, plus a few other things that Avie wouldn't admit to. She gave it to pregnant werewolves to keep them from shifting. There was no guarantee that it would help me, but it wouldn't hurt.

An hour later, I'd gone through a second pot of tea and was no closer to finding my giant. The supper crowd had begun to trickle in. I questioned a couple of imps and a human. No one knew any giants. The third time I questioned one of his patrons, the barkeep scowled. My welcome was wearing thin.

I pushed away from the bar, not bothering to leave a tip. Mr. Dragon Pony Inn had taken enough of my coins for no information of any worth.

Outside, the wind had died and a light rain misted the street. I zipped my jacket and pulled the collar up around my neck to ward off the damp.

"Eh, missus?" The voice came from the shadowed alley beside the inn. The errand boy. He stepped into the light only long enough to show me his face. He was pale, dirty and stick-thin. Greasy, matted hair stuck out of a worn wool cap, and an old bruise yellowed the skin under one eye.

My first thought upon seeing him up close was…Raven. This was the life he could have expected if Hub had taken him away from his father. I might have failed to reach him so far, but at least he wasn't soliciting people in back alleys.

"Da giant won't be 'ere today. 'E only comes on 'is days off." He spoke with a thick French accent and wiped snot trickling from his nose with his sleeve.

"You know him?" I asked.

The boy shrugged. "Everyone knows 'uyn."

"Huyn?" The name struck a memory bell. "Huyn Gillingrson?"

"Maybe. I dunno."

"You said he only comes on his days off. He works for the Knackers, is that right?"

"*Oui*."

"Do you know where?"

He shrugged. "Could be anywhere."

The Knackers hosted illegal fight rings. Hub was always trying to shut them down, so they moved around a lot.

"Can you find out where?" I asked. "There's fifty credits in it for you."

The kid snorted, then spat on the ground. "Credits no good. Gold."

Now I scoffed. "And where would I get gold? I've got silver. Three pieces if you come back with the giant's location in less than an hour."

In fact, I had a small stash of gold hidden in the false bottom of a dirty rag bucket in my truck. But it wasn't a good idea to flaunt your wealth in Hedge.

He stuck out his filthy hand. "I want it now."

I practiced my mom glare at him. "Do I look stupid to you? You get paid when you deliver."

The boy shrugged as if he'd expected as much and disappeared into the shadows. I went back inside The Dragon Pony Inn. No point in waiting in the rain, and Little Bean was hungry again.

I FINISHED A plate of roast venison—or so the scowling barkeeper said—with root vegetables. Either I'd been really hungry or the chef was better than I'd expected for a shanty town inn. The boy from the alley bumped my chair as he passed. He made eyes at the door before ducking back outside. I paid for my meal and followed.

In the alley, he waited with his hand outstretched. I placed a coin in it.

"Did you find the Knackers?"

He nodded.

I added another coin.

"There's a bulla. Just popped up outside of town. The scavengers 'aven't found it yet."

Bullas were little time capsules from the pre-war world. Terra spat them out from time to time. No one really knew why. They could be houses or factories or entire neighborhoods. Scavengers prized them for the treasures they brought—things that were no longer easily obtainable, like copper, lithium and diesel.

I placed the third coin in the boy's hand and held up two more. "These are for you, if you take me there."

The kid grabbed for the coins, but I held them back.

"Take me first."

He disappeared so fast only my keening let me know that he'd run off down the alley. I followed.

We left the noise and bustle of Main Street behind and emerged from the alleys at the outskirts of town. It was full dark now, so the boy stopped trying to hide behind every wagon or pile of junk heaped on the road. The rain had fizzled out, leaving the dirt roads mushy underfoot.

We passed several camps that looked semi-permanent. A lot more people were taking refuge here than I remembered. That wasn't a good sign. More refugees meant more unrest in the Inbetween. When the opji vampires were on the move, the population in the shanty towns swelled to overflowing. I hadn't heard definite news of opji unrest, but mainstream channels rarely considered the plight of non-citizens.

Maybe it was the wet conditions dampening tents and spirits, but the refugees looked like lost and forgotten souls waiting at the gates to the afterlife. Fires were low and sheltered. Garbage was strewn about and dogs fought over choice bits. Dirty children watched us pass, half-hidden behind canvas tent flaps.

The boy scuttled through this maze like a rat through the sewers. Wary eyes watched us, and I was glad when we finally left the camps behind even though the road ahead was dark and empty.

"What's your name?" I called out. The boy looked back and shook his head. I wasn't name worthy yet.

"You shouldn't be out here alone." I pulled my sword from its sheath.

"Don't be fraidy cat. We're almost there."

I mumbled something about small boys being eaten by monsters. In truth, I regularly went farther into the Inbetween to dump critters that I'd trapped in the city. And we weren't really alone. I could already keen the ruckus of human and fae bodies ahead. Within minutes, I could smell it too. Someone was burning damp wood, giving off a lot of smoke.

Then, in that strange way of bullas, we went from walking on a loamy, leaf-littered path, to the cracked pavement of a suburban neighborhood.

I'd seen bigger bullas, but it was big enough—an entire street of nearly identical homes on half-acre lots. The fire burned at the end of the street, illuminating a large boxy structure. As we neared, I recognized it as a high school.

"There." The boy pointed. He held out his hand and I gave him the coins with an extra as a bonus. He didn't grace me with a thank-you, but turned and ran away. I wanted to call after him, to offer him…what? A safe place to sleep? A chance to escape the shanty town? I couldn't save every lost boy, and he wouldn't take up my offer anyway, so I kept silent.

I watched him disappear back into the forest before heading for the school.

An ogre, a troll and an elf stood by the fire that burned in a metal drum. And no, that wasn't the opening to a bad joke. They were the bouncers. If I didn't get past them, I wouldn't find my giant tonight.

Faint music filtered through the closed door, and I keened a mass of bodies inside.

The ogre sat on the pavement, but his head was still taller than the troll who stood whittling a stick with a long knife.

"What do you want?" said the elf. Tall and stooped, with black hair and black clothes, he had none of the grace of the elves I'd seen at the fae court. These were hard characters, blunted by hard lives.

"I want to go in." I pointed to the double doors that led to the school's gymnasium.

"It's a private party. Invitation only."

I took a chance and dropped the only name I knew. "I'm a guest of Huyn Gillingrson. Tell him Kyra Greene is here."

The elf eyed me for a long moment, then he nodded to the troll who growled and set down his whittling stick. He sauntered over to the doors and opened them. Music blasted into the night before they swung shut behind him.

We waited ten minutes for him to return—ten minutes where I tried not to fidget and reveal my worry. It was a long shot. Would Huyn even remember me?

We'd met a lifetime ago for mortal creatures. The last test for a Valkyrie novice was to be dropped off in the wilds outside of Asgard with nothing but her sword. I wandered in the forest for days, surviving only because the weather had been kind. But it hadn't lasted. And if Huyn hadn't found me on the third evening as I struggled to light a fire with nothing but wet sticks and my magic, I'd have frozen to death. He was journeying from his father's court in Jotunheim to meet with my grandfather. We traveled together for three days. We weren't exactly friends, but I hoped that Huyn would be intrigued enough by my sudden appearance to let me in.

Finally, the troll returned with another blast of music.

"She's true," he said.

The elf glowered, but nodded toward the door.

And so I went in to witness my first cage fight.

CHAPTER

7

Only one gleam lit the gymnasium, but it was a big one, floating above the cage set in the middle of the old basketball court where a cyclops troll was desperately trying to fend off a manticore. The cyclops landed a solid hit from a club spiked with nails. The manticore trumpeted out a scream and shot poisonous quills from its mane. The spectators roared.

Humans and nonhumans were packed shoulder to shoulder on bleachers lining both sides of the gymnasium. More people milled around the open space in front of the door where I'd come in. Smoke from pipes, cigarettes and other less legal options hung over their heads in a haze of carcinogenic fumes. Maternal instincts screamed at me to get away, to protect Little Bean, but if I didn't find the giant, there would be no Little Bean.

I yanked my blade from its harness—the Knackers didn't seem to have a no-weapons policy—and pushed my way deeper into the throng of shouting, gesticulating spectators. More cheers rose as the cyclops or the manticore scored a hit, but I could no longer see the cage through the crowd.

A wooden structure rose beside the fight stage. Burly guards blocked the stairs that zig-zagged up its side. A viewing box for VIP guests? From this distance, I couldn't see anyone in the box, but it was a good bet.

I glanced around, looking for Huyn. Lone females weren't the Knackers' normal clientele. Faces turned my way. Eyes followed me though the smoke. Someone whistled.

My fingers tightened on my blade. It might not sing anymore, but it was wickedly sharp. It would do if push came to "I'll slice you into so many ribbons your next-of-kin won't recognize you."

44

Fingers tried to pinch my butt and missed, getting my hip instead. I whirled to find a grinning goblin.

"Come sit with me, dearie. I've got the best seats." He nodded toward the stairs leading to the raised box. He was well-dressed for a goblin in a velvet suit of deep blue. He probably thought it made him look like part of the elvish court.

"No, thank you." I scanned the crowd over his head, but didn't miss the scowl on his face. I moved on before he could make a scene.

I scrambled past the first row of spectators in time to witness the end of the fight. The manticore's viper tail struck the cyclops in the throat, and he went down convulsing as venom coursed through him, his one eye bulging like a full moon. The crowd booed at the lack of blood, then cheered when foam frothed from the cyclops's mouth. His legs kicked out once more and he lay still.

The manticore did a victory lap, snarling and hissing at the faces on the other side of the cage.

Someone jostled me and I felt hands trying to pick my pockets. They'd find nothing. My silver was securely stashed inside my waist band. I jerked my elbow, catching the intruder in the ribs and he moved on.

The intermission lasted just long enough for patrons to refill their mugs from a keg set up in the corner of the room. And for the fight attendants to clear the body.

A man stepped onto the stage. He looked human, but the cage was only ten feet in front of me, and I keened the rank magic streaming off him. It tasted like rot. So not human. His glamor was painstakingly average, like he'd taken great pains not to stand out. Neither tall nor short, he was dead-eyed with hair the color of dirt. His skin was beige with a sickly green undertone.

"And now for the fight you've all been waiting for!" Unlike his appearance, the man's voice was rich and full of drama. It seemed to pull excitement from the audience and they began to chant and stomp their feet.

A giant joined him on the stage and the crowd went wild. He was clearly a fan favorite.

Contrary to myth, giants aren't huge beings. This giant was taller than the average human and burly, but in a crowd, he could have passed for a mundane. Except for his magic. That *was* giant. It filled the cage and seeped into the crowd. I didn't need to taste that magic to recognize Huyn. He hadn't changed in the twenty years since I'd traveled with him in Asgard. He was broad-shouldered as an ox, with an open, handsome face bronzed by the sun, and hair as blond as wheat. His full mouth spread in a delighted grin as he pumped a fist at the crowd.

A third man stepped into the cage. He was short and wiry with black eyes that shifted around the audience. The emcee stood between the contenders and pointed at Huyn.

"Returning champion, Huyn Gillingrson!" The applause was deafening. Across the room, feet stamped out a drumbeat on the wooden bleachers.

"And facing the giant tonight, we have Tom 'The Swarm' O'Brian!"

The crowd hushed as the opponents faced off.

Above the cage a face poked into the light at the edge of the box. My VIP goblin. He saw me in the crowd and pointed. Beside him another man nodded, then caught my eye. He was black-haired and blunt-featured and had the look of a man in charge.

Uh-oh. This wouldn't end well.

Inside the cage, the emcee raised a fist and shook it. "To the death!" He stepped aside to let the opponents face off.

Huyn struck first. His massive fist swung for O'Brian's head. The man didn't duck. When the fist connected, his flesh exploded into thousands of flying beetles. The rest of his body collapsed, slithered behind the giant and reformed, head and all.

Uh-oh. O'Brian was an entomo. A bug man. They were notoriously hard to kill. He punched Huyn in the lower back, a hit that would have bruised kidneys on a human. Huyn swung around, but his fist went right through his opponent again as The Swarm scattered.

While the fighters circled each other, I kept one eye on the VIPs. Another head appeared in the box, the brute who'd been standing guard at the stairs. The dark-haired man spoke to him and pointed in my direction. The guard nodded and disappeared back into the box.

O'Brian pummeled Huyn with his fists, but the giant stepped into the assault and grabbed him by the throat. The Swarm dissolved again, but this time, Huyn managed to grip onto some part of him. Instead of slithering away, the beetles attacked, swarming Huyn's face as if trying to choke him.

To my left, spectators were being pushed roughly aside as a guard stalked toward me.

Blood streaked down Huyn's face. The beetles tore off bits of flesh, but he hung on.

Good for him, I thought. Everyone always went for the head, but the only way to kill an entomo was to get the core, the bit of magic that held it together as a whole. Huyn needed to outlast the swarm of stinging insects and squeeze the life out of O'Brian's core.

The guard was nearly on me.

O'Brian materialized in his human form. His eyes bulged as he clawed at Huyn and gurgled out a scream. Something went "Pop!" I keened it rather than heard it. Huyn had snuffed out the entomo's life. O'Brian sagged, then seemed to drip out of Huyn's grip as he devolved into a puddle of dead bugs.

Ew.

The crowd loved it, but I didn't have time to cheer for Huyn's victory. The guard stepped in front of me, blocking my view.

"Mr. Gaffer would like to see you." His voice was exactly what you'd expect from a brick wall.

"I don't know any Mr. Gaffer."

I tried to turn away, but he gripped my arm. "You will."

I rammed the pommel of my sword into his groin. He grunted like a wild boar that had stubbed its toe, but he let go.

I spun, bringing up my blade. Everyone else moved back to clear a space for the new entertainment. I stood with an easy stance, not brandishing my blade, but not backing down either. The guard flicked open a wicked-looking blade. It was puny next to my sword, but he had arms like a gorilla, and if I missed a strike, he could easily get inside my space.

Over his shoulder I spied Mr. Gaffer watching with a frown. Anger flared through me. What did he want with me anyway? Was I just a prize for his goblin guest, or had I caught the Knacker overlord's eye for some other reason? Either way, I wasn't getting out of here alive without making a good show of it. And when I did get out, I knew some Hub agents who would kill for the Knacker head honcho's name and description.

I let the guard come. He reached with his meaty left hand while menacing me with the blade in his right. I let him get close enough to tag him on the sleeve with the tip of my sword, not drawing blood, but just letting him know I meant business. A grin split his face.

One strike of a Valkyrie blade was normally enough to kill a mortal. But I didn't know a) if this guard was human, and b) if my sword would perform like usual in its dormant state. I really didn't want to find out, but it didn't look like this tugboat in jeans wasn't going to give me a choice.

I lifted my sword and pointed it at the guard's chest. He parried with a grin that would frighten small children and reversed his blade, getting ready to throw it.

"My lord!" Huyn leaned against the cage with his fingers twined through the steel bars. He looked toward the VIP box. Mr. Gaffer waved for him to speak.

"This is my tenth victory. By your own rules, I am due a boon." The gymnasium was silent as everyone waited for Mr. Gaffer's approval. Finally, he nodded.

Huyn's chest expanded as he drew in a breath and pointed at me. "I ask for the woman."

The Knacker chief frowned down at him. The snooty goblin gabbled in his ear, but Gaffer held up a hand. After a moment, he waved away the guard that menaced me. The man spat at my feet before turning back to the stairs.

Classy.

The crowd settled down, ready for the next fight, but the space around me didn't fill in. No one wanted to mess with the giant's woman.

I watched two shifters—bear and wolf—tear each other to shreds while I wondered how to get backstage to speak to Huyn. Five minutes into the fight, I had my answer when a nervous young man found me.

"Huyn says to join him now." His hands twitched at his sides as if he didn't know what to do with them.

I nodded, but glanced up at the VIP box before following him. Mr. Gaffer watched me still.

I followed Huyn's messenger into the locker rooms. Huyn sat on a table, naked but for a towel around his waist. Even slumped as he was, muscles ridged his abs. His hair fell in sweaty curls to his shoulders. His bare legs, as wide around as my chest and fuzzed with more blond curls, hung over the table and nearly brushed the ground.

A flutter of pixies swarmed him. Some hovered by his neck to pat away moisture. Others rubbed cream on his bulging shoulders or dabbed at the wounds on his face. The room stank of eucalyptus.

He glanced up through a curtain of hair and straightened. "Kyra! So glad to see you!" His voice boomed like he was a clacker and all the world was his bell. I winced.

That is the magic of the Jotnars. Yes, they're big and solid, but it's more a force of personality than a physicality. The word Jotnar means devourer and the giants seem to devour every space in a room, no matter how big the room.

Huyn jumped off the table and swung me into a hug. My cheek pressed against his bare, sweaty shoulder until I squirmed away to face his big grin.

"I'm glad to see you too. You haven't changed a bit."

"Neither have you. As beautiful as ever."

I bit my tongue on the denial that came to my lips. There is nothing worse than putting down a well-meant compliment.

"That was some fight," I said. "How did you know how to kill the entomo?"

"Ah, we used to catch 'em for a lark as kids. I had to make of a show of it first. Damn but I hate those things. Look at the bites." He inspected his upper arm. Red welts puckered the skin. The pixies tsked and dabbed more cream on him. He waved them away.

"Enough. I'll survive the night. Go pester someone else." The pixies fluttered out, taking their baskets of herbs, pots of cream, and dirty towels with them. The remaining towel barely covered Huyn's important bits, and I was glad it stayed in place. He grabbed a fresh towel off a nearby stack and rubbed his damp hair.

"I heard you were in Montreal," he said. "Nasty business with your cousin a few months back."

"I believe you had a hand in that." I kept my tone light. No matter what had happened with Gunora, I needed Huyn on my side now. "I know a couple of goblits who still talk about the giant who took them to the old fairgrounds."

"Aw, you're not here to bust my balls over that, are you? They were never in any real danger, you know." Huyn grinned and shook his curly mane. He really was a handsome devil—chiseled chin and cheekbones, blue eyes that danced with humor, a full kissable mouth…

I shook my head as if to clear it of cobwebs. The Jotnar charm was strong with this one. Even now, I could feel his magic twining around me like I was a bug in his web. It would be easy to let myself sink into that web.

I sighed and strengthened my personal wards.

"No, I'm not here to bust your balls. Though we will have a conversation about that at some point. Right now, I need your help."

"Go on." He poured two glasses of water from a pitcher and handed one to me. I accepted it but didn't drink.

"Did you know Gunora was sick?"

"I did." He watched me over the rim of his glass.

"Did you know that the only cure for her illness was to pass it onto another Valkyrie?"

He frowned and his eyes narrowed. "I did not. Did she do it?"

I bit my lip and nodded.

"And now I need to get home to Asgard. Fast."

"The Golden Apples, eh? Gunora was after them too." He sipped his water. His gaze fixed on the gray brick wall that seemed to be standard in every high school locker room, but he was seeing a horizon on another world.

"Yes, but I don't need them for me, or not entirely, at least." My throat constricted as I thought of the tiny life inside me, of never getting a chance to see her face. My hand strayed to my stomach as it did so often these days.

Huyn's eyes widened. "Oh, I see."

"This illness, it will…" I couldn't even say the words.

"It will kill the child." He laid a massive, warm hand over mine. "I'm so sorry."

"Sorry enough to take me home?" I sniffled.

"I'll make you the same deal I made Gunora. Gold. Not for me. I'd be going home at some point anyway, so I don't mind the company. But there will be bribes to pay. Call it tax for safe passage."

He named the price and I accepted without hesitation. As I turned to leave, he stopped me.

"And Kyra?"

I turned.

"The door to Jotunheim is sacred. I will not let it become common knowledge so the humans can invite any damned demon through it. They ruined their world. I'll not have them ruin mine. You come alone, and the secret path to Jotunheim dies with you." He quirked an eyebrow, waiting for my response.

"Understood."

I went home to say my goodbyes.

rrol was walking the perimeter of the yard when I arrived home. Since Errol is a bodach and only three inches tall and was easy prey to hawks and other ambush predators, Angus walked with him. I parked as they reached the gravel driveway. Even as I got out of the car, I could feel the strong pull of Errol's magic. Not a breath of wind blew in the yard, but the leaves stirred around him, kicked up by his magic as he concentrated on our ward line.

"Hey, guys. What's up?"

"Ghrtbtwvth." *Coy-bears.* The word popped into my head effortlessly.

"Coy-bears?" I turned to face the shadows darkening under the trees. The Inbetween could cough up all kinds of weird and savage creatures. Coy-bears got their name because they looked like black and white pandas, but with a canine snout. They ran on four nimble legs like a dog, and had the temperament of a grizzly.

Unlike the coy-dogs that plagued the suburbs of old Montreal and other North American cities before the wars, coy-bears weren't actually a hybrid of two cousin-species. They were neither coyotes, nor bears, but some monstrous creature that came through a crack in the veil. And usually, they shied from interactions with people, unless something disturbed their den…

"What happened?" I asked, but I already knew.

Angus scratched his backside and pulled up his sagging pants. "Oh, don't be mad now. Boys will be boys and all that."

I closed my eyes and took a tempering breath. "Just tell me."

"Raven and the two other laddies were playing hide-and-seek, so they say." I already doubted that story. Raven and the goblits didn't get along well enough for that. "And Raven disturbed a den nearby." Oh, gods. "There were cubs inside." Angus saw my face and rushed on. "Now don't be throwing fire on ice. The boys are fine. Nobody's been hurt. Errol, here, just thought it would be a good idea to reinforce the wards."

I rubbed the spot between my brows where a headache was starting to bloom.

Errol pounded his walking twig into the dirt, and I keened the ward snap to attention.

"Htbnt hrnmw." *All done.*

"Thank you, Errol."

The little bodach nodded. "Thptn." *You look tired.*

"You have no idea."

I left them to finish up and went inside. Raven was sulking in his room. I poked my nose in to be sure he still had all his limbs, but couldn't muster the energy to scold him. No doubt, he'd already had a good lecture from Gita and Suzt. So I said, "You okay?"

He nodded, shoulders tensed as he waited for his punishment.

"We'll talk about the coy-bears tomorrow, okay? How about hamburgers for supper?"

He nodded again. "I can help."

"That would be great. We both had long days."

He smiled and scrambled out of his bed. Punishments were over-rated anyway. I followed him into the kitchen, glad that on our last night together, we didn't have to argue.

THE HARSH LIGHT in our bathroom was unforgiving. I studied myself in the mirror. Were there more wrinkles around my eyes? Was that a gray hair or was it just sun-bleached? My long days (often without lunch) and my demanding job left me lean. Now my face had filled out, my cheeks were plump and pink. My hand slid down a curvy body that felt completely alien, even though my rational mind told me I didn't look much different. In fact, an unbiased eye might even say I looked healthier than normal.

I didn't feel normal.

How long did I have before the curse kicked me into crone mode again? The not knowing was a curse in itself.

I took a swig of Avie's potion and turned off the light.

It was midnight. I needed sleep. My bag was packed. I had provisions for a few days, weapons and a change of clothes. That was all I would take from this world. I planned to leave in the hour before dawn. Dutch wouldn't be awake yet and the gargoyles would be sleepy. With any luck, I'd slip away without anyone noticing. I'd left instructions for Tak and Gibus on caring for the critters and places where they could be re-homed if they found the job too onerous.

I'd also written private notes to Gita, Jacoby, Grim, Errol and Raven. I would leave them all behind, but I was a big chicken and couldn't face the goodbyes.

I refused to consider asking anyone to come with me. Apart from the dangers of a trip through giant country, their home was here. I couldn't rip them away from that. I wouldn't. No matter how much it hurt to leave my family behind, they were better off here.

But there was one person I couldn't say goodbye to in a note.

Jacoby had fallen asleep on the couch, so I brought my old computer into the bedroom and closed the door. Mason had given me Kester's personal address. It was a secure link and a stable one. I tapped it in and pushed magic through my fingertips into the keyboard. After a moment, the screen lit with a wrinkled face, crowned by white hair pulled into a bun.

"Good evening. Is that you, Miss Greene?" said Kester's housekeeper, Havia.

I kept my video feed off.

"Yes, I must have a bad connection."

"Mr. Mason has just retired. Shall I wake him?"

"Um, yes please." I stopped short of telling her it was an emergency, but she caught my tone. One eyebrow rose.

"Of course. Just a moment."

It was longer than a moment, but Kester's house was huge. I waited five long minutes—minutes where my resolve flip-flopped and I almost shut the computer. By the time Mason arrived, looking rumpled from sleep, tears flowed freely down my cheeks. With the video off, he couldn't see me, so I took a deep breath to hide the tremble in my voice.

"Mason?"

"Kyra! What's wrong? Is Raven okay? The baby?" He was suddenly wide awake. I hiccuped through a bad explanation of the past two days, the curse diagnosis, finding Huyn. All of it.

Mason listened. His eyebrows crept down lower and lower until they shaded the black fire in his eyes.

I ended with, "I'm going to Asgard. The Golden Apples will keep me safe until I deliver."

"When?"

"Tonight."

"Kyra, please. Turn on your camera." His eyes seemed to reach through the screen to grab me.

"I…can't."

"Please." He sounded hurt.

"I don't…" I hiccuped, "I don't want you to see me like this. I've changed already. I want you to remember me the way I was."

Mason swore in old French and ran a hand through his hair so it stuck up every which way.

"Kyra, I have two things to say to you, and you're going to listen carefully."

I nodded, then remembered he couldn't see me. "Yes." *Hiccup.*

"First, you forget how old I am. Do you think age scares me? I will love your wrinkles and gray hair whether they come tomorrow or in fifty years. I love you. Period. Full stop. Tell me you understand that."

My chest was aching with love and sorrow. I couldn't believe this was how we had to say goodbye. I turned on the camera.

I endured a long silence as he took in the new crows feet around my eyes and the slight sag at my jowls.

Then he sighed, not a sigh of weariness, but relief.

"Thank you. I don't want you to think you are anything but beautiful. Not now. Not ever."

My fingers touched the screen as if I could connect with him over the vast distance that separated us.

"And the second thing?" I asked.

"I will find you."

I let out a small laugh. "You can't. There is only one door to Jotunheim and Huyn refuses to give me its coordinates. And once I go through that door…"

"Kyra!" His voice was sharp. "I. Will. Find. You."

I nodded and sniffled. I knew he believed it. "I love you."

"I love you too. More than you know. Be safe. And take care of our Little Bean."

I raised my hand in a last wave. It seemed so inadequate for the feelings coursing through me. And then the screen went black.

I reached for the pillow on the other side of the bed. It smelled faintly like Mason. I hugged it and waited for dawn. The memory of his voice—*I will find you*—anchored me in the darkness. It wrapped my splintering soul and kept me whole for a little while longer.

I lay awake staring at the ceiling for hours. My room suddenly felt stuffy and hot. Sweat tingled down my spine. I flung off the blankets, but still the room was close and smothering.

I need air. I needed to breathe the sky.

I ran for the doors that led to our patio, praying to a god who'd never answered me, to stave off the shifts. On my way out, I grabbed Avie's tincture and downed another gulp.

By the time I reached the patio, I was hyperventilating. The cool night air felt like a balm in my lungs. I leaned against the stone wall of the patio that overlooked the garden.

Once, Mason and I had watched dragons fly across the moon from this vantage point. I could almost feel the heat and strength of his body pressed up against mine, his arms circling me, lips catching the soft spots that only he could find…

By the All-father! That wasn't the way to calm my nerves. I sucked in a deep breath. My fingers pressed against the rough stone.

It was two hours before dawn. I should leave now. I was all packed. There was no use putting it off. I could…

"You're leaving, aren't you?"

I turned to find my banshee huddled in a patio chair like a wraith. Her eyes were lost in the shadows, making her face cadaverous. Wind tossed gray hair about her head like Medusa's snakes. If I hadn't known her, I would have run screaming into the night.

"I have to." My voice hitched on the words. I'd never been able to lie to Gita.

"It's the babe, isn't it?"

My hand brushed my stomach.

"Gunora got her way. I'm cursed with MMC."

"You'll be going home to Asgard then?"

I nodded. "I have to keep it at bay long enough to deliver her."

"Her?" Gita quirked an eyebrow, but then nodded. "And what about the boy?"

"Raven? He's asleep." A pang of heartache hit me. I knew what she was asking.

"You'll just leave him? When he needs a mother now more than ever?" She leaned forward and moonlight caught the tears streaking down her cheeks.

"It's a dangerous road to Asgard. He'll be better off here. They all will be."

"Some maybe. Not him."

"He's already lost one home. I don't want to tear him away from another."

Gita gripped my arm in both her bony hands. "You are his home."

I scoffed at that. "He doesn't even like me."

"He's a teenaged boy. Almost, anyway. He's not supposed to like his parents. But if you go, he'll have no one."

"He'll have Mason."

"Mason will follow you."

"He won't be able to." I couldn't fault Huyn for keeping the secrets of his people, but I wished I could leave some breadcrumb for Mason to follow.

Now it was Gita's turn to snort. "He'll find a way. That man would find you in Hell if he had to." She patted my arm then dropped it. "Go. Wake the boy and give him a choice. I think you'll be surprised."

She favored me with a quick hug before fading back into the shadows. Her last words drifted back like the voice of a phantom. "And don't worry about the others. I will take care of your family."

I stood in the quickly fading night for several minutes, wrestling with indecision. Then I sighed and went back inside.

I paused at the door to Raven's room. He slept curled in a ball like he was trying to protect his vital organs. Princess heard me the moment I stepped into the room. She lifted her nose from her paws and let out a soft woof.

"It's only me," I said, though her nose would have already told her that. My words stirred Raven. He sat up and rubbed his eyes.

"What's…Kyra?"

I sat on the edge of his bed.

"I'm leaving. For good." I let the words sink in for a moment. I could see apprehension creep over him. His shoulders hiked up to his ears. He wrapped his arms around his legs and rested his chin on his knees. In the dim light, his eyes were all pupil.

"Without being too dramatic, it's a matter of life and death. And if you decide to come with me I'll tell you all about it on the road."

He straightened. "If I decide…"

"It will be dangerous. And we won't be able to come back."

"Not ever?"

"Well, not me. Maybe one day, you'll be able to."

"What about Mason?" He was fighting hard to keep his voice from breaking. He loved Mason already. They'd spent hours together in the small lab in the basement. Every time Mason said that Raven had the makings of a great alchemist, the boy seemed to grow an inch taller.

"Mason will join us," I said, then I shook my head. I wouldn't lie to him. "Mason will *try* to join us. But you have to know, there's little chance of him finding the way. We're going through the veil to Asgard."

Raven lowered his head. The white lock on his forehead glowed in the faint light from the window. He was considering my proposal, but the dawn was already lighting the sky.

"I don't mean to rush you, but I have to leave now."

"And you really want me to choose?"

My stomach turned in knots, and I had a vision of Little Bean riding a roller coaster in my womb. Was this choice too much for him? How could I drop the decision of his entire future on those scrawny shoulders?

I nodded.

"Thank you." A slow smile completely changed his face. "I'll come. And Princess too?"

Princess heard her name and poked her nose between us. "Aroo?" I ruffled her fur.

"Of course, Fur-face will come too."

"Okay." Raven jumped out of bed. "I have to pack a bag."

"Keep it light. And be quiet. I don't want to wake the others before we leave."

He paused, and I realized that sneaking out sounded shifty, but if I had to say goodbye one more time, I wouldn't make it out the door.

Raven whispered. "I'll be fast. And quiet."

"Good. Meet me outside in ten minutes."

I left him to pack and went to add extra provisions to my bag. On the way, I spotted Jacoby on the couch, arms and legs flung wide. His light snores ruffled the ridiculous fringe of fur around his eyes. Grim was also asleep by the hearth, curled in a ball with his back pressed against Willow. More soft snores came from the little house beside the bonsai tree. I imagined Mason sitting beside the fire, a book on his lap, but one eye on me as I untangled my braids at the end of the day.

I soaked it all in, then turned away. It was the hardest thing I'd ever had to do.

orion Park lit up in shades of pink as we walked the western access road toward the highway. Every step took me farther from home. Every breath felt like a shard of ice in my chest. I'd made my choice and I would not go back on it, but by the One-eyed Father, I could feel myself slowly turning to ice, and not only because of the cold.

Raven hadn't said anything since he'd joined me on the front stoop with his backpack and the hound at his side. He neither questioned me nor complained, and since I couldn't make conversation around the lump in my chest, we walked in silence.

At the junction of Dorion Park's access road and the old highway, we stopped to wait for Huyn. Hub crews kept the highway clear of the encroaching forest. To the east, it led to Gallop Bridge and the gate into Montreal. Westward, it wound through orchards and fields of greenhouses that fed the city. After that? Unguarded wilderness, rampant magic, marauders and monsters.

I tapped a quick message to Mason: *We're west of Dorion.* That meant we would be heading north or west. For any other direction, Huyn would have asked to meet outside another gate. I didn't know how long my widget would work as we moved away from the apex stones, but I wanted to give Mason as much information as I could.

It wouldn't be enough. If the giants had managed to keep the location of their door secret this long, he wouldn't find it.

"Are we really never coming back?" Raven asked. He looked small and lost in the early morning shadows. The pack over one shoulder seemed almost as big as he did.

I smoothed back the white lock on his forehead and for once, he didn't push my hand away.

I'd explained as much as I could about the reason for our journey on the short walk through Dorion Park.

"I won't be able to come back. I'll have to eat the Golden Apples for the rest of my life." However short that might be. "But when you're older, you might choose to return." I left out the struggles that journey would entail. He'd soon discover them first hand.

Was it really fair to have let him make such an important decision? Maybe I should have chosen for him, left him at home where he'd be safe and cared for. Isn't that what good parents did? They made the hard choices for their kids until they were old enough to choose wisely. Was bringing him along selfish? I hoped not. I wanted to believe I did it for the right reasons and not because Raven was a link to the home I was losing.

"Now, I need you to shift. Is that okay? Huyn said I had to come alone. But I don't think he'll mind me bringing my pet pony and hell hound." I smiled to make those words less disrespectful. "Do you think you can keep your horse form until we're through the door to Jotunheim?"

"Sure. It's easier to travel like that anyway."

"Good. I'll carry your pack."

"I can do it. Look. Mason made it for me. It's waterproof and everything." He moved the strap of his bag from over his shoulder to around his neck. It was thick and padded. He pulled a string and the pack split in two like a saddlebag. He shifted to his horse form and the pack settled over his withers with the strap now securely around his neck.

He pranced in place, pearly white wings shining like little fiery suns in the morning light. Princess dashed around us in circles. Their enthusiasm affected me, and my spirits brightened by a fraction of a lumen.

The trick was to not look back. I would keep my thoughts on happy things: hugging my mother and grandfather again, seeing the beautiful city of Asgard against the forever snowy mountains, meeting Little Bean for the first time. Those thoughts would give me energy to keep one foot moving in front of the other. At least during the day. I had no doubt that my nights would be filled with visions of Mason, Jacoby, Hunter and the others I'd left behind.

I took a deep breath and it hitched in my chest.

"Happy thoughts only."

Raven cocked his head, and I realized I'd spoken aloud. I waved a hand at him as a "never mind."

Princess suddenly stopped pacing. Her body language said she sensed something coming—ears pointed forward, tail straight back, hackles raised. Her lip curled and a low growl rumbled from her chest.

A figure appeared on the road to the east. I shaded my eyes against the rising sun and watched Huyn approach. For a giant, he was oddly graceful, walking with the loose-jointed gait of a dancer.

"Stand down." I waved a hand at Princess. She let out a woof of protest, but relaxed her posture.

"Glad you're on time!" Huyn's voice boomed even though he was only a few feet away. "Nothing like an early morning departure."

"You're on foot," I said.

Huyn glanced at his massive feet dressed in beaten up combat boots. "I am. Is there a problem?"

"You said you'd arrange for transport."

He frowned and a twinkle lit his eye. "You got feet too, don't you? See? Transport arranged."

I sighed but he was already onto another topic. "Who are these little fellas?" Huyn tried to ruffle Raven's mane, but he danced out of reach.

Princess wasn't giving him an inch. The growl intensified. Her head hung low and her back legs bunched, ready to pounce.

"Princess, *hael*!" I pushed magic into the command. She stopped, but trembled with the need to attack.

"You remember me, don't you, girl?" Huyn held out his hand, fist closed for her to sniff. Princess showed him her finger-long fangs. "Look, no hard feelings, okay? It was just a job. I wouldn't have hurt the goblits."

Ah. Now it made sense. Huyn had been there when Gunora's contacts had kidnapped Tums and Tad. Princess had tried to defend them and ended up in a pit for her efforts.

Princess's growl erupted into an explosion of barking.

Huyn stepped back and held up his hands. "Can't you put her on a leash?"

I grabbed a fistful of Princess's ruff. "You try putting a hell hound on a leash and see how that works out for you."

I managed to calm Princess down, but she kept one eye on Huyn, and little woofs kept escaping her lips as if she couldn't hold them in.

"She won't forgive you any time soon," I said. "Best to keep out of her way for now." I sighed. A complicated trip just got more complicated.

"Well, if she's gotta come, let's get moving. We're burning daylight."

We headed westward, away from civilization as we knew it. With my widget hidden in my pocket, I sent blank text messages to Mason every few kilometers. Our geo position relative to the apex stones would be embedded in the metadata of those texts, and I hoped it would be enough for him to follow our trail.

Huyn sang a jaunty tune as if we were on a holiday stroll. I recognized only one in ten words of the Jotnar language, but he seemed to be singing about going home and seeing the smile on his sweetheart's face.

I let Princess and Raven run ahead as long as they checked in every few minutes. The trees were in their last blush of autumn and the road was littered with brown leaves that swished and crackled under our steps. Luckily, we weren't concerned about stealth. This section of road was protected by Hub, and we didn't have to worry about marauders yet.

Raven and Princess came bounding through the trees ahead. A huge hare dangled from Princess's jaws. Raven grabbed it in his sharp teeth, and they played growly tug-of-war until Huyn and I caught up.

Huyn's eyes widened as he watched my pet pony dig into the hare with carnivorous glee.

"He's not a normal horse, is he?"

"He's really not."

With full bellies, Princess and Raven lost their initial exuberance, and we continued at a more sedate pace, each lost in our private thoughts. Every step further from home tore a little piece of me away. I second-guessed and third, fourth and fifth-guessed my decisions. What if I didn't make it to Asgard before I shifted again? I'd be in the wilds, dealing with a miscarriage alone. The thought brought a jolt of fear and I stumbled.

"Whoa!" Huyn grabbed my arm to support me before I landed flat on my face.

"Sorry," I mumbled. Then the morning sickness hit me and I lurched off the path to throw up in the bushes. I knelt in the dirt dry-heaving and trying to convince myself that morning sickness was a good thing. It meant that Little Bean was still very much alive. I wiped my mouth and the sweat trickling down my face with a bandana and tucked it away in my pack. My hand brushed against Avie's bottle. I pulled it out and gulped down the bitter tincture. Only half a bottle left. I had no idea if it was really working. I guessed I'd find out when the bottle was empty.

Returning to the trail, I found Huyn waiting with a frown.

"I'm okay," I said, but I must have looked a fright because his frown deepened. "Really. It's a pregnancy thing. Let's just keep going." I walked on before he could object.

My breadcrumbs to Mason dried up about midmorning, when my widget no longer connected to Montreal's apex stones. I kicked myself for not taking the time to visit Oscar again and pick up one of his long-range widgets. But time wasn't something I had in abundance, as the ravenous Little Bean kept reminding me.

Nagging hunger was my constant companion and the flip side of nausea. I pulled another bag of trail mix from my pack and offered it to Huyn.

He waved it away frantically. "The way you're packing it down, I wouldn't get between you and a bag of snacks."

"It's not easy to make a human. I'd like to see you try it."

"No, thanks. I'll leave that business to the stronger sex." He grinned, and I felt the tug of his peculiar flirtatious magic again. Did he even realize he was doing it?

"Are you going to tell me where we're going now?" I asked. "We're out of communication range. It's not like I could tell anyone."

Huyn side-eyed me and didn't speak. I humphed and dug into the trail mix again.

Princess was still wary of Huyn. Every time he came near, she growled low in her throat. Huyn, being a good-natured sort, kept trying to make friends with her anyway. When we stopped for a brief rest at lunchtime, he offered her a stick of jerky, but forced her to take it right from his hand. The hound wanted that meat, but she also didn't want to get within the giant's striking range. She whined and bowed and pranced.

Huyn took a bite from the jerky and held the smaller piece on the flat of his hand. "You'd better take it before I eat it all."

Princess aroooed in frustration, then snapped up the meat. Huyn grinned.

"See, she'll come around. No one can resist Huyn Gillingrson's charms for long."

"About that," I said. "I want to know what happened with Gunora. How did she rope you into kidnapping the twins."

Huyn took a swig from his canteen before answering. "I made her the same offer I made you. But we couldn't follow through with her stuck on Grandill. She seemed pretty sure you'd free her, given the...uh...proper incentive."

"It wasn't about going home for Gunora," I grumbled. "At least not *only* about going home. She needed me to pass on her curse."

"I know that now. I didn't then. And I'm sorry for it."

I nodded, fighting back tears.

His big, warm hand covered my shoulder. "You must believe me, I would not have been part of it, if I'd known her true plans."

"But what about the boys? You didn't seem too worried about hurting them."

"I would never!" His tone seemed truly affronted. He put a hand over his heart like he was swearing an oath. "That's why I went with her crew that night. So they weren't mistreated. And I insisted on keeping them myself, to make sure they were well cared for. We had a grand old time, in fact."

"So I heard. The boys are still telling tales of their big adventure with the giant."

"See? It's only your dog who hates me."

"She's a hell hound. If you want to be her friend, you'd better get that right."

"Hell hound. Got it."

I stowed the rest of my lunch in my pack for later, and we moved out. While we walked, I considered my new traveling companion. I wasn't sure what to think about Huyn's involvement in Gunora's nefarious plans. He clearly saw himself as a good guy. "I only kidnapped a little bit" wasn't a great argument in my books. It was like saying I was only a little bit pregnant. But he had taken good care of Tums and Tad. And regardless of my feelings, I needed him at least until we reached Asgard.

Still, his motivations weren't entirely clear. Twice, I'd asked him why he would go out of his way to help Gunora and me get back to Asgard, and twice he'd dodged the question. Yes, I was paying his so-called transport taxes in gold, but the son of King Gillingrson of Jotunheim wouldn't be cash poor. He had other reasons for helping me, reasons he chose to keep to himself.

I stowed my irritation and doubt for the time being and kept walking. We had a long way to go—worlds to travel—and only our feet to get us there.

CHAPTER

10

My legs trembled and my arches ached. Princess panted at my side. Every now and then, I'd feel her leathery tongue on my hand. She was thirsty and we'd run out of water. It was almost nightfall.

I didn't want to be *that* person—the whiner who begged to stop, but the words erupted from me. "Are we there yet?"

"A little further. Come on, now. You're not tuckered out already?" Huyn was eternally chipper. His gait never slowed. He didn't sweat or lose his smile. It was really annoying.

"Just tell me where we're going already!"

He dug another piece of jerky from his pack and handed it to me.

"Stop trying to shut me up with food!" I nearly shouted.

"It's worked so far."

My heels ground into the dirt. Raven, who had been a step behind, bumped into my legs. I crumpled to the road and crossed my arms over my chest.

"I'm not moving another step until you tell me where we're going."

Huyn bit into the jerky and considered me with that infuriating smile. "Cornwall."

"What? That's another fifty kilometers! We'll be walking for days!"

"Come on now. Don't be a baby. There's a crossroads just ahead. We're bound to meet a caravan there."

He reached out a hand. I groaned but let him pull me up.

CARAVANS OF HOMESTEADERS weren't unusual in the Inbetween. The land was alive with magic. It shifted constantly. A few villages were able to put up wards strong enough to keep the forest from reclaiming their land, but many homesteaders were nomads, moving from site to site. Some traded goods between wards, dangerous work that needed a small army of guards.

Since I didn't spend much time this far outside the ward, I didn't realize how organized these caravans were.

Huyn stopped us just after dark at a crossroads between two highways. These weren't the highways I remembered from my youth. They had once been great six-lane roads with cement medians running down the center. Most of that was gone now. The asphalt was cracked and overgrown, but enough traffic passed this way to keep a narrow lane clear.

The crossroads was an open space with little shelter, but it allowed us a clear line of sight far up the road in every direction. We'd see others coming with plenty of time to decide if they were friend or foe. A well by the side of the road provided much needed water and we refilled our canteens.

"A caravan should be along any time now." Huyn sat and patted the bare dirt beside him. "Get some rest."

I didn't need a second invitation. I sank to the ground and was asleep in minutes.

"Kyra, wake up!"

Huyn was shaking me. It felt like only minutes had passed.

"Huh?" I sat up straight. I'd fallen asleep with my head on his shoulder. There may have been some drool involved.

Huyn grinned. "You've got the print of my sleeve pressed into your forehead."

"Sorry." I rubbed my eyes. "That couldn't have been comfortable for you."

"Nah. I don't need much sleep."

A menacing growl from Princess had me suddenly alert.

"Tell your hound to relax. There's a caravan coming and we don't want to spook them."

I finally heard what Princess had been listening to for some time. The creak of wagon wheels, the crunch of boots on hard ground and other small noises made by a large group moving together.

The lead wagon paused at the crossroads and the rest rumbled to a stop behind it. The train was a dozen vehicles long and included carts, wagons, single riders on horseback, and even an old diesel truck. A pack of dogs darted in and around the train, making Princess's lip tremble. Dirty-faced children poked out of tented wagons, only to be scolded by parents who yanked them back into hiding. At least a dozen guards walked beside the caravan. They held torches to light the way and warn off predators.

A man with a grizzled beard sat in the driver's seat of the lead wagon. He had brown skin that hung on his face like cheap curtains. The sclerae of his eyes were a sickly yellow. He held the reins of two draft horses who already seemed bored by the interruption in their journey. A second man, younger and pale-skinned under a film of dirt, sat on the bench beside the caravan leader. He leveled a blaster at us.

"Do you know them?" I whispered.

"No. But I know their kind." Huyn spoke from the corner of his mouth without taking his eyes off the newcomers. He stepped forward to put himself between the wagon and me. It was a sweet but futile gesture because from the other wagons, I spied a dozen blasters trained on us. Huyn spread his big hands wide. He dazzled them with his mega-watt smile. The wind picked up a lock of golden hair and tossed it over his forehead. With his broad shoulders, massive legs and easy fighter's stance, he looked like a hero from the old tales—like Heracles, Erik the Red or Robert the Bruce—champions from the epics who will never go out of fashion.

"We're heading to Cornwall. Can you use some extra hands?" When he spoke, his voice projected for all to hear, but the caravan leader's eyes watched Huyn's fingers flickering in a complex gesture, and the tension in his shoulders relaxed. The man beside him lowered his blaster.

"We travel all night," the leader said. "And we don't need more guards."

Huyn had warned me that they would want gold, and I had already supplied him with an ample payment for our bribes. He held up a small pouch.

"Then maybe you can provide an empty wagon bed?"

The man considered him only a moment, then nodded toward the rear of the caravan. "Second to last wagon. And keep your beast away from my bitches. They're not pets."

Huyn dropped the bag of coins in his hands as we passed. The dogs watched us with sharp eyes but didn't challenge us. Princess let out a woof. I grabbed a fistful of her mane and hauled her along beside me. Raven, who had grown up among shifters and murderers of all sorts, trotted along behind me without a sound.

We nodded at the woman driving the second to last wagon. She nodded back, and we climbed aboard. Princess hopped up beside me. Huyn lifted Raven and the pony whipped his head around to snap sharp teeth at the giant.

"None of that." Huyn shoved him onboard. I patted Raven's soft wings and whispered, "Thank you." He could have shifted back to boy. It would have been easier for him to climb onto the wagon, and probably more comfortable to sleep. He blew out a whuffle, and curled into a ball in one corner.

The wagon wasn't covered, and the night was growing chill. I settled beside Raven with Princess pressed against my other side. The caravan moved on. The pace was slow and it jostled us from side to side.

"What was that sign you made," I asked Huyn. "You part of some kind of brotherhood?"

As long as men had gathered together in groups, there had been secret handshakes and unspoken languages. From the Freemasons, to the Brotherhood of the Holy Cross, to the Portal Wardens who fought off demons after the Flood Wars. But I had never seen the sign Huyn had made.

"Not really. Just a caravaner's surety. Tells him I've done caravan work before, and I know their ways." He stretched his legs out and they filled the wagon from one end to the other.

"So you were a guard?" I asked.

"I ran with the caravans when I first arrived in Terra. I've done a bit of everything—fishing, fighting, bouncing. I was even a carpenter for a while. You know what it's like for a king's second son—master of all trades, king of none."

When I'd first met him, Huyn had been on a diplomatic mission to Asgard. But I'd seen him hunt and I'd seen him fight. It wasn't hard to imagine him holding his own in any arena. Which made me once again wonder at his real motives for helping me.

"How much are they paying you to bring me in?" I asked. It was a long shot, but not an unreasonable guess. I'd fled Asgard with Aaric's blood on my hands. And then, just to ensure my eternal damnation in the eyes of the gods, I burned down Bifrost.

Huyn didn't speak, but I waited him out. Finally, he sighed and leaned his head against the wagon's bulkhead.

"It's not what you think."

"Oh, so you weren't planning to cash in on the price on my head? No wonder your escort fee is so cheap." I couldn't keep the sneer out of my voice. I could hardly blame him though, and regardless of what waited for me there, I had to go back to Asgard.

"Don't go off all half-cocked and misguided," he said. "There's no bounty on your head. I swear."

I wished I could see his eyes, but the wagon was dark and hid his secrets too well.

"Then why? Why are you helping me?"

"Because King Baldyr asked me to keep tabs on you."

"Grandfather? You saw him? Is he well."

Huyn nodded, then shook his head.

"I saw him last year. He wasn't well." Huyn's big hand wrapped around my knee and squeezed.

Then Huyn cleared his throat. "Kyra, he's dying."

The words hung in the darkness. I couldn't believe it. *Wouldn't* believe it. Grandfather was larger than life. He couldn't die. The Aesir didn't die!

But, of course, they did. Girls perished from MMC. Aaric had taken his own life. And the gods of old had all retired from life centuries ago. Death happened, just not often.

"How long does he have?" I asked.

"I don't know. I've been away for over a year." Huyn's hand retreated and I instantly missed its warmth.

"But why did he send you?"

Huyn shifted and his boots scraped against the wagon's boards. The sound was gratingly loud in the quiet night. "He wants to you come home to rule in his stead."

That made no sense.

"What about Dana? Surely she will take over." It was what she'd always wanted.

Huyn shifted again. "Dana has become…unpredictable. There are rumors…" He faded to silence.

I prodded him with a toe. "Tell me."

"Rumors that she's into dark magic. Even rumors that she poisoned Baldyr, though he doesn't believe those. What truly worries him is the treaty with Jotunheim."

Of course. Dana had been a most vocal opponent of the treaty. After all, what use did a society have for Valkyries if they had no enemy to battle?

"If she becomes queen, she'll disregard the treaty. There will be war."

"But what can I do about that? I have no influence over Dana."

"That's why you should be queen."

I let out a harsh laugh, but Huyn was serious. He patted my hand and settled himself to sleep. There would be no more sleep for me. *You should be queen.* His words echoed in my head as the wagons rumbled through the night.

CHAPTER

11

Cornwall had once been a thriving city on the St. Lawrence River. Its claim to fame was a paper plant that dominated the skyline for over a hundred years. The plant's closure lurked on the periphery of my childhood memories. It was big news for a company that had once had the largest payroll in the area.

Giant polluting factories were the first things that Terra reclaimed after the wars, but she'd never had a chance in Cornwall. The small city was the site of a terrible battle between an elemental demon and a fae-human coalition. The demon, a water spirit, had come through a breach in the veil that had opened offshore. She made Cornwall her new home and changed the landscape to suit her needs. Entire neighborhoods were flooded. Roads transformed into canals. And the demon set up her castle in the new bay she'd gouged from the land.

The humans and fae eventually beat her back. No one knew exactly how because none who took part in that final battle survived. Their graves lay at the bottom of the river.

A strange byproduct of the battle was a blight left on the city. Terra didn't reclaim the land, as if the foul taste of demon prevented her trees and vines from rooting. The canals remained, along with a few ancient industrial buildings. Years later, squatters took over. They became gangs who ruled Cornwall and patrolled the caravan routes, demanding taxes for safe passage.

Our wagon let us off just outside the city. The caravan would take its chances on the road north, around the city, rather than pay the gangs' taxes.

We walked the rest of the way. I noticed Raven favoring his right back leg.

"Are you hurt or did you just sleep badly?" I asked. He shook his mane and trotted ahead.

"You talk to him as if you expect an answer back," Huyn said.

"He answers in his own way."

"I'm sure he does." His tone was smug, but I didn't bother to correct him. He could find out about Raven once we were in Jotunheim and there was no turning back.

It was strange to see a city looming ahead. The Seaway Bridge that had once linked old Canada to old USA was gone, but the frames of several tall buildings were still ghosted against the sky. No where else in the Inbetween would you find a city without a ward.

The road ended abruptly at a wide canal cutting into the mainland. A ferry waited to cross, but it was guarded by a band of feral-looking men and women. They sat on and around several trucks that looked too battered to even run. As we approached, a man pushed away from leaning against a truck and met us on the road.

"What's your business in the city?" He was a big man who had been worn down by poor nutrition and a hard life. His shoulders sagged and his back was stooped. Wind-reddened cheeks bulged as if he were storing nuts for the winter.

"We're just passing through," Huyn said. "On our way to Toronto Ward."

"On foot?" The guard squinted and spat something brown and foul on the ground between us.

"We like to walk." Huyn bared his teeth in something like a smile. "We can pay for passage."

"Extra for the beasts."

"Of course." One of my gold coins flashed in Huyn's fingers like a magician pulling it out of thin air.

The man snorted. "I hope you got more of those."

Five minutes later, after a brief haggle, we boarded the ferry. It was little more than a raft pulled by a small tug boat. The boat's engine was too quiet to be fueled by gas, and I wondered where these people got their hands on alchemy tech.

"Are we really going to Toronto?" I asked.

Huyn shrugged. Maybe he didn't want our plans overheard, but I wasn't about to let up. "Why are we walking? Wouldn't it be faster and safer to go by ship?"

Cargo ships sailed the seaway all the time. It was easy to book passage on one. The only reason someone would travel inland and risk marauders and wild beasts was for lack of gold or because they feared being caught by the Hub soldiers who regularly rode the cargo ships as extra security.

We didn't lack gold.

I wondered why Huyn would need to hide from Hub, but he remained tight-lipped until we disembarked from the ferry. But then Huyn had said many things to make me wonder in the last hours. I mean, come on. Queen of Asgard? Me? That was just ridiculous. But when I'd questioned him more, he said I'd have to wait until we reached Asgard for answers.

The whole situation nagged at me as we disembarked the ferry and walked along a seawall.

"We're not going to Toronto," Huyn said in a low voice. "The door to Jotunheim is here. But no more questions. The gangs have eyes and ears everywhere in town. Just follow my lead and don't engage in any chit-chat."

"I'll be chit-chat free," I said.

The seawall held the canal back from a narrow strip of land. On the other side was another canal, this one no wider than a suburban street. As I gazed inland, I saw more canals branching off from this one. Small boats, some motorized and others powered by oars, traveled up and down the waterways. Buildings were crammed onto the spits of land between canals. These were mostly shacks, but a few looked pre-war in design.

We approached a man standing beside a tow-scow tied to a mooring. It was a flat-bottomed boat, square at both ends. An alien-looking ox with six legs and sawed-off horns was yolked to a harness that was attached to the boat's bow. Huyn paid our toll to a gruff-looking man who had wood-troll somewhere in his lineage. He nodded us toward benches at the back of the boat and pulled up his jacket collar to block the wind coming off the river. I huddled into my coat too. The morning was chill. My breath came in misty puffs. Princess sat on my feet, keeping them warm, and Raven pressed against my left thigh. I sank my fingers into his thick mane.

The captain made no move to untie the boat. The ox-beast munched lazily on a bag of oats tied to the mooring. Two more passengers boarded and sat on the benches.

"What are we waiting for?" I asked.

"It's more of a water bus than a taxi," Huyn said. "It leaves on the half hour."

I'd packed away my widget when we lost contact with the apex stones, so I had no idea how long we'd have to wait. I dozed. The red-eye trip on the wagon had left me tired and stiff. When the scow finally jerked into motion, I found myself leaning heavily on Huyn's shoulder, more than half way to dreamland.

I glared at him. "What's so funny?"

"You snore even when you're sitting up."

"Do not."

"Do too."

Rather than get into a juvenile slapping contest with him, I turned to watch the canal and the bustling town built alongside it. Many dwellings had boats parked beside them. Children ran along the wall, tossing sticks and rocks into the water. We passed a smith, sweating beside his forge, and several small shops.

The tow-scow came to the end of the canal and we stepped off, only to board another boat pulled by another alien ox. This one took us deeper into the city. Each tow-scow had its particular route, at the end of which, the navigator would turn the boat around and head back the way they came. We changed boats twice more.

The waterway was as jammed as Denis Street in Montreal at rush hour, but everyone moved out of the way for the large tow-scow bus. At one point, we passed a market on the banks. Vendors peddled their wares from tents or the backs of wagons. I was surprised to see an abundance of fresh produce. The scent of cooking meat made Little Bean turn over inside me. I nibbled on my trail mix, hoping I could keep it down.

"That's the water demon's palace." Huyn nudged me and pointed beyond the market with his chin. It was hard to miss the monstrous building that rose like a spiraled shell. It looked organic, as if some giant hermit crab had abandoned its house for a new one. The shell was so black, it seemed to suck in the sunlight. The only door was visible because a reddish light glowed from inside. "I never realized that such...civilization was possible outside the wards," I said.

"Ironic, isn't it. That the demon's blight is the reason they were able to build here." He gazed at the bustle passing us by on shore. "Makes you wonder if they didn't kill her too quickly."

I made a noncommittal noise. Considering I had the spawn of a so-called demon in my womb, I had my own opinions about the shoot-first-ask-questions-later mentality that most people had when dealing with demon-kind.

Even so, the palace gave off an unsettling hum of magic, and I couldn't imagine why anyone would want to live or work nearby. I was glad when the scow moved on.

It took several hours, but we navigated the breadth of the city and disembarked at the last scow terminal near noon. Only one other passenger got off at the same stop. Huyn held me back, pretending to watch the tow-scow make its lumbering turn to head back into the city.

"Wait for him to go on ahead," he whispered. I didn't think the passenger was spying on us, but we waited until he disappeared into a cluster of buildings before leaving in the opposite direction. We followed a narrow road into an abandoned industrial complex. Steel girders and cement towers jutted into the sky.

Before the wars, these little towns of offices, warehouses and factories grew up outside every city. As a teenager, I spent one summer working as a receptionist for a moving company in such a complex. The job had been mind-numbingly dull, and I remember thinking that the corporate park was so ugly, someone should tear it down. And of course, Terra did just that to many of those parks.

This one sat just inside the perimeter of the dead demon's influence. The forest hadn't reclaimed it, but vines grew up around the metal joists and beams. Walking through the empty doorways and staring up at the building's rusted bones felt like walking through a graveyard of steel leviathans.

Huyn stopped at a pile of rubble grown over with bramble and began pulling off branches. Princess, happy to help, dug around the base, tossing clods of earth behind her.

I took the respite to eat. Again. I was almost out of trail mix, so I pulled out a travel cake. I'd bought them in Montreal in preparation for this trip. The baker had assured me they'd keep for several weeks. He'd failed to mention that they were hard enough to break teeth if you didn't soak them in tea or water first. I munched on a dry biscuit, and choked it down with water. At this rate, I'd wear down my molars in no time, and then I'd be a toothless old…crone. A jolt of panic shot through me at that thought. The business of travel and Huyn's revelations about Baldyr had occupied me so much, I'd almost forgotten the reason for the journey.

Thankfully, Huyn didn't give me long to dwell over my angst. He piled branches to one side and revealed an opening in the rubble. You had to squint at it just the right way to even consider the crack in the rocks as a door.

"This is it? The door to Jotunheim?"

"Of course not. Come on. Before someone sees." He waved us through. One step into the shadows, I saw stairs descending steeply into blackness.

"Wait here. If you've got a flashlight, get it out." Huyn left us at the top of the stairs to re-barricade the door. I fished a gleam from my pack, shook it and tossed it up to float above my head.

Huyn returned and nodded at the gleam. "Fancy."

"My…um…boyfriend is an alchemist."

"Nice." He didn't seem to notice my hesitation. Calling Mason my "boyfriend" sounded ridiculous, like we were teenagers who dated on Friday nights. But technically, he wasn't my husband. I knew no good word to describe what he meant to me. Lover? Soul-mate? Missing limb? Those were a bit too dramatic.

We descended the stairs in single file—Huyn in the lead with Raven and Princess clattering along behind him, then me. The stairs led to a basement walkway with metal doors along both walls. Most of these were closed and Huyn didn't try the rusted handles. At the end of the hall, a sliding metal door stood partly ajar to reveal more stairs.

Down we went again.

After a few steps, the stairs changed. Instead of industrial cement slabs, they were carved from rock, rough-hewn and slick with ancient moss. The tiled walls also gave way to naked stone. The air felt heavy with the burden of solid rock overhead.

Princess whined at nothing and pressed against my leg as we walked.

A noise came from ahead—something like an industrial fan or air conditioner.

We hit the last step and moved into a large cavern. Huyn didn't stop, didn't hesitate. He found another tunnel and kept going. Only his forthright confidence kept me moving forward.

The humming intensified, and I realized it wasn't a fan, but the faint and growing sound of rushing water.

We finally stopped when the tunnel ended at the edge of a river. The water looked deep and cold, its surface black as an obsidian mirror. The current was slow, but somewhere ahead rapids were making that rushing noise. I couldn't help thinking of River Styx and half expected to see a ferry taking the dead to their final home.

Huyn was cursing in old Jotnar, and I noticed a boat tied to a crumbling mooring. Or half a boat. The rest had rotted away or been torn off by the current.

"We're going to have to swim." He was already sitting on the dock, getting ready to slip into the water.

"Hey! Hold on a minute! I'm not going in there." I crossed my arms over my stomach. They say parents can't protect their children from everything, but I could certainly protect Little Bean from dying of hypothermia in a freezing underground river or from getting eaten by sea serpents.

"You will if you want to get to Asgard. The door is in there." Huyn pointed downstream. He jumped into the river and turned on his back to watch me as he paddled into midstream. "Come on. It's not so bad."

Raven leaped, but instead of splashing into the water, he spread his wings and flew over Huyn's head.

Wow. I still thought of Raven as that little pony with stunted wings, but he'd grown. His wingspan was wider than an eagle's.

Huyn gasped and swore in Jotnar as Raven's hooves barely cleared his head. Eagle wings or not, he was struggling to keep to the air. Princess leaped after him. Her bone-white wings appeared from nowhere and she zoomed around the low-ceilinged cavern.

"Show offs," I mumbled, crouching down on the dock to let my feet dangle in the water. Ever since we returned from the Nether, Princess had been able to conjure those wings at will. I wasn't so blessed.

I sucked in a breath as the icy water seeped into my boots.

Huyn treaded water in the middle of the river. "Hurry up. I'm freezing my balls off here."

I muttered something else he could do with his balls, and lowered myself into the water.

It was too deep to stand. I kicked away from the dock. My pack and sword limited my arm strokes, but I only had to paddle out to meet Huyn. After that, the current took us on a gentle ride downstream. It might have been fun, like lounging in a tube on a lazy river on a summer's afternoon, except, of course, for the crush of black stone on every side and the numbing cold. Luckily, the gleam kept pace and we weren't forced to make the trip in darkness.

The rapids bumped us around. I banged a knee on a submerged rock but managed to keep my head above water. I cried out as I got sucked through a rock funnel, but then the river widened and we were once again floating in deep, black water.

Raven gave up trying to fly and dropped into the water with a splash. I had a moment of panic when he didn't resurface right away. Then his curly black head with the glowing white forelock popped up. He thrashed, snorted out water, and found his sea legs.

A bark came from ahead. I glanced up, wondering how Princess had gotten so far ahead, but she was right above me. She'd heard the barking too. Her wings fluttered, holding her still like a bumblebee over a fat flower. Her ears pricked forward and a woof burst from her trembling lips.

A sleek, black head popped up in front of me. It let out a chilling howl— halfway between a hyena's laugh and the chitter of an angry squirrel. Princess launched into a frenzy of barks. The creature dove. Its fanned tail thumped the surface and sprayed us with water.

Princess's wings disappeared and she dove after it.

More heads popped up, chittering and splashing. We were surrounded.

I twirled in the water, desperately searching for Princess who hadn't come up again. The creatures weren't attacking, but they were in my way as I paddled and turned in circles. Raven was snarling and snapping his teeth at any that came too near.

"What are these things?" I yelled over the noise.

"We call them water hounds," Huyn yelled back.

Then Princess breached like a whale with a loud "Aroooooo!" The creatures pounced on her.

They were playing!

The water hounds were as large as sea lions but with more wolfish muzzles and longer ear flaps.

"Are my eyes deceiving me or did your hell hound just trade wings for fins?" Huyn asked.

"What?"

Princess soared through the air again in a dolphin dive. Huyn was right. Her tail and back legs had merged into one great, fan-shaped tail.

The hounds tussled and romped like a tumble of puppies. Raven seemed agitated and swam around me, snorting angrily.

"She'll be fine," I told him, then turned to Huyn. "Right? They're not dangerous, are they?"

"They can give you a good nip, but it's just for sport."

The hounds kept us company as we floated downstream. I gave up trying to swim. My water-logged boots and sword made it a struggle just to keep afloat. I turned onto my back and let the current take me down a narrow corridor of bare rock. The gleam kept up with us, but its light was starting to fade. I didn't want to be stuck down there when the light went out.

"How much longer?" I asked.

"Not much. Just around that bend." Huyn pointed forward. The blackness ahead was just a little less black as the gleam reflected off stone. It looked like we were about to sail right into a wall, but the river took a hard turn to the left, and we were suddenly in another underground cavern.

The current spiraled in a lazy vortex as if it had no clear exit, and the walls seemed to press in on me. I fought down panic with hard breaths.

A water hound yipped and dolphin-dived straight into the wall. I cringed, expecting to hear its head splat against rock. There was no splat. And no water hound. It simply disappeared.

More hounds followed it. I moved closer and saw that the wall shimmered slightly like a black mirror hit by stray moonlight.

It was a portal. We'd made it.

Princess barked as the last water hound dove through.

"Princess, *hael*!" I shouted, but it was too late. She followed them.

Raven let out a whinny of despair and frantically swam toward the portal.

"Raven! Don't you dare…"

He dove through.

Some parenting authority I had.

"Don't worry." Huyn was also heading toward the door. "It's what we're here for after all."

"Jotunheim? You're sure?"

"That's right. Come on, now. Before they get too far ahead."

We swam forward. I put the last of my energy into each stroke. I didn't want to leave Princess and Raven alone, but I paused.

"What's on the other side?" I asked.

"Hard to say. The door isn't stable. It moves around a bit. But I expect we'll come out under blue skies."

That would be an improvement over this black tunnel.

"See you on the flip side," Huyn said with a grin before the portal swallowed him.

I hung in the water, staring up at the door. If I'd had second thoughts about this, Princess and Raven had taken that choice away.

No going back now.

I pushed through the portal. It washed over me like a warm shower of jelly. I panicked as the vacuum compressed me. I couldn't breathe. And then I was through...

...into a bright day under a blue sky. Birds sang from green trees along the shore as I floated down a cerulean river and right over a waterfall.

CHAPTER

12

When I was ten, my mother dated a man with three kids, all a bit older than me. We all went camping one weekend at a small cabin on a cliff overlooking a lake. My almost-step-siblings taunted me to jump off the cliff. I stood on that ledge looking down at blue-black water. It felt a hundred feet high, but was probably closer to thirty. Looking back now, I should have wondered why they made me go first. Maybe it was because I was naive and easily manipulated. I'd never had siblings before. I wanted them to like me. So I closed my eyes and jumped.

They say it's not the fall that kills you. It's the landing. But the falling part was enough to panic my ten-year-old self and I flailed like a turkey in a tornado. When I landed I broke my right elbow. My soon-to-be ex-siblings blamed me for ruining our trip. When the weather is damp, that elbow still aches.

This time, as I fell, I had a lot more to protect than my elbows.

I shot over the falls and for a heart-stopping moment, I was suspended in the air. Water droplets misted around me in a blinding cloud. Then I dropped. Feet first, I tucked my arms in tight and prayed to the All Father to protect me and Little Bean.

The surface of the river slapped me. Hard. My head snapped back. I gasped and my mouth filled with water. I sank, but only for one stunned instant. Then I kicked and thrashed. I clawed at the water churning around me, with no idea which way was up. Pack, sword and boots weighed me down, but I had no time to shuck them. I needed air, and I needed it now.

Something caught in my braid and yanked me. I burst through the surface into sweet, sweet sky and sucked in a watery breath. Then I coughed and spat while Huyn hauled me to shore.

"What the hell Huyn!" I gasped. "You could have warned me!"

His lips were pressed as flat as the hair plastered to his skull. "I didn't know. I told you the door moves around on this side. But it's never opened at the falls before."

I heard barking.

"Raven! Is he okay?"

"The pony is fine. Or should I say the boy is fine." Huyn's expression went from contrition to indignation. He pointed upstream where Princess was prancing around a wet, bedraggled boy on the river bank. Raven must have panicked when he tumbled over the falls and reverted to his human form.

"I told you to come alone," Huyn said. "I allowed the beasts against my better judgement, but we're in Vanlandi territory here. Their scouts will stop any travelers, and they don't like strangers sneaking along their border. I'm allowed some leeway due to my status, but…"

I cut him off before he worked himself into a rant. "What's done is done. He's here now. Besides, you don't get to be mad. I'm still mad. That fall could have killed…" My words trailed off. I crossed my arms over my stomach, even though my keening told me the life inside was still thriving.

"I'm sorry. I should have been more careful." Huyn squeezed my shoulder. His thumb scooped away a wet lock of hair stuck to my cheek. The gesture was so like something Mason would do, I was almost undone. I sniffled, and my sinuses burned from their cold-water bath.

"It's okay. I can ask Raven to change back to his pony form, but he's coming with me."

"No. Better he stays human for now. The Vanlandi have powerful sensates. They can sniff out glamors and shifters better than most. If they think he's hiding his true form, there will be more questions."

"You make it sound like it's a done deal that they'll catch us."

He shrugged. "Hope for the best and expect to be eaten by a rabid ogre. That's always been my motto."

"It's catch…tchy." My teeth were chattering.

"Let's get moving. You'll warm you up faster. It's a long walk to a hot meal and a bed."

Raven wouldn't leave the river until we found his pack. The current had ripped it away when he shifted. Huyn wanted to head inland, away from the mountains and the deep river gorge, but Raven was adamant.

"Mason made that pack for me. Said to keep it with me at all times. I'm not going without it." He stalked off along the river bank.

"Want me to grab him?" Huyn asked. "He'll kick and scream, but I've handled worse."

I had no doubt he had. Huyn was a bouncer for the Knackers, after all.

"Will it be much out of our way if we follow the river for a bit?"

Huyn rubbed his chin and thought about it.

"It's not so much the distance. That river heads straight toward Vanir, the Vanlandi stronghold."

"Surely, these Vanlandi aren't as bad as all that. They're Jotnar, just like you, aren't they?"

I was trying to remember my Asgard history lessons, but was coming up with a blank about the Vanlandi.

Huyn's eyes darkened. "Yes and no. They're Jotnar, but a clan that keeps mostly to themselves. And they don't have much use for the Aesir. We should avoid them at all cost."

Raven had stopped not far away. He'd listened to the exchange between me and Huyn. Now he waited for my decision. His feet were planted and hands fisted at his sides. He'd lost so much. He really needed a win. If I was being honest, I wanted to give him that win. I wanted to be the cool mom who listened.

I didn't feel like a mom. I was still that kid standing on a cliff, hoping others would like me if I leaped.

"Let's follow the river for a bit," I said. "Maybe the pack got caught on some rocks."

Huyn shook his head, grumbled in giant tongue, something about dumb Aesir blood, and we headed out.

We followed a well-worn path along the river bank. Twice, I called a halt so I could run into the bushes and throw up. The morning sickness had been exacerbated by swallowing river water. After the second run-and-barf, I sat in the dirt and tried to tidy my wet and bedraggled hair with shaking hands. Hunger and cold were making me weak. Princess poked her nose over my shoulder and snuffled my ear.

"I'm okay." I patted her neck. She spied the pile of vomit, and lunged for it. "Don't you dare!" I yanked her away. Princess had a habit of finding the smelliest, rottenest things and rolling in them for sport.

I got to my feet and hauled her back to Huyn and Raven who were waiting by the river.

"You okay?" Huyn asked.

I nodded, though I felt strangely numb all over, like the cold had seeped into my bones and taken over my thoughts.

"Just need some food." I rifled through my pack with stiff fingers until I found my last sack of trail mix, and made a silent thanks to Mason for creating the waterproof travel bags. Even when he wasn't with me, he was still taking care of me.

I also found my first aid kit and wrapped myself in the emergency blanket. I ate the rest of my rations as we walked with the mylar blanket over my shoulders like a cape. I'd expended a lot of energy and my hands shook as I offered the bag to the others. They all declined. No one wanted to get between the hungry pregnant woman and her trail mix.

We found Raven's bag a half-hour's walk from the falls. It had snagged on some rocks and driftwood in the middle of a rapid current that surged around the rocks with white caps. It was too far to reach with a stick.

Raven and I turned to Huyn.

"What are you looking at me for? I just got my ass dry. I'm not going back in there." He crossed thick arms over his chest.

"So, you'd make the pregnant woman do it?" Yes, I played that card.

He scrunched up his face and glared at me.

Raven made one of those disgusted noises that all teenagers seem to perfect and pushed past us. "I'll get it."

"You will not!" I grabbed him, but his arm melted as he shifted. In boy form, he was scrawny and gangly. As a pony, he was all legs. Either way, he looked shaky and exhausted. He flexed his wings and could only manage to raise himself a few inches off the ground.

"Forget it. If you get caught in those rapids you'll break your neck." That sounded perfectly reasonable and mom-ish. But his wings gave me an idea.

"Princess, fetch." I pointed to the bramble of driftwood with the backpack. Princess cocked her head. Her tongue lolled from the side of her mouth and hung halfway down her chest.

"Fetch!" I pointed to the pack. She pawed the ground at the river's edge.

"She's not stupid," Huyn said with a grin. "She doesn't want to get wet again either."

I flapped my arms. "You can fly there. Fetch!"

Princess rolled in the dirt and begged for belly rubs. Critter wrangler rule number sixteen: Sometimes a hound is just a hound.

I was considering what I had to bribe Huyn with, when a sound had us all turning toward the thick hedge that ran along the river's edge. It was a muttering, buzzing noise with the cadence of gabbling geese.

"Oh no." Huyn face-palmed himself and walked off a few steps.

"What's the matter?" My head swiveled around. I was trying to pinpoint the source of the noise, but it seemed to be coming from everywhere.

"Yggies," he said with the same disgust as if he'd said "maggots."

"Really? I've never seen one."

"You'll soon be wishing for that blessed ignorance again. Trust me."

Despite his words, I turned eagerly toward the hedge that was now rustling. The pest expert in me couldn't resist an encounter with a new critter. All I knew about yggies was that they were small sentient tree beings and generally moved in flocks.

The hedge churned and a mass of two-foot high bodies surged through it. The yggies came right at us, then like a school of fish with one mind, they balked at the giant in their way and turned, only to come up against a snarling hell hound. They stopped sharply. The ones in the back plowed into those on the front, causing a traffic jam of squawking tree limbs. Eventually they sorted themselves out, and they milled around the space between the river and the hedge.

About two-feet high, the yggies were thin like saplings, though their bark-like skin ranged from smooth and silver to craggy and gunmetal gray. They had many stubby feet that crept over the ground and dozens of branch-like limbs sticking out of their trunks. Some yggies seemed more evolved than the others. These had definite arms that ended in spindly fingers, and tufts of green shoots sprouting from their heads. Most were faceless or with only the hint of features, but these others had distinct eyes, noses and mouths hidden among the branches.

They clucked and strutted and seemed to be conferring with each other. One yggie cooed at his neighbor and touched him with twiggy appendages. The second yggie clucked and turned to his neighbor, passing on the message with more touches. It was like watching a game of broken telephone played by octopuses.

"What are they doing?" I whispered.

"Nothing. Just don't make eye-contact." The yggie conference had ended and one of the little bushes gripped my leg in several of its hands. The branches spiking from his head were covered in bright green leaves. Dark eyes peered through a beard of prickly branches.

"Travelers? Helping?"

Huyn studiously examined the clouds in the sky.

"Um, no thanks," I said. "We're just about on our way."

"No helping?"

"Yes!" Raven cried.

"No!" Huyn shouted at the same time.

Raven pointed to the bramble in the middle of the river. "See that pack. It's mine. *He's* too chicken to go get it and *she* won't let me." He pointed at Huyn then at me. "But you could help us get it back."

Huyn swore. I'd never heard someone combine so many expletives in one sentence. He was an artist, really.

The yggies went through their little touch-and-coo dance again. Their spokesperson glided over to Raven and grasped his ankles.

"Helping travelers. For great Yggdrasil. Helping!"

"Of course." Raven didn't know what that meant, but with all the arrogance of a pre-teen he agreed anyway.

I vaguely remember that yggies were said to be the spawn of Yggdrasil, the great Life Tree that linked nine worlds, included Terra, Asgard and Jotunheim. I also remembered that they were big on karma and doing good deeds to impress Yggdrasil.

And we were their next good deed.

They scoped out the problem with much cooing and touching as they considered the distance, the sun's angle and wind speed. Huyn dropped his bulk into the grass.

"Might as well take a rest. We'll be here a while." He laid back, shaded his eyes with an arm, and pretended to sleep.

The yggies settled on a plan. I'm not sure how, but all the touching and clucking had come to an end. One yggie jumped on the back of another, its tiny feet scrambling in the twiggy limbs. A third yggie climbed on top of the second. A fourth climbed onto the growing tower of bodies. The rest surged around them, boosting and supporting their brethren. For little creatures, they were strong. A fifth climbed on top. The tower started to lean over the water. More yggies scrambled up. With all the rushing around and cooing, I couldn't keep track of them. Three more yggies went up. The tower swayed. The yggies cried, "Ooooooooh!" as it almost toppled and, "Aaaaaaah!" as it swayed back over the water.

Another yggie mounted the scaffolding of tree bodies. He reached the top, let out a squawk and waggled his twiggy limbs.

The tower of bodies dipped low over the water. The yggies were interlocked tightly, and they made a perfect ladder. The last yggie, the one who'd spoken to me, reached for the backpack. His many arms grasped at air. They were an inch too short.

An yggie inside the tower cried out and the structure collapsed in a splash of bodies. Terrified yggies flailed in the rushing current. They scrambled over each other in a rush to save themselves from drowning.

Their screams roused Huyn, who marched into the water, cursing and yelling at the creatures to get out of his way. He tossed soggy yggies onto the bank like he was piling cordwood. They clung to his legs, climbed onto his back and hung from his arms. He stomped through the water, then waded when it reached his waist until he grabbed the last yggie clinging desperately to the driftwood bramble. He plucked the critter off, untangled the pack, waded back to shore and dumped both at Raven's feet.

His eyes were as dark as storm clouds.

"And that is why you never ask an yggie for help."

Yggies: Big heart in a small sapling

May 4, 2077

In the forests around Asgard and Jotunheim you might find a small sentient tree being known as an yggie (pronounced iggy). In fact, if you see one yggie, you'll probably see a whole bunch. They tend to move in packs. A group of yggies is called a thicket. Ha! That makes me laugh. I know it's supposed to refer to a hedge but, let's face it, yggies are a little thick.

They have one purpose in life: to become a Life Tree like Yggdrasil, the great Ash whose roots and branches hold up the nine worlds of Norse legends.

The yggies have some work to do to achieve this lofty status, considering they generally stand about two feet tall. More of a bush than a tree, really, an yggie has dominate limbs that it uses like arms and tiny root balls for feet—so many feet that it sort of glides across the ground like a centipede. The rest of its body is covered in bristly, branch-like spikes. Mature yggies develop distinct facial features among these bristles.

In a twisted sort of mythology or religion, the yggies believe they can attain Life-Tree status through good deeds. Rack up enough karma points, and BAM!, your spirit can suddenly penetrate the veil between worlds.

Seems a little hinky. But I suppose it's not much different than the Christian view of sainthood.

Unfortunately, the yggies roam in packs that can reach great numbers, and so they become pests. In their driving need to do good deeds, they can trample each other to death. Innocent bystanders have been known to get caught in an yggie stampede too. Entire crops have been lost to a frenzied thicket. I, personally, have never met an yggie. This information comes from reliable sources who have encountered them, but I'd love to hear from you. Have you ever run into a thicket?

*Update November 18, 2081

Since I wrote this post four years ago, I have had an actual encounter with a thicket of yggies. Yes, they can be a nuisance, but the worst offenders are the very young yggies. As they mature from sprouts to saplings, they develop a greater sense of self and dignity. They may even go off alone, leaving the dubious safety of their thicket.

I have witnessed one yggie perform a great and selfless deed. And yes, he was rewarded by becoming a tree that pierces the veil between worlds. So perhaps there is some truth in sainthood too.

COMMENTS (8)

They sound very much like creatures we call cactus cats, though I've never heard one speak. If you break off one of their arms, they leak enough milk to keep a man alive in the desert for a day. Tastes a bit like chicken.
SaguaroHero (May 5, 2077)

Where do you come up with these crazy-ass stories?
Potpie4U (May 5, 2077)

DO NOT COMPARE YOUR BLASPHEMES WITH THE STORIES OF CHRIST AS HIS DISCIPLES
his-word333 (May 5, 2077)

> his-word333, STOP YELLING!
> *Iamnotarobot (May 5, 2077)*

I'm glad you rediscovered this amazing creature. I think they get a bad rap. Like children with over-active imaginations and restless legs, they just need to have that energy refocused on a worthwhile activity.
ClassAct913 (November 18, 2081)

Yeah, let's harness them to a wheel and generate some electricity—you know put them to use at something important instead of this twaddle.
CheeseSandwich4044 (November 18, 2081)

> CheeseSandwich4044, feel free to scroll on by if you don't like my twaddle.
> *Valkyrie367 (November 18, 2081)*

>> CheeseSandwich4044, and don't let the door hit ya where the good lord split ya.
>> *Iamnotarobot (November 18, 2081)*

CHAPTER

13

otunheim doesn't do seasons like Terra. It has winter, spring and summer, but these are a patchwork of places rather than times, as if a long dead god had pointed at the ground and demanded snow, or green rolling hills, or whatever his current mood fancied.

Heading into winter didn't mean longer nights. It meant the lush greenery suddenly gave way to tundra-like desert. By midday we had to break ice on a small stream to drink and pull warmer coats and hats from our packs. Sand and dirt became snow, hard-packed and crunching underfoot. A white sun shone in an impossibly blue sky, and the wind bit with icy teeth.

Princess, who didn't like the heat, bounded ahead to find some dead and frozen thing to roll in. Despite Huyn's warnings about the Vanlandi, Raven kept to his equine form for warmth, and his fur was thick and fluffy like an Icelandic pony's.

Since leaving the river, we'd seen no one else. This was the land of frost giants and they had all been slumbering for centuries.

"Look, there is Bestla, mother of the gods." Huyn pointed to a mountain range in the distance. "See how she sleeps with her arms encircling the land. Even now she protects her offspring."

I shielded my eyes against the sun and gazed at the distant mountains. It was like trying to find the archer in the stars. I was never very good at that game. But if I turned my head and squinted, the lowlands did vaguely look like arms spreading from the mountain.

"And that big one, spiking into the sky is Ymir, the first giant born from the icy drops of chaos itself. Legend says the mountains where Bestla and Ymir slumbered are unreachable. We could walk for months or years and never reach them.

"Fascinating." I let him ramble on about the births and relations of gods. Luckily for us, we weren't heading toward the unreachable mountains, but skirting along the flatlands within Bestla's embrace.

None of it mattered.

As I doggedly put one foot in front of the other, my heart beat only for my unborn child. Once she didn't need it anymore, I was certain it would shatter like glass.

There isn't much to tell about that journey over the ice. It was cold, mind-numbingly bleak and treacherous. Once my foot crashed through the top layer of snow and I sank to my thighs. Raven screamed and back-pedaled on his hooves. Huyn stepped away too, so the crust wouldn't crack under him. He threw me a rope and I dug my way out. After that, the boredom of one step after another became fear that each step might be my last.

We camped that night huddled in a small cave carved from the only rocky outcropping we'd seen all day, with the wind howling like a pack of wolves around us.

We found wood to make a fire big enough to melt snow for tea. We ate cold pack rations. Raven was asleep before he finished his. Princess wrapped her body around him with a huge sigh and closed her eyes.

Against the odds, the yggies had kept up with us all day. The thicket had thinned when we left the warmer realms, but we still had a dozen of the odd creatures tagging along. Now they too slept in a jumble of stick-like limbs. Small snores came from the pile.

I dug through my pack for Avie's tincture. The bottle was nearly empty, and I downed the last drop. How long would that hold off the change? Not long enough. I could feel it coming in my bones.

I was counting liver spots on my cold-chapped hands when Huyn spoke softly.

"You know, you'll make a great queen."

He sat across the fire. The flames did little to warm us, but they lit his face in golden light.

I shook my head. "I'm too reasonable to rule."

"And reason isn't a good trait for a queen?"

"Not really. I like the happily-ever-after stories. I always want everyone to kiss and make up. Political negotiations don't work that way." I'd had a front-row seat to Mason's political wrangling. Only a few weeks into his term he already came home fuming in frustration.

The thought of Mason was like a cold wind down my back. For a moment—a blissful moment—I'd forgotten that I would never see him again.

"As I said, I'll think you'll be great."

I tucked my hands under my arms to warm them and stared at the fire so I wouldn't have to see the adoration in his eyes. Had it always been there? Had I been blind to it, or had his affection for me grown as we'd traveled? It didn't really matter. It would come to nothing. My heart was as frozen as the ice shelf we rested on.

Huyn thought I could challenge my aunt Dana for the throne of Asgard when the time came. Chances were, I'd never have to make that challenge. Huyn had said Baldyr was ill, but the king was older than dirt. I couldn't imagine Asgard without him. Surely, the Golden Apples would give him many more years—more years than I had.

"You said my grandfather was sick. How sick exactly?"

"Hard to tell. Last time I saw him, he looked perfectly fine. But you Aesir are like that. Fit and strong until the day you drop dead."

I nodded though he couldn't see me in the dark. "It's the apples."

"Yep. Those apples have started wars. Some say they were the original source of strife between Asgard and Jotunheim."

I didn't know about that. The Aesir and the Jotnar had been fighting for so long, the origins of their disagreements were lost in the mists. My grandfather had been the only one brave enough to stop the fighting.

And now he was dying. It seemed impossible. Every memory I had of him was happy. He laughed loud, drank hard and loved with fervor. He was a stern leader, but fiercely protective of his people. All his people—even the half-breeds that everyone else looked down on.

Asgard had no one to compare with King Baldyr, no one else who could lead with such a fair and strong hand.

And that's what the giants feared.

"You know, the Aesir will never accept me as queen." The fire had burned low and I spoke into the near-darkness. Huyn rested against his pack with his eyes closed. I thought he must have finally fallen asleep, but after a moment he answered.

"You might be surprised."

I wondered just how bad things were in Asgard, if Huyn thought they'd want me as queen.. "All I can do is challenge Dana. It will be up to Baldyr to name his heir."

"He can't name you if you're not there. So that's the first step. Getting you home. Now get some sleep. We'll be walking again tomorrow, and I'm not carrying you."

The wind howled through the icy mountains. I listened to Huyn breathe until the rhythm of his breaths became deep and even. But despite my exhaustion, I couldn't sleep.

My thoughts turned back to my larger-than-life grandfather. It would be wonderful to see him again, but I had no intention of becoming his heir. I would convince Grandfather to name another heir, someone other than Dana. At least one cousin must have distinguished themselves in the years that I'd been away.

There was Marika, a young Valkyrie novice who hadn't quite finished her training when I left. She would be a full-fledged Valkyrie by now, though I remembered that she had a weakness for the young men who came to watch us train. Other girls sniggered about her behind her back, saying that she'd get knocked up and would have to take her final test with a full belly. So maybe not Marika.

There had been a boy too. What was his name? Freddie or Frodo. No that was a hobbit. But something like that. He was a scholar. Too young maybe, but everyone said he was brilliant.

I ran the names of a dozen other cousins through my head, but they all had some deficiency that would keep them from making good leaders.

Water dripped from the ice shelf above and hissed on the embers burning low in our fire. My eyes felt gluey and my muscles were starting to ache. I sighed. I wouldn't solve any of my problems tonight.

Princess made puppy noises in her sleep, then tucked herself behind my legs. I turned and laid my head on her fluffiness. The rise and fall of her breaths finally tipped me over into sleep.

THE NEXT MORNING we continued over the bleak landscape. Then, like walking off a stage set, winter became spring. We stepped from the ice onto a dirt road. Within an hour of walking, grass and wildflowers grew by the roadside. By late afternoon, we were deep in a lush forest full of flying insects and creeping vines.

We shed our warm coats. My fingers and toes thawed, but not the bubble of ice I'd wrapped my heart in.

The yggies followed us for the rest of the day. When he hit a boggy patch, the one yggie who could speak jumped to my aid.

"Kale helps!" he said.

"Is that your name? Kale?"

The creature nodded vigorously. The buds on his branches seemed bigger and greener today. I didn't need help, but he was so earnest, I let him take my hand.

The other yggies tripped all over themselves trying to help too, until we wasted precious minutes pulling them out of the bog. One yggie insisted on carrying my pack, then left it behind and we had to backtrack for half an hour to recover it. They brought me a wild pear to eat, but couldn't agree on who should get the honor of presenting it, and by the time the winning yggie put the fruit in my hand it was nothing more than pulp.

If helping was their ticket to paradise, they had a long road ahead.

I was dragging my feet by the time Huyn announced that we should stop for the day.

"The next village is only a few hours away, but we won't make it before dark."

"I'm happy here." I dropped to the ground and laid my head on my pack. "I'm just going to rest my eyes for a moment, then I'll help you set up camp."

At least that was my intention, but I was exhausted. When I opened my eyes, some time later, the blanket from my pack covered me. A small fire warmed me from the front and Princess was slumbering at my back.

I sat up and pulled the blanket around my shoulders. The sun had taken all the warmth when it set. Two large rodent-like creatures were browning on a spit over the campfire.

Raven had shifted back to his human form, and now he stared into the flames with glassy eyes, his knees drawn up under his chin. Beside him, the yggies were piled in a heap of twiggy arms and legs. I would have mistaken them for a bramble bush except for the tiny snores coming from the jumbled mass.

Huyn returned carrying an armload of wet tubers.

"Found these growing by the river. They're a wild yam, of a sort. Should be tasty once they're baked." He dumped them around the edge of the fire where they hissed and popped.

"I'm so hungry I could eat them raw," I said.

"Not a good idea. My brother dared me to eat one raw as a lad, and I chipped a tooth. They're harder than a witch's heart until they're cooked. But no worries, they should be done soon."

I sighed. Little Bean would just have to wait for supper.

An hour later, I was licking grease off my fingers. The meat—I didn't dare ask what it had been—was gamey and tough but I didn't care. I'd needed the protein. And Huyn's wild yams were the best thing I'd ever tasted.

"It's amazing how everything tastes better when you're hungry," I said.

The sun had just set, leaving a faint glow above the trees. Coyote hour, I thought. The time of day when small creatures ventured out in search of food, and larger creatures crept among the growing shadows to feed on them.

A large beetle hummed out the song of his people behind me. Frogs trilled along the creek and something hooted in the trees. I wasn't afraid of night critters here. Yes, wolves prowled the forest. Monstrous brutes descended from Fenrir, the wolf of legends. And the thick trees hid others beasts, but they were beasts I knew and understood, not like the Inbetween's magic-addled monsters. These worlds—Jotunheim and Asgard—hadn't suffered the apocalyptic Flood Wars. Those wars had broken the veil between Terra and countless other worlds, letting in alien species and twisting the Terran animals into unrecognizable horrors. Here, I could enjoy the campfire and listen to frogs calling to potential mates and owls hooting directions for the hunt.

My belly was full and my eyes felt heavy again.

"We should stop in the village and buy horses," Huyn said, breaking me out of my lull.

"Is it that far to Port Utgard?"

The River Ifing separated Asgard and Jotunheim. The only ferry across it left from Port Utgard, and it was closely guarded by both sides. Anyone caught crossing elsewhere would be considered up to no good and detained, if they were lucky. Border patrols were known to shoot first and not bother with questions.

"Two days on foot," Huyn said. "And we need to stop in Utgard city."

That made me sit up and pay attention. "We can't!"

"We must." Huyn frowned. "My father would be insulted if you didn't pay your respects."

I ground my teeth and my jaw popped. I'd been grinding them a lot lately. Utgard City was the capital of Jotunheim. It sat on an island in a tributary of Ifing, a short boat ride from the port. It wasn't a particularly long detour, but being presented at King Gillingr's court wouldn't be quick.

Huyn saw my hesitance and said, "Your grandfather will not be pleased when he finds out you spurned Gillingr's hospitality. We're allies now. There are protocols to follow."

He was right. Aesir could only travel through Jotunheim with the king's permission. I couldn't get that permission unless I presented myself at court.

But my bones ached like an old woman's. Like a crone's. "Huyn, I know you want to do the right thing, but…" I felt the heat of tears flood my eyes. "Tomorrow, I could wake up a dried up old husk…" My hands strayed to my belly. Huyn scooted over to put his arm around me.

"Shush, now. That won't happen. We'll get there. No palace visit, then. Better to ask forgiveness than permission, right? Come on now, it will be all right. We'll get horses in town tomorrow and we'll be across the river in no time."

His magic twined around us, making me feel safe.

I sniffled and wiped my nose on my sleeve. And now I had the hiccups. Huyn rubbed my back, and I let him. I knew it was wrong. I knew he had feelings for me that I didn't return. But he was warm and solid and I desperately needed comfort in that moment.

"If I were bigger, I could fly you across the river." It was the first thing Raven had said all night. He rose to toss another log on the fire. When he sat, he pulled his backpack onto his lap and hugged it between his chest and knees.

Huyn pulled away from me. His magic jangled and I realized he was embarrassed. "Unless you plan to gain a few hundred pounds in the next hour, we'll have to find other mounts," he said.

We all fell into staring at the flames, thinking our private thoughts. The quiet was broken only by my persistent hiccups. After a moment Huyn said, "What's so important in that bag anyway?"

Raven didn't look up but shrugged. "Just stuff. Stuff Mason and I made together."

Oof. My heart was squished flat. I'd been so hung up on my own misery and fear, I'd forgotten that Raven had lost his second home too—and his new dad—just when he was starting to settle in.

"I miss him too." I reached over to squeeze Raven's knee. He didn't respond, but he didn't pull away either. I took that as a win.

The yggies suddenly stirred. One moment they were a jumble of slumbering twigs, the next they jumped up and waddled around like a bunch of drunken geese, jabbering and bumping into each other. Then they gave a communal shriek and ran off into the dark, leaving us in stunned silence.

"Hey, Kyra, what do you call a group of yggies?" Raven asked.

I shrugged. "A thicket?"

"A pain in the ass."

I felt my jaw drop open.

Did my kid just tell a joke? It was a terrible joke but I laughed anyway. And Raven shot me a shy grin.

"Any idea what that was about?" I asked Huyn.

"None." He stood and stared into the shadows thrown by our fire. His hand went to the knife at his belt.

An arrow struck the dirt between his feet.

"Touch that blade and the next one goes through your heart," said a voice from the darkness.

14

We were surrounded. A dozen Jotnar stepped into the ring of firelight. Six of them held bows, ready to shoot. The others gripped swords or axes. One stepped forward. He was taller than the others but still short and slender for a Jotnar. He wore supple leather breeches and a vest with no shirt underneath. Black hair fell over his brow in a boyish mop, but his eyes were hard and his lips pressed thin. He pointed a sword at Huyn.

"Rangvald, is that you?" Huyn rose from the campfire and all the arrows took aim at his chest. He held up his hands in surrender. "It's me. Huyn."

"Huyn?" Rangvald lowered his blade. The men met in two strides and clapped each other on the back. "How long has it been, my friend?"

Huyn stood back and grinned. "Too long. The last time I saw you, your skinny arms couldn't even lift that sword." He turned. I still sat by the campfire with Princess bristling by my side. "This is my friend, Kyra Greene and her ward, Raven. Rangvald was billeted at Utgard as a boy. We had the same tutors and sword master."

Rangvald's eyes swept me up and down, leaving me feeling raked over and exposed.

"What are you doing traveling with one of Odin's lot?" he asked. Someone behind him spat on the ground, as if to curse the All-father's name. Despite the friendly greeting from Rangvald, the rest of his party hadn't relaxed. Huyn took in the military stares and weapons-ready stances and pulled Rangvald aside.

Princess pressed her shaggy body against my leg. Her chest rumbled. I sank my fingers into her ruff.

"Silence your hound or I'll shoot it," a soldier said.

I unsheathed my sword. The soldier wouldn't have much to fear from a normal sword. Giants healed fast and the magic humming around this lot sent my keening bells ringing. But my sword wasn't average either. It was a Valkyrie weapon—a sword of mercy and death on the battlefield—and the Jotnar would recognize it. The soldier's eyes widened when firelight hit the dull metal.

"That's right. It's a Valkyrie blade." I grinned, knowing full well that after days on the road I looked like some wild woman with a dirt-smeared face, tangled hair and crazy eyes. I was betting they couldn't tell the sword was dormant.

The soldier who'd threatened Princess lowered his bow. The others relaxed, but weapons weren't sheathed. Princess sat back on her haunches, ready to attack at my signal.

Huyn and Rangvald returned. Huyn took me aside and spoke quietly.

"Rangvald's mother is the Freya of the Vanlandi. He insists that we travel with them tomorrow."

"Where?"

"To Gottvaer, the Vanlandi stronghold. They were on a hunt and will be returning in the morning." He saw me hesitate. "They have...their own ways. It's not a good idea to insult the Freya. And we're moving in that direction anyway."

I glanced at the hard men and women arranged around our campfire and nodded.

Rangvald clapped Huyn on the shoulder.

"Good. It is settled. Tomorrow we ride for home. Tonight we drink!"

THE RATTLE OF harnesses and stamping of hooves woke me before dawn. I was amazed that the hunters were able to stand after the amount of ale they'd consumed the night before. The Jotnar were big at everything, eating and drinking included.

Rangvald had hobbled their horses down the road in order to sneak up on us the night before. We were a day's walk from the stronghold, so I was glad when they offered us extra mounts. Actually, if it weren't for the horses, I might have snuck away in the night. Gottvaer was on the road to Utgard, so it wasn't out of our way, but playing tea party with some Vanlandi Freya looking to pick a fight with the Aesir was not on my to-do list.

I woke Raven and packed up my bedroll before finding Huyn, who was conferring with Rangvald. Fog hung around their shoulders and misted Rangvald's beard.

Rangvald saw me and smiled. "I hope you slept well, Lady Kyra."

"I did. And it's just Kyra."

Rangvald didn't lose his smile. I suspected he knew it was a good one that pleased the ladies, but it had a hard edge this morning.

"Are you not the granddaughter of King Baldyr of Asgard?"

"Yes, but—"

"Then Lady Kyra it is." He turned and patted the horse next to him. "I chose this mare for you. She's fierce but runs with a smooth gait. A mount well suited to a Valkyrie. Her name is Tordenbitt. We call her Tory."

Tordenbitt—Thunder Bite. It was a good name for the mare. She stood sixteen hands tall and was all black with a white blaze on her forehead.

"Thank you." I took the reins and stroked the mare's neck, letting her taste my magic. All animals, and horses in particular, are sensitive to magic. She felt my calm assurance through the energy pinging back and forth between us and let out a welcoming snort.

"We should be enjoying my mother's hospitality in time for a late dinner," Rangvald said.

"Your mother is the Freya of Gottvaer?"

"Yes, and I'm certain she'll be interested in the tale of the Jotnar and the Valkyrie who walk together." He glanced at Huyn and grinned.

"It's not really so interesting," I mumbled, but Rangvald only laughed and clapped Huyn on the shoulder again. How could anyone be so good humored before the sun rose? I hadn't even taken part in the drinking the night before, and I had to drag my butt into the saddle. Thankfully, Tory was a very patient mount.

Huyn gave me a brief rundown about the Vanlandi as we walked through the growing dawn. They were Jotnar, in that they were subjects of King Gillingr, but they enjoyed a certain independence that other clans didn't have.

Rangvald's mother, Disir, kept the title Freya, which meant clan chieftain.

Somewhere, a millennium ago, the Vanlandi giants mingled and married with the Vanir. Like the Aesir, the Vanir boasted a divine lineage. They were the *other* gods who'd ruled in the early days of Asgard—gods of wisdom and fertility. Their wise-women could see into the future. What they saw there must have terrified them because they tried to wipe out Odin and his crew. When that didn't work, they made a truce, and the two sides exchanged hostages to keep the peace. In this way, the lines between the Vanir and the Aesir blurred until no one in Asgard remembered why they'd been fighting in the first place.

The Vanlandi remembered. For an eon, they'd kept up a healthy distrust for the Aesir who'd plotted against and killed their people.

King Gillingr might have made peace with Odin's offspring, but not all the Jotnar agreed, and the Vanlandi were the treaty's most vocal opponents.

And I was about to greet the Freya of this clan at her own hearth.

Rangvald called a halt when a ratatosk scout returned with news of the road ahead.

Ratatosks were rodents about the size of a large dog. They were descendants of the giant squirrel that ran messages up and down the great Yggdrasil. As such, they had the clear language skills of one favored by the gods and the dexterity of their squirrel cousins. They made excellent scouts, scribes, pages and servants. Many ratatosks lived in my grandfather's castle in Asgard, though I had never been comfortable with how the Aesir treated them as second-class citizens.

I drank from my canteen, watching the scout give his report. His tail twitched in agitation and his tiny, strangely human hands would not be still. Rangvald listened with an expression that went from curiosity to anger. His eyebrows met as he frowned. In the morning light, he seemed to go pale under his beard.

Not good news then.

The ratatosk scampered away and Rangvald moved among his hunters, giving short, quiet instructions. When he reached me and Huyn, he stopped to drink from his own canteen.

"We've got trouble. The…uh…*quarry* we've been hunting attacked a homestead nearby. We have to stop and investigate."

"How can we help?" Huyn asked. "Are there wounded?"

Rangvald shook his head. "There's no help for those poor souls now."

Suddenly, I had the strong need to know where Raven and Princess were. I craned my neck to see over the resting hunters.

Rangvald saw my concern. "They're by the river. Safe for now. But I cannot promise that safety much longer."

"What exactly have you been hunting?" I asked sharply.

"Draugs." His voice was flat. He didn't seem to be mocking me, but surely he couldn't be serious.

"Draugs? As in ghouls? As in undead eaters of flesh?"

Rangvald nodded.

"As in draugs, plural?" I could hear the note of hysteria in my voice, but couldn't stop it. One draug was bad enough. One draug could kill an entire flock of sheep in a night. Aesir ghost tales were full of these evil ghouls who killed indiscriminately until villagers worked together to drive them out. It was a favorite folk tale about the evils of being independent.

I'd never heard a story with more than one draug.

"Draugs, plural," Rangvald confirmed. "The reports are confusing, but there are definitely multiple ghouls in the area. Freya Disir sent us to investigate, but so far we've shown up too late to help. It seems that is the case again. But we must stop at the village regardless. I hope you don't mind the delay." The firm line of his lips told me that my minding or not, we were stopping. I nodded.

"And I would like your opinion on the matter," he said.

"My opinion? Why?"

Rangvald's gaze pierced mine and I keened his strange magic, like fingers trying to pry open the door to my thoughts.

"Because on the eve before the first ghouls began attacking our villages, we chased Aesir raiders off our shores."

Perfect. The Vanlandi's reasons for hating my kind just went from vague prejudice to concrete hostility. When I found out which Aesir had broken Baldyr's treaty to raid in Jotunheim, they'd be explaining their reasons at the tip of my sword.

DRAUGS—LIKE VULTURES WITH TEETH

November 14, 2076

Since this is a fairly new blog (thank you to everyone who commented on my first posts!), I'm going to continue with my examination of creatures both mythical and real. This is not a definitive encyclopedia by any means. I think of it instead as a bestiary, like the ones that travelers to the far reaches of the world used to catalogue the strange and wonderful creatures they found.

This blog's mission is to document my experiences with fae creatures and to gather information from you, my readers. Together, I hope we can pool resources about caring for these beings and learn to live with them instead of against them.

Today's topic is ghouls.

Almost every culture has stories about the undead. In my formative years, the stories around the campfire were about draugrs or draugs—a creature closer to ghouls than to zombies or vampires on the undead spectrum. Like ghouls, draugs frequent graveyards to feast on dead flesh, the more putrified, the better. But where I grew up, the residents were long-lived. There wasn't much dead flesh to go around, so draugs weren't above killing to create more rotting flesh.

But where do they come from? Legend says they were made in error by a witch clan long ago. The witches, mostly women, were tired of their men going off to war, so they created the ghouls from corpses of soldiers who fell in battle. They were meant to be a new army, one that would fight their enemies and leave the men to tend the fields and raise their families.

Of course, like most black magic, it didn't quite work out that way. The witches lost control of their undead constructs. The draugs, which have the mental capacity of a psychopathic first-grader, decided killing soldiers was too much work. They turned to easier prey, like small children and untended sheep.

No one quite knows how the draugs reproduced, but thousands of years later, shepherds still blame draug ghouls for lost sheep. The fact that draugs are able to shape-shift into almost any animal form—including wolf—makes it difficult to verify these claims.

There are always stories about black witches creating new draugs, reanimating corpses (Aesir, human or animal) to do their bidding, but it takes a lot of power to create a draug. Most witches just don't have it in them. Thank the gods for small blessings.

A last word about draugs: they are solitary creatures. Put two draugs alone in a room and there would be a cannibalistic feast. To a draug, any flesh is good flesh.

Tell me tales of the undead from your culture!

COMMENTS (5)

Mmmm. Putrefied flesh—nom-nom-nom.
LeGourmand55 (November 14, 2076)

Now I have a plan for all those bitches who are too high and mighty to date real men. Draug bimbos for all!
Incel69 (November 14, 2076)

> Don't bet on it. Even ghouls have eyes, dickhead.
> *LeeryLamb (November 14, 2076)*

My Malaysian grandmother used to tell me stories about toyols—little goblin thieves made from the reanimated corpses of stillborn babies. Gran has been gone for nearly fifty years, but those stories still keep me awake at night.
DelimaD (November 14, 2076)

Thank you, DelimaD. Unlike the other commenters, these stories are exactly what I want to hear about. Scary or not, they shouldn't be forgotten.

Valkyrie367 (November 14, 2076)

e rode two-by-two with Huyn and I in the middle of the hunters. After a good night's rest, Princess and Raven in his pony form bounded back and forth along the line. I yelled at them twice to stay close, but my warnings kept their attention about as long as a kitten spotting a butterfly.

Rangvald rode just ahead and Huyn spurred his horse to catch up to him.

"What exactly are we looking for?" he asked. "The walking dead?" He raised his arms and lolled his tongue in a zombie pantomime, then glanced over his shoulder at me and winked. Rangvald wasn't amused.

"Not zombies. Draugs are ghouls, but these are unlike any we've encountered before."

Now I was curious. "What's different about them?"

Rangvald frowned, turned in his saddle and spoke softly. He didn't want the other hunters to hear.

"Do you know how draugs are made?"

I nodded. "Sort of. They're born from necromancy. A type of undead."

"Exactly. It takes a powerful witch to raise a man from his grave. Only these ghouls aren't...manlike. And they move in a pack."

That *was* odd.

"Not manlike?" I asked. "What are they like then."

"Monsters. Short, no taller than a child, but monstrous. Teeth like Fenrir's fangs. They've taken out entire herds of cattle." Rangvald shuddered. His expression was bleak.

"You've seen them, then?"

He nodded. "I was sent to investigate the first reports."

While the draugs of legend were mostly humanoid, they had strong magic and could shape-shift, so it wasn't entirely unreasonable to believe that Rangvald had seen some kind of draug that had shifted to animal form. What bothered me most was his implication that Asgard was involved.

"And you really believe an Aesir came across the river to create these monsters?"

"Aesir, plural." He smiled grimly at the echo of our previous conversation. "Boats have been spotted on the shore several times in the past months."

"That doesn't mean they created the draugs. I don't know any Aesir with that level of dark magic." That wasn't exactly true. Old Asha was capable of raising the dead, but she hadn't left her mountain cabin in centuries.

"It would make sense, wouldn't it? Build an army of ghouls to take out your enemy. It's efficient and no one can pin the blame on you."

"The Aesir are not the enemy of the Jotnar," I said.

"So you say." Rangvald favored me with one of his brilliant smiles and spurred his horse into a trot to check on those who rode ahead.

"Are things this bad all over?" I asked Huyn.

He shook his head. "No. The treaty stands. Most Jotnar like the new trade between our worlds. They won't do anything to jeopardize it. The Vanlandi are stuck in the past."

And I was stuck in their lands, surrounded by armed soldiers. How easy would it be to make one Aesir disappear? I could only hope that Huyn's presence would keep them in line. I itched to kick my heels into my mare's flanks and speed up our journey. As if I didn't already have enough need for haste.

Not long before sunset, the line of horses stopped.

"What's going on?" I asked Huyn, but he shrugged.

"Dunno."

I took the moment of pause to drink from my canteen and look for Raven. Their morning exuberance had long since worn off, and Raven and Princess now lagged behind. The hound's tongue hung from her mouth and she panted after hours at a run.

"See if you can get Princess to drink," I said to Raven. He immediately shifted to human form and fished a bowl and canteen from his pack.

"No matter how many times I see that, it always amazes me," Huyn said. "It's like watching one ocean wave flow into another. Never seen a shifter that fluid before."

"He is pretty amazing." I spoke around a mouthful of trail mix.

"I know some shifters who would love to learn that trick."

"I don't think it can be taught. It's a product of his unusual ancestry."

"Which is?" Huyn raised both eyebrows. We'd had this discussion before, and I'd somehow squirmed out of telling him that Raven might be the son of Thunderbird or that when he hit puberty, he might turn into a raging, skinless, bull-like equine.

"We're not exactly sure."

I was saved from more interrogations when Rangvald rode back from the head of the line looking grave.

"The first homestead is just ahead. Everyone's dead. The draugs are still in the field eating the sheep."

"Now? It's not full dark yet," I said. Draugs were usually nocturnal feeders, preferring the cover of darkness to stalk and terrorize their prey.

"As I said, these aren't normal ghouls." Rangvald's eyes were troubled. I was starting to doubt that we were, in fact, dealing with ghouls.

"So what's the plan?" Huyn asked.

Rangvald took off his helmet and wiped sweat from his brow on his sleeve.

"We try to take one alive so the Freya's mage can study it. Maybe we find out where they're coming from."

"And the others?" Huyn stretched his shoulders and spine just like he did before the Knacker's cage-fight.

"We kill them all."

RANGVALD DIDN'T WANT me in the fight. I wasn't sure if that was chivalry or if he didn't trust having an Aesir at his back. In any case, I had to stay behind and monitor Raven and Princess. Both were eager to hunt draugs.

"Mason would let me!" Raven protested when I told him he would be staying back too.

"He would not."

"Would too!"

I had no comeback for that logic. Before I could spout off another mom platitude, Huyn took him aside and spoke quietly. Raven listened. He stared at his feet and kicked dirt. Then he nodded, shifted into pony form and trotted back along the trail.

"What did you say to him?" I asked.

"I told him it was his duty to keep you safe."

"I don't need anyone's protection." I already had my sword unsheathed, and it shone dully in the sunlight.

"I know that and you know that, but he doesn't. It helps that you're pregnant with his little sister. He's very eager to be a big brother. He told me so. And I told him that being a good big brother starts now."

"Huh." It was all I could think of to say. Raven hadn't shown any indication that he was excited about the baby.

I laid a hand on Huyn's arm. "You be careful. Don't leave me alone with all these Vanlandi."

"A kiss for good luck then." And before I could protest, he dropped a quick, light kiss on my lips.

"Good luck." My throat was thick with emotion. Not lust, at least not in the way Huyn would have preferred. His kiss reminded me of the many times Mason and I had gone into battle together.

He clamped a helmet on his head (provided by the Freya's hunters) and followed the others down the road to the homestead.

I mounted Tory and trailed behind them. A soldier blocked my passage. He was the youngest of the crew, no more than a teenager by the plumpness of his cheeks and the blond fuzz on his lip that was trying very hard to be a mustache.

"My lady, it would be best if you waited here."

"I want to see the draugs. I won't get close enough to get in anyone's way."

"Rangvald said to keep you here."

I sat taller in my saddle and gathered my Valkyrie confidence around me like a cloak. I unsheathed my sword and pointed it at him.

"Neither Rangvald nor the Freya have the authority to tell me what do to."

"I'm s...sure they just...just want to keep you safe." The poor kid turned red and could barely get a word out. Rangvald probably thought he was giving the newbie the easy babysitting job.

I dug my heels into Tory's flanks. The mare snorted and blundered forward. The soldier barely pulled his horse out of the way as we galloped past. Raven whinnied and matched our speed with Princess on his heels.

The forest opened up at the top of a rise. I pulled up. Tory stamped and turned in circles. She'd been ready for a good run and wasn't happy when the fun was cut short.

The homestead lay in a valley below us. A stone cottage sat in the middle of a yard with several small outhouses clustered around it—barn, chicken coop, smokehouse, shed. Smoke rose from the cottage chimney. The crofters hadn't been dead long. Fields of newly planted corn and wheat rolled over the hills to my right. Grazing pasture was on the left. In the distance, I spotted sheep. In the dying light they glowed like giant white puffballs against the green. They weren't moving.

"Do you have binoculars?" I asked the soldier who had just caught up to us. He shook his head.

Raven shifted to boy form and slid the pack off his back. He rummaged around inside and held out a small pair of binoculars.

My heart clenched. They were a new design that Mason had been working on. Small, but powerful even in low light.

"What else have you got stashed in there?" I asked.

"Stuff." Raven shut the pack's flap and clutched it to his chest.

I took the glasses and held them to my eyes. They auto-adjusted to the light and the distance, but it took a moment to understand what I was looking at.

The sheep were gutted. I scanned the glasses from one dead animal to another. Entrails spread behind one, glistening red and wet in the grass. A head was missing from another. It lay a few feet away, eyes staring glassily into the sky. Bile rose in my throat. I lowered the binoculars. So much blood. The ground was soaked in it.

Just like a draug to spread out its kill and let it putrefy before eating it.

A head popped up from behind a sheep carcass. What in the the All-father's name was that? It didn't look like a draug. Standing perfectly still beside the dead sheep, it lifted its nose as if trying to catch a scent above all that blood.

I peered through the lenses again. The creature's back was to me. All I could make out were pointed ears and a tail rising up like a fluffy question mark behind it. Another head and fluffy tail popped up. I panned the field. There were dozens of them.

Were those ratatosks? They couldn't be. Few homesteaders could afford to keep even one ratatosk in their employ. And why would the draugs feed on sheep and leave the ratatosks?

I brought the binoculars to bear on one of the creatures. It stood as tall as a jackrabbit. Slender ears pointed straight to the sky with no bend or curve. More like horns than ears. Its fur was longish and dun brown as if it belonged in a desert climate instead of the lush green hills of Vanlandia.

And it moved…wrong. It didn't hop like a rabbit or scamper like a squirrel. Its arms were longer than its legs, and they grazed the ground as it pushed forward in an ape-like gait.

Then its head swiveled toward me, and a face from nightmares filled the binoculars' field of vision.

Dear gods. That was no ratatosk. It had a bat-like face, and not the cute fluffy bats that look like foxes. This was monstrous. Its mashed-in nose was topped by a thorn-like spike that pointed back toward its forehead. A big, wide mouth opened in a creepy grin to display a jawline of serrated teeth. Purple-rimmed eyes with yellow irises stared toward my binoculars with that distinct glassy stare of a ghoul.

I lowered the glasses. These weren't the prey. They were predators. Draugs unlike any I had ever seen or heard of in tales.

A last ewe came stumbling and bleating out of the bush. The draugs turned as one and fell on the poor sheep. It screamed its last breath as a draug tore into the wool at its throat. The sheep staggered and fell with six more beasts clinging to it while the others fought for their turn at the kill.

Raven tugged on my sleeve. "Look!"

He pointed beyond the pasture. The Vanlandi stalked through the shadows between the trees. There were twenty men and women in the Rangvald's hunting party. I did a quick count in the pasture, and estimated at least two dozen draugs. They were small, but that didn't mean they'd be easy to kill. Ghouls could take a lot of abuse before going down.

Rangvald's hunters approached from both sides of the pasture. Several draugs left off worrying at the carcasses to stand up and peer into the trees.

Fuzzy ears twitched, sensing movement. Hunters stepped into the light with swords and bows primed.

Draugs froze.

Hunters froze.

Two men leaped into the pasture and stood poised for attack while the rest of their crew cleared the fence. Huyn was the last to cross.

The Vanlandi spread through the pasture. The draugs hadn't moved. The hunters slowly walked forward, closing on the ghouls like a net.

The draugs moved so fast, I didn't understand what I was seeing until one of Rangvald's hunters fell. Blood spurted in the air as a draug clung to his neck, tearing away hunks of flesh. And suddenly more men and women were down. Screams pierced the morning—shouts of pain and anger. A draug tackled Huyn and they fell. He was instantly lost in the slaughter raging around him.

My heels dug into Tory's side.

"No!" My babysitter yelled, but I wouldn't listen to him, not with the blood of rage boiling in my ears.

The mare flew on light feet. Wind around me as I tugged at my sword in its sheathe across my back. It was an awkward position to pull the blade, but I finally got it as Tory leaped over the fence rail and mowed down the first draug we encountered.

In that moment, I had no thought for myself, no worry for Little Bean, Raven or anyone else. I was a Valkyrie riding into battle.

I decapitated a second draug with one slash of my sword. Another fell under my blade as it feasted on an open chest. We reached the far fence. I pressed my right knee into Tory to turn her, but she didn't need my guidance. She wheeled around and flew back into the melee. I lost count of how many draugs I killed. My blade was eerily silent, but that didn't make it any less efficient.

I fought my way to where I'd seen Huyn fall. He was still down with a bloody leg. Raven and Princess stood between him and an angry draug. Princess bared her fangs. Her head hung low in a ready-to-pounce stance. Raven's pony fur stood on end like a pissed-off cat's, and his curled lip displayed sharp kelpie teeth. They weren't going to let any draug near Huyn.

I felt a moment of pride washed in guilt. I'd left them unguarded when I made my mad rampage into the fight. On the other hand, they'd been brave and selfless to protect Huyn.

The draug facing them hissed, a sound more like a buzz saw than an animal. It was missing an arm and dark blood oozed from the stump, but it didn't seem to notice.

I took in all this detail in the seconds before Tory swept onto the scene and trampled the draug into the mud. I hopped from the saddle, ready to finish the beast with my blade, but Raven beat me to it. The little kelpie pounded the draug's chest with his front hooves and tore into its neck.

"Raven, no!" I was too late. The draug twitched and Raven finished the job. One more chomp and he severed the draug's head.

Raven looked up from his kill. Blood dripped from his teeth. His muzzle was covered in gore.

By the One-eyed God. My only thought was, what kind of mother lets her kid kill ghouls?

CHAPTER

16

nlike zombie bites, ghouls don't infect their victims with an undead virus. Still, a ghoul bite is nasty. They feed on rotten flesh. Their mouths are cesspools of bacteria. Infection is a real danger.

The bite on Huyn's thigh had missed his artery, but the punctures from the draug's fangs were deep. Pain turned his complexion waxy. Even though the morning was cool, sweat beaded his brow when two hunters hoisted him back onto his horse. He swayed in the saddle and his knuckles were white on the reins. I'd tied off his wound with a bandage, and it now only oozed blood, but I had no idea how he could ride in such pain.

"We'll have to take him back to Gottvaer. You will ride with the wounded." Rangvald spoke to me, but his eyes didn't leave the battlefield, as if he expected another attack. He was bloody and dirty, but had escaped the fight without injury. Others weren't so lucky. Five hunters lay dead on the field. Six others were wounded. One wasn't expected to last the journey home. All the draugs were dead, and though the bleak expressions on the remaining hunters' faces didn't reflect it, the fight had been a victory for the Vanlandi.

Now we had to get the wounded home to be cared for.

I gazed over the pasture. Sheep carcasses lay next to the corpses of men and women waiting for their graves to be dug. I was still gripping my bloody blade. "Do you want me to…I mean, I can help dig graves." I pointed with the fist that was wrapped around my blade's hilt.

For an instant, Rangvald lost his usual friendliness. His lip curled and he sneered out the word, "Valkyrie." Then he shook his head and his charming smile returned. "The Vanlandi do not need the help of a Valkyrie witchcraft. We will see to our own dead."

"Of course." My sword was still dormant. There would be no Valkyrie "witchcraft" clearing lost souls from the battlefield. But Rangvald couldn't know that, and the Vanlandi hostility toward the Aesir was too deeply rooted for him to accept my help.

He turned his back to me and started shouting orders at his hunters. I sheathed my blade with shaking hands, hoping that Huyn's wound didn't worsen. A lone Valkyrie wouldn't last long among the Vanlandi.

THE VANLANDI STRONGHOLD was more of a fortified homestead than a castle. Cottages lined the road leading up to it. We dismounted and left our horses with stablehands in a muddy courtyard surrounded by a dozen outbuildings.

Two hunters took the wounded away as soon as we arrived. Huyn's face was sickly green as he fought the pain of his wounds. I hoped the Vanlandi had good healers.

"This way, Lady Kyra." Rangvald waved me toward the main building with his signature smirk. With a last glance at Huyn, I steadied myself to enter enemy territory.

Inside the main hall, several people sat steaming off the chill by a hearth big enough to roast an entire cow. Three long tables with benches filled the room and people gathered around these, scattered in groups of two or three. Plates were scraped clean on the tables, and diners lingered over mugs of ale or mead. Fur rugs covered the floor by the hearth. The stone walls were etched with runes that made my teeth buzz. Torches burned in wall sconces, adding to the smoke and flickering light from the hearth. The whole place smelled of damp earth and stale beer.

All eyes in the room turned when we entered. The rumble of low conversations stilled. The dogs lounging by the hearth growled at Princess, but she ignored them. She was cool that way.

Rangvald strode to the back of the hall where a woman sat at a long table. He knelt before her in a quick gesture of honor and rose.

"Freya, we met our friend and cousin, Huyn Gillingrson on our hunt. I bring you his traveling companions, Kyra Greene and young Raven."

Raven, who had been quiet for most of the trip to the clan hall, stood taller when his name was spoken. The Freya studied him for a long moment, and he held her gaze without flinching. He was tough stuff, my kid.

Then Disir turned her gaze on me, and I keened the weight of her stare. She examined me not just with her eyes, but with a not-so-gentle thrust of magic too.

From what I'd seen so far, the Vanlandi were smaller and slimmer than the average Jotnar, owing no doubt to their Vanir heritage. Not so for Disir. She was a big woman, in body and in presence. She wore her blond hair in elaborate braids that hung in loops around her shoulders. She was too hard-featured to be pretty, but her strong jaw, straight nose and piercing blue eyes were striking. Her magic was bold and spicy, and I took a moment to ramp up my personal wards.

"And where is our cousin now?" Her voice boomed, and it was laced with magic.

"With the healers," Rangvald said. He didn't seem to notice the magic that the Freya was weaving around us. Or he didn't care. "He was wounded by a draug in the hunt."

Disir had been watching me like a hawk watches a mouse until now. At the mention of draugs, her gaze turned sharply to her son.

Rangvald's expression was grim. "They're all dead. We arrived too late."

Disir sank into her chair.

"You bring nothing but bad news along with enemies into our hall tonight."

"Be kind, Mother. Kyra is the granddaughter of Baldyr, and she fought well today." My fighting skills meant more than my heritage to Rangvald.

Disir flicked her eyes to me and sniffed as if testing bad air. It would take a lot more than help with a few draugs for the Vanlandi forget their feud with the Aesir.

Two ratatosks entered the hall. Their tiny hands held trays and they moved with that quick grace of their squirrel ancestors. Tails flicked as they placed mugs of ale and plates of stew before us. Two more ratatosks brought a bench so we could sit facing Disir and her attendants at the long table.

The rich scent of spiced meat and root vegetables made Little Bean turn over in her bed. I sat and dug in, glad that even enemies were well fed in the Freya's hall.

Conversation returned as everyone decided that the excitement of new arrivals was over. I took a moment to study the runes. They were everywhere—carved onto the stone walls, into the wood mantel above the hearth and the frames around doors and windows. They were even underfoot, beneath the sand and dust that covered the floor.

Sometimes it's hard for me to separate my keening from my other senses, in the way that you can tell what something tastes like just from its scent. So I wasn't sure if the runes glowed with actual light or with activated magic.

Raven nudged me. "Is there more?" His bowl was empty. Disir heard him and signaled for the serving maid.

"Bring the growing boy another helping and add a second bowl for the hound so the boy can keep his own meal."

Raven blushed. "I'm sorry…ma'am. We've been traveling for a long time and Princess was hungry."

The hell hound in question had her head on the bench and she gazed up at Raven with adoration shining from her eyes.

Disir smiled, a real smile that softened her edges.

"No apologies for taking care of your beast. A good man always thinks of those in his care before himself."

The serving maids returned and placed a bowl of stew in front of Raven and another on the floor for Princess.

"So have you come over the river to raid our lands, Valkyrie? Or are you just here to create monsters and leave?"

Disir's blunt question came out of the blue, and I nearly choked before answering her.

"Mother!" Rangvald's tone was sharp, but Disir smiled.

I showed her my teeth.

"I came from Terra, not from across the river. I'm going home to Asgard. Huyn has been kind enough to escort me."

Disir studied me for a moment longer. Her magic twined around me and the runes at her back pulsed with power. I let her probe do its work. I had nothing to hide. Eventually, seeming satisfied, she nodded and said, "Tell me what you know of these ghouls that have been attacking my people."

"Very little. Only what Rangvald has told me, and what I saw at the homestead." I paused, not sure if I should continue. "Rangvald seems sure that the Aesir are connected somehow. If that is true, I will have to inform my grandfather when I return."

Disir snorted. Several grumbles came from the others around the room. Clearly no one thought that Baldyr would care.

I spoke louder to be heard over the rumbling. "Do you have proof of these Aesir raids that I can take to the king?"

Disir shrugged. "I don't need proof. We recognized the boats that slunk to our shores during the night. In fact, they flew Valkyrie sails. Sisters of yours, no doubt."

"I have been in Midgard these last fifteen years," I said, giving the old name for Terra. "I have no sisters in Asgard anymore, but I will take this information to the king."

Disir leaned in. "I don't need the king's permission to protect my borders from draugs or the Aesir."

Huyn saved us from a bigger disagreement when he shuffled into the hall, leaning heavily on a crutch. The healer helped him to sit in a chair by the hearth before giving her report to Disir.

"The bite missed the bone, but he'll be sore for a while. He shouldn't ride for at least a week."

"Thank you," Disir said. The healer nodded and left. A ratatosk server brought Huyn a plate of food and mug of ale. He smiled from across the room and lifted his mug in salute.

Now I was left with a dilemma. Did I wait for Huyn to heal, or did I push on without him?

The ratatosks returned with pots of tea, and served us with quick efficiency. A piper and fiddler played softly in one corner. The music was more relaxing than festive. The light was low and the fire had burned down to embers. On the walls, most of the runes weren't active. Only one or two glowed with that unearthly light. I thought I understood them better now. They were like the music, contributing to the atmosphere in the hall. Disir, or maybe her sorcerer, could activate certain runes to nudge the crowd's mood in a certain direction. I wondered if the Vanlandi were aware of this manipulation.

"They are good, aren't they?" Disir spoke softly beside me. She pointed with her chin toward the duo of musicians. "The piper is my grandson. He has a natural gift from the gods."

"He's very good."

Disir didn't look old enough to be a grandmother, but like the Aesir, the Jotnar aged slowly. A lack of wrinkles was no way to estimate someone's age. Keening their magic was a better test. And I'd tasted Disir's magic. It was ancient.

"Did you know that Huyn plays the pipes?" A rune above Disir's head glowed in a mesmerizing pulse like a slow heartbeat.

"I didn't know." I sipped my tea. It was growing cold, but I didn't want to disturb a ratatosk for a refill. I glanced at Huyn, propped in a chair near the hearth. The healer had given him something for the pain and he dozed with his head back against the chair and his mouth hanging open.

"There's probably a lot about him you don't know." Disir's eyes never left the musicians, but I felt the weight of her words.

"You're probably right," I said. "We haven't been traveling together for long."

"He's a good man. He deserves better than to be caught up in Aesir politics."

What she really meant was that he deserved better than to be caught up in a romance with an Aesir.

"I assure you my business here is not political. It's…personal."

"Is that his child you carry?"

Wow. She wasn't holding back.

"No. But it's for the life of this child that I must get to Asgard as soon as possible." I wouldn't go so far as to tell her about my disease, but I hoped that appealing her maternal instincts would soften her opinion of me.

"Then you should leave Huyn behind and continue alone."

"The king's treaty forbids any Aesir from traveling alone within the borders of Jotunheim."

"I know the limits of the treaty," Disir snapped. Then her voice softened. "For your bravery in the fight today, I will grant you an escort of six warriors. They will take you to Port Utgard and make certain you get on a ship bound for Asgard. You will leave at first light."

"Thank you, Freya. That is very generous." I would've taken the offer even though Disir's tone made it plain I had no choice. The warriors would be more of a guard than escort.

Her gaze met mine. "As one mother to another, I hope you get there in time."

Shouting came from the beyond the great door to the hall. The music fell silent and all eyes turned. A soldier strode into the room. He wore heavy mail and he carried a helmet under one arm. A sword hung on one hip and a knife on the other. He was sweaty and dirty from a long ride. Four others in similar dress followed him into the hall and waited by the door. They all wore the symbol of King Gillingr on their breast—a sword crossed with a hammer.

The lead soldier bowed perfunctorily before our table and greeted Disir with a curt, "Freya."

Disir rose slowly, the line of her mouth hard.

"What is the meaning of this? How dare you come into my hall uninvited." Her voice was full of the authority of a kindergarten teacher faced with unruly glue-eaters.

"I am Captain Hagen. I come at King Gillingr's request. We are on an urgent mission to Terra and sought permission to pass through your lands." His gaze slid sideways to fall on Huyn. "But I see Prince Huyn at your hearth and now our mission is at an end. My Prince." He strode to the hearth, knelt in front of Huyn and handed him a folded letter sealed with red wax.

Huyn, who had only just woken, looked dazed from the medication. He took the letter and the captain snapped back to attention. He turned to Disir and gave a short bow. "Freya, I apologize for the intrusion. We will wait outside for the prince's answer."

Huyn broke the seal, read the letter, and frowned.

"Bad news?" Disir asked.

"Not bad. Just inconvenient." Huyn turned in his chair. "My father sent his guard to find me. It seems they were ready to travel all the way to Terra to do so. And in turn they wanted me to find someone else."

"Who?" I asked.

He smiled. "You, Kyra. King Gillingrson wants to see you in Utgard."

CHAPTER

17

isir gave us a private room for the night. Raven and Princess were already asleep. The warm food and fire after the long walk had knocked them out. I paced around the small room, still full of restless energy.

"I can't go to Utgard!"

"My father doesn't like to be ignored" Huyn was sitting in a chair by the fire with his bad leg propped up before him. I stepped around him as I paced.

"Can't we just send back a letter, telling him of our urgency?"

"We can try, but the King's Guard is rather single-minded in their purpose. They were sent to bring you back. They won't just let you walk away."

"You mean they'd confine me?"

"Possibly."

"For what reason? Why does the king want to see me?"

Huyn raised his great shoulders. "Don't know."

I grunted in aggravation. A summons from the king was not trivial. We couldn't ignore it without causing an inter-dimensional incident. I knew the stipulations of the treaty. Any Aesir traveling through Jotunheim needed to be escorted by a Jotnar. Permission to travel could be revoked at any time at the king's discretion.

If we ignored his summons, King Gillingr would certainly revoke my right to travel. And then the guards who'd been sent as an escort would become my jailers.

Huyn stopped my pacing by grabbing my hand. "Just give me the word, and we'll sneak out tonight. We can put at least a few hours between us before they even know we're gone."

I bit my lip and looked down at his flushed face. The candle's soft light flattered him. It highlighted the square cut of his jaw and chin. He really was ridiculously handsome. His warm hand enveloped mine and he squeezed.

"You would do that for me?" He wouldn't make it far in his condition but I appreciated the gesture.

"That and much more." His lips were parted in a slight smile. I could see the tension in his shoulders as if he were holding himself upright with effort—as if he were holding himself back from pulling me into his lap.

I lowered my eyes and stepped back.

"It's not a good idea." I was talking about running from the king's guards, but the words were more than that, and we both knew it. Huyn sucked in a sharp breath.

"Of course." He leaned his head against the chair and closed his eyes.

I sighed.

"I guess we're heading to Utgard."

FROM THE BACK of a wagon, I watched Port Utgard as we passed it. Two long piers jutted into the river like arms hugging the harbor. A dozen ships were moored, either loading or offloading cargo. The cobbled streets around the harbor were crammed with Jotnar—buying, selling, strolling, picking pockets. Water taxis and small boats filled the harbor, all vying for a spot to dock. Sailboats drifted along the horizon.

The Ifing, while technically a river, was an immense body of water. Asgard lay on the far shore. It called to me. I wanted to hop off the wagon, run onto the pier, and commandeer a ship. Home was so close, just a boat ride and one trip through the veil away. But the twelve guards escorting us through the busy port would never let me go that easily. The king had commanded my presence at his court. No argument would deter them from that goal. I'd tried.

For two days, I'd pleaded with Captain Hagen to leave me at the port instead of dragging me all the way to the castle. I'd pleaded for the life of my unborn child, but either he didn't believe me or he was unmoved by my plight. I was going to Utgard and nothing I did or said would change that.

That didn't mean I'd be welcome in the capital city. The treaty between the Jotnar and the Aesir held because the Ifing was a strong border between the lands. The Jotnar and Aesir didn't mingle for social reasons. Their communications were limited to trade and politics.

But we could be friends, as Huyn and I had proven. We felt no need for animosity, just because some long-dead Aesir had stolen Jotnar brides and the Jotnar had retaliated with death and destruction. Those people were dead and gone, as Grandfather had once said in his impassioned speech to both courts.

"We shall not be held accountable for the lusts and the crimes of our ancestors. And we shall not pass their follies onto our children. Instead, we shall build new worlds. Worlds of peace and collaboration."

I'd been in Utgard for that speech and signing of the treaty when I was a novice Valkyrie. It was the first and only time I'd been to Utgard.

The King's Guard were questioning people who tried to enter the city, but no one stopped us. Traveling with a prince of Jotunheim had its perks.

"My father will be waiting for us," he said.

"How? We just arrived."

The bumpy cart ride hadn't been kind to him. His brow was damp with sweat, and his jaw bulged as he fought against the pain. He nodded toward the guard tower beside the gate.

"News travels fast. Hagen sent scouts ahead with news of our arrival."

Utgard hadn't changed in thirty years. It was a busy metropolitan city with Jotnar and ratatosks living together in relative harmony—relative only because the ratatosks didn't dispute their lot as a serving class. They were easy to overlook, being so much shorter than the giants. A sorcerer with magic strong enough to make ghouls would be smart to take victims from the ratatosk community. And if he—or she—wanted an army of ratatosk draugs, he had to look no further than Utgard for stock.

I put away those dark thoughts to enjoy the splendor of Utgard.

Terran stories made giants out as big, bumbling oafs, or devious tricksters who enjoyed deceiving Thor and his contemporaries. In reality, they were just people, and perhaps more artistic-minded than most.

The city was clean and beautiful. White stone and pale wood dominated the architecture, so the buildings seemed to glow with fire in the afternoon light. Every door and lintel was elaborately carved, down to the lowliest baker's shop. What the Jotnar lacked in color on their buildings, they made up for in their dress. Even basic brown homespun was embroidered with colorful stitching. The wealthier Jotnar dressed in bright wool, finely worked leather or animal skins. It was a startling effect to watch the sea of color winding between buildings.

The castle sat like a jewel at the city center, visible from almost any avenue. It was an oddly delicate structure of white stone, topped with thin towers like upended icicles. Pedestrian traffic thinned as we wound our way toward it. In the more affluent neighborhoods, people traveled by mule carts or rickshaws. By the time we reached the roundabout in front of the castle, the mules had been replaced by glossy horses in livery pulling ornate carriages. Our dirty, ragtag appearance turned a few heads. Huyn ignored the glares and whispers. He thanked Hagen for the escort and beckoned me to follow him into the castle.

He spoke to a squire who waited inside, and the boy ran off.

Huyn turned to me. His handsome face was drawn with exhaustion and pain.

"I've asked for an audience with my father. I know you want to get this over with quickly, but I think it would be best if we got cleaned up first."

I nodded. Urgency or not, I didn't want to greet the King of Jotunheim in blood-stained travel clothes.

An elderly Jotnar woman came hurrying over and hugged Huyn. He grimaced as she jostled his bad leg, but patted her on the back.

"It's good to have you home, Master Huyn."

"Good to be back, Gertrude. My father will be waiting to see us. Can you find our guests a room to bathe and maybe some clean clothes?"

Gertrude eyed me up and down. She was a plump woman, with gunmetal gray hair and cheeks softened with wrinkles.

"You've been on the road for a while, have you?" she asked.

"Feels like a lifetime," I said.

"No worries. We'll get you tidied up in no time."

She whisked us away to a suite of rooms. A huge bed decked out with silk pillows begged me to fall on it and sleep, but I had other duties before I could rest.

Raven and Princess followed the smell of freshly baked bread into the adjoining room.

"The boy could use a bath too," I said to Gertrude while she laid out a dress. "He needn't join me for the audience with the king, but he might not welcome the bath."

"Don't you worry. I have plenty of experience with grubby young boys. Master Huyn has five strong brothers. You've never seen a messier crew. But I wrangled each one into the bath a time or two."

Gertrude called for a fleet of serving maids who deftly stripped me, bathed me and combed out my hair. An hour later, my skin was bright pink from scrubbing. I'd shooed the maids away, preferring to dress myself. Now I stood naked in front of a full-length mirror with a robe puddled at my feet. My hair lay in a damp, tangled mass across my back, and I wondered who that stranger was looking back at me. I hadn't seen myself in a mirror since the night I left Montreal—the night I first shifted to Mother mode.

I had wounds I didn't remember getting—an abrasion on my right forearm and a cut under my chin. Most likely they'd happened in the draug battle. I traced the scab on my arm with my finger. My jawline felt plump. New lines crinkled the edges of my eyes. Were those the first sign that the Mother mode would soon turn into the Crone?

My hand cupped the tiny swell of my belly. It was my first baby bump.

My throat closed and I fought back tears. I had no one to share it with. Mason should be here to see this milestone. Instead, I was alone in the court of giants, my future uncertain.

I wiped away tears and turned from the mirror. I could do nothing about Mason, but I could hurry these proceedings by not delaying in my bedroom. I braided my hair and dressed in the fresh clothes. The skirt was too long, but I folded the waistband so I could walk without tripping and covered it with a vest. The effect was clumsy, but it was the best I could do.

I checked in on Raven and Princess before leaving. They were already asleep, curled together on the huge bed in their room.

A ratatosk page waited to lead me to King Gillingr. Night had fallen while I bathed, and the hallways were lit by pale gleams in sconces all along the wall. I assumed we were going to the main hall, but when we reached the stairs, the page led me upward. The upper landing was brighter. Guards stood at attention by the stairs and at intervals along the hall. We stopped at wide double doors that were open. The page cleared his throat and said it that peculiar chirpy voice of ratatosks, "Lady Kyra, my Lord."

"Send her in," rumbled a deeper voice from within the chamber. The page nodded and disappeared back down the hall. I hesitated on the threshold.

"Come in, Valkyrie. I don't bite. Much," came the voice again, followed by a low chuckle.

I stepped inside a surprisingly elegant room. Light came from the hearth where a fire licked at freshly laid logs. The furniture was maroon silk over ornately carved wood, except for the two couches by the fire. These were plush and worn, obviously the favorite seating for many years. Huyn sat on one couch with his leg propped up. King Gillingr sat on the other. Like Huyn, he was sandy haired, but edging toward gray. He had the build of a warrior with broad shoulders and long limbs. A massive hand was wrapped around a flagon of ale. The slight paunch around his middle suggested he'd spent more time on the couch lately than in the training yards.

Having grown up on modern Terra, I didn't have the knee-jerk reaction for bending to royalty that most Aesir and Jotnar did. Still, I attempted an awkward curtsy.

"None of that." Gillingr waved me over. "I asked to meet you here so we could forgo all those formalities. Sit."

I perched on the other end of his couch. Huyn smiled. It was meant as an encouragement, but his eyes were sad. The look sent tremors through my chest. Something was wrong.

"A drink?" Gillignr asked.

"Tea, please." I didn't think I could drink it. My stomach was in knots, but the tea would give my hands something to do so I didn't fidget.

Gillingr waved to a ratatosk attendant who brought me a steaming cup from the sideboard. Then he said, "Leave us."

The attendant left, closing the great doors behind him. We were alone.

"My son tells me of your bravery against an unusual foe." Gillingr's tone was light, but his eyes hinted at intensity.

"Thank you. The draugs were frightening."

"But not the most frightening thing you've ever faced?" He smiled and it transformed his stern face into that of a kind old uncle. "Huyn also told me about your work on Terra as a...what did you call it?" He turned to Huyn.

"Pest controller." Huyn smiled.

"Pest controller, yes. Seems like a suitable job for an ex-Valkyrie."

I didn't think anyone could ever be an ex-Valkyrie, but I didn't correct him.

"Yes, I guess you could say I've faced some frightening creatures." I sipped the tea.

"That's good. Overcoming fear is more important than overcoming foes."

I made another noncommittal sound. One did not rush a king, but I wished he'd get to the point so I could be on my way.

Gillingr leaned back on the couch. "Huyn has had much to report. Apart from the draugs, it seems the Vanlandi have been visited by the Aesir too. They might even be the cause of the draug attacks."

"According to the Freya," I said.

"According to the Freya," he acknowledged. "You don't think that's possible?"

"I only know of one sorcerer in Asgard capable of creating a ghoul, and she would never cross the river."

"But you've been gone a long time. Ten years?"

"Fifteen." My keening was picking up magic from the corner of the room, making it difficult to focus on Gillingr's words. All my alarm bells were going now.

"Things are much different these days." The king watched my face for any reaction. I tried to give him nothing. "You are a big reason for those changes, aren't you? I heard about the way you left."

Was that why Gillingr had summoned me? Because I'd destroyed Bifrost? Why should he care? Unless he and my grandfather had made a deal. Perhaps the Aesir had grown tired of waiting for me to return on my own to atone for my crimes.

My legs tensed, ready for my fight-or-flight nerve to kick in.

"Is that why you brought me here?" I asked. "Is this about Bifrost? Did my grandfather ask you to bring me back in chains to pay for my crimes? Well, you went through a lot of trouble for nothing. I was going home anyway. Once my child is born, I will accept any punishment King Baldyr and the Elder Council of Asgard see fit."

I glanced from Huyn, who frowned deeply, to Gillingr, who watched my outburst with a smile twitching the corners of his mouth.

Gillingr rose to pour himself more ale.

"Your child," he said. "Huyn also told me of your illness. I'm sorry that I have delayed your return to Asgard. If I had known, I would have instructed my men to put you aboard a ship right away and met you in port."

"Met me?"

"Yes. Despite your haste, we have urgent matters to discuss."

"This isn't about Bifrost?"

"No. That is for you to work out with your Aesir family." Gillingr retreated to the corner of the room that was lost in shadows—the corner that hummed with magic—and came back carrying a long box.

"This is for you." He laid it on the couch beside me.

My fingers traced the carved tree on the lid. Its magic circled me like a warm hug. I knew that magic and I knew this box. They were my grandfather's. I flicked the latch and opened it to reveal Baldyr's sword lying on a bed of red velvet.

Tears fell down my cheeks and my hands shook as I traced a finger along the sword's hilt. If Baldyr's sword was here, it could only mean one thing.

My grandfather was dead.

"He wanted you to have this too." Gillingr handed me a letter. I cracked the red wax sealed with Baldyr's ring and read the words through eyes blurred by tears.

My Dearest Kyra,

I am writing this with my own hand, though it shakes with tremors, so please forgive the disordered penmanship. This will be the last letter I write, so the healers tell me.

Please don't weep. I have lived longer than any man has a right to. I have only two regrets. The first is that I lived long enough to become old and infirm instead of dying on the battlefield. But those desires belong to an Asgard that no longer exists. I worked my whole life to create a world where men no longer die in battle for senseless causes. I believe that is my greatest victory, one that will be sung about in the halls of Valhalla.

My second regret is that I leave Asgard rudderless. My advisors beg me to name my successor, but there is no one here I trust to rule in fairness and in peace.

Aaric was supposed to take my place. He had the gentle heart that could have kept the course I plotted. But perhaps his heart was too gentle.

I know that he took his own life, and that he used you as his weapon of choice. I hope in the years you have been away, you have been able to forgive him for that betrayal.

And yes, I know what you did to Bifrost, but be assured, I forgave you the moment I learned of it.

A sob wrenched from my chest, and I was too overcome to continue. I dropped the letter and covered my face in my hands.

For so long, I had lived with the double-edged sword of guilt and rage over Aaric's death. He'd needed a Valkyrie and a Valkyrie blade to end his long life. And he chose me because he knew I loved him and I could deny him nothing. But that truth couldn't wash away the memory of my blade—my hand—stabbing him through the heart.

I felt a hand rubbing the spot between my shoulder blades. Gillingr sat on the couch beside me.

"You should read on," he said.

I nodded and wiped my eyes. The letter was crushed under my fist. I smoothed it out and turned to the second page.

I am entrusting this letter, my sword, and my signet ring to my friend and ally, King Gillingr. He has sworn that on word of my death, he will send soldiers through the Jotunheim gate to Terra and find you wherever you may be.

Please, daughter of my heart, come home.

I would not seek you out if my need was not urgent. You never asked to rule, which may be why you are the one to take my place. You may not want this legacy I am firmly placing on your shoulders, but I am going to my rest knowing that you will do the right thing, whatever that may be. All I ask is that you grant this old man one last wish:

Do not let Dana wear the crown.

It was signed in Baldyr's scrawling signature.

CHAPTER

18

The king's healer had Huyn up and walking the next day with the help of crutches. As dawn began to run its fingers across the sky, we stood in the courtyard outside the king's private residence. A carriage with two horses and a sleepy driver waited to take me to the harbor. King Gillingr had arranged for one of his ships to take me home to Asgard.

"I wish I could finish this journey with you." Huyn's hand found mine. His grip was warm and comforting. I would miss his company too, but so close to my destination, I wouldn't be delayed any longer. And now I had the extra burden of my grandfather's legacy.

"Be careful," Huyn said. "You don't know what kind of reception you'll find. Dana has been the acting ruler for months now. She won't give it up easily."

"I know." I had no idea how I would deal with Dana yet. It still seemed impossible that my grandfather was gone, and even more impossible that he wanted me to be queen. When Huyn first proposed the idea, it had seemed preposterous, but now his absurd idea of challenging Dana was becoming all too real.

"I'll miss you. Maybe we can keep in touch. I'll write." His thumb was running across my wrist in a manner that suggested something way more than penpal status. "And you're welcome here any time...for any reason. Maybe in a few months, after the baby is born, I can come for a visit. You know, official welcome from the King."

"That would be nice." The smile on my lips was real, even if my stomach was in flutters.

Huyn pretended to tuck a stray lock of hair behind my ear, but my braids were freshly done by the expert castle maids. It was just an excuse to touch me. I held myself rigid, though a small treacherous part of me wanted to lean into his touch.

"Goodbye, Huyn. And thank you for all your help." I kissed his cheek. He held me there for just a moment too long. Then I extracted my hand from his and turned toward the waiting carriage.

The maids had cajoled my sleepy ward out of his bed before light. I wished I knew their secret. Raven came stumbling out of the castle, clutching his pack to his chest and yawning. Princess lumbered along behind him. I bundled them into the carriage and just as I was about to join them, I heard that distinctive yipping that I thought we'd left behind in Vanlandia.

"Mistress! Mistress! Let me help!" Kale skidded to a halt and crashed into the open carriage door. The door smacked my elbow and I cried out.

"Sorry! So sorry, Mistress. Let me help you into the carriage!"

I turned to find Huyn grinning at the yggie's antics.

"You might as well let him. He'll just follow you to the port."

Kale held out one slender hand, as if to boost me into the carriage seat.

"Hello, Kale." I took it his proffered hand. "Is it my imagination, or are you taller than last time we met?

Kale beamed and stood up even taller. "Good deeds make me strong, Mistress."

"They seem to make your speech better too."

Kale nodded vigorously. "Soon I will be as strong and as wise as the great Yggdrasil!"

I doubted that, but I let him hand me into the carriage. Really, it was more difficult for me to climb inside while clinging to his small, brittle appendage, but if good deeds were like vitamins to him, how could I say no? And then there was critter wrangler rule number seventeen: even the smallest creature can be big in magic. The gods seemed to keep throwing Kale in my way. Who was I to turn him away.

Kale stood beside the open door, hopping from foot to foot.

"Well, come on then." I beckoned. He yipped in delight and jumped into the carriage.

"Not him again," Raven moaned.

"Be nice," I said. "You might be glad for his company."

"Doubt it." Raven crossed his arms and slouched into the carriage bench. I was about to lecture him with the wrangling rules, but I let it slide. We were all tired and grumpy.

Raven indulged in his sulk while I watched the city pass by outside the carriage window. Utgard sat on an island in a smaller river that branched away from the great Ifing. I spied the gleam of water between buildings as we got closer to the port. Kale chattered on like a tour guide, pointing out historical buildings, neighborhoods and markets.

"And there is the statue of great Skrymir who once ruled Utgard," he pointed with his dominate twig. "And see that stone in the market? Some say it's the cap to Mimir's Well. And only a descendent of Odin himself will be able to move it."

"How do you know so much about Utgard?" I asked.

Kale squished up his face, thinking hard.

"Yggdrasil knows, so I know." He smiled as if the answer pleased him.

Interesting. I would have to delve more into how one yggie could tap into the knowledge of the ancient Life Tree. But for now, we were coming into port. I scanned the ships, wondering which one would be ours.

The pier was busy even in the early morning hours. The market wasn't too far away and local farmers and fisherfolk were already haggling over produce and the day's fresh catch.

Our carriage bore the king's insignia and foot traffic moved out of our way. We pulled up to the *Vergen*, a large ship with two square sails in the king's deep burgundy. The first mate met us and ordered a ratatosk to help with our bags.

"No bags," I said. "We're traveling light."

"Of course, my lady. Harald will show you to your cabin."

Harald, the ratatosk, brought us below decks and left us at our cabin with a twitch of his whiskers.

I thanked him and went inside. The cabin wasn't luxurious. It was small and cramped with two narrow bunks, but aboard ship, only the captain would have roomier accommodations.

Princess puked in the corner, then immediately sprawled in a heap of legs and fur. She took up all the floor space, and now the small cabin reeked of dog vomit.

"Let's go up top and find something to clean that up with," I said.

Raven was holding his nose. "I think she's seasick."

I hoped he wasn't right. It would be a long sail with a seasick hell hound.

Back on deck, I found a deckhand and asked for mop and bucket. Kale had been "helping" him coil ropes and had tangled himself in the loose end. The sailor looked kind of desperate. He'd probably been told to treat the king's guests with all honors, but the yggie could try anyone's patience.

I took the rope from his hands. "Raven, why don't you show this nice sailor the mess in the cabin. And take Kale with you. Keep him there until we're underway so he doesn't bother anyone else."

Raven mumbled something I didn't really want to hear, but he grabbed Kale by one twiggy limb and steered him below decks.

I set about untangling the ropes. It was the least I could do for bringing that disastrous yggie on board. I had no idea how to properly coil a rope, suspecting that sailors had some mystical way of doing it, so I just unknotted it and left it in a tidy heap.

"Kyra!" A voice called from the wharf. I ignored it because no one here knew me. Also, the voice sounded much too familiar, and that probably meant I was finally overwrought with fatigue and worry and starting to hallucinate.

"Kyra!" The call came again. My head whipped around. There, pushing through the crowd at the end of the pier was a familiar black-haired head.

Mason.

Little Bean did a somersault. Or maybe that was my own nerves reeling at the sight.

It couldn't be.

The crowd shifted and I lost sight of him. I planted my hands on the ship's rail and leaned over, willing the crowd to move.

Mason pushed through the throng of market-goers, leaving a few angry remarks in his wake. I ran to the gangplank, but a sailor blocked my way.

"I'm sorry, my lady. We're about to leave."

"I have to get off!" I tried to shove him aside, but he was as immovable as the ship's mast.

"Captain's orders! No one disembarks."

I gave him my best crazy eyes. "If you don't move this second, I will bring the gods' wrath down on you. By the One-eyed Father, your blood will boil in your veins."

His eyes goggled. I shoved him aside. Most Jotnar still had a healthy fear of old Odin. He didn't have to know that the All-father had never before answered one of my prayers.

I loped down the gangplank, tripping as I hit the pier, but Mason was there to catch me. Like always.

"Kyra!" My name escaped him like an anguished sigh.

"You found me!" Tears blurred my eyes and streamed down my cheeks. He kissed them away. His hands cupped my face, holding me like I was a precious egg that he was afraid of breaking.

"I told you I'd come."

"But how?"

Instead of answering, he kissed me. It was a deep renewal, like finding a lost treasure. His lips opened mine. His tongue tasted me, first hesitant, then frantic as if he needed to reaffirm the connection between us.

"Kyra-lady!" A small body slammed into me and I broke off the kiss.

"Jacoby?"

My dervish clung to my legs. I laughed and crouched to hug him tight. Mason crouched too, circling us in his arms.

And I had to revise my assumptions about Odin. For once, he'd answered my prayers.

CHAPTER

19

he *Vergen* left with two more passengers. Raven came back on deck just as Mason and I re-boarded. He dropped his pack and flung himself at Mason.

"It's okay, son. I'm here. You did well."

Raven smiled. His lips wobbled as if he might dissolve into tears, but it was the first genuine smile I'd seen on his face in weeks.

The ship's captain wasn't waiting for any more delays. Ropes were flung off their moorings, and we backed away from the pier. In the old days, a ship of this size would have been outfitted with oars for dozens of rowers. But the *Vergen* was a modern Jotnar ship, powered by an engine that ran on magic. Asgard and Jotunheim might not have taken part in the Flood Wars, but they'd learned a few tricks from their Terran neighbors.

We all stood by the rail, watching boats in the busy harbor. The Ifing was wider than any Terran river. It would take days to cross. I didn't care. My family was here. I didn't know what lay ahead for us—Mason and I would have a serious talk about that later—but for now, I had everything I needed.

Jacoby scrambled to see over the rail and Raven boosted him.

"What did you mean when you told Raven he'd done well," I asked Mason. Raven caught his eye and Mason nodded. He set Jacoby down and rifled through his pack, coming up with a small black disk.

"This." He handed it to me. I turned it over in my fingers, then weighed it on the palm of my hand. It was dull black and featureless, made from something other than metal or stone. Pearl, I thought, or onyx.

"What is it?"

"A prototype of a tracking device," Mason said. "Something I've been working on since our little adventure in the Nether. It tracks across any distance, even between worlds."

"You're kidding." I couldn't fathom the magical mechanics of such a thing. Mason wasn't just an alchemist. He was a genius. I turned to Raven. "And you brought this with you? How did you know?"

Raven shrugged, but it was less about adolescent apathy and more of a shy, self-effacing gesture.

"I've been helping Mason in his lab. He talked about the tracker a lot. I thought maybe..." He shrugged again.

"You thought right. I'm just glad the prototype worked." Mason ruffled his hair and Raven grinned. Wow. If I'd tried that move, I would have lost fingers.

"So you tracked us through the door to Jotunheim?"

"It wasn't easy. I had to do some fast-talking to some pretty irate giants. Seems they don't like strangers sneaking through their doors."

No kidding.

"But I met a group who called themselves the Vanlandi. You'd just been through that way. You must have left an impression because they gave me an escort here."

I ran a finger over the disk. Such an innocuous looking thing, and yet right now it was worth more than all the treasures of Odin's hall.

I grinned. "You alchemy boys have all the best toys."

THE CABIN WAS cramped with a teenage boy sleeping on one bunk, a seasick hound and a dervish curled up together in the middle of the floor, and an yggie perched on the small galley table along one wall. Mason and I tried to get comfortable on the other bunk that was meant for only one. I was glad for the comfort of his body pressed against mine, but I wasn't sleeping. He ran a hand over my belly in silent communication with Little Bean. I shifted, trying to find more room in the cramped space. He pressed his lips against my ear. His breath was hot as he whispered, "Let's go up top." I nodded my agreement. We slipped out of bed, tiptoed over the sleeping critters and left the cabin.

The passageway was dark with only one dying gleam in a wall sconce to light the way. Mason held my hand until I needed it to climb the ladder up to the main deck. I felt like a schoolgirl sneaking out of my mother's house late at night, and I giggled as I tripped over the last step.

Mason caught me before I sprawled onto the deck. In the dim light, I could just make out the grin on his face too. "What is it?"

"Just that I feel like I'm sneaking out after curfew."

"You always were a naughty girl, then?" He quirked one eyebrow, the way he did when I amused him. I couldn't help myself, I ran a finger along his brow. I'd thought I'd never see that look from him again. He caught my fingers and kissed them, then pulled me up.

The night was cool, but not frigid. The crisp air felt good after the stuffy cabin. We nodded to the second mate who stood by the ship's wheel with a ratatosk sailor by his side. They nodded back, but didn't stop us from moving about the deck.

We leaned against the rail on the port side and stared at the black river as big as an ocean with a sea of stars overhead.

"It's beautiful," I said.

"It is."

I could feel his eyes on me. I cut him a sideways glance.

"You're supposed to be admiring the stars."

"I'd rather look at you."

I tried to hold steady under his gaze, but that little insecure girl inside me cried for the Kyra I used to be before getting sick. She couldn't believe that Mason could still love me, not with my plump jowls, crows feet and matronly curves.

"Please don't." I turned my back to him.

His hand crept under my braid and fingers trailed along my jaw. Did he feel how different it was? How the skin had begun to give up its fight with gravity? Was he imagining the old hag he'd have to care for one day soon?

"Kyra, please look at me."

I sniffled back a tear. Damn those pregnancy hormones.

"Kyra..."

I turned to him, lifting my chin and trying for defiance.

"I know you must have been shocked when you first saw me. It's okay to say it now. I won't crumple."

His fingers continued to trace the lines of my face, my chin, the swell of my cheek…my lips.

"Why are you smiling?" I snapped. "You think the fact that I'm going to turn into an old crone is funny?"

He pressed his finger to my lips.

"No. It's not funny. But it amuses me that you think you could be anything but beautiful. You are the mother of my child. That alone makes you beautiful in my eyes. But in truth, you have not changed so much as you made me believe. A little sturdier, perhaps. A little softer in some places." His fingers ghosted along the side of my breast and I shivered. "But I love these changes because they are part of you."

I swallowed hard, downing the lump of anxiety that had been riding in my chest for so many weeks now. I was almost home. The Golden Apples would keep me alive long enough to birth my daughter. And Mason was at my side. I could almost believe that everything would turn out all right. He kissed me. The touch of his fingers had been all the foreplay I needed, and even as my mind screamed at me to hold back, I melted into his embrace.

Later—it could have been minutes or hours—I stood with my back cradled against his chest and the enormity of the Jotunheim-Asgard sky spread before me. Mason rubbed the side of my head with his chin, as if he needed the reassurance of skin-to-skin contact.

"Do you remember the stories I told you about my previous wives?" he said.

"Yes. You nursed your second wife through her final years. That must have been hard."

"Not as hard as letting my third wife go. Jeanne would not let me love her simply because she was aging without me. Please don't…" Now it was his turn to have a catch in his voice. "Please don't break my heart like that again."

"No." I wouldn't. I couldn't. I leaned my head against his shoulder. It was so good to have him with me again, but he needed to know everything before he decided if he wanted to stay. I turned to face him.

"There's more. My grandfather is dead." I told him about Baldyr and his letter. "He doesn't want Dana to rule Asgard. Neither do the giants. It seems my aunt hasn't been making many friends since she took over."

"And you? What do you want?"

It was a good question. What *did* I want? I sighed. "I want to go home. To

Dorion Park. I want to have tea with Gita and toss shrimp into Hunter's tank. I want to sleep in our bed and raise Little Bean in our home. I want you to be Prime Minister of Montreal—"

He cut me off with a raised hand. "I agree with home, but don't make this about my career. I never wanted to be Prime Minister. Oscar bullied me into it. You know this. And I will follow you, wherever you need to be. You know this too, right?"

I nodded. Not trusting my words. Asgard wasn't so bad. It never got too warm or too cold. The food was good. The air was clean. I knew all the monsters that lived there, including Aunt Dana. And besides, the fickle gods knew I wouldn't have to endure it for long. When the MMC took over for good, Mason could return to Dorion with our daughter.

Until then, I would enjoy the time we had together.

CHAPTER

20

y feet left the pier and landed on solid ground. Asgard ground. The magic of the land zinged up my keening, at once familiar and strangely exotic. I had a love-hate relationship with the land of my mother's people. Love-hate might put too strong a spin on it. Asgard had welcomed me and my mother when we had nowhere else to go. It had healed her. It had given me my sword and my Valkyrie strength. But it had never felt like home, and it would be now, for the rest of my days.

No one in Asgard knew we were coming, so I was surprised when a ratatosk messenger scurried up to meet us.

"The captain says you need a guide to the capital, is that right?" He asked in that high-pitched squirrelly voice. He sat back on his haunches with elbows tucked at his sides and hands held forward in that peculiar pose that made it seem like ratatosks were always ready to accept a nut. He wore short pants that left his bushy tail fluttering freely behind him, a white shirt with a lace collar, and a green vest embellished with needlework of vines and berries. It was hard not to smile at his costume, but I held it in. Ratatosks knew they were ridiculously cute. The smart ones used that to their advantage. Others could be touchy about it.

"I guess a guide would be a good idea," I said. "It's been many years since I've been to the capital."

"No worries. No worries. None at all." The messenger twitched his whiskers. If you'll follow me, it's all been arranged. Horses, provisions and a guide. That's right. All taken care of. Follow me now. Follow me."

144

He scurried off. I caught Mason's eye and he shrugged. I could probably make it to the capital on my own, but we'd be walking all day. Horses would be a blessing.

We followed the messenger to a small office near the port authority.

He had me sign for a letter.

"It's all there," he chattered. "Read it if you like. All right as rain. His Majesty King Gillingr has made arrangements. You just take that chit down the road to old Fenrir's tavern. He'll see to the horses and provisions. And I'll send along a guide. Go on now."

I nearly dropped my backpack as he shooed us out the door, but Kale was right there to earn his existential brownie points.

"Please, my lady. I'll help you with that pack." Yes, his diction was definitely getting clearer.

Jacoby snarled and shoved Kale, then shouldered the bag that was much too big for him.

"Jacoby! That was rude. And I can manage my on my own." I took the bag from him. Jacoby stuck his nose in the air and sniffed dramatically before trudging after Raven and Princess.

"What's that all about?" I asked.

"Just give him some time," Mason said. "He was very upset when he learned you were gone."

I sighed, feeling both annoyed and worried. In truth, I had given little thought to those I'd left behind, other than Mason. The idea of never seeing Jacoby, Gita or Hunter again had been unbearable. Thinking about their hurt was just the pain-filled cherry on top.

But I had wronged Jacoby by leaving him behind. I would have to address that soon.

Our new guide met us outside the tavern. He was another ratatosk, but thankfully, a much less chatty one than the port messenger.

"If we head out after lunch, my lady, we'll be in Asgard proper by mid-afternoon." His voice wasn't quite so chirpy as the other ratatosks we'd met.

"Thank you," I said. "But we need to make a stop at Iduna's orchard. And it's urgent, so we'll be eating on the road, if that's all right with you?"

"Perfectly," he said. "I'll make sure provisions are ready."

His name was Raol. He wore hunting leathers and when, a few minutes later, Mason and I mounted our horses, he sprung lightly into the saddle of a small pony. I worried that they wouldn't be able to keep up, but the mount had some spunk and didn't like being third pony on the string. He set the pace and Raol perched on the saddle with his furry tail sticking straight up like the plume on a hat. I'd never seen a ratatosk ride a horse before and wondered how he would steer it. But pony and ratatosk seemed to be in tune with each other and moved as one.

Jacoby rode in front of Mason. Raven ran as a pony beside Princess who seemed thankful to be back on solid ground. Kale, for reasons of his own, had decided to attach himself to me. Perhaps he sensed that I was someone often in need of service. The gods knew he was right. I seemed to attract trouble whatever world I was on. Kale must have figured that by following me, he'd fill his quota of good deeds in no time.

As we rode away from the port and into the countryside, the crowd of travelers thinned. The road was wide, bordered on both sides by green rolling hills dotted with stands of pine and oak.

Mason and I rode side by side. Jacoby sat in the saddle staring straight ahead and white-knuckling the saddle horn. The dervish wasn't comfortable with horses, and the animals weren't any happier to have him on their backs, as if they could sense the fiery potential they were carrying.

"Are those new pants and vest?" I asked him, trying to take his mind off the horse's clop-clop gait.

"Yes."

"They're very nice. You look sharp."

His lips pinched flat and he wouldn't look at me. I sighed. I'd keep trying. He'd talk to me eventually.

An hour into the journey, the terrain started to look familiar.

"Are we nearly there?" I asked Raol as we came to a crossroads. He slowed his pony to speak, and pointed with a gray paw to the left fork. "That would take us straight to Asgard, my lady." Then he pointed right. "But to visit Iduna's orchard, we must pass through the Vale of Heimdall first."

"Of…of course. I hadn't thought of that."

Raol nodded and nudged his pony into a quick walk.

"Something wrong?" Mason asked.

I bit my lip and shook my head. "Yes. No. It will be all right."

Heimdall was the rainbow bridge's warden. His valley was the site of my worst crime, where Bifrost had once soared from the mountains of Asgard, across the veil and into Terra. Now nothing remained of the rainbow bridge, and if Heimdall caught me, he'd kill me on the spot.

"Let's just get this done," I said, and spurred my horse forward. Nothing, not even a raging demigod, was going to keep me away from those Golden Apples now.

Jacoby and Kale grew bored in the saddle. Since we were resting the horses and moving at a sedate walk, I let them down to trot alongside Raven and Princess.

"Stay close," I called after them as all four ran ahead. We were deep in the wood now, and even at high noon, only a spattering of light made it through the canopy. Raol rode at the head of our little caravan, and I could just spy the jaunty curl of his tail.

Mason and I were alone for the moment.

"What should we expect when we reach the orchard?" he asked. "Are the apples guarded?"

"Iduna keeps watch. She probably already knows we're coming."

Mason frowned. "Iduna, the goddess?"

"Not exactly. It's complicated. The guardian of the Golden Apples is always called Iduna, and she's long-lived, but not immortal. More like a reincarnation of the goddess."

"I see…and she has the sight?"

"She has spies in the woods." I waved a hand at the shadows between the trees.

"What kind of spies?" Mason's hand instinctively went to the knife on his belt.

"Relax. I mean birds, squirrels and brownies. She has a way with the forest folk."

We rode in silence for a bit, then I said, "You haven't told me about your visit with Kester. Was he able to help you?"

Mason glanced at Raol and the others. They rode far enough ahead that they couldn't hear us. The forest was unnaturally still and quiet. This wasn't the Inbetween where monsters lurked around every hill, but I couldn't help feeling like eyes were watching and ears were listening from the shadows.

Mason felt it too. He kept his voice low. "We didn't get much time to talk before I had to leave, but he agreed to help in any way he can. He says that my peculiar power, my demonic traits, will get stronger with time. He suggested that I master it now, before it gets away from me."

Demons could manifest a variety of dark powers. Some ate the life-force of magical creatures or even humans. Others, like Kester, could control darkness itself. Mason's particular power was necromancy. It had manifested in a spectacular way when we fought Gunora and her pet nuckelavee. I'd killed the nuckelavee, but Mason had reanimated his corpse to defend us against Gunora's army of kelpies.

"Did he have any suggestions about how to master this power?" I asked.

"None. It's not like I can walk into the morgue and ask if I can make the corpses dance." Mason had a bitter twist to his lips. That battle with the kelpies had taken a lot from him. It had taken a lot from all of us. Raven had lost his home. I'd been infected with MMC and I'd even lost my sword, or at least I'd lost the magic side of it. My hand went to the hilt sticking up over my shoulder.

Don't worry, I thought. We'll bring you back to life one of these days.

To Mason, I said, "We'll think of something. Kester's right. You need to understand your magic now, before you're forced to use it again."

Mason grunted an agreement.

"And did he say anything about…about the baby?"

Mason reached across and grabbed my hand in his. "No. I'm sorry. He has no children of his own. He's never known one of our kind to sire a child."

I nodded through a prickling of tears. I wasn't worried that Little Bean would sprout horns and come out spitting fire. Nor did I expect her to be evil because of her demon genes. I'd learned that evilness, like time, was only a construct. Kester was a demon and he wasn't evil. And I'd met plenty of pure humans with black souls. Mason's magic might be dark, but I trusted no one more with my life or my child. Little Bean might be part demon, part gargoyle, dryad, Valkyrie…it didn't matter. We would love all aspects of her.

He reached across the gap between our horses and squeezed my fingers. "It will be all right. I promise."

"I know."

These were the words people say. *All will be right.* We say them, not because we believe them, not deep down where the magic of our souls wells up. We believe them with the forced bravery that gets us through the day, through the next step on the road, through the days-months-years of not knowing for sure. Until I held my baby in my arms, counted her fingers and toes, and keened the magic in her heart...until then I would believe that the child of a demon and a half-blood Valkyrie would be all right.

The narrow path we followed opened up to a grassy plain. Our horses tugged on the reins, wanting to stop and graze the sweet grass.

Raol circled back to us. "We could rest here, my lady, but the orchard is just over that rise. About another hour's ride."

"Let's push on," I said. "The horses can rest once we arrive."

"Very good." Raol swung his pony around and took the lead again.

"Are you sure we shouldn't rest now?" Mason asked. "You look tired."

"I'll feel better once we reach the orchard."

I didn't want to stop. This was Heimdall's Vale. I let myself glance at the mountains to my right where Bifrost once soared into the sky and through the veil to Terra, then I firmly urged my horse to follow Raol.

CHAPTER

21

The orchard of the Golden Apples spread over dozens of acres of rolling hills. It was surrounded by a hedge so dense that even the local rabbits couldn't get through. No one entered the orchard without Iduna's consent.

She met us at the grandly arched gate in the hedge.

I jumped from the saddle and gave my reins to Mason. "You should wait here and keep the kids out of trouble."

Mason eyed Iduna and the gate behind her. "I would rather go in with you."

I shook my head. "This is something I need to do alone. Please." I didn't want to test Iduna's goodwill or hurt Mason's feelings. If she sensed his demon magic, she would never let him pass under that arch.

Mason's eyes were hard. "Fine. But if you're not back in an hour, I'm coming in and no goddess in a fancy dress will keep me out."

I nodded. He would do it too. He'd followed me through worlds. Iduna wouldn't know what hit her.

Raven, in his pony form, was dancing around me.

"It's okay." I ran my hand along his withers. He let out a little neigh. "I'll be back. I promise."

I turned and walked up the hill to the orchard.

Iduna was tall and willowy, with loose blond hair held back by a crown of flowers. Her dress was simple and white and flowed around her feet like ragged daisy petals.

"Welcome, Kyra of the Valkyrie. You have been gone too long." Standing on the rise, she towered over me.

"Thank you, Iduna. I hope I am welcome."

Her smile was soft. "And why shouldn't you be?"

She was going to make me say it. I'd known she would. The price of entry into her garden was only—and always—the truth.

I steeled myself and stepped forward. The day was hot and still, but Iduna's gown fluttered around her on some inexplicable wind.

"I ask permission to visit the Golden Apple Tree and to partake of its fruit." I spoke the formal words. "And in return I will tell you my truth."

Iduna inclined her head for me to continue.

"When I last rode through this vale, I committed two sins. I severed the rainbow bridge, cutting Asgard off from its ally world, Terra." My voice quavered, and I paused to take a deep breath. Iduna's eyes seemed to darken from periwinkle to icy ocean blue. I keened the magnitude of her magic swirling around me. I couldn't have held back my next words if I'd wanted to. "And...I killed my lover Aaric before I fled."

Iduna's magic swelled. She seemed to grow bigger until she loomed over me. Her beauty was no longer sweet. She was imposing. Forbidding. Downright scary. Her dressed whipped about her as if she were caught in the eye of a storm.

"Speak truth!" Her voice cracked like thunderous whip.

I fell to my knees. "It is the truth! I killed Aaric. It was my hand, my blade that pierced his heart."

"Speak truth!" Iduna thundered again.

I looked up at her through tears. Her face was haloed in sunlight. Her magic felt like a thousand tiny needles jabbing at me, looking for a way under my shields. My shields had been built a lifetime ago and reinforced through years of fear and denial, but Iduna's magic was stronger. She peeled away those layers to what lay at their heart.

A scared young woman who only wanted Aaric to love her. A woman who realized that he never would, that his heart had been given away long ago and never returned to him. A woman who was easily manipulated because of her love for him.

Baldyr's words came back to me.

...he used you as his weapon of choice...

"I didn't kill Aaric." My voice was barely above a whisper. "He killed himself."

Iduna smiled. Her eyes paled back to periwinkle and her gown settled around her feet.

"There now. Was that so difficult?"

I laughed and sobbed at the same time. I'd always said that Aaric killed himself, but part of me had kept the idea that it was my fault like a rock in my shoe to punish myself with every step.

Iduna leaned down and tipped my chin up, forcing me to meet her gaze. "The truth. It is a powerful thing and a worthy price for the Golden Apples. You may go in, and I hope you find what you are looking for."

I sniffled and rose to my feet. I glanced back at Mason. He'd run halfway to the arch but stopped himself from interfering. I knew what it must have cost him. I gave him a smile and mouthed, "It's okay." His hands were fisted at his sides, but he backed off.

I followed Iduna under the arch and along a walkway covered in a bower of flowering vines that ended at a hill overlooking the orchard. The grass under our feet was as smooth as a carpet, and I had the sudden urge to take off my boots and sink my toes in it.

"You should listen to your instincts," Iduna said. "The orchard will speak best if you are connected to it. Go on. Feel its love against the souls of your feet."

I side-eyed her, wondering how she'd gotten inside my head, but I kicked off my boots and left my socks tucked inside them. The grass was soft as velvet. Its magic hummed against my bare skin, and I laughed at the tickling sensation.

Iduna smiled. "Go now. She's expecting you. Take what you need for you and your child. For today and the days to come."

I turned to thank her, but she was gone. I left my boots by the bower, but kept my sword in its harness. A Valkyrie never went anywhere without her sword, not even into the heart of a goddess's domain.

I strolled through the orchard, not on any particular path.

Iduna usually brought the Golden Apples to Baldyr's court. They were the secret to the Aesir's long life, and so she doled them out carefully. But I'd been here before. Every Valkyrie took a pilgrimage to the orchard before her graduation.

Last time, I'd wandered for hours without finding the Golden Tree. I'd been frustrated and almost turned back before I spied the distinctive leaves shining in the sunlight. This time, I didn't bother to search. The tree would make herself known when she was ready.

The orchard boasted hundreds of trees, all varieties of apples, and many with healing powers of their own, but there was only one Golden Tree. I found her at the orchard's heart, in a clearing surrounded by smaller trees that seemed to bend toward her in homage.

Her leaves were pale green and gilded in gold. And no matter what the season, she always bore white blooms and plump yellow fruit at the same time.

I filled my pack with the golden apples and sat cross-legged in the grass by her roots. I chose one apple to eat straight away and admired its perfection. A simple orb, full of life-giving nutrients—sweet, juicy, and clothed in golden skin with a blush of peach.

My sword harness was uncomfortable, so I took it off and laid the sheathed blade across my knees. The sun warmed my back. A few insects buzzed around my head, but even those seemed cheeky rather than annoying. I thought if I never set foot in paradise, this would be close enough.

I didn't know what to say, but felt I should say *something*. The Golden's magic was calm and reassuring, but I keened her anticipation. She was waiting for me.

"I, uh, come for your help. I paid for my entrance to your orchard with a truth, but the truth that I kept even from Iduna is that I'm scared. Not for me, but for my daughter. This body I wear is sick, but she needs it, for a little while longer. Will you bless me, and help me to keep her safe?"

Leaves rustled. Petals burst from the blossoms and rained down like pink and white snowflakes. They landed on my head, my shoulders and my stomach. I lifted an arm to examine the petals. They were perfectly formed half-hearts, pearlescent white with a stroke of pink down the center. They didn't fall flat like normal petals. They didn't slide off my arm either. They clung to me, quivering with life.

I felt my daughter shift inside my womb.

The petals covered my sheathed sword, and for the first time in months, my blade sang out. The sword's magic burst forth and circled me like an aura of warm light.

My sword was awake.

I rose and nodded to the Golden. "Thank you."

I left the orchard, munching on the sweetest apple I'd ever tasted.

sgard is a world and a country, or a country that fills an entire world. Its founders weren't the most imaginative and when it came to naming the capital city, they decided to keep it simple and call that Asgard too. No point in burning brain cells over it.

The castle in Asgard City had been built by Odin and the wall around it by a giant he tricked into service over a millennium ago.

I knew the streets of Asgard well. They wove uphill from the main gates to the castle that was shoved against the highest wall at the city's upper edge. The king's quarters and the Great Hall nearly hung off a cliff, overlooking a valley where many battles had been fought.

I'd lived in the castle with my mother and spent many evenings on my balcony staring over that valley. On the far side, the mists of the Gudsov mountain range obscured the road to Valhalla where the gods waited for great warriors to join them in their feasting and drinking.

The faces of those gods were etched into the massive gates marking the entrance into Asgard City. Odin with a raven on each shoulder dominated the scene. Thor's hammer featured prominently and Loki was a small figure in the corner, looking off into the distance as if plotting his next prank. The other gods were represented too—a sword crossed with a sheath of wheat for Freya, an arching bridge for Heimdall and Hel's pet wolf Garmr.

These giant faces were meant to intimidate those seeking entrance to the city. The gates rose four stories high and were wide enough for ten carts to pass through at once. But they were closed to traffic today.

We waited in line at the smaller side gate, where guards were scrutinizing everyone who passed through.

The Aesir lived long lives, and children were cherished for their rarity. They took care of their elderly and their sick and worked at whatever job needed doing. No one went hungry in Asgard.

So, when I saw a beggar woman harassing the waiting travelers, I reined in my sympathy and ignored her. Her clothes were rags hanging on her wasted frame. Blue eyes rimmed in red wept as she clawed my leg and called out, "See me! See me!" Two raw X marks had been slashed into her cheeks. They weren't yet healed and oozed blood. When she tried to grab my stirrup, I kicked my horse forward.

Mason cut me a glance and pulled his mount closer to mine.

"Not like you to ignore the needy," he said. It was true. In Montreal he'd seen me empty my pockets as we walked down the street.

"She's been shunned. Aiding her in any way is a crime. No one will interfere with her."

"Shunned? For what?"

I shrugged. "Had to be something terrible." The only other person I'd seen shunned had murdered a child. I glanced back at the woman who was already trying to latch on to the next riders in line. She would be ignored until she gave up. Then she'd go live in the forest, if she could. If not, she would die. Usually, the shunned died.

Aesir laws might seem harsh by other standards, but Asgard had only one prison, and it held those awaiting trial. Executions were rare, as death was considered a privilege of the gods. Sentences for minor crimes were meted out as community service. Only killers and rapists were shunned.

I could still hear the woman crying and shouting for someone to pay attention, and then she was lost in the crowd.

Jacoby was perched on the saddle in front of Mason. His eyes were wide as he took in the white walls of Asgard and the impressive gate.

I squeezed his arm. "It's beautiful, isn't it?"

He frowned and pulled away.

I met Mason's sympathetic gaze over the dervish's head. I still had some work to do.

Raol wheeled his pony around.

"This is where I leave you, my lady. You can find your way through the city?" His tail twitched and he was already looking at the far horizon.

"Of course, but won't you come with us? Get a hot meal before heading back?"

"No, my lady. Too much fuss to get in and out of the city. I wish you success on your errand. Should you need the services of a guide again, you can leave a message at the Gardsbruk Inn. We passed it on the road."

He made a chirping sound and his pony turned back the way we'd come. He was the only mounted ratatosk, and people stepped out of his way. In a moment, I could no longer see the curl of his tail over the crowd.

We were nearing the gates, and I told Raven and Princess to stay close. Kale was still gripping the saddle behind me, but he was so quiet I'd almost forgotten he was there.

Six Valkyries lined the road just inside the gate. They wore full battle regalia and their armor shone in the sun. None made a move to intervene with the flow of traffic but their eyes scanned the crowd constantly. They were supervising. That was odd. The Valkyries didn't get involved with municipal affairs. Luckily, I didn't recognize any of them, so they couldn't know me.

Two guards wearing the king's colors had the menial task of questioning people as they entered. One was young and looked bored. The other was a little more gray than I remembered and his shoulders were more stooped.

"Hello, Karl."

The old guard's lips pinched, and he peered at me through squinted eyes. "And who's this?"

My heart thudded. Maid Mother Crone had changed me, but surely not so much that I was unrecognizable?

"Kyra Greene...er, Valkyrie Kyra." I gave him my old name. When I left Asgard, it had been difficult to get used to being Kyra Greene, but already I felt my old title slide around my shoulders like a familiar shirt.

Karl's eyes widened. He leaned forward to get a better look. "Kyra? By the gods, it's true! Welcome home!" I thought he might shake my hand or try to hug me, but then he remembered his duty. He straightened and tamed his grin down to a stiff smile. "It's good that you're home." His eyes were troubled, as he stepped aside to let us through.

"A good first encounter," Mason said.

"Not everyone will be so welcoming."

He nodded and kept his hand on the grip of his dagger.

Coming home was strange. Everything was familiar, and yet odd after living in Montreal for so many years. Asgard was a city from another time. The Aesir kept to the old ways. The roads were cobbled and the vehicles horse-powered. Technology meant a new forge or better braking system on a carriage. Women dressed as they pleased, but gowns were still favored. And men wore their weapons with pride.

A lamplighter was coming around to activate the gleams on every corner. Like their technology, Aesir magic had only progressed so far. Gleams and magic apples were accepted, and no one would look twice at a talking squirrel dressed in a waistcoat, but they had never taken to technomancy the way the Terrans had.

My thoughts strayed to my memories of living here as we made our slow way across town. Every corner reminded me of my grandfather. Hawkers plied us with sweet cakes and meat pies—grandfather's favorite—hoping to sell out their stock before the day's end. Farm carts blocked the way as we neared the market that was shutting down—the market that grandfather had built.

We dismounted while we waited for the road to clear. I spent the few silver coins Huyn had given me on meat pies for everyone. Since leaving the orchard, I'd felt Mason's eyes watching me almost constantly. I could feel the weight of his stare now. I swallowed the last of my meat pie and washed it down with water from my canteen. I turned to catch him frowning, and smoothed the crease from between his brows.

"Didn't your mother ever warn you that if you make a face too long it will stick?"

His expression softened. "I'm just worried. You don't seem any different. How do you know the apples worked?"

I turned my keening inward, and felt the blood coursing through my veins. "I just know. For one, the morning sickness has been better."

"That could be a coincidence."

"Maybe. But I feel...stronger." I took his hand and rubbed his thumb with mine, not looking into his eyes. "You know they won't cure me. But I'm confident that their magic will give me enough time."

"Enough time." Mason's eyes were hard. "Is there such a thing?"

"No." I leaned my forehead against his shoulder and breathed in his scent, so glad that he hadn't given up, that he'd followed my trail and found me.

Then the farm carts moved out, leaving the road clear, and we were on our way again.

We left the horses with a groom in the yard outside the castle proper. I kept my own blade in its harness across my back, but unsheathed Baldyr's sword. I slipped his signet ring on my thumb. It was too big to fit any of my fingers.

"Are you ready for this?" Mason asked.

"Not in the slightest." I gave him a wobbly smile.

I grabbed the sleeve of a page running by. "Who's in court now?" I asked. The boy frowned at my hand on his sleeve. He was old for a page and had that look of a man who'd begun to lose patience for being ordered around like a boy.

"The usual. Valkyrie Dana, the council and Lady Natalia. What's it to you?"

I resisted the urge to scold him for his impertinence.

"You will announce that Valkyrie Kyra is here on urgent business. I require an immediate audience with…the council." I didn't know for sure who was in charge these days, but the council was a good bet.

"I won't!" The page seemed incensed by the idea. "You have no right to be here. Be away, now." He turned to rush away, but found Mason standing in his path. I knew that Mason was a big softy underneath, but to others he had a dark glare that made him look tough and immovable. The page stopped and looked back, probably wondering what mess he'd stepped in.

I held out Baldyr's sword.

"Do you recognize this blade?"

The boy's eyes widened. His mouth hung open and he nodded.

"This blade says I have the right to enter court. You will announce me now."

He braided his fingers in front of him. "My lady, I don't have the authority!"

"Then find someone who does."

He nodded and disappeared into the castle.

I waited several long minutes, standing stock still. I could feel eyes watching me from the many outbuildings in the yard. It wouldn't do to look nervous.

Finally, a short, burly man dressed in a blue coat with tails hurried across the yard. His beard was red, flecked with white and the red hair continued in a ring around his nearly bald head. His broad mouth was spread in a wide grin.

"Kyra! It's true! I thought the boy was playing a prank."

"It's not a prank, Sten. I'm really here."

He took my free hand in both of his and pumped it up and down.

I couldn't help grinning. Sten had been Baldyr's chancellor, his closest advisor and his friend. Of all the council elders, he was the only one who had ever shown me kindness.

"You are a sight for these old, weary eyes." He took in the sword and the ring. "So you've been to see Gillingr. That's good. Very good." He glanced around the yard. People were staring at us now. Grooms congregated in the stable doorway. Two ladies whispered behind their hands, eyes fixed on the group of strangers with the chancellor.

Sten leaned in and whispered, "I wish you'd sent word ahead. I could have managed your arrival better. But there's no stopping it now. They'll already be talking about you inside."

"Good." I hefted Baldyr's sword in my grip. "Let's give them something to talk about."

"Right behind you," Mason murmured.

It was customary for the doors of the main hall to remain closed while the Council of Elders was in chambers. Sten stalked through the outer atrium and called for them to be opened, but before the guards could comply, a dozen Valkyries marched out of a narrow hallway on the atrium's far side. They wore full battle regalia—leather armor, drawn swords, shields and golden helmets with white wings. Gods, how had I ever worn such a get-up with a straight face?

But the Valkyries weren't laughing. The few stragglers in the atrium moved aside, recognizing a fight in the making. More onlookers had come in from the outer yard to witness the confrontation.

I put my family behind me. Mason held Raven and Princess in check.

Kale was gone or hiding. Good. I hoped he wouldn't get underfoot if it came to a fight.

One Valkyrie led the others. Her breastplate wore the crest of a captain.

"Valkyrie Kyra!" Her voice rang with magic. She was using a thaumatic amplifier to be heard throughout the atrium. "You have been charged with murder and treason for the destruction of Bifrost."

More armed Valkyries poured into the atrium. They surrounded us and separated me from Mason and the others.

"It's all right!" I called to him. "It will all be sorted out. I promise. Don't do anything rash!"

His face was dark as a storm cloud and I hoped he'd listened to me. Then the Valkyries were prodding them toward a far corridor and I lost sight of him.

Sten was arguing with the guards by the main doors, but they remained closed. I faced the Valkyries. Better to get this over with.

I smiled and held out my hands. The swords were taken from me, but I'd snuck the signet ring into my pocket.

The Valkyrie captain got right in my face and sneered. I recognized her now. Valkyrie Anni. She'd graduated a year behind me.

I gave her my best smile. "You need twelve Valkyries at your back to confront me? You never could stand a bit of competition."

"Hello, Kyra. You shouldn't have come back."

She raised a fist and dashed me over the head with the hilt of her blade.

CANINES OF MANY COLORS

November 22, 2076

I happened upon a pet adoption event at Abbott's Agora today. A local animal shelter was showcasing its adoptees at the market. Since my apartment is tiny and already packed with cages and critters, I had to pass up the chance to adopt. But it was a close thing. So many cute puppies! Maybe one day, when circumstances allow, I'll get myself a little dog—one of those fuzzy-slipper-with-eyes kind of dogs. For now, I have to be content to window shop at pet stores.

Looking at all those wonderful and needy faces got me thinking about our love-fear relationship with canines. It has always struck me as a little odd that mythology is riddled with stories of evil canines—from hell hounds to werewolves, black dogs to monstrous wolves—and yet the lowly dog is supposed to be man's best friend. That makes me think that many old tales sprouted from fear but also maybe a grain of truth.

I grew up running with hell hounds and can attest that they can be gentle, loyal creatures. They can also rip out a man's throat if needs be. And since their coming-out party, werewolves have proven to be no more or less evil than anyone else.

There is one hound whose very name still makes my bones shiver. That is Garmr, Hel's pet and guardian of the gate to the underworld. Maybe it still affects me because my older cousins took delight in scaring me with tales of Garmr. If Ragnarok really happens, Garmr will be the one to open the gates and let the demons loose. But what really makes me sad is the legend that evolved around his offspring. It was said that the blood from a pup of Garmr's seed could cure any illness, bring fertility, prosperity and wisdom. Too many dogs were killed in the Garmr's name, both on Terra and in other lands. So many innocent dogs lost to human and Aesir foolishness. I think that's why his legend still sticks with me.

What are some of your favorite canines—real or imagined?

Comments (4)

There's an Abenaki myth about Azeban, the trickster dog. I may have some literature on it, but the Abenaki are from up your way.
cchedgewitch (November 22, 2076)

> Good to know. I'll look it up in Montreal's archives.
> *Valkyrie367 (November 22, 2076)*

——•——

Blood sausage will get you through any cold winter. Don't knock it til you try it.
HomesteadingWhizard (November 23, 2076)

> You spelt wizard rong, dum-ass.
> *Peeky00you (November 23, 2076)*

CHAPTER

23

thought I'd only blacked out for a moment, but when I came to, I was alone in a cell. The only light came from a tiny window too high to look through.

I pounded on the door, and yelled for the guard, for anyone. No one came. The door was solid metal except for a small slot six inches from the ground, through which I assumed someone would eventually slide a meal. At least I hoped so.

My head ached. I touched the lump above my ear where Anni had struck me. Blood had already crusted over a small cut, but I had a spectacular bruise that spread down my jawline.

They'd taken my weapons, but left my pack. I pulled out another Golden Apple. It would solve two problems—hunger and the wound on my head.

I ate it listening to the whine of my sword. It was nearby—probably at the guard's post—and not happy about our separation. I could do nothing to soothe it now, but the brittle sound of its agitation was comforting after its long silence.

I considered my prison cell. The floor was damp and there was nowhere else to sit. I paced. Six steps one way, six steps back.

What had they done with Mason and the others? And when had the Valkyries become the Asgard Police? This whole thing stank of Dana's manipulations.

I still had Baldyr's letter and signet ring in my pocket. They were proof that Baldyr had pardoned me before his death and that his intentions were for me to rule in Asgard. But they were worthless unless I could get the Council of Elders to listen. Dana wouldn't make that easy. I could only hope that Sten was pleading my case before the council right now.

I glanced at the slot in the door. At some point, someone would come, if only to feed me. I had to get them to listen. The Aesir weren't barbarians. I'd be given my day in court and then they'd have to let me go. At least that's how it had worked when Baldyr was in charge. But Dana was the de facto ruler in Asgard now.

Dana. The one who regularly abused me in the name of "training."

Another hour passed. I gave up worrying about the damp floor and slid down the wall until my chin hit my knees. I wrapped my arms around my ankles and tried not to panic. The apple had soothed my most basic needs.

I closed my eyes, not expecting to sleep. Instead, I sank into memories of the life I'd run away from fifteen years ago.

I DIDN'T HAVE to dig deep to bring up the memory of Dana commanding me and another Valkyrie novice to fight. It was a hot morning. I'd passed all the tests to fulfill the Valkyrie training, but Dana wouldn't give me my wings as was my right. Instead, she set me to train with girls years younger than me.

I'd been at it all morning. She threw me into one fight after another. I was bruised, cut and weary, but she wouldn't stop until I begged her to. And I wouldn't beg.

The current bout was against a novice named Anni. She was a year behind me and the best fighter in her class. Some even said she was better than Gunora who was set to make Captain. She was certainly out of my league, and even if I wasn't exhausted from a dozen fights already, I wouldn't have been able to beat her.

Dana counted on it. Looking back later, I realized that my stubbornness had brought me to this point. Why did I want to be a Valkyrie so badly anyway? Why couldn't I just walk away? It seems silly now, but back then, I wanted my Valkyrie wings more than I'd wanted anything before.

And since I wouldn't give up, Dana decided that maiming me would be a good alternative.

"Anni! Don't check your strikes!" Dana yelled from the sidelines. "Your enemy will give you no quarter!"

Other Valkyries had gathered to watch us fight as if sensing the brewing storm.

Anni's face was flushed, but not from exertion. This was her first bout of the day. She was embarrassed to beat down a rival who was so obviously beaten already. It wasn't the Valkyrie way.

But Dana's strident commands wouldn't let up.

"Take her down! Show no mercy!"

Anni's sword fell like Thor's hammer. Metal slid on metal with a hideous squeal as I blocked one more time. I could barely hold my arm up.

"Finish it!" Dana shouted.

We used blunted practice swords, but that didn't matter. Anni struck with the force of thunder. I had nothing left to give and she easily sloughed off my parry. I heard my collar bone crack with her next hit, but before the pain registered, I saw shock on her face, and thought, "She is a victim here like me."

Then pain ignited like fire inside me. I gasped and crumpled to the ground.

Anni dropped her blade and knelt in the sand. Her sister, Rini, who'd been watching with the others, joined her. Together they tried to help me stand. I could barely breathe.

"Leave her!" Dana shouted. "She will walk off this field on her own strength or not walk at all."

"But Freya," Anni said, "she's injured."

Dana slapped her. I didn't see what happened next. The slap jostled Anni, and I fell back on the sand. The new flush of pain brought blissful blackness.

I recovered in bed for weeks, despite the old healer's tinctures. Even Iduna's apples could only do so much. During that time, I learned that Dana had punished Anni and Rini for stooping to help me. She said it was for defying her orders, but I knew it was for showing solidarity with the outcast.

The punishment she chose was a reflection of me too. She knew how much I loved hell hounds. Years ago, she used to make me clean the kennels, but that stopped when she realized I enjoyed the work. So to pour salt on my wounds, she commanded Anni and Rini to travel into the Razor Mountains, find the hell hound Garmr and bring back one of its pups. Alive or dead.

The silly Valkyrie girls who'd visited me to tell the tale had gasped with gleeful horror at those words.

"Alive or dead. Can you believe it?" one of the girls said. "Her exact words were 'Whichever is easier to carry.'"

"I believe it," the other girl replied. "I just wish it was me. What an adventure!"

I closed my eyes and told them I was too tired for visitors.

I couldn't even remember their names, those silly girls who pretended to be my friends just so they could be the ones to tell me about Anni and Rini.

Alive or dead. An innocent beast would die.

And worse, the Razor Mountains were made of ice so fine it sliced through any armor. Anni and Rini would be cut to ribbons before they found Hel's gate.

Alive or dead. Innocent lives wasted because Dana hated me.

And that was the first time I wondered, was it hate or fear?

It was also the reason Dana couldn't be allowed to rule in Asgard. She had no love in her heart—no love for others, for the gods, or even herself. She'd lived alone for all the years I'd known her. No spouse, boyfriend or girlfriend. No platonic friends either. She had a heart of stone that wouldn't let anyone in. Her reign would be marked by fear, hate and prejudice, enough to wipe out Baldyr's legacy altogether.

The slot on the door rattled. I rolled to my knees. They were stiff from lying on the cold floor. How long had I been lost in memories best forgotten?

The slot rattled again and a stick poked through.

"Mistress Kyra? Are you there?"

I knew that voice. That wasn't a stick. It was a finger.

"Kale?"

"Yes, mistress! I bring you a visitor. This is a good deed, right?"

"Definitely." It didn't matter who the visitor was, I was grateful to the little yggie. "I will sing your praises to the great Yggdrasil."

"Thank you, mistress! Thank you!"

I heard scuffling outside my cell. I strained to see anything through the slot in the door.

Fingers poked through.

"Kyra?"

My heart backpedaled in my chest.

"Mom?" My voice cracked. I grabbed the fingers like a lifeline. They were warm and wrinkled and covered in brown spots.

"I can't believe you're here!" I could hear the tears in her voice, and I knew, without a doubt, I should have come sooner.

"I'm sorry, Mom. So sorry…"

"Shush. We don't have time for that. The council is convening now. Dana wants your head."

I stifled a sob. Not because I was afraid of Dana—though I was—but I was just so damned glad to have my mom back.

"Now listen," Mom whispered urgently, "Dana can't keep you here indefinitely. The council hasn't ratified her as queen yet, and now they won't. Now that you're home."

"I have a letter from Baldyr." I fumbled in my pocket for the letter. "It explains everything." I shoved the paper through the slot.

Mom took it and I waited while she read it.

"This is good. It confirms what Sten has already told the council. Don't worry. You have allies here at court. Baldyr made his wishes known. Dana won't be able to ignore that. Just hold the faith for another little while, baby girl. I have to go. The council is waiting. And my darling, I'm so glad you're home. I love you to the moon and back." Her fingers slipped away, leaving me to smile through tears at the old expression we used to say to each other every night before bed.

"I love you too, Mom," I whispered. "To the moon and back."

CHAPTER

24

The sound of a key grinding in a lock tore me out of a fitful sleep. I jumped up, shook out the tingles in my legs, and faced the door, not knowing who was on the other side. A friend? A guard to take me to my trial? Or worse, a Valkyrie sent by Dana to simply dispose of me and save her the aggravation of having to prove her case to the Council of Elders?

I waited with clenched fists as the heavy door swung open.

"Hurry," Sten said. "We haven't much time." The old advisor's face was red under his beard and he was puffing from the long walk from the council hall carrying Baldyr's heavy sword.

"This is yours for now." He handed it to me.

"Where is my blade?" I rubbed my temples. I could still keen its despair at being apart from me.

"In the council hall, along with Baldyr's letter." Sten smoothed down his long beard. "Both will be returned to you shortly, but I thought you should enter the hall with Baldyr's sword. It makes a statement."

I took the blade. It was far heavier than mine, and a big part of that weight was the responsibility that came with it. I didn't hang it on my belt. It was too long, and I'd look ridiculous staggering under its weight, so I unsheathed it and gripped the blade in front of me. Iduna's apples had made me strong, and my hand didn't even shake.

"I'm ready." I turned for the door, then paused. "No, I'm not. What should I expect in there?"

Sten rubbed his beard again. Two yellow lines marred the beard where his fingers incessantly worked out his nervousness.

"The council has agreed that Baldyr's testament is legitimate."

"So I'm to be queen."

"Perhaps. That still has to be ratified. Dana won't let go that easily. But come now, let's not keep them waiting. An impatient elder is a grumpy elder."

Right. I hefted the sword and he led me through the dank, stone-walled corridor. We came out briefly under a darkening sky, crossed a courtyard and entered the main hall from a back door. The council hall was just ahead.

A herald boomed out, "Valkyrie Kyra!" as I walked through the great doors. All eyes—and there were hundreds—turned to watch me. I suddenly wished I'd had a chance to bathe and change my clothes before making my appearance at court, but there was no helping it now. I straightened my spine, lifted my chin and hefted Baldyr's sword above my head. I wore the signet ring on my thumb and its ruby gleamed like fresh blood.

As soon as I was recognized, a murmur went through the hall. I waited for the ripple of curiosity-outrage-disdain to die away. My breath was heavy in my chest, and my heart pounded hard to send blood to the arm that still held the king's blade steady.

The Council of Elders sat or stood around a huge oak table on a dais at the front of the hall. Baldyr's chair stood empty at the table's head.

I recognized several elders. Torsen, the old Captain of the King's Guard sat to the right of the empty chair, and Sten sat beside him. Nut, the king's physician was there, and Ivar, the huntsman. Ulf, another lieutenant in the guard, and Frode, my younger cousin who had been studying to become the court archivist when I left. He'd attained that goal, apparently. Others that I didn't recognize filled the remaining chairs.

Dana sat at the table's far end with her Valkyries fanned out behind her. They were all tall, strong women. I knew many of them and their gazes ranged from surprise to outright hostility. Dana's expression was deceptively calm. She was master of her emotions, hiding anger behind manners and protocols, letting it out to sting like a scorpion when needed.

A large man wearing hunting leathers leaned against the wall behind the table. He had a grizzled beard and wild mane of hair, more white than brown.

Heimdall. Warden of the rainbow bridge. His gaze tracked me as I moved down the aisle. Given the chance, he would gladly throttle me for destroying his beloved Bifrost.

These were men and women who advised the monarch. Some were ancient by Terran standards, but the Golden Apples kept them young. Except for one woman who sat beside Sten. She looked ancient. Almost lost in the big chair, her wizened legs barely touched the floor. White hair was pulled back in a long braid. Her hands were clasped on her lap, over a simple blue gown.

Like Dana, this woman also had retainers spread out behind her. Many were Baldyr's personal guard. Mason and my crew stood by the wall beside them. Raven hunched into himself like he could disappear if he tried hard enough. Mason's jaw was set and his arms crossed over his chest. Tension rippled along the lines of his shoulders, and I knew he was only a heartstring away from lashing out at someone.

The old woman glanced back at my ragged band, then raised her head to meet my gaze.

Her eyes were blue quartz, exactly like mine.

I froze in the middle of the aisle and nearly dropped Baldyr's sword. The crowd's murmurs became a dull wash in my ears.

Mother!

In the cell, I'd thought it was a trick of the light that made Mom's hand look wrinkled and spotted. But now the truth hit me like Thor's hammer.

Mom was old. She'd either stopped eating the Golden Apples or they were no longer able to fight off her cancer.

She nodded and a smile creased her wrinkled cheek.

My feet stumbled over each other as I mounted the few stairs to the dais. Baldyr's letter lay open on the great table. Beside it lay my Valkyrie sword, humming contentedly now that I was nearby. I wanted nothing more than to drop Baldyr's hulking monstrosity and scoop up my own familiar blade. Instead, I sucked in a breath and nodded to one end of the dais and then the other.

"Hello, Mother. Aunt Dana."

The room was so quiet you could hear the dead.

Dana rose and within a few strides, she was close enough to grip the hilt of Baldyr's sword. She tried to wrench it away.

"You have not yet proven your right to bear this sword."

I yanked my hand back. She would have to try harder than that to take my grandfather's legacy from me.

171

From the corner of my eye, I spied Mason, his face clouded with rage.

A small figure streaked forward and a high-pitched voice shrieked, "Die evil witch!"

Kale kicked her in the shin and she stumbled back. It wasn't much of a hit, but enough for me to wrench the blade away. Mason pushed away from the wall to stand between us and my hell hound joined him. Princess's fur stood on end. Her lips curled back to reveal finger-length fangs. Drool slid to the floor. A low growl rumbled from her chest.

Dana straightened and sneered. "Call off your hound, Kyra and your human. Or I will have them both shot."

I smiled.

"You have no authority here, Auntie." I picked up Baldyr's letter and waved it in her face. "You were never meant to rule in Asgard."

Dana slugged me. Pain burst through my jaw.

The courtroom erupted in shouts. Benches overturned as people jumped to their feet. Valkyries swarmed Dana. Heimdall held onto Mason, whose face was twisted with rage. His eyes had gone black.

"Mason, don't!" I shouted through the pounding in my head. I knew that look. He was one minute away from harnessing his demon magic and taking out the entire council.

"Quickly! This way!" My mother grabbed my sleeve. A dozen of Baldyr's guards pushed past me and blocked the Valkyries. The clang of steel on steel filled the air. The crowd of onlookers had erupted in shouts of anger and fear.

I hesitated. I wouldn't leave Mason.

"Kyra! We must go. Now!" Mom was frail, but she still had mom-voice. From across the hall, Mason saw my concern and mouthed, "Go!" His eyes had faded to their normal gray. Now he was just fighting to get away. He tugged Raven by one arm as he herded Jacoby and Princess before him. I dragged my eyes away and followed my mother into the castle's dark, twisting hallways.

CHAPTER

25

The old king's guards flanked us and blocked the door, enabling our escape to Baldyr's private council room. Scratch that. It was now *my* private council room. Before I could sit or even unload Baldyr's blade, my mother caught me in her arms.

"My girl!" Her arms closed around me. It was an awkward hug. I stood there, arms wide unable to hug her back because I held the unsheathed sword in one hand and the letter in the other.

I must have looked like a deer caught in the sights of old Ullr, god of the bow. A guard smiled grimly. He took the sword and letter, and I sunk into my mom's embrace.

"I never thought to see you again," she said through tears. Emotion surged through me at her touch, at the scent of her hair—so familiar—and the catch in her voice.

"Let me look at you." She leaned back to study my face. I studied her in return.

The Golden Apples were a boon to the Aesir, but they didn't stop aging altogether. Eventually nature, age and sickness did their job. My mother's cancer had caught up to her. I could see it in the yellow tinge around her mouth and the bones showing at her collar. If I had known she had so little time left, I would have moved earth and aether to get back here.

But I hadn't wanted to know. For the last fifteen years, I'd lived my life in a vacuum, as if I had sprouted from Terra with no history at all. It had been easier that way. I'd left my guilt, anger and sadness behind as if coming through

173

the veil had washed them all away. The price was that I'd also suppressed memories of happy times and people I loved.

Until this instant, when I keened my mother's magic surrounding me like a favorite blanket, I didn't realize how steep that price had been.

"Mom." My voice was thick and barely louder than a gulp of air. I wiped the tears running down my cheeks on my sleeve and sniffled.

"You look so grown up."

I sobbed out a laugh. That was mom-speak for "how much weight have you gained?"

I gripped her hands in mine. They were warm and dry and lined with a map of blue veins.

"I've missed you. It's good to be...back." I hesitated to say "home," though of course, Asgard was my home now. Maybe it always was. Maybe my years on Terra were just a dream and now I'd been rudely awakened.

But then Mason burst through the door followed by Raven, Jacoby, Princess and Kale. Mason grabbed me in a desperate hug, feeding me the warmth of his body and the magic of his spirit. He was proof of that other life—him and Little Bean.

I untangled myself from his embrace.

"Mom, this is Mason, my...um, friend."

Mason raised eyebrow at that introduction, and I gave him my exasperation face—*what?* I didn't know how to introduce him. *Boyfriend* was too tame for our relationship. But he wasn't my husband either. Maybe I should I have said, "Hey, Mom, meet my lover, the father of your grandchild-to-be."

"Nice to meet you, Mason." Mom smiled at him then turned to Raven. "And who is this?"

Raven ducked his head shyly. I hesitated over this introduction, then said, "This is Raven, our son." That introduction felt strangely natural.

I squeezed his shoulder. He lifted his gaze and grinned. His hair—long overdue for a cut—fell into his eyes, and I brushed it away.

Jacoby popped up between us. The fur fringe around his eyes bristled.

"And this is Jacoby, my apprentice." The dervish was hopping from foot to foot. The excitement in the council hall had riled him up.

"I helps, Kyra-Lady. We captures monsters."

Mom laughed. "I bet you do."

Princess jumped up and slurped a kiss across Mom's cheek. Mom yelped in surprise and would have been trampled under the massive hound feet, but Mason caught her.

"Princess! Down!" I scolded. Princess dropped to her haunches, but her lolling tongue said she wasn't sorry.

I turned to my mother. "Are you okay."

She laughed and wiped drool off her face with a handkerchief. "I haven't been slobbered on like that since Jimmy Halbert took me to prom."

Princess wagged her tail.

"And this is Kale." I gestured to the yggie who stood shyly apart. "But you've already met."

Kale's round face beamed in delight. He tried to bow, but it was more like a sway. He'd grown again and the top of his head nearly reached my shoulder

Sten strode into the room. He was sweating under his beard. "I've managed to settle them down, but Dana wants a full accounting. She'll press any weakness to her advantage. We've got to rally the council and have Kyra's reign ratified immediately.

Mom leaned heavily on my arm. I helped her onto a couch. She wouldn't let go of my hand, so I sat beside her.

Sten pulled a chair up to the couch.

"You need to speak to the council," he said. "And soon. We had a letter from Gillingr, backing up your claim."

"That will work both for and against her," Mom said. "Not every elder was in agreement with Baldyr's peace treaty."

"Tell the council I will speak to them tomorrow," I said. "Unless you think that's not soon enough."

"Tomorrow will do," Sten assured me.

Good. I needed a bath and a night's rest. And a few hours to decide what I would say to the Council of Elders.

Mom sighed and sat back on the couch. "What assurance do we have that Dana will let Kyra speak and not attack her outright?"

Sten bristled, as if she'd insulted his ancestors going back ten generations.

"You have my assurance, my lady. And that of the King's Guard. There will be no bloodshed in my council hall." He sighed and smoothed down his beard with two fingers. "Of course, ratification or not, Dana has the right to challenge Kyra to a duel."

"She can't!" Mason said. The outburst was so unlike him. He was usually the quiet contemplator, speaking out only when he'd weighed arguments from every side.

Sten turned to him. "But she can, sir. Despite Baldyr's best efforts, the Aesir are one step away from blood-thirsty Vikings. They loved Baldyr. That is the only reason they will even consider his last bequest. Otherwise, the strongest shall rule."

And Dana had always been the strongest.

Mason turned his back on Sten, pulling me up from the couch so we could confer in relative privacy.

"Can you take her in a fight—in your condition?" His eyes were dark and full of concern.

I twisted my lips, considering. I had never beaten Dana at swordplay, but I'd learned a trick or two in my time on Terra.

"I don't know."

Mom rose from the couch and intervened.

"Let's rest and eat and talk this over." She turned to Sten. "We'll be ready to present our case tomorrow."

"Milady." Sten bowed and left the room.

Mom smiled and briefly touched Mason's arm. Even wasted by sickness, she was still elegant. She had a quiet way about her, a sense of confidence and command that made people feel comfortable enough to put aside their own stories and listen to reason.

She had a lot in common with Mason.

Mother leaned in to him and spoke in a conspirator's whisper. "Could you be a dear and take the boy and the...others to my rooms. I'll have dinner laid out for you. I would like to speak to my daughter alone."

"Of course." Mason squeezed my hand, then motioned for Raven and the others to follow him.

Everyone shuffled out of the council chambers, leaving Mom and me alone except for the guard at the door. Mom swayed and closed her eyes.

"Are you all right?" I helped her back to the couch, and she sank into it.

"I'm fine. Just too much excitement." She smiled, but fatigue tightened the lines around her mouth and eyes.

"Are you in pain? Is there something I can do?"

"You can come sit and tell me why you're really here. I've been in contact with Gillingr. He only sent his soldiers a few days ago. There's no way they found you so quickly."

"I was already here. They met us in Vanlandia."

The door opened and Mom held up her hand for me to wait. A ratatosk maid came in and placed a tea tray on the table. A second ratatosk followed with a plate of fruit and sandwiches.

"Will that be all, my lady?" Mother nodded and the maids scurried out with their tails swishing behind them.

Mom poured the tea.

"Now tell me everything. What is this condition Mason spoke of? Are you sick?"

I told her about Gunora, her crimes and her cure for MMC. Mom's expression was furious by the time I finished.

"And when I returned, I moved into Mason's house."

"Well, at least there is some good that came out of all this. And you have a son."

The thought of Raven made me smile. "Mother and son are titles we're currently trying on for size. He's had an unconventional upbringing, and he's not used to the structure of family."

"I'm sure you'll figure it out."

We had a lot of things to figure out. Such as our living accommodations. I had no choice but to stay in Asgard. Mason was free to leave, but he wouldn't. That would make him consort to the queen. I didn't think that was a title he'd wear easily.

"Mom, there's more."

She focused her sharp eyes on me.

"You're pregnant."

Of course she knew. Any woman who'd been pregnant could read the signs.

Mom's eyes sparkled with delight, but I cut her off before she could say anything.

"Don't get your hopes up. I may not carry to term. Not if the MMC isn't controlled."

"I see." Mom looked thoughtful. "The baby won't survive in a crone's womb."

I nodded. "That's why I came. Before the MMC changed me."

Mom squeezed my hand. "You did the right thing. As soon as you get some Golden Apples in you, everything will be right again.

"I have." I cleared my throat. "I mean, I've been to see Iduna already."

"Good. That's one problem solved then."

"For now."

"Everything will be—"

I cut her off. "It won't be fine. The apples will only delay the inevitable. You of all people should know that."

Mom pinched her lips. It was such a familiar expression, I almost laughed. How many times in my teen years, had she favored me with exactly that look of disappointment? It was so much better than punishment. I had never worried about making Mom mad, but garnering her *disappointment* was a great deterrent.

She sighed then pulled herself up to her full height, which wasn't very tall. "You will live long enough to see your child born. Everything after that is a gift. Now tell me more about this rite Gunora performed."

I explained how she drained the magic from my blade and used that to fuel her spell. How she blended our blood, like a childish blood-sister oath.

"And she invoked some power words. I recognized the magic in them, but I can't remember the actual words." That whole night was a blur, and since I'd spent most of it tied spread-eagle on a sacrificial altar, I was glad for that.

"I have her journal. It has a few more details, but none of that matters. I won't cure myself at the expense of another Valkyrie."

"Not even if that Valkyrie was your enemy?" Mom's bland expression belied the deep wrongness of those words. Could I inflict this disease on Dana and rid myself of two problems at once?

I shook my head, not ready to voice my objection out loud.

Mom clapped her hands on her lap. "Well, I'd still like to see that journal. I've been working with Asha, the hedge witch. Her tinctures have helped me as much as the apples. She might know more about it," Mom said.

"It doesn't matter. The only *cure* is to pass it on to another Valkyrie. And that's no cure at all." The more I thought about it, the more I was certain I couldn't use the disease as a weapon.

"Well, it's not like those Valkyries have ever done you any favors."

"Mom!"

"Don't get your knickers in a twist. I understand. Infecting Dana is off the table. But maybe this rite can be modified to send the curse away without hurting another. We should still consult with Asha."

"Maybe." I mumbled, not believing it. If there was a cure, Gunora would have found it.

Mom stroked my braid. "I wish your grandfather could be here to see you."

"Me too. I wish I could have said goodbye." My eyes were hot with tears again. I could blame it on the pregnancy hormones, but in truth, I was simply overwrought with the emotion expended that day—joy, anger, fear. It was all too much.

"He was very worried in his last days. Dana has become unhinged, and sending his last will to Gillingr was the only way he could assure it would be carried out. It put his mind at ease." She smiled. "You were always his favorite, you know."

I felt that tightness in my chest again.

"Do you think Dana will challenge me to a duel?"

"No. She has no reason to. She's been ruling for months already. Since Baldyr took to his bed the final time. People are used to her. She won't feel the need to prove herself."

I rose and paced. "I, on the other hand, am an outsider."

"Exactly."

I had always been an outsider, and nothing I had ever done had changed that opinion in the eyes of the Valkyrie or many other Aesir.

"So maybe I should challenge her to a duel. Would she accept?"

"She would have to or look weak in the eyes of her supporters. But can you beat her?"

That's exactly what Mason had asked.

"I don't know. Maybe. But to be honest, I don't really want to rule as Queen of Asgard. I'm not fit. The MMC might be slowed down, but it's not gone. Maybe Dana is the right one to rule."

A shudder ran through Mom. "I doubt that. There's a lot more you don't know about the changes she's already made around here. But before we go any further, I want you to see Asha. She'll be able to give us a better picture of this disease. And you must meet with Frode. You remember him?"

"Cousin Frode? He was in the council hall. I hardly recognized him. Last time I saw him, he was a skinny kid with bad skin and hair that was always sticking up."

Mother smiled. "He's outgrown the bad skin, but not the hair. He took over the archives after old Jarno retired, and he's been a huge help in these last few months. He has a firm grasp on law and tradition. Without him, Dana would have already taken over completely."

I rose and stretched my back. Too much time in the saddle had made me stiff.

"All right. I'll meet with Asha in the morning, and then Frode. We'll come up with a plan." My words were more confident than I felt.

Mom rose too and put her arms around me.

"Everything will work out. You'll see."

I really wanted to believe her.

CHAPTER

26

sha didn't make house calls. She was arguably the most powerful witch in Asgard, which is why I'd thought of her when Disir accused the Aesir of creating the draugs. But she hadn't left her cabin in the foothills of the Gudsov mountains in decades. Her healing prowess was legendary, but few sought out her talent because her temper was even more legendary. She was just as likely to turn you into a scabby toad as to heal you. Stories of the witch in the mountains were still used to frighten children into obedience.

And now, here I was riding into those mountains to find that witch.

It was a bright morning when Mom, Mason and I left Asgard. The sun hid behind thin clouds, making the sky a white sheet, and mist swirled about us like ghostly fingers. Our horses were jumpy, and my mood was dark. Somewhere far ahead, the mist would coalesce. It would become an impenetrable wall separating Asgard from Valhalla, the land of the gods. My grandfather and his fathers gathered beyond the mist. They were as close as the sky and just as unreachable.

Mason was jumpy too. We couldn't see more that a few meters ahead and his head kept swiveling from left to right as he tried to make out shapes in the fog.

"Relax," I said. "This isn't the Inbetween. The worst thing we'll face in here is a bear. Or maybe a wolf."

"That's supposed to make me feel better?" he grumbled.

The fog damped all sound. As we rode closer to the mountains, the light dimmed and the colors were muted too, so it felt like we rode through an old silent movie.

To break the tension I questioned Mom about her visits to Asha.

"You've really been coming here a lot?" I didn't like that idea. Mom looked small and frail on her pony. Her cloak was pulled tight around her and the cowl's fringe was wet from the mist.

She made a "mmm" of consent and pulled the cloak tighter.

I worried about her out here in the damp. It was a tough journey for me and I was more-or-less fit.

"Maybe we should turn back." I glanced at the road behind us. It was already lost in the fog. "I can come again tomorrow on my own."

"Asha won't see you without me," Mom said. "Stop fretting. We're almost there, and a bit of a chill won't do me in."

I wasn't so sure about that, but I kept my horse's nose pointed into the hills.

"I heard the guards talking about Asha this morning," Mason said. "She's got a reputation."

"She's not so bad," Mom said. "Most stories about her are all hype."

I wasn't so sure about that. "Didn't she give old Gorm boils when he sought her out for help with his, uh…romantic difficulties?" I asked.

Mom snorted out a laugh. "Gorm was a randy old goat, who should have learned to keep it in his pants. Honest to gods. The man wouldn't know what to do with an erection anyway!"

"Mother!" I felt my cheeks heat and glanced at Mason. He was grinning.

Mom sniffed the air like she smelled something off, but said, "Please forgive my forthrightness."

"No need to tame your words for me," Mason said. "So this Asha is really a witch?"

I nodded. "One of the best. And the scariest."

That brought Mason's brows together. We'd faced some pretty scary things together. If I said Asha was one of them, he would be on his guard.

We'd started out following a well-worn path, but as we rode deeper into the mountains it narrowed to nothing more than a goat trail. The trees thinned and the terrain became more rocky.

We came to a small depression. A rock face blocked the way forward. The path wound around the bluff and into the trees again. Nearby, a spring burbled over a tumble of rocks into a small pool. It had all the hallmarks of a shrine with a small stone effigy sitting on top of it—Freya, goddess of love, beauty and magic.

"We'll stop here," Mom said. "Asha will find us and decide if we're worthy of her attention."

"And if we're not?" Mason asked.

"I keep telling you not to worry. We're old friends."

We waited. We drank from our canteens. I fidgeted in my saddle. Mason scanned the scrubby trees and rock formations looking for trouble. Mom dozed in her saddle.

A figure rose from the mist behind Freya's shrine. It was big as a bear, covered in black fur with a wild mane of tangled golden hair sprouting from its crown like the fronds of a palm tree.

"Who disturbs my peace?" The voice boomed. It bounced off the rocks with an unnatural echo. My horse shied and I struggled to keep my seat and tighten the reins.

"It's just me, Asha." The voice had jerked Mom out of sleep.

"Natalia?" The creature stepped forward. She stood straight and shucked her cloak. It was a bear skin with a yellow mane of horse hair attached to it like a hood.

A tall, handsome woman stood before us. Her silver hair was long and combed straight. Wrinkles creased the edges of her lips and eyes, but she wasn't as ancient as I'd imagined. Her eyes were sharp. She wore a simple gown of gray homespun, a fine weave that could have been accessorized to fit in at court.

"Sorry about the theatrics," she said. "I can't be too careful about welcoming strangers."

"I understand," Mom said. "This is my daughter Kyra. We come to ask for your help."

"You haven't by chance been making draugs, have you?" I asked.

The witch looked startled, then she let out a cackle. "I bet there's a story behind that question. Come inside and tell me all about it."

ASHA'S LOG CABIN was hidden behind the rocky bluff, and so well-camouflaged, we were at the door before I spotted it. Inside wasn't the hedge-witch lair I'd expected. It had all the witchery accoutrements—pots of salves, skulls, pouches of dried herbs, crystals, tinctures, and jars with recognizable animal parts floating inside—but these were neatly organized on shelves around a large table. The rest of the space was surprisingly homey. Colorful tapestries hung on the walls to cover rough logs. A fire burned in a small hearth, with two chairs snugged up beside it. Gleams shone from sconces on the walls, filling the space with soft light. A privacy curtain sectioned off a smaller room, where I could just spy the end of a bed.

Asha pulled another bench up to the hearth and offered us seats. Mason waved me over to the more comfortable chair, but I was too nervous to relax. Instead, I perched on the edge of the bench beside him.

"So, you have a draug problem?" Asha asked as she tipped the contents from a kettle into a teapot.

"Not really. I met a few in Jotunheim, and the giants think us Aesir are responsible."

"And you couldn't think of anyone else who could raise a ghoul." Asha's eyes twinkled as if that thought was amusing more than insulting.

I shrugged. "I told them it wasn't you."

"Quite right. Draugs are abominations."

Asha placed the teapot on a low table beside the hearth and sat in a chair. She closed her eyes and seemed to fall into meditation. I glanced at Mason. He shrugged. Mom made a placating gesture with her hand. We waited in silence. I could almost hear the tea leaves steeping. Then as if some ethereal clock that only she could hear chimed, Asha stood and poured tea into four cups. She handed these around and settled herself again with a serene smile.

"Well, then. Drink up and tell me what I can do for you." Her smile was placid, her magic calm.

I sniffed the tea. It had a spicy, lemony scent. I put the mug back on the table without taking a sip.

"I should tell you first that I'm pregnant."

Asha reached across and gently pushed the mug toward me. "I know." She winked at Mason. "I would do nothing to harm you or the babe. It's a simple concoction of ginger and lemon balm. It soothes morning sickness and anxiety. Your magic is twisted tighter than a sailor's knot."

I smiled, but I was sure it looked forced. I picked up the mug and drank.

I didn't have high hopes for any of its curative properties, but at least it was warm.

Asha said nothing more, but sipped her tea and watched me. I glanced from her to my mother who nodded, prodding me on to speak.

The words seemed close to the surface. They were fighting to get out, but my own shields—the ones I'd grown and fortified for decades—held them back.

"Tell me, child. I can't help you otherwise." Asha's eyes were warm brown, a rarity among the Aesir. Mason's arm slipped around my waist, a weighty and soothing comfort.

"I've been infected with Maid Mother Crone, and now I worry I'll lose the baby if I shift before she's born." The words spilled out. This was my second telling, and I remembered more details than I'd shared with my mother. I told her about the pain and terror of my first shift, of my theory that it had come on more quickly because I'd inherited the disease from Gunora. I also told her about Baldyr's bequest and my impending battle with Dana over the right to rule.

"I need to be fit enough to take on Dana. And soon."

Asha listened without comment or expression.

"I also need to know how long the Golden Apples will keep me healthy."

Asha sighed. "Maid Mother Crone is a nasty disease." She set down her tea and grabbed my hand. "It's all the nastier because it originates with a curse. But it seems that Gunora has already given you the key to your cure."

"No! I won't go that route. I refuse to save myself at the expense of another." I tried to tug my hand away, but she flipped it over and examined the lines on my palm. After a moment, she let me go with a grunt. It was a noncommittal noise. I didn't know if she liked what she saw.

"What if passing the curse on is the only way to save your child? Would you do it then?" Asha raised one eyebrow.

I hesitated only a nanosecond before shaking my head. "There has to be another way." I rifled in my pack and found Gunora's worn leather journal "Gunora detailed her search for a cure in here."

Asha reached for the book, but I held it back and ran my thumb over the wings embossed on the cover.

"I've read it a dozen times. She doesn't mention the rite or the power words she used."

Asha said nothing, but simply held out her hand until I gave up the book, then she pushed herself up.

"Let's have a look-see and find out what's to be done."

During my Valkyrie training years, I was a regular visitor to Baldyr's healer. I went to him with contusions and broken bones from the practice ring, and he'd cluck and fuss over me. He worked mostly with potions that sped up healing and good old-fashioned sutures. I'd also witnessed Nori heal Jacoby and Berto. Her power was unique. I'd keened her magic as she dug into Berto's wounds and stitched them closed with the sheer force of her will.

Asha's magic was more subtle. She invited me into the back room behind the curtain and asked me to take off my shoes and lie on the bed. Then she watched me for a solid three minutes. That's a long time to sit still under someone's scrutiny. At first, I thought she was meditating with her eyes open, but no. She was looking at me. All of me. Her eyes flicked to my hands when my nervousness had them gripping the blanket. She tilted her head sideways while she examined my lips, nose and eyes in minute detail. She stared at the top of my head for so long, I thought she must be counting hairs.

"Relax," she finally said. "Put your shoulders down before they're swallowed by your ears."

I did have a bad habit of hunching my shoulders when I was tense. I elongated my neck and heard it crack.

"That's better. Now I'm going to put my hands on you. Shouldn't feel anything except some heat."

I nodded my consent.

She started at the top of my head. Her fingers roved over my cranium, lingering over bumps and divots in the bone. They brushed over my face, light as whispers. She moved to my neck, manipulating lymph nodes and down to my shoulders, massaging and prodding.

She smiled when her hands rested on my stomach.

"She's a busy one."

"I haven't really felt her move yet."

"Too soon. You're about ten weeks?"

I nodded, but her eyes were closed. She didn't need confirmation. I had a feeling her fingers saw more clearly than any ultrasound.

She brushed past my legs and spent several minutes communing with my feet. Her strong thumb dug into the sensitive pad beneath my toes. I might have groaned, it felt that good. Days of walking and clinging to stirrups had made my feet cranky. I sank six inches deeper into the bed while she massaged me.

"What can you tell about the MMC from my feet?" I asked.

"Not a thing, but you looked like you needed a boost. You should get that strong man out there to rub your feet. They'll be worn out by the time you're full term. Now, you can sit up. I want you to tell me again about this rite Gunora performed. Try to remember the words of power she used."

I sat up and crossed my arms over my chest.

"I told you, I won't pass this disease on to another."

"So you said, but understanding that rite, might give us a clue to the nature of the curse."

"And you'll be able to counter it?" For the first time in days, I felt hope trying to dig through my wards.

"I can't promise, but I will try."

I went over everything I could remember again. Asha dug into the details, pulling surprising impressions from me. When I was done, she sat lost in thought for some moments, then she clapped her hands again as if she'd come to a decision.

"I think you should know the worst of it," she said.

"Wait. I want Mason and Mother to hear it too."

When we were all settled back before the hearth, Asha sank into her chair. Healing was strong magic that took a lot of resources. She looked wilted and older than when we'd arrived.

"I won't sugarcoat it. MMC is always fatal. It usually strikes a girl just as she becomes a woman and can take years to fully manifest. That isn't the case here. I know she looks healthy, but Kyra is in the full throes of the disease."

"But how can that be?" Mom asked. "She was only infected a few months ago."

Asha held out her empty hands to show she didn't have the answers. "Maybe it's her age or the unconventional way she was infected. Whatever the case, it will progress faster than normal. It's hard to explain, but I can feel the…the grain of the disease. Like the seed that unfurls into branches and leaves. It has already spread throughout her system."

Mason's hand gripped mine. His dark eyes looked thunderous. Someone else might have thought him angry, but I knew better. He was scared. So was I.

"But then why hasn't she shown more symptoms?" he asked. "Why hasn't she shifted more?"

Asha smiled and I knew the answer before she spoke. It was the same reason why my sensitivity to magic was dulled.

"The baby."

"Yes." Asha laid her hand over Mason's and squeezed us both. "She's powerful, your daughter. She's protecting her mama. Oh, I can't wait to see that magnificent young woman. She's strong and healthy and full of magic. She'll do great things!"

A sob slipped from my throat. It was all wrong. I was supposed to be the one protecting her. I turned to Mason, ready to face the fear and anguish in his eyes, but he wore a silly grin.

"We have a daughter?"

I couldn't help but smile back. I'd forgotten to tell him.

"Yes, we do."

I'd wanted to give him time, to give him years together. That wouldn't happen. But at least I could give him a daughter.

CHAPTER

27

n the end, we postponed our meeting with the council by a day. The elders wouldn't like it, but I decided that, if I would be queen, they could wait for me.

After meeting with Asha, we returned to Baldyr's castle and I begged off having lunch with my mother. I needed rest. Mom had made up a room for us in her private wing.

"Look in on Raven and the others," I said to Mason, but didn't even hear his answer before I was asleep.

I woke when I heard the rattle of a tray being put down on the side table.

"How are you feeling?" Mom hovered over me. She laid a cool hand on my forehead, and I felt about nine years old.

"As good anyone who's growing a human in their belly can."

Mom smiled. From the tray, I smelled savory broth and hot buttered bread and waited for the usual nausea. It didn't come. Iduna's apples were working their miracle, and I was suddenly ravenous. Mom watched me slurp down the bowl of broth and mop it up with bread.

"Mason told me your morning sickness has been bad."

I nodded with a mouthful of bread.

"She's going to have a full head of hair, just like you did. I was sick morning to night too."

"That's just an old wives' tale."

"Sometimes old wives know best."

I finished my soup and leaned back against the pillow with a satisfied sigh.

I couldn't remember the last time I was clean, dry, rested and full from a hot meal.

"Where's Mason?" I asked.

"He took Raven down to the main hall for supper. Then he promised they could see the stables and the kennels."

"They're going alone?"

"No. I asked a guard to go with them. They'll be safe."

I nodded. Mason could take care of himself, but he didn't know his way around Asgard, and Dana would be looking for any weakness to exploit.

"I like him," Mom said.

"Me too." I grinned.

"Then why do I see sadness in your eyes when you speak of him?"

"You don't. I mean, I don't..."

She raised one eyebrow in disbelief. I never could keep my feelings hidden from Mom.

"Fine. I'm not sad exactly. Just worried. He came here to be with me, but I won't be able to leave Asgard. You know he was just elected Prime Minister of the Alchemist Party in Montreal? It's a big deal. And he has his Guardians to look after. I made him leave his entire life behind."

Mom held up a hand to stop me.

"He's a grown man, Kyra. You didn't make him do anything. And if you had to choose between Mason and the baby or your job, what would you choose?"

I chewed my lip and fidgeted. Mom didn't wait for an answer.

"Exactly. Now instead of brooding about what might have been, let's take care of the here and now. The council will convene tomorrow to hear arguments from you and Dana. You need to prepare. I've arranged for you to meet with Frode."

"I still don't see how he can help. He still looks like such a kid."

Mom smiled patiently. "You've been gone a long time. Kids grow up."

I hadn't even said hello to Frode in the council hall. For that matter, I'd hardly spoken to him when we were kids. He was always tucked away in some part of the library while I was either running with the hounds or dodging sword strikes in the practice ring.

"Besides," Mom said. "You need dirt on Dana, and he's got it." She thumped the mattress with the flat of her hand and stood. "Now get dressed and put on something that makes you feel like a warrior."

"The old fake it 'til you make it trick?"

"Exactly."

KALE HADN'T BEEN pleased that we sneaked off to visit Asha without him. He had a severe case of fear-of-missing-out, but his FOMO was all about lost chances for good deeds.

As Mom and I headed out to meet Frode, I found him camped outside my door.

"My mistress is leaving? Do you need an escort?"

"I'm not your mistress, and no, I don't need an escort."

The bright green fronds sprouting from the top of his head shuddered as if a stiff gust of wind shook them. He definitely had more fronds than the last time I saw him.

"Very good, Mistress."

He turned to follow us. A small figure shot from the shadows and tackled him. Kale squealed like a chipmunk caught in the fox's paws. His numerous twiggy appendages flailed.

"Jacoby!" I grabbed the dervish by one skinny arm and hauled him upright. His teeth gnashed and his hands made fists as if he could strangle Kale by sheer will. Kale was panting and his fronds drooped. He looked terrified.

"I ams 'prentice! Not...not...freaky stick man." Jacoby's eyes blazed with the light of vexation. I knelt and smoothed the fur from his eyes. He flinched at my touch. Still mad then.

"You *are* my apprentice, but this isn't work. And Kale is a friend. If you come, you have to treat him like a friend."

Jacoby stamped a foot and turned away mumbling, "Stinkin' stick man."

I sighed.

"I see the boys are still fighting over you," Mom said with a sarcastic drawl.

"Ha ha. You're not helping."

I decided to ignore my groupies. They would follow me no matter what I said, so I motioned for Mom to lead the way.

I wasn't surprised when she took me to the library. It was a huge, windowless hall with books lining every wall. Gleams hung on chains from the ceiling, but much of the room was lost in shadow.

Three scholars sat at tables with piles of books around them. A fourth had fallen asleep with her head on an open book. Frode was nowhere to be seen.

Mom wove through the tables. Kale straightened books and quills as he past.

"Good deed for you," he said. "And good deed for you. Send thanks to great Yggdrasil!" His helping hands elicited angry looks from the scholars and a "stupids stick man," from Jacoby.

At the back of the library, Mom headed down a narrow hallway neatly camouflaged by the shelves. I hadn't even known it existed. The hall ended at a locked door. Mom fitted a key into a lock and the door swung open to reveal stairs leading down into darkness.

"A secret lair?" I said.

Mom gave a small shrug. "Not secret, exactly. Just private."

I turned to Kale. "Maybe you should stay here to stand guard."

"Yes, Mistress." He nodded vigorously. So did Jacoby. But when Mom and I headed down the stairs, they followed.

The stairs were steep and the few gleams threw nauseating shadows. Halfway down, Mom had to stop and rest.

"Are you okay? Maybe we should go back." I had become used to her aged appearance. It was easy to forget how ill she really was.

"Nonsense. I'll be fine. Just a dizzy spell. It's already passed."

At the bottom, we found another door, this one open to let out the the dim light from what appeared to be a forgotten storage room. Junk was piled on every available surface, matted with dust and cobwebs. There were machine parts, tubs, carts, tubes and wires. Many, many wires all snaking together in a tangled mess.

"Frode?" Mom called out. Her voice was quavery and her hand shook on the door frame. No one answered.

"Let me clear the way, Mistress." Kale pushed ahead and swept away cobwebs.

"I clears the spiders!" Jacoby said too loudly. They shoved and scuffled, colliding with tables and tools as they fought for dominion over the cobwebs.

"Knock it off, you two!" I said in a loud whisper. Mom rolled her eyes.

"It's all clear now, Mistress." Streams of webs were tangled in Kale's fronds and hung from his twiggy limbs like a ghostly cloak. Jacoby spat out dust and glared at the yggie.

"Thank you," I said. "But you guys really need to settle down."

"Frode?" Mom called again, and again she was answered by silence. Then a patter of feet came from far away, and I realized the lab was much bigger than it seemed.

A ratatosk appeared from the darkness. He wore a smock with goggles on a cord around his neck.

"This way." He beckoned with a furry hand. "This way."

I hurried to keep up with the ratatosk. I could just follow his gray swishy tail as he scurried around and through the piles of junk. We turned a corner and came to a well-lit work area. A man was welding something to a large contraption in the middle of the room. He wore a helmet and visor. Sparks burst around him like fire works.

"Please wait here for master Frode," the ratatosk said.

I nodded and looked around Frode's impressive lab. Like the outer room, it was cluttered with stuff, but here, the clutter seemed more ordered. At least, everything was clean and dust free. I wished now that Mason had joined us. The magic zinging around had the distinct tang of alchemy, and I was sure he could make more sense of it.

Finally, Frode put down the welding torch and flipped off his helmet.

"Kyra!" His face was flushed from the heat, and his voice was much deeper than I remembered.

Nothing reminds you of how time goes by like seeing kids you once knew all grown up. Frode was well over six-feet tall and thin as a spear. He had a mop of red-blond curls and sharp features that might have been handsome if he put on a few pounds.

"It's so good that you're home!" He swung me into a big hug. His arms were long enough to wrap around me twice, and I'd seen grizzly paws smaller than his hands.

"It's good to be home. You've grown." I grinned and untangled myself from his embrace.

"So they tell me." He grinned back.

He'd been a quiet teen, but had a sharp eye and keen observational skills. He turned that eye on me now.

"You look like you've been dragged through Hel's kitchen by the hair."

"Thanks. I've been better." I slapped Jacoby's hand from reaching for the welding torch. Kale was busy tidying the worktable. The ratatosk hovered behind him, grabbing precious books and pots out from under twiggy fingers.

"Balan, stop hovering," Frode said. The ratatosk flicked his tail.

"Sorry about that," I said. "They don't mean any harm. They just need to be kept busy."

"And Balan is fussy." He glared at his assistant. Balan made a chittering sound and moved another book out of Kale's reach.

"Maybe you could find some task to keep them busy? Something menial, but time-consuming?" Mom said. And that was why she was the mom. Why didn't I think of that?

"Excellent idea!" Frode said. "I think we have some nuts and bolts that need sorting, don't we?" Balan nodded and turned to scamper back into the depths of the lab.

"Come on, you two." Mom prodded Jacoby and Kale to follow the ratatosk. "Let's sort some hardware."

"She's so good with them," I said, maybe a bit wistfully.

"She's had a lot of practice," Frode said. "I remember when we were kids, Natalia would organize all the outings—picnics with games, scavenger hunts and races."

"Yeah. She was a good mom." I could only hope that I'd be half as good. Frode saw my hand go instinctively to my stomach.

"Oh, I see. When are you due?"

"I have a while to go." There was no point giving him a date. I hadn't converted my Terran due date to the Aesir lunar calendar. I'd have to figure that out soon. Add another thing to my to-do list.

"May Odin favor this new life," he said. It was somewhat formal, but Frode had always been an odd kid. I just nodded. I hoped that Odin was only one of many gods looking out for Little Bean.

"We'll have this matter with Dana settled long before then," Frode said.

"I mean to challenge her to a duel." It sounded absurd, hearing myself say it aloud. Dana was the master of dueling. Not once in all my years of training had I bested her.

Frode nodded. "I figured that. Not that I agree. We should have progressed past the whole rule-by-might-of-the-sword thing."

"You'd think, but what are my chances if I leave it up to the council to vote?"

Frode shook his head. "It could go either way." The Aesir were one step away from the Vikings. Alliances were made over mugs of mead, and dynasties were established over the blood of a sword fight.

"I hope it won't come to a fight, but I'm ready if I have to." I said. "That's why I'm here. Mom said you have some information about Dana that I can use."

Frode snorted. "Information, yes. Is it useful? I don't know. She's a wily one. For the past year, I've been documenting her crimes, but nothing sticks. It's like water off an otter's back." He pulled off his welding gloves and smock and rummaged on the mess of a work table until he found a small book.

"These are all the dubious things Dana has done since taking over for Baldyr." He flipped through pages of notes. "It started small. She undermined the authority of the King's Guard and let a group of Valkyries go after they were caught brawling. Small stuff that nobody really cared about. But lately, her misdemeanors have multiplied as her influence has grown. Last month, she renounced a trade agreement with Jotunheim, one that the guilds had been working on for months."

"Why would she do that?"

Frode shrugged. "Who knows. She must have benefited somehow. There have been other minor disturbances. She imprisoned a visiting Jotnar envoy for over a week, alleging that he stole from the market. Bogus charges that almost caused an incident. Luckily, Baldyr was able to smooth things over. It was his last official business before he took to his bed for good."

I flipped through the pages, reading Frode's scribbled notes. "She seems to have no love for the Jotnar."

Frode shook his head. "She'll continue to undermine our alliance. And next time, Baldyr won't be here to fix things. But that's not the worst. There's something you need to see."

He beckoned me to follow him to a cold room at the back of the lab. A body lay on a table covered in a sheet. It was too small to be a man. Frode hesitated with one hand on the sheet.

"I hope you have a strong stomach."
He pulled it back to reveal a dead draug.

CHAPTER

28

The draug had been dead for some time. Long thin arms curled against its chest like dried seaweed. The ribcage was smashed and bone protruded from a desiccated wound. Dried blood matted the bushy tail coiled around the body. But its face was the worst. Shrunken lips revealed nightmarish fangs. The bony spike on its snout had been severed and a deep scar cleaved through one eye.

"It's not a ratatosk," Frode said.

"I know. It's a draug."

He looked at me sharply.

"You've seen one before?"

I swallowed down the acid rising in my throat and nodded.

"In Jotunheim. We fought a more than a dozen. They're hard to kill. How did you kill this one?"

"Not me. It came from Toftir. That's a village about a two day ride along the Gudsov foothills."

Then Frode told me a story that made my blood run cold.

The first sheep went missing in Toftir three months ago. Others disappeared more frequently over the next weeks. At first the villagers suspected raiders coming down from the mountains to steal sheep in the dead of night. But then they started finding carcasses, many torn to pieces. Still they thought it was a mountain lion or pack of wolves.

"The killings escalated." Frode stared at the dead creature as he spoke. "A shepherd's family was killed. His name was Miro. He came home to find his cottage empty and blood streaks in the dirt as if bodies had been dragged away.

"Miro ran to warn the village elders, but they wouldn't believe him. They still thought it must be a wolf or big cat. So Miro when hunting. And he found the draugs eating his children."

My hand covered my mouth as I sucked in a breath.

"He told me that he doesn't remember much after that. His only thought was to get his children away." Frode shook his head. "They were dead, of course, but grief has no reason. Miro was bitten but he managed to kill one of the beasts. The others ran off as the sun rose. When he brought the dead draug to the village, they kicked him out, said he was cursed and would only bring more monsters down on them." Frode sighed. "Some of these outer villages are very isolated. They still live in an age of superstition."

"What happened to Miro?"

"He came here. It took him nearly a week, dragging that carcass the whole way with an arm that festered from the bite wound. This was just after Baldyr's death and Asgard was in turmoil. But that's exactly why the Council of Elders was created!" He pounded a fist on the table, making the dead draug jump. "No one man or woman can rule effectively in all situations. The council means continuity. Despite the commotion around Baldyr's funeral, Miro should have been heard by the Elders. But he had the ill-luck of presenting his case to Dana first. Again, he met with only disbelief, ridicule and threat of banishment.

"I heard about it only because the ratatosks were in an uproar about the dead draug that looked so much like one of them. And ratatosks gossip among themselves. Balan made me aware of Miro's plight. The poor man had found himself an inn with the last of his coins. He just wanted a comfortable place to die."

He paused to drop the sheet back over the corpse. "I was too late to save him, but I promised I would make someone on the council listen. And so I've spent the last weeks examining this abomination with every test I can think of, and I finally know what it is. Or rather, what it's not." He met my gaze. I knew already what he was about to say. Some part of me had known since the draug fight.

Frode laid a hand on the sheet as if he felt some connection to the body underneath. "It's not a draug at all. Not a magical construct. And it's not native to Asgard or Jotunheim."

"That can mean only one thing."

Frode nodded. "It's from another world."

I thought so too. The draugs were too alien. Every creature's magic tasted a little bit like the land it sprang from, but the draugs were unlike anything I'd keened before.

"Can you prove it?"

"It's all here." Frode ran his hand over reams of notes on the table beside the corpse. "Autopsy report, eye-witness accounts, and thaumascans. The magic signature of this creature is not from here. Somewhere, there's a tear in the veil between worlds. We need to find it and close it."

"We will," I said with more confidence than I felt. "But the Vanlandi giants blame us for the draugs we fought in their territory. They think we're raising an army of undead to raid their borders. We need proof that this isn't the case."

The crease on Frode's brow deepened. "They might be right, in part, anyway. The rift might not be natural. What if someone opened that door on purpose? Someone like Dana."

It took a minute for his words to register. Creating ghouls was one thing. Opening a door to another dimension was stupidity on an entirely different scale. That's how Terra was nearly destroyed.

When magic seeped back into the world, humans harnessed it. They weaponized it. They learned to breach the veil and open doors to other worlds, letting in more magic that escalated the whole process. They also let in demons. Maybe that was a mistake. Or maybe some arrogant humans thought they could control the demons. Spoiler alert: they didn't. These weren't the cute, fluffy kind of demons like Mason or Kester. These were the rampage, rape and murder kind. Demons decimated cities across the globe and governments responded with armies of mages that dropped magic-fueled bombs of devastating power. The effects of these bombs are still felt in pockets of rogue magic in the Inbetween. The demons were eventually destroyed, but the price had been too great. The world was forever changed.

And now, someone had spun the wheel of chance and opened a door to another world on Asgard. And Frode thought that someone was Dana.

It was the ultimate act of treason. If true, not only would she lose any bid for the throne, she'd be executed as a traitor.

"If we find that rift, can you close it."

"Yes. No." He ran a hand across his face and over his hair. His fingers were black with dirt and left smudges on his skin. "Maybe. That's what I was working on when you came in. It's a device, like a syphon that draws magic from the atmosphere. In theory, if I can pull enough magic from the rift, it will collapse."

"Perfect, but before you destroy it, we need to test that rift. It's the only way to find out if Dana is responsible."

"So you believe me? That Dana is responsible?"

"I do."

His face lit up and he looked like a puppy who'd just been told he was a good boy.

"This has the stink of Dana's arrogance all over it." I said. The Vanlandi were right. She was trying to start a war. But her blind ambition was going to get us all killed. "We need to find that rift."

Frode frowned, pulling his brows together. His expressions were so plastic and malleable. He'd be a terrible poker player.

"That means going where the draugs are," he said. "It will be dangerous. After Miro…I asked for a squad of soldiers as an escort. But so far the council hasn't seen fit to grant my request." He gave a wry scoffing laugh. "The danger is too much to risk the soldiers. Seems to me that is the very reason we should be going."

"Agreed."

I sized up Frode. He was a distant cousin, a nephew or grand-nephew of the old king. It was difficult to keep track of my convoluted family tree. I had to meet with the council tomorrow and plead my case. And I still had no idea what I would say to them, but I was glad to have Frode on my side.

"If I get the council to agree, will you come to Toftir and find that rift?"

Frode dragged his dirty fingers through his hair again and stared at the sheet-covered monster.

"I'll come."

I returned through the maze of work benches and junk piles to find my mother with a new plan germinating in my head.

29

I stood on a hill outside the city kneeling at the granite obelisk that marked the final resting place of Baldyr Odinson, King of the Aesir and my grandfather. The walls of Asgard rose behind the tomb, and the castle hunched on the cliff high above those.

For once my hormones left me dry-eyed. I didn't feel like crying. Grandfather wasn't really here. I turned to gaze over the hills where Odin's hall lay hidden in the mist. If my grandfather was anywhere, he was there.

Wind whipped through the valley, buffeted the great stone wall, and pulled loose hair from my braids. It was peaceful here. I wished I could stay a while longer.

The crunch of a shoe on the grass told me someone approached. I'd asked for a moment alone to gather my thoughts, strength and wits. That moment was over.

"They're waiting for you," Mason said.

I nodded but didn't move.

"It's ridiculously beautiful, isn't it?"

"The mountains?"

"This place. All of it." I waved a hand in the air. "Like some god dreamed the most idyllic place to live then willed it into creation."

"I suppose so."

His hand crept into the small of my back and I keened his magic, strong and confident beside me.

"Then why do I miss Montreal so much?"

I thought of the house that had become ours, my barn with all my critters, my office with Emil in my old apartment. My job that I loved. I looked up at him with a shaky smile. "I even miss cleaning guts and blood off my tools. How stupid is that?"

"Not stupid. Everything has changed. It'll take some getting used to."

"I'm sorry you have to."

"I'm not. Ever since I met you, I've been on an adventure." He smoothed the loose hair from my face, then pulled me against him. "I'm not ready for it to end. And who knows, maybe we'll find a way back to Montreal one day."

I sighed. "In the meantime, I have to convince a bunch of wannabe Vikings that Dana isn't the best choice to be their leader."

"So you're still going through with this?"

I banged my forehead against his chest and ground out a growl. "I don't see how I have another choice. I don't want to be Queen of the Aesir. It's not my style. But I can't let Dana lead either."

I'd spent the morning with Sten and Nut. They'd filled me in on the happenings since Baldyr's death. Dana hadn't wasted any time in dismantling the work Baldyr had done to modernize Asgard. She'd already implemented strict new tariffs on any goods coming in from Jotunheim. Sten worried that she would go after the treaty as soon as she was made queen. It wasn't a far stretch to imagine she'd start a war with the giants by creating a pack of ghouls. In Vanlandia, I had discounted the idea because making ghouls needed precise magic. Dana didn't have it. But what if Frode was right? What if the draugs weren't made, but brought here? Did Dana have enough magic to rip a tear in the veil? Maybe.

I shuddered. Mason rubbed my upper arms vigorously as if to pump life back into me.

"Let's go convince some Vikings." He took my hand and we walked back to the city.

The council hall was packed even though no formal court was in session. Standing at the great doors to the hall, we stared at the throng of people blocking the only path to the dais where the council waited.

Frode popped out of a side corridor and waved to us.

"This way. The back door is clear."

We slipped through the servants' quarters and came to the council hall from a small door used by the maids to clear away clutter after the council left for the day.

Dana stood beside the massive oak table. She turned as we entered and spoke in a voice that carried over the crowd.

"Isn't that fitting. The half-blood uses the servants' door. She wants us to believe she's humble. Too bad her real intentions are to usurp the throne." Dana didn't sneer. She didn't cross her arms over her chest in defiance. Dana always had complete control over her body language. When I was younger, this lack of emotional cues had unnerved me. She seemed capable of violence at any moment, and you wouldn't know it until the flat of her sword struck with bruising force. A ghost of that old anxiety flitted through me, but I squashed it.

The one good thing about having been taught by Dana was that I could play her games too.

I sat in Baldyr's chair at the head of the enormous table. Dana's eyes narrowed and I smiled sweetly. At least I hoped it was sweet. My nerves were a tangle of vipers in my gut.

The other council members were spread around the table. My mother sat to my left and Frode was next to her. Torsen sat on my right. Sten had explained that he was now Speaker of the Council, and had been acting as regent since Baldyr's passing. During my time in Aesir, Torsen been Captain of the King's Guard and spent much of his time away from the castle, so I didn't know him well enough to guess whose side he would take.

Sten sat beside Torsen. Then came Arne, the renowned scholar. He was tough but fair. And good at persuading others. I needed him on my side. Ulf came next. While I was away, he'd been promoted to Captain of the Guard. Allegiance unknown. Sif, the kennel master, had often indulged my need to get away from Dana and run with the hounds when I was younger. She favored me with a small smile, and I was fairly certain I could count on her support. Old Nut was Baldyr's personal physician. He could go either way.

Three other elders who I didn't recognize filled out the chairs. Twelve council members in all, including Heimdall, who'd accepted the role, but refused a seat at the table. Instead, he leaned against the wall, arms crossed over his chest, and favored me with a scowl.

I rose and willed my voice to be steady. "Before we begin, I want to inform the council that Valkyrie Gunora is dead." The twelve faces around the table met this news stoically, but I had to speak over the murmur that rose from the gathered crowd. "She was convicted of murder in Montreal and died on the prison island of Grandill." I left it at that and sat down again. They didn't need to know about my involvement in her death.

Dana met my pronouncement with her usual impassivity, but a Valkyrie behind her snarled out a curse. "And that's your fault too, isn't it. She was only on Terra because she had no way to get home." She jabbed a finger at me from across the table.

Torsen leaned forward and interrupted her. "Baldyr exonerated Valkyrie Kyra for that crime before his death. We are not here to debate what is already a matter of public record."

The Valkyrie sneered and shook her head, but she didn't argue further.

My hands were clenched together under the table. I could feel the weight of Heimdall's stare. It wouldn't matter to him that Baldyr had pardoned me for my crimes. We would have a confrontation, Heimdall and I. And soon. He would make me pay for destroying his beloved Bifrost.

Torsen continued. "We are here today to resolve the matter of King Baldyr's succession. Before we open the discussion to the general court, I am hoping we can come to an understanding."

Dana rose and interrupted him. "I understand perfectly. I have been maintaining order since Baldyr's death." She turned to face the people of Asgard who'd come to witness this debate. "Has anyone gone hungry? No. The markets are running, the garrisons are manned. Life has gone on as usual because I have seen to it." There was a general response from the crowd, some dissenting voices, but more nodding heads and agreement. "These things don't just happen by accident," Dana continued. "I stepped in and took care of business. And now this mongrel," she swung her arm to point at me, "who ran away from her family and her duty as a Valkyrie comes back only because she needs the healing power of Iduna's apples." She paused and focused her attention on me with a cold smile. She wanted me to know that my secrets were no longer my own. "And now she expects to take up the mantle of rulership. It's not just absurd, it's dangerous."

Dana sat. She didn't smile or gloat. She folded her hands on the table and waited for my rebuttal. Her tone had been measured and calm. No one could accuse her of hysterics. And, if I was honest, her words made sense. Even when I'd lived here, I hadn't been Miss Popularity. I'd had my family on my side—Baldyr and Mom and Aaric. No one had expected great things from me. Now only Mom was left and she held a single vote on the council.

The hall was silent. How could hundreds of gathered people not make a sound? The eyes of the council were all trained on me. I briefly met each gaze. Sten nodded. Nut looked unhappy. I couldn't read Ulf's expression through his shaggy beard. Sif nodded in encouragement. The others met my gaze without giving anything away.

Mason mimicked Heimdall's pose on the other side of the hall. I shot him a glance and he nodded.

Here goes nothing. Or everything.

This was it. I had to prove myself in the eyes of the council and those Aesir gathered here today, and I had to do it now.

I cleared my throat and took a page from Dana's playbook. I didn't raise my voice, but spoke softly, forcing all in the room to pay attention.

"It is true that I have been away from Asgard for many years now. But that time has not been wasted. I learned much from living on Terra, a world that was nearly torn apart by the careless use of magic. The Terrans waged war, opened rifts to other worlds and brought chaos to their own. Asgard chose to stay out of that war. We closed every door to Terra but one." I took a deep breath. That last door had been Bifrost.

"We all know what happened to Terra, Valkyrie Kyra," Torsen said. "Tell us why we should care about the plight of humans—why this has anything to do with you becoming queen."

Torsen's words ruffled me and I lost my train of thought. I needed to make them understand the dire situation we were all in. If an unsanctioned rift had opened in Asgard...

Frode's chair scraped loudly as he rose.

"Valkyrie Kyra's words are more relevant than you know. Last month a shepherd from a village to the north brought news of attacks by what he thought were draugs."

This caused a stir. Necromantic magic was forbidden in Asgard.

Frode held up a hand and raised his voice. "Before you all start shouting about witches and dark magic. I studied the creature in question. It was not a draug, at least not one that came from within the borders of Asgard."

"What does that mean?" came a shout from the crowd. "Find the witch!"

and "Kill the beast" were shouted above the general confusion.

"Please!" Frode shouted. "Please listen! My thaumascans prove that the creature came from another world, which can only mean that somewhere, there is a tear in the veil. Someone has opened a door to another realm."

Torsen banged his staff of office on the floor to quiet the outbursts from the crowd.

"As interesting as this...*story* is, I do not see its relevance to today's proceedings."

Frode flapped his big hands in the air. His face was turning red. "It's relevant because Valkyrie Dana knew about this creature and the attack on the village three weeks ago and did nothing about it!"

More shouting and banging of the staff. I sank to my seat. No one was paying attention to me now.

"Valkyrie Dana is not fit to rule this house, if she ignores such extreme danger to our people!" Frode shouted. He was really worked up now. Dana didn't respond, but her Valkyries were all shouting. I rubbed my eyes. Had I ever felt so tired? I wished I'd consulted with Frode about synchronizing our story. This wasn't the way to win over the council.

Finally, after several tries, Torsen got the room calmed down.

"Is this true, Valkyrie Dana. Did you repress information of this potential threat?"

Dana wasn't looking at him. For a long moment, she studied the grain of the wood table as if it held the secrets of the universe. Then she put both palms on the table and rose with a confident smile.

"Elder Frode has over-exaggerated the ghoul problem," she said. "I have been kept aware of the situation, but I didn't feel it warranted further investigation. I didn't want to alarm the council and cause panic among the general population..." The rest of her words were lost among the shouting.

Torsen pounded his staff furiously. When the crowd refused to calm down, he motioned for the guards to clear the hall. Ten minutes later, the massive doors shut with a slam and the Council of Elders was alone in the great hall.

"Now. Let us proceed with the business at hand," Torsen said. "Valkyrie Kyra, do you wish to claim your rights as Baldyr's heir?"

That was the million dollar question, wasn't it? Did I really want to be queen?

"Please forgive the interruption, Speaker Torsen." Ulf held up several papers. "But I believe the real business at hand is this draug problem. This report came in this morning. We have lost contact with the garrison at Toftir. Had Valkyrie Dana not made the unilateral decision to withhold vital information, I would have understood the seriousness of the report sooner." His icy blue eyes fixed on Dana. I rose before she could respond.

"I have a solution to both these problems. But first, I want to address some issues put forth by Valkyrie Dana. It's true that I left Asgard under less than auspicious terms. But I didn't return only to heal. I didn't know that coming home to Asgard was even possible. I would have come sooner, if for no other reason than to see Grandfather and my mother." I smiled at Mom and she nodded for me to keep going. "My illness was simply the impetus that forced me to find a way. And I did. My only regret is that I was too late to see Grandfather one last time." This at least was the truth.

Torsen leaned in to speak. "But isn't this illness reason enough to keep you from wearing the crown? We just lost our king. Transitioning to a new monarch will cause an upheaval no matter what. This curse that you are afflicted with is fatal, is it not?" He looked at Nut for confirmation. The old healer nodded, and Torsen continued, "Do we want to subject our people to a second transition so soon after losing Baldyr?"

I ground my teeth. I hadn't realized that my illness was common knowledge. Dana had been busy this morning too, filling the council's ears with worst-case scenarios. I might live for decades still, but to the Aesir who lived for centuries, that was a brief term.

I sucked in a breath and reordered my argument. This didn't really change things.

"It's true that my health may fail me at some point, but the Norns don't reveal what's in store for any of us. I might fall off a horse tomorrow. What I do know is that Baldyr didn't want Dana to rule."

Dana's eyes were glassy with anger, but I rushed on before she could interrupt. "Baldyr had no faith in Dana. She has no love in her heart, not for anyone here, not even for Asgard or the gods." There was no point in sugarcoating it.

Dana rose to speak, but I kept going.

"And if any of her Valkyries could be trusted to speak honestly, they would tell you I speak true. Now, I ask you, do you want a queen who rules by fear and intimidation? A queen who is the antithesis of everything Baldyr stood for? A queen who would hide information about the murder of Asgard citizens?"

Nut pushed away from the table and stood. His face was red. "I want a queen who will rule with the authority to keep our borders safe and our merchant guilds from squabbling. Do you have that authority?"

"I have the authority of Baldyr's last will and testament," I snapped.

We both knew that wasn't enough.

Nut glared at me. I'd hoped that he would take my side. He knew of Dana's cruelty better than most, having treated many of my injuries at her hands. More importantly, of all the council members, Nut had the strongest keening sense. If we found that rift, he'd be able to determine its magic signature. So would I, but the council—and the general public—would accept Nut's appraisal before mine.

I glanced at my aunt, but she showed no smugness at having gained an ally.

I squared my shoulders and took a deep breath.

"If you're truly worried about our borders than you should know that Valkyries have been spotted on the shores of Jotunheim near Vanlandia. This is yet another thing Dana has hidden from the council."

"Liar!" Dana shouted.

Torsen banged his staff of office on the floor and called for quiet.

"Do you have proof of these claims?" he asked.

"Freya Disir told me that Aesir ships had been spotted…"

"…never trust a giant!" Arne said. "They are lying bastards!"

Torsen banged his staff once, and Arne sank back in his chair with a grumble.

"The Jotnar have also been victims the draugs," I said. "Along with Captain Ulf's report, this points to a much bigger problem. Perhaps Valkyrie Dana would like to explain why she has done nothing about the draugs roaming our land. Or better yet, how she plans to stop them."

Several people spoke at once. Nut shouted about the absurdity of my accusation. Sten muttered something. Torsen called for quiet. I cared about none of them. Only Dana mattered. Would she rise to the bait?

Dana leaned far over the table as if she wished she could reach my throat.

"How dare you make such an accusation? You who walked in here with no knowledge of our lives or our struggles. How dare you?"

Mason and Heimdall pushed away from the wall. Heimdall looked ready to break something. Mason's stance was tense, a fighter ready to attack or defend. He scanned the room while he decided who his opponent would be.

I met Dana's glare. "I dare because I have it on good authority that these draugs are killing Aesir sheep and cattle and even raiding villages. Children have gone missing from Toftir. A shepherd brought proof of the draug killings to the council! But you sent him away to die!" I scanned each face at the table. Some shook their heads. Others remained defiant. "Somewhere in Asgard, there may be an open door to a world of ghouls. I mean to find it and close it." I turned to my aunt. "Why, Valkyrie Dana? Why would you want to keep the people of Asgard ignorant of such a danger?"

The room fell silent. A sneer flitted across Dana's face and was gone. She filled her lungs and stood straight.

"I will not stand here and be accused of incompetence! Baldyr's last wishes are only that. Wishes. He is not the highest authority. The gods are." She turned so her gaze pinned me to my chair. "Valkyrie Kyra, I challenge you to a duel. To the death. And for the crown. Let the gods decide who shall rule."

Gotcha. I knew her pride could only lead her in this direction.

Several council members shouted their approval or disapproval, including my mother who grabbed my arm as if she could pull me away from the danger.

"I accept," I said, though no one heard me. I raised my voice and laced it with magic so my words echoed in the empty hall.

"I accept Valkyrie Dana's challenge! On one condition…" I turned to Dana. She smiled smugly, no doubt thinking that I wanted a way out of the duel. I didn't. She'd terrorized me for years, but I wasn't a novice Valkyrie anymore. I'd battled a rock troll, a water dragon, a nuckelavee and even vampires. I had more experience with battle than she'd ever had. And I had a few tricks up my sleeve that she wouldn't expect.

I waited for the noise to die down. Then I locked my eyes on Dana's.

"We will fight in a fortnight. But first you and I will work together to find these ghouls and drive them out of Asgard."

I felt Mason's hand on my shoulder. He'd come to stand at my side.

Dana watched me with eyes half-lidded.

Come on, come on! Take the bait.

If she rejected my proposition she'd seem either weak or uncaring about the plight of farmers facing the draugs.

Dana nodded once. "I accept."

CHAPTER

30

ana announced that she would ride for Toftir at first light with a party of twelve Valkyries. She left to get ready. The Council of Elders broke up and the hall slowly emptied.

Sten, Frode, and my mother stayed behind to make plans. Heimdall stayed to glower at me too. I tried to ignore him, but his eyes followed my every move.

"You'll need as many in your party as Dana brings, if not more," my mother said. "I don't trust her not to attack you on the road."

"I'll bring twelve. Any more will make me look weak. Frode will come?" I turned to my cousin, making it a question, and he nodded.

"I'm not much of a fighter, though. You might remember."

"It doesn't matter. We need your expertise. With Mason, that means I need ten more hunters. Sten, can you manage to find them for me? Soldiers who were loyal to Baldyr, if possible."

Sten looked up from a notebook where he'd been taking notes. "Yes, my lady. I have a few names in mind already." He tapped the page with his pen. "Give me two hours and I'll have them muster in the yard outside Lady Natalia's private rooms for your inspection."

I thanked him and turned to Mason. "Will you take care of them?"

He nodded and agreed to meet Sten to inspect our guards. Sten hurried off to make preparations.

"Are you sure you want to do this?" The worry in Mom's eyes made her look more haggard than usual. She remembered the times I'd come home with broken bones after training with Dana.

"She can't hurt me. I promise."

"Maybe not in a fair fight, but don't expect her to be fair."

"I'll watch her back," Mason said.

I wanted to lean against him for support, but the other councillors were still milling about. Heimdall's eyes followed my every move from across the hall.

Kale let out a yip and I turned to find him in a tug-of-war with Jacoby over my sheathed sword. I had set it down when I joined the council table and forgotten about it. Now my apprentice and my self-appointed servant were arguing over which one had the right to carry it. The sword screeched out a gleeful song. It enjoyed being fought over.

Kale's bright green hair was sticking straight up. His nose and mouth were scrunched as he strained to pull the sword from Jacoby. Jacoby bared his teeth, and smoke slipped from his ears.

Oh, no.

"Jacoby!" I called out. "Just let him have it."

Jacoby's fingers released the blade. Kale fell backward in a heap of tangled branch-like limbs. Jacoby faced me. His little furry fists were clenched in rage. He stamped a foot, then scooted out the door before I could stop him.

Kale rose. He hugged the sword to his chest before handing it to me.

"Here, Mistress. I recovered this for you. It is a good deed, yes?"

Heimdall chose that moment to confront me. He pushed away from the wall, heading my way. His eyes were dark as storm clouds.

I took the sword. "A very good deed, Kale. Thank you."

"You should go after him," Mason said, nodding to the door where Jacoby had disappeared.

"I really should." I glanced at the godling bearing down on me, and slipped away before Heimdall rounded the table. I'd have to face him at some point, but I wanted to end this business with Dana first.

The outer hall was cluttered with people, all gossiping about the news from the council chamber. Voices stilled and everyone turned to watch as I ran by. I didn't care.

I found Jacoby outside. He was kicking dirt into dust devils beside one of the castle's magnificent gardens. Poor guy. He looked small and lost. I thought about the time we'd found him in the Nether and how the magic of that place had made him as tiny as a mouse because that's how he'd felt. If Asgard had that kind of magic, he'd be as small as a flea right now.

I sat on the rock wall that surrounded the garden.

"Hey." I reached for him, but he scooted away and continued to kick dirt. His head hung down and his bottom lip stuck out in a pout.

I sighed. "Are you going to tell me what's wrong?"

Kick. Kick.

"I know you're upset that I let Kale take my sword."

Jacoby whirled. His big eyes fixed on me. They were filled with tears.

"I ams Kyra-lady's 'prentice! Not stupids stick man. I holds Kyra-lady's sword! I carries Kyra-lady's pack. I goes…with her everywheres!" His voice broke on the last word and it released a torrent of tears.

There it was. Jacoby finally admitted he was mad because I'd left him on Terra.

He covered his face with his hands. Bony shoulders shook with each sob. At least the deluge of tears had put out the fire and smoke stopped streaming from his ears.

I gathered him in a hug. "I'm sorry."

"Kyra-lady lefts me behind!" he wailed.

I patted his back and could feel ribs under his fur. "I know. I shouldn't have left you. I see that now. I thought you'd be happier there with Mason and Gita. I thought having a home was more important than being with me."

Jacoby untangled himself from my hug and wiped his nose across his furry arm.

"Kyra-lady was wrong."

I smiled. "It happens. More often than you know. But I'm glad you came with Mason. I understand now that my home isn't in Dorion Park or in Asgard. My home is where my family is. And you are that family. You and Mason and Raven. Will you forgive me?"

Jacoby turned his huge eyes on me. They were fringed in damp gray fur like some exotic wildflower. His mouth pursed in a stern frown.

"*I* is Kyra-lady's 'prentice. Not stupid stick man."

"Of course. I only let Kale take my sword because good deeds are important to him. It's kind of like a religion with the yggies. But you will always be my apprentice." I dared to rub behind his ears, and he leaned into my touch. My fingers dug through his bristly overcoat to the soft fur underneath.

"I'm glad we got that sorted," I said, "Because tomorrow we leave on a dangerous mission and I will need my apprentice at his full strength."

"I be's ready!"

Sten found us in the courtyard and came hurrying over with a dozen lists in his arms.

"I think we should have at least two scribes in our company," he said. "Three would be better, but hard to get on short notice."

"Scribes? What for?"

"For transparency." Sten grunted and shifted his notes from one hand to the other. "There can be no doubt about what happens on this trip. The council must have a full accounting. The public too. The scribes will see to that."

I agreed it was a good idea. "I thought we should have representatives from the council there too."

"Oh, we will." Sten nodded absently and made a note. "Frode and I will represent the council."

"Not good enough," I said forcefully enough that Sten raised his eyes from the papers. "Everyone knows that you both support me. We need other, more unbiased representatives. I thought Nut and Ulf could come. They were the most vocal opponents in there. They should see Dana's handiwork up close."

Sten considered. "Hmm. Ulf is a natural choice, as Captain. But Nut? The old man hasn't left the castle grounds in years."

"I know, but you could appeal to his duty as a healer. We might need one if we find the ghouls."

"I'll try, but I can't guarantee anything. Now who among your party will be coming?"

"I comes!" Jacoby popped up between us. "I's 'prentice for Kyra-lady."

"Ah, yes. Well isn't that nice," Sten said. "Any others?"

I couldn't leave Raven and Princess behind. And Kale would follow me whether I wanted him to or not.

I sighed. "We're all coming."

CHAPTER

31

Sleep didn't come easily that night. I spent an hour staring into the small mirror in the guest bedroom in my mother's suite. I could find no signs that I was turning into a crone, but the Golden Apples hadn't rejuvenated me to my former self either. I ran a finger over the crow's feet beside my eyes and sighed. Maybe it was better this way. A woman shouldn't live for almost eighty years with nothing to show for it.

My hand rested on my stomach. I felt a little flutter but couldn't decide if it was Little Bean's first kick or just nerves. Probably nerves.

I put the mirror away. Agonizing over every new wrinkle wasn't productive. The apples wouldn't cure me. They only had to get me through the next few months.

I got into bed and opened a book that was sitting on the side table. It was a retelling of Loki's escapades, written for children. I flipped through the first pages, not really absorbing anything I read. Soon the book lay open in my lap as I stared at nothing on the wall.

Raven and Jacoby had worn themselves out and were already asleep on cots in the next room. I was supposed to be asleep too. I'd need my strength for the long ride to Toftir in the morning. But sleep seemed a long way off.

My mind circled around the events of the past days—Dana's fury and her challenge. Frode's rightful worry over the draugs and a possible tear in the veil. And for some reason, Asha's eyes—dark and secretive—kept floating through my thoughts like she was trying to warn me of…what? I had enough forebodings that I couldn't pick out just one.

I wished Mason were beside me in bed. He was the only one who could talk me off the cliff I was standing on, but he was still out in the yard with Sten, choosing the soldiers who would accompany us to Toftir.

Mom came in carrying a tea tray. She laid it on the bedside table.

"I saw the light under your door and thought you might want something to relax you. Big day tomorrow. You should sleep now."

I sighed, stretched and closed the unread book.

"I am tired. At least my body is. My brain just hasn't caught up."

She handed me a cup and I sipped the tea. It was earthy and fruity with a hint of spice.

"That's good."

Mom smiled. "Drink up and get some sleep."

I let her tuck me in like I was eight years old again.

"I'm glad to be home. I just wish it weren't under such dire circumstances."

Mom brushed the hair from my forehead. Her hand was cool and soft.

"I'm glad you're home too. Everything will work out for the best. You'll see."

I was asleep before she even closed the door behind her.

AND I WOKE in a panic to the sensation of being lifted from the bed. I struggled and tried to scream. A gag muffled my cries. My arms were pinned by a blanket wrapped tightly around me. I couldn't open my eyes. I'd been blindfolded too.

The blanket was hot and smothering. I tried to thrash, but sleep wouldn't leave my limbs and they reacted like sandbags.

I heard muffled speech. My captor wasn't alone. My fuddled mind couldn't make out the words, only that it was a man. Even my keening seemed off, leaving me feeling adrift in the dark.

I must have dozed again, only to be woken by that voice.

Heimdall! It had to be him. Dana would have sent a Valkyrie to do her dirty work. But Heimdall's angry gaze hadn't left me since I arrived at court. He was taking no more chances and had snatched me.

But where was Mason? Why hadn't he been in bed beside me? And my mother?

By the All-father! My blood froze. The only way Heimdall could have kidnapped me from my bed is if he'd killed Mason and my mother to get access.

Now I really did thrash about. I heard a pained grunt as my elbow dug into my captor, but he didn't let go.

I was dumped onto a hard surface—the back of a cart, I realized, as it started to move and I was jostled around.

"She's coming around." I recognized that voice.

"Give her some of this. Quickly."

And that voice too. Confusion replaced my rage.

A pin pricked my arm, and all thought disappeared into darkness.

IT WAS THE smell that alerted me to my surroundings even before the muzziness of the drugs wore off—that mingled scent of earth, stone and drying herbs.

I was in the hedge-witch's cabin.

I struggled to sit up, but something held down my left arm.

"Hold still." Asha's grip was firm on my wrist as she wrapped my forearm in a bandage. My nerve endings came alive again, and I felt the sting of a new wound under the dressing.

"Here now, have some water." She helped me to sit and handed me a mug. My unbandaged hand shook and my fingers felt like rubber bands. I couldn't grip the mug. Asha held it to my lips. I took a sip, without thinking, then spat it back into the cup.

"You drugged me." The words slurred around my thick tongue. Why would Asha kidnap me?

"It's just water."

"The tea…" I remembered the odd spiciness in my tea—tea that my mother had brought me.

"Don't fret. It was nothing that will harm the baby. You're both safe now, but you need water. It will help to clear your head." She offered the mug again. I pushed it away.

"But why?" Panic hammered at my ribcage. Something was very wrong. "Why am I here?"

"I'll let them explain. Just rest now."

Them?

Then I remembered the wagon ride in the night and the voices…

All-father help me. Mason and my mother had been in the wagon with me.

 Had Asha taken Mason too? And my mother? But no. Mason had been the one carrying me. My mother had urged him to drug me.

That couldn't be right. My thoughts were still shadowed and chaotic. Mason would never hurt me, nor would my mother. They were the only two people in all the worlds I could trust.

I flexed my tingling fingers, wishing I had a blade to grip. My sword was somewhere nearby. It was agitated by my state and hummed a strident note.

I had to get out of here. I had to find Mason. Make him explain. I threw off the blanket and felt like a lead weight had been lifted from me. As soon as I stood, the room tilted, and I steadied myself on the sloping ceiling.

"There now. Steady on." Asha hurried over and caught me before I fell. "Shouldn't take things so fast."

"I need to go." I shoved her with both hands, and pain flared up my wounded arm. "I need to find Mason."

"I'm here."

The sound of his voice hit me like an arrow to the heart. I turned and saw him standing in the open doorway. Darkness stretched across the mountains behind him. It was still night, then. His eyes were hidden in shadow, but I keened tension streaming off him like a fog of fear and worry.

"What's going on. Tell me now." My voice rasped with an edge of hysteria.

"Kyra, please understand. We did what had to be done. For you and the baby."

A terrible, murderous feeling crept up my legs and pooled in my stomach. This wasn't real. It couldn't be. A sob hiccuped up my throat. My sword screamed in its sheathe from the wooden table in front of the hearth. I grabbed it and ran for the door. Mason blocked me. I tried to push past him, but my good hand held the scabbard and my left hand burned with pain. I had no energy to shove him, but I tried anyway. He caught my wrists and held them fast.

"Kyra stop! Let me explain."

"No!" I didn't want to hear it. Nothing he said could make it better, and a bitter suspicion back in the depths of my mind was telling me that his words would only make things worse.

"You're safe now. Safe and healthy."

I gripped his shirt in my left hand, not caring that blood bloomed on the bandage. "What did you do?"

He raised his gaze and nodded over my head. I turned and saw a second bed across the room. It was lit by only one candle. I ran over and knelt beside it.

Mom lay on a cot. Her eyes were closed and fluttered as if she were in the midst of a busy dream.

It was my mother…and not.

Her magic pinged me with familiarity, but I recognized her only because I'd seen old school photos of her in the nineteen-eighties, when big hair and jewel tones had been all the rage. Her hair was big now. It lay across the pillow in a swath of chocolate brown. The gray was gone. So were the wrinkles around her eyes and mouth, and her cheeks were flushed as if she contemplated her first kiss.

My mother was a maid again.

"I had to sedate her," Asha said quietly. "The changes came on fast and hard. More so than we expected."

I fondled the bandage on my arm. "You did this. You performed Gunora's rite." The words fell out of me like stones. "You gave the curse to my mother."

Asha nodded slowly. Her eyes were sad, but unrepentant.

My blade was unsheathed before I knew what I was doing. I pointed it at Asha's heart.

"You killed her!"

Asha held her hands wide, not trying to protect herself. "She was dying, sooner than you knew."

"Kyra, it's what she wanted." Mason's hand fell on my shoulder.

"You!" I snarled and turned to threaten him with the tip of my blade. "How could you? I trusted you…" My sword shook. My other hand went to my belly, to take reassurance from the life growing there. "I trusted you and you betrayed me."

Mason nodded. "I did." His voice broke and his eyes pleaded. "You can go home now. To Montreal. Or stay here. The choice is yours. She…your mother… wanted to give you that choice."

"You didn't give me a choice! *You* chose for me!"

His magic was as still as stone.

"Yes, I chose for you and for our child."

I couldn't meet his eyes. I could only see his lips moving, flinging each word like knives at my heart. "I knew you would never agree. And I knew you'd hate me for it. But I'd do it again. Even if you leave me and take my child with you. I'd rather live in a world where you hate me than a world without you."

My sword clattered to the floor.

Mason caught me before my legs gave out. He gathered me into his arms. I sobbed and beat at his chest. I hated him. I loved him. I needed the comfort of his body, but at the same time, I keened the scent of betrayal coming off him like the sweat of fear.

After a moment, I shoved him away.

"Go away. Both of you. Just go away!" I screamed and wiped my tears on my bloody bandage.

I sank to the bed and took my mother's hand in my own. It was bandaged too, no doubt to hide the wound where her blood had mingled with mine in the damning rite that passed my curse on to her.

"Oh, Mom. Why would you do this?" Tears flowed freely down my cheeks now. I let them fall.

Her eyes fluttered and opened. She smiled and I had the strange, errant thought that this is how my father must have seen her when they first met— young, sweet and beautiful. In the shape of her jaw and the color of her eyes, I could glimpse the woman who would become the mother I knew, the one who coaxed me through my homework and drove me to soccer practice and school concerts. The one who let me cry without judgment when I came home with a broken heart. The one who fed me, clothed me and always put my needs first even when her illness left her exhausted.

"I wasn't sure it would work." Her voice quavered. "I'm Valkyrie by blood, but not by training. Gunora's book was adamant that the curse could only be passed on to another Valkyrie."

"The book." I ground my teeth. "I gave that to Asha so she could find a cure."

"And she did."

"This is not a cure!" I waved my bandaged hand at her. "This is just passing the buck."

"It's not." She sat up, moving with grace and fluidity that I hadn't ever seen in her. "The buck stops here. I'll take the curse to my grave."

"But why?"

"Oh, Kyra. Don't cry." She folded me in her arms. She smelled like Mom and she keened like Mom, but it was all wrong.

"I'm going to die. The Golden Apples haven't been able to stave off the cancer for some time now. But don't you see? You gave me one last gift." She cupped my face in her hands and forced me to meet her eyes, to see the love and happiness in them. "I can go knowing that you'll be safe. And if I get to spend a few days between now and then with this sweet ride, that's just a bonus." She ran her hand down her waist and thigh. "I mean, look at me! Brigit Bardot has got nothing on this bod!"

I laughed through my tears. "Brigit Bardot has been gone for years, Mom."

"Oh, who's considered sexy these days?"

"I don't know. You'd have to ask Mason."

"I bet he remembers Brigit Bardot."

"I do," came Mason's voice from behind me. "And she doesn't hold a candle to the Greene women."

"Flatterer." Mom made a shooing motion with her hand. I didn't turn around. I wasn't ready to forgive him. I didn't forgive my mother either, but I wouldn't spend what little time we had left arguing.

Mom squeezed my hand. "Don't blame him. I made him do it."

I shook my head and tears leaked down my cheeks.

"It's true!" Mom tried to sit up. She gripped my hand more fiercely and shook it until I looked at her. "I told him I would do it with or without his help. And he only wanted you to be safe." Her words and the sudden movements brought on a fit of coughing and she fell back against the pillow. I soothed her with nonsensical words until she calmed.

After a sip of water she said, "So what now? Will you stay and take your place as Queen of Asgard as Baldyr intended? Or will you go home to Montreal."

"I don't know yet. There's a lot to think about."

She gripped my hand tightly. "Just be sure you're thinking about yourself and what you want. I shouldn't factor into that decision."

"How can you even say that?"

"I can say it because…becau—" Her mouth hung open and she made a *zzz-zzz-zzz* noise as she tried to get the word out. Then her eyes rolled to white, and she fell back against the mattress as muscles seized. Her fingers curled into claws and jerked against her chest.

"Mom!"

Asha pushed me aside. I sensed panic in her swift movements.

"Do something!" I grabbed for Mom's arm, but Mason pulled me away. Mom's face seemed to melt. Skin slackened and softened. For a brief moment, she was the mother I remembered, then the shift went too far, and she was the ancient crone again—gray-haired with withered lips and skin as creased and fragile as antique paper. One tear crept from the corner of her eye, finding a path through the wrinkles down her cheek.

She shifted again. Maid.

And again. Mother.

Crone.

The shifts came so fast, she had no time to scream, but I keened the painful surges of magic coming off her. So much magic. It was like an acorn bursting its shell, sprouting, clawing for the sky, budding with leaves, then turning brown and dying all in a moment.

Asha laid both hands on Mom's chest and shouted a word—a power word from the old gods. It erupted with magic as she let it loose in the world. I clamped my hands over my ears as the word screamed into existence. Seconds later, I couldn't remember what Asha had actually said. Power words were like that. Only a true adept could capture them and keep them.

Magic pulsed into my mother like the shock from a defibrillator. She bucked on the bed. Her back arched hideously. Then she lay still. Once again, she was young and fair, but pale like a maid wasting away from grief.

Asha slumped at her side. She looked like she'd aged a decade.

"That's all I can do for now," she said. "One more episode like that and I won't be able to stop it."

Mom's chest rose and fell, stopped, then rose again. I watched this frail intake of breath for a minute longer, then fled outside.

The sun was about to rise and the rocky alcove that hid Asha's cabin was washed in pink tones. Birds were busy chirping out their morning agendas. I leaned against the rock face and studied my hand. It was my same work-worn appendage. Not too old, not too young. Without a mirror, I couldn't check my face, but I felt like me again, a bit lighter in my step, a bit less stiff in the joints.

Despite my heavy heart, a great weight had been lifted from me. Little Bean was safe. I didn't have to worry that my womb would suddenly lose its precious cargo.

I could go home.

"I've said my piece and I won't apologize for something that needed to be done." Mason's voice didn't startle me. I'd expected him to follow me. I stared at the mist burning off the hills below.

"If you want me to go," he said. "I will. I won't fight you. But know this, I will be a part of my daughter's life. No matter what."

I didn't answer him. I couldn't answer. How could I say the words that would send him away? But how could I ever look at him again and not think of my mother dying because of me? Because of him.

"What will you do now?" he asked.

"I don't know. Stay and sort out the draug problem, if nothing else." I kept my back to him.

"Then I'll stay and fight too."

I nodded.

I felt him move closer and tensed, thinking he might reach for me. He didn't.

"We should leave soon. The hunting party will be gathering."

"Fine. Let's go." I turned and walked past him, then stopped. "I'm not ready to forgive you. I don't know if I ever will be."

I went inside to say goodbye to my mother.

CHAPTER

32

The journey from Asgard City to the village of Toftir took three days. We rode in the lowlands of the misty Gudsov mountains. Before we left, the council had made us sign a binding pact and sealed it with blood magic. Dana and I would travel to Toftir to pick up the trail and try to discover who was making the draugs or if there really was a tear in the veil. At the end of fourteen days, whether our mission was successful or not, we would duel for the crown of Asgard.

Sten, Nut and Ulf rode with us to make sure the pact's terms were upheld. They brought two scribes to make an accounting of the journey for the council and the general public of Asgard. Frode came along because he was the only one with the knowledge to close a rift, if it came to that.

Dana may have been forced to work with me, but apparently that didn't include any form of communication. She rode with six Valkyries and six soldiers. They kept to themselves on the trail and camped apart from us every night. That was fine with me. I hadn't expected any aunt and niece bonding.

I spent the days of travel worrying about my mother. I'd had no choice but to leave her in Asha's care. The damage was already done and whatever Asha's role had been in the whole affair, I believed she would care for Mom. I'd said my goodbyes before I left because I wasn't sure either of us would live through these next two weeks.

No one with modern surveying equipment—modern by Terran standards—had ever mapped Asgard. There were maps, but they were colorful and varied, showing far-flung villages, rivers and great forests. The seas had krakens and sea-serpents among the waves. Dragons and wolfish monsters lurked in the margins by the forests.

I'd studied several of these fanciful maps before leaving Asgard City, but none could agree on the distance to Toftir. So, I'd sent word to Raol, our ratatosk guide. The other ratatosks in our party were cooks and servants. Raol stood out in his hunting leathers, riding proudly on his chestnut pony. It seemed that Raol was well-known as a guide, and both parties agreed to follow his lead. That was about the only thing we agreed on.

My group consisted of the ten guards plus Ulf, their captain, Sif the kennel master, and Frode. Sten, Nut and their scribes, kept to themselves. As arbitrators they wouldn't be seen as partial to either group.

Mason rode out with me as promised. I was still angry at him—so angry my stomach burned with acid—but a traitorous part of my heart was glad to have him along. I wasn't sure how I felt about that. For now, I decided to ignore my turbulent feelings about Mason.

Raven, Princess and Jacoby came too, of course. At least I could try to manage the mischief they got up to. Kale, to Jacoby's ire, had followed.

The guards had been chosen for their loyalty to Baldyr and for their ability to fight. All were broad-shouldered men with red, blond or gray beards and eyes as blue and cold as the fjords. Watching them, I felt like I'd been transported back a thousand years into the time of Vikings.

During the day, they rode in formation around me. Their hulking bodies covered in thick leather armor blocked my view of the road ahead. At night, Ulf kept them on a tight leash. They made an efficient camp, ate from their rations and slept. That was it. No drinking. No carousing.

On this third night of our journey, Raven and Princess were already curled up together as puppy and pony to share their warmth. The only thing more tiring than spending all day on horseback had to be running along beside the horses and Princess had the added burden of teasing Sif's hounds every chance she got.

I felt stronger than I had just days ago—thanks to Mason and my mother—but pregnancy and a long journey weren't a good combination. I was weary from the days in the saddle.

Dinner was done and my bedroll was calling, but I lingered by the fire's warmth, comforted by the small noises of the soldiers around me. Unlike

Dana who had brought an army of ratatosk servants, we mostly took care of ourselves. Except for Jacoby and Kale, who were currently fighting over which one would roll out my bed. During the day their arguments had ranged from who should tack and untack my horse to which one was faster at filling my canteen.

Frode watched them tussle over my bedroll and said, "Don't you find them exhausting?"

I sighed. "I really do. But it's more exhausting trying to sort them out. Unless things get violent, it's best to leave them alone."

"You should get some sleep," Mason said. I ignored him, and he ignored that I ignored him. This was our new method of communication.

"Do you think we'll make it to Toftir tomorrow?" I addressed my question to Frode because Raol was already asleep. The guide didn't waste energy socializing around the fire.

"Raol says so. But it will be a late arrival."

Laughter rose from the Valkyrie campfire. Dana had clearly relaxed the rules and let her people indulge tonight.

"They'll be regretting that on the morrow," Ulf said.

"Don't you want to join them?" I asked. I still didn't know exactly where Ulf's loyalties lay.

"No. We won't be celebrating until the job is done." He paused and added, "My lady." Then he said his goodnights and rose to retrieve his bedroll from his saddle bags.

The fire had burned low, and I watched it with mesmerized eyes. Shouts of laughter from Dana's camp seemed out of place in the forest. I could see her sitting beside her fire. Anni sat beside her, laughing at something another Valkyrie said. A mug of ale or mead hung from Dana's hand, and she also stared into the flames, ignoring the others. Was she thinking about our pact too? She looked up and through a crack in the darkness, our gazes locked. She raised her mug in a salute.

"If it comes to a fight with the draugs," Mason said in a low voice, "don't turn your back on her. She's going to get her duel with you, no matter what."

His voice startled me, and I spoke before I remembered I was mad at him.

"I'm not planning to fight her. Not here and not back in Asgard. I only need to get Nut to that rift."

226

"Why Nut?"

"Because his keening is at least as good as mine. If Dana made that rift, he'll keen it."

Mason grunted. "Let's hope the old guy makes it that far."

Nut had fallen asleep sitting up, his chin resting against his chest, shoulders rising and falling with each snore. Maybe it had been cruel to insist that the old physician make this trip, but no one would believe me—the half-breed usurper—if I keened Dana's magic at the center of this draug fiasco.

I hunkered down in my coat. The dew was settling and it brought a chill.

Mason turned away and rummaged in his pack. He came back with a large, thin blanket and wrapped it around us both. I tensed.

"I know you're angry," he said, "but two bodies are warmer than one."

I relaxed into the crook of his shoulder. He was warm. He smelled of the road—sweat, dirt and hot stone. It wasn't unpleasant, and I was sure that after days in the saddle, I wasn't a sweet rose either. Those little things didn't matter with Mason. He always saw past my grime to the person underneath. I'd never had to pretend to be girlie and dainty for him.

But we were at a standoff. I couldn't forgive him and he refused to be forgotten. There would never be anyone else like him for me, and unless I could find a way past this knot of betrayal that sat in my chest like a lump of shattered glass, I would lose him.

One by one, Ulf and the other guards lay down to sleep. Mason cleared the ground beside us, and we lay back to back.

"Goodnight," he said.

Goodnight, I answered, but not out loud.

We continued in the shadow of the Gudsov mountain range all the next day, stopping at a shrine to Odin just before dark. The shrine was an old one with a dark pool fed by a spring that was said to originate at Mimir's well—the same well where Odin sacrificed his eye in the search for wisdom. I remembered Kale pointing out another shrine in Utgard that came from Mimir's well, and wondered how many of them were dotted around the two worlds, and if any were real or only stories told by long-dead hero-chasers.

I jumped down from my saddle and shook out my legs while waiting for my turn at the spring. I didn't believe the waters would make me wiser like in the old tales, but they would go a long way to quenching the thirst brought on by a day's travel. Many guards knelt and said a small prayer before taking a drink. I didn't think Odin answered prayers. He wasn't that kind of god. He might have ruled this land once, long ago, but when he went through the mists to Valhalla, he never looked back. Still, I said a silent thank you to him and to Mimir for good measure before I filled my canteen.

Jacoby and Kale burst from the trees, arguing over a burlap sack. Their faces were smeared with red.

"We founds berries, Kyra-lady!" Jacoby held up the sack that was dripping as if it held a severed head. Kale jumped up and tried to grab the bag with his long, twiggy limbs.

"I will give it to the mistress!" he cried.

Jacoby held the bag just out of Kale's reach with a smug smile on his face. Kale's green cheeks flushed even greener. His lips pressed together in a bunch. He lowered his head and rammed Jacoby in the gut. The dervish let out an "oof!" and dropped the bag. As soon as he caught his breath, he tackled Kale. They rolled in the dirt, biting and kicking and screeching like hellions.

"Enough!" I yelled. Dervish and yggie stopped cold. Kale had his hands around Jacoby's neck. Jacoby's teeth were about to sink into Kale's arm. They both looked up, saw the anger on my face, and scrambled to their feet. The bag of berries sat leaking juice into the dust.

"Thank you for the berries." I leaned down and picked up the soggy bag.

"I found the bushes, Mistress," Kale said. Jacoby shot him a black look.

"Thank you *both* for the berries. Now why don't you offer them to the guards."

Jacoby pouted. He wanted me to have them. But Kale only wanted to do my bidding, so he happily jumped up, grabbed the bag and started offering the sweet treat to the guards around the spring.

Dana's troop was already watered and remounted. She steered her horse to walk past me and muttered, "Only a few more days of this charade, and then I'll meet you at the end of my sword, *Valkyrie*." She sneered on the last word. Dana never had felt I was worthy of that title even though I'd passed every test she'd thrown at me. In the end, she would have refused to let me graduate if Baldyr hadn't intervened.

I showed Dana my teeth. She knew enough about predators to know it wasn't a smile. She dug her heels into her mount and rode off.

"Once this draug mystery is cleared up, she won't give you any more leeway," Frode said as he came up beside me.

"I'm not really sure why she agreed to it in the first place."

"Because of Nut. None of the old king's inner circle welcomed Dana. Nut is the only one she might be able to sway to her cause. He's tough but fair. He's waiting for her to show how she'll use her new authority. If she's really been hiding the truth about the draugs, she won't win over the council. She has to come out of this fight not just the winner but the queen."

"And what are my chances of gaining the council's favor?"

Frode fiddled with his horse's stirrup.

"It's okay." I let out a harsh laugh. "You can tell the truth. It's no big secret that I'm no one's favorite."

Frode gave me a sheepish grin. "Well, you've got my vote, for what it's worth. And Sten's too. The others...they'll take some persuading. Hal will do whatever Nut says. So getting Nut to your side is vital. Frida is a quiet one. She was close to Baldyr, but her daughter and granddaughter are Valkyries. She could go either way." Hal and Frida were two elders I knew nothing about. I listened while Frode listed the virtues and vices of every member on the council.

"You know them all well," I said. "Have you ever thought of putting your name in the ring? You are my cousin, after all, you must have some claim to the throne."

"Third cousin," he corrected. "Baldyr's younger sister was my grandmother. But I would make a terrible king. In case you hadn't noticed, I prefer books to court life. People are just too...peoply."

I got that. Give me a nest of cerastes over a tea party any day.

For most of the day, Mason had ridden at the back of the train of guards and ratatosks, he probably thought that if he gave me some space, I'd come around to his viewpoint. Now, he was the last one to fill his canteen at the spring. I was already checking my stirrups and girth when he rode in.

"You won't have much chance to rest," Frode said. "We're already heading out."

"I don't need a rest," Mason said. "Just a drink. How are you?" His eyes bore into mine, asking more than his words implied.

"I'm fine. Better than fine, thanks to you. Isn't that what you want to hear?" I jammed my toes in the stirrup, swung my other leg over the saddle, and kicked my horse forward without giving him a chance to answer.

I brooded the rest of the way to Toftir, about Mason and about this ridiculous challenge with Dana, but talking to Frode had given me an idea. Maybe there was a way for me to go home to Montreal after all this was done.

King Frode. It had a nice ring. At least it gave me something to think about while we rode through the darkening forest.

CHAPTER

33

e rode into Toftir after dark. The village was nothing more than a few dozen buildings at a crossroads with farmsteads farther out. But even a village this size shouldn't have been desolate after the sun went down. No one walked the streets. No lights burned in the windows.

As we passed an inn, I saw the door frame was splintered and the door hung open. The front room was empty and dark. Chairs and tables were toppled and broken.

Market stalls in the village square had goods displayed as if the vendors had just stepped away. Rat eyes shone from the shadows as we disturbed their feasting. I risked letting out my keening and tasted the distinct magic of death.

"They left in a hurry," Ulf said. He motioned for his men to spread out.

I dismounted and tied my horse's reins to a post. "We should check the buildings. Someone might be left to tell us what happened here."

Ulf set the guards to the task. They worked in twos, going from house to house. Dana's soldiers joined them, but the Valkyries hung back, protecting their Freya. Dana made no motion for them to do otherwise. She was going to obey the letter of the pact, but not its spirit.

Well, I wasn't going to stand back and let the others search. I was used to dirty work. I asked Frode to watch Raven and gave stern instructions for my charges to stay put. Jacoby scowled but did as he was told. Good apprentice.

Mason followed me and I didn't stop him. I didn't encourage him either.

We entered a small cottage. Little light penetrated the shuttered windows. Mason rummaged in his magic bag of alchemy tricks and pulled out a gleam.

He shook it and tossed it in the air where it hovered near the ceiling, casting enough light to fill the small cottage.

The main room was sparse but neat. A large table dominated the space with a kitchen and hearth behind it. Mason headed for the kitchen. I peeked behind a curtain to find a king-sized mattress on a bentwood frame. The blankets had been left in a tumble. I imagined an entire family—mother, father, a bunch of kids—all packed together in that one bed, only to be disturbed in their sleep by something frightening enough to make them flee.

"There's blood in here," Mason called from the other room. I let the curtain drop, hiding the bed, and returned to the kitchen.

Mason kneeled by a small back door. Old blood was spattered on the floor and smeared on the wall.

"Where does that lead?" I pointed to the door.

"Garden." His expression was locked down tight. He pushed the door wide. The wind had picked up. It brought the stench of dead and rot mingled with sweet garden scents of basil and thyme.

I stepped outside.

Someone had once cared for this garden. It was walled to keep out rabbits. Vegetables were growing in neat rows, with herbs in pots filling in the unused spaces. The beans had been staked to let the vines climb. Garden tools were leaning against the wall in a corner.

At least it should have been neat and serene. Instead, the bean stakes had fallen. Pots were smashed. The trellis had been torn down. A shovel lay across the mess, its blade coated in dry blood and shaft broken. And everywhere, laying among this mess were body parts.

Parts.

Of bodies.

"Oh, gods." My hand went to my mouth as if that could hold back the bile rising in my throat.

Blood had pooled and dried in black stains on the dirt. The flies were gone for the night, but the stench of rotting meat remained. It was impossible to tell how many people had died here. I spotted a torso under the trellis and a head lay nearby. The toe of my boot nudged a dismembered hand with obvious teeth marks. I jumped back, crashing against Mason's chest. His arms enveloped me.

"Come away." His voice washed against my ear. "There's nothing we can do."

I was choking back hysteria as we ran from the house. I bent and retched into the shadows beside the cottage. Mason rubbed my back as I brought up trail rations. It wasn't the first time he'd nursed me through a bout of nausea.

"I'm okay." I stood up, still feeling queasy. Without a word, he handed me a handkerchief and his canteen. I took both and followed him back to the square.

Ulf and the others had completed the search of the village. I caught his eye and he shook his head. The grim look on his face told me that he'd found similar scenes to ours.

The hounds were restless. They prowled around the market, snapping at shadows. Even the kennel master couldn't settle them down.

I stalked over to Dana. Her Valkyries had huddled at the square's far end. Someone had started a campfire by burning pieces of a farm cart left in the market. They sat around the fire drinking and eating.

"The village is empty," I said as I approached.

Dana smirked. "I knew this mission was a waste of time."

"They're gone because the draugs got them!"

"So *you* say," Anni said. "We should just go home. This is ridiculous."

I pointed to their horses that were tacked and ready to leave.

"We're not going anywhere. There are bodies in the houses. We must find out what happened. And at the very least, we have to give them a decent burial."

"So you say," Anni repeated, this time with a false smile. Another Valkyrie snickered.

I heroically resisted the urge to deck her.

Ulf and Raol joined us.

"Sif says the hounds may be able to track the ghouls back to their lair," Ulf said. "But I won't risk it before sunrise."

"Whatever attacked these folk is long gone," Dana said. "I'm done with this so-called pact."

"Not so long gone, my lady." Raol had that quiet, confident way of speaking that made people listen. "Some of the attacks are days old, but we found at least two cottages with fresh blood. Families that had probably holed up, hoping the draugs would move on. They didn't."

I closed my eyes and tried not to picture those poor families, the last of their village, hiding in the only safe place they knew—their homes—while listening to their neighbors getting picked off, family by family.

"I don't care," Dana said. "I'm not staying another minute." She turned to mount her horse.

Sten's commanding voice stopped her. "If you don't at least attempt to find out where these draugs are coming from, you forfeit your right to challenge Valkyrie Kyra. In that case, Baldyr's testament will stand."

A scribe scribbled notes in a journal beside him.

Dana paused with one foot in the stirrup. Her eyes landed on the scribe, then moved to Sten. He stood straighter, quietly accepting the pure hatred coming from Dana.

She opened her mouth, but I never found out if she was going to give in or rebuke Sten because a snarl from one of Ulf's hounds made us all turn to peer into the darkness.

A horse screamed.

Another horse reared, snapping its loosely tied reins. It ran through the market until a draug leaped on its back. The ghoul sunk teeth into the horse's withers and tore out a hunk of flesh.

And then the market square was overrun by the undead vermin.

"Raven!" I turned and dashed into the confused melee of guards, Valkyries and horses, all running in different directions. I couldn't find Raven or the others.

"Draugs! Draugs!" Someone was yelling hysterically, and then the sound was cut off by a choked scream. All around me was chaos.

We'd come looking for the draugs, but they'd found us.

My sword hummed with anxiety, sensing the coming battle. A squirrel-like creature rushed me. I unsheathed it just in time to skewer it. My gut seized. I'd killed a ratatosk! Then the thatching on a nearby roof caught like a wick, filling the market square with light. I put my foot on the creature I'd killed and pulled the sword.

It wasn't a ratatosk. The filthy, matted fur and over-large, bloody teeth were unmistakable. Someone jostled me as they ran and I fell. My sword thudded on the hard-packed dirt. I scrambled to pick it up. Something snarled and snuffled in the bushes nearby. I whirled and slashed, nearly beheading the draug. Its lifeless body toppled, but another ghoul was right behind it. I lashed out again, and ran, not waiting to see if I'd wounded it.

"Kyra! Here!" Mason's call was a beacon in a raging storm. My guards had barricaded themselves behind a couple of overturned carts. I ran to them and scrambled over the makeshift wall. Mason grabbed my arm and yanked me forward just as a draug leaped for my back. His stone arm bashed in the creature's skull, and its dying scream was lost in the frenzy of shouts and the roar of fires that now raged all around us.

More draugs were pouring into the square. Dozens of them. Hundreds. We had maybe twenty-four fighters, and half of those were already down. Their bodies were backlit against the burning cottages. Ghouls pounced on the fallen, fighting with each other to disembowel and feed.

Sif's hounds were in the middle of the battle. She commanded them from behind another barricade. I watched a hell hound slap a draug out of the air as it leapt, and it broke the ghoul's neck. But like us, the hounds were about to be overwhelmed.

"Raven?" I grabbed Mason's arm. He wiped sooty sweat from his brow and nodded behind him. Raven knelt beside Princess, protected by the guards and the barricade. His face was as white as his forelock. Skinny arms were wrapped around the hound's neck, holding her back from the fight. Her fur was puffed and her eyes wild. I couldn't see Jacoby or Kale, but I had to hope they were hiding somewhere.

"We can't stay here," I shouted to be heard over the screams, the snarls, and the crackle of burning thatch.

"If we run, we're dead," said a guard. I couldn't remember his name and I thought that was a shame. I should know the people I would die with. He was right though. If we ran, we wouldn't even make it out of the village.

"Maybe we can find a better holdout." I looked around. Thatch smoked on the one cottage behind our barricade. We could take refuge there and hope it wouldn't go up in flames. Or we could suffocate in the smoke and give the draugs a feast of cured meat.

No. Our only choice was to fight. I gripped my blade in a hand slick with sweat and made a small prayer to the All-father, asking him to protect me for the sake of my unborn child.

Only a few paces ahead, a dozen draugs mobbed a corpse. It was surreal to watch. They looked so much like cute, fluffy squirrels feasting on a pile of peanuts. They chitted. Fluffy tails snapped. Cute, until you spotted the gore covered muzzles and dagger-sharp claws raking dead flesh.

Two ghouls decided the corpse wasn't enough and turned their attention toward us.

I stood up, making myself a clear target behind the barricade. The draugs leapt. I slashed in a wide arc, hoping to take out both ghouls.

I missed.

Because the draugs twisted in midair and clashed with each other, snarling and ripping out chunks of fur.

What the...?

The pack that had been worrying at the corpse stood on their haunches. Tails twitched. Their squirrelly forearms were pulled back at their sides, and blood dripped from their claws. One draug raised its bloody muzzle to scent the air. Then it whipped around and sunk its fangs into the draug beside it.

"What are they doing?" said the unnamed guard beside me.

"I don't know."

Then I keened the dark magic streaming from Mason. It was black and heavy like the air a moment before a tornado. His arms were stiff and straight before him, the left one gray stone. The veins on his neck stood out. His lips were pressed to white, and his eyes had gone black.

I felt his magic pass over me like an oily fog and shivered.

Here's hoping he can only affect the dead.

His magic blanketed more draugs, and they turned away from their victims to tear into each other. The chittering turned to shrieks as draug tore into draug. Blood sprayed. Fur flew. The undead fell in true death. It was quick and violent until no draugs remained standing.

A pall fell over the square. Smoke billowed around the dead, hiding the worst of the blood. The only sound was the crackle of flames.

I heard someone puking. And someone else crying.

One last draug twitched amid the pile of bodies. Ulf's sword scraped against the cobblestone as he dragged himself from behind the barricade. He raised the blade and plunged it into the ghoul's chest.

Beside me, Mason made a strangled sound and fell over in a faint.

CHAPTER

34

The survivors of our party spent several fearful hours waiting and listening for more draugs. Ulf ordered everyone to stay put until sunrise. From behind his barricade, he ordered both his guards and Dana's to sound off. As names were called out from different hiding spots around the market, it became painfully clear that we'd lost more than half our crew.

Dawn brought the scene at the market square into vivid focus. With no more attacks, we emerged from behind our barricades. Smoke from the burned cottages swirled like mist in the morning sun. Flies descended on the corpses and pools of sticky blood. There were bodies everywhere—Aesir, hounds and ghouls.

I checked on Mason one last time before joining the search for survivors. He was still unconscious.

Sten saw me fussing over him and came to check on us. He lifted one of Mason's eyelids. His eyes were still black as coal.

"Necromancy?" Sten asked. His puckered his lips were almost lost in his dense beard.

I nodded. "He burned out his magic, but he'll be all right." I had to believe that.

"He's done this before?"

I nodded again. I'd seen this effect of his dark magic when we fought the nuckelavee, but I didn't want to divulge all Mason's secrets.

I laid my hand on his chest and felt the slow tolling of his heart and the steady thrum of his magic. He'd be okay. He had to be. We couldn't leave things as they were. A tear leaked from the corner of his eye and I wiped it away, wondering if he was worrying about the same thing.

No. He'd be fine. He just needed rest.

Sten gave Mason a last once-over and frowned. "Necromancy is dangerous magic. Your husband may recover this time, but it will change him. Every time he brings that dark magic to bear, you risk losing him. One way or another."

I closed my eyes and sucked in a ragged breath. "He's not my husband."

I heard Sten sigh. His knees creaked as he rose. "If we had any to spare, I'd set a guard to watch him. Necromancy makes everyone nervous—even hardened soldiers. But we won't worry about that now. Here. I came to show you this."

He handed me a small scrying glass. It looked like a ladies hand-held mirror but with a stubby handle. Sten touched several runes around the rim, and a moving image appeared in the glass.

"The scribes recorded the battle last night," he explained. "It's new technology. Frode would be able to explain it better. But the council has a synchronized glass in the castle. Anything recorded on this glass will appear there too." He grinned and twisted his long beard. "And just to be sure the council doesn't suppress it, I left a third glass with the merchants' guild."

It always amazed me how technomancy evolved on different worlds with different needs. Asgard had no Ley-net, but they'd found a way to communicate over great distances by modifying old-fashioned scrying magic.

I watched last night's battle play out on the small glass. Much of the horror was lost in the dark playback, until the cottages caught fire and lit the scene like a dramatic film. Suddenly, the blood reflected in wet pools under the dying and glistened in the draugs' teeth as they attacked one victim after another. It was brutal, fast and all too real.

When Sten had insisted on bringing the scribes, I'd assumed they would write an account of our journey for posterity and for the council's debriefing. I hadn't counted on their ability to project actual footage from the battle. I could only imagine the reactions back in Asgard. I'd lived through it, but even I watched the tiny, arcane video with panic and dread tingling over my tired muscles.

"That ought to make them pause for reflection back home." Sten's smile was grim.

The recording didn't inspire quiet reflection. There would be all-out panic in Asgard when this was made public.

Sten packed away the glass and moved off to help with the cleanup, leaving me with a churning stomach. I wolfed down a travel cake and some water, trying not to recall the images from the scrying glass. At least the scribe hadn't recorded Mason's part in the massacre. From the footage I'd seen, the draugs seemed to attack each other without provocation. But the question would come up in council.

"Raven! Princess!" I called and they trotted over. Sometime in the night, Raven had shifted to his pony form. In stressful situations, he felt more comfortable with four legs.

"Stay with Mason," I said. "Guard him. Understand? Princess, guard!" The hound cocked her head and lolled her tongue, but then heaved a sigh and lowered her bulky body to rest beside Mason. "Make sure she stays here," I said to Raven. The pony tossed his head.

I told myself I was being extra cautious. Sten was just being kind to warn me about the effects of Mason's magic. But a small niggling doubt wormed its way into my thoughts. The Aesir frowned on all dark magic and necromancy in particular. Dana could use Mason against me. Or worse, she could decide to quietly take out the necromancer herself.

I took a deep calming breath. I was jumpy from a sleepless night after a bloody battle. Still, I was glad to have someone watch over Mason, so I could find Frode and start the real work of this mission—finding the tear in the veil.

The guards from both parties had united under Ulf's command. Some were collecting wood for a funeral pyre. Others picked through the bodies, tossing draugs to one side and laying out our dead.

Dana watched the proceedings with an unpleasant frown, as if this whole situation was a nuisance. Besides her, only four Valkyries survived the night— Captain Anni and three young novices. One of the younger women sat crying over the body of another fallen Valkyrie. Dana glared at me as if all this death was my fault. I turned my back on her and went to help collect the dead.

I found Nut first.

The elder lay on his face by the edge of the square. His hands were stretched above his head, fingers clawing the dirt as if he'd been trying to crawl to safety. His lower back was flayed open. White rib bones poked through the viscera. I placed a hand on his neck, knowing I'd find no pulse, but still feeling the need to try.

"Damn the fickle gods." Frode's curse was just loud enough for me and the gods to hear.

"Help me roll him over," I said. Frode grunted but leaned in to grab Nut's shoulder. Lying on his back, with his wounds hidden, Nut looked almost peaceful.

"Now we have no one to corroborate your keening when we find the rift." Frode's face was pale under the streaks of dirt and sweat plastered his hair to his head. Except for his exceptional height, he looked like a grubby kid. A scared, grubby kid.

"We still have to find it and close it, even if we can't pin the blame where it belongs," I said.

Frode nodded. He absently ran his hands ran down his pant legs as if trying to wipe off the caked-on blood.

"Any claim to the throne will be moot if we fail." He stared into the distance where the trees met the sky. "It's only a matter of time before more draugs come through—draugs and maybe something worse."

"Do you remember anything more that Miro said?" I asked. "Any hint about where the draugs might be coming from?"

Frode shook his head. The shepherd had died after delivering his ill-fated news. We'd planned on relating that news to whatever family he had left in Toftir. That seemed unlikely now. If he'd had any family left in Toftir, they were dead.

"Help me move him?" I indicated Nut's body. Frode grabbed him under the shoulders and I took his feet. We hauled the old physician to the funeral pyre, where another dozen bodies were already burning. Despite the grim task, Ulf had the cleanup well in hand.

"Drop your weapon!" A guard shouted. All heads turned to the sound. At the edge of the market square a guard stood in attack stance with his sword ready to strike. Beside him, the remains of a cottage smoked.

Frode and I ran. Ulf met us there. "What is it?" he asked.

The guard's face was slack and white under the grime. "A kid. I thought it was a draug, but it was just a kid. With a knife. He came at me with a knife. Right through the smoke. I thought it was a draug."

The man was rambling. Constant fear, the need to be on alert and the sleepless night had overcome him. He swung his sword in a dangerous arc as he pointed toward the smoldering ruins. "He came right through the smoke. I thought…I thought…"

I met Ulf's eye and he shook his head.

"Come and sit down, son," he said. "Have some water."

"I thought he was a draug."

"I know. Come on, now." He led the guard back toward the barricade.

"I'm going after the kid," Frode said.

"Right behind you." I had my sword out. Maybe it was just a kid, but I was going to be ready for the worst.

We crept around the burned out cottage and moved deeper into the village. We spied him twice as he dashed around corners. He led us on a chase around the village, until we circled back to where we'd started.

"He's playing with us," Frode said.

"Or he's just scared. Think of what he must have seen in the past weeks. There, look!" The flash of a dirty white shirt set us running again. Frode growled in frustration and put his long legs to good use. He overtook the kid and tackled him in an overgrown garden behind an abandoned cottage.

"I got you!"

"Let me go!" The kid squirmed. Frode screamed as teeth sunk into his arm.

I channeled my best mom voice and shouted, "Stop!" Both grubby faces turned to me in shocked silence. I may have laced my command with a touch of magic.

"Frode, let the boy stand."

Frode untangled his long limbs and stood. The kid sprung up like a weed.

"I'm not a boy!" She snarled and showed me her teeth.

"I see that now. Would you like something to eat?" I held out a travel cake from my pack. It was full of nuts and dried fruit and looked enough like a cookie to entice any wild child.

The girl grabbed the treat and Frode grabbed her collar before she could run away with it. She glowered at him, but hunkered down to eat.

THE GIRL'S NAME was Liva. She was scrawny and dirty with matted blond hair. Her legs and arms were covered with cuts and bruises. She'd been living wild for some time.

Only after bribing her with another travel cake did we get any kind of history from her. She lived with her aunt and uncle. She was ten years old, and had been sent to watch over her sheep when the draugs first attacked. I had a few choice words for people who would send a ten-year-old to protect the sheep at night after some unknown creature had already attacked once, but her aunt and uncle had been gone when she returned. No doubt they were victims of the first draug attack on the village. Despite their poor parenting skills, sending Liva to the fields had probably saved her life.

She didn't seem too upset by their loss. She spoke with little emotion as she ate her way through my rations and emptied my water bottle.

"How have you managed to stay away from the draugs since then?" Frode asked.

Liva shrugged and stuffed her cheeks with cake. "Easy. The monsters mostly come out at night. I hide after dark, and during the day I stay away from Lundr."

"Lundr?" I asked. My Aesir was rusty.

"Literally, the grove." Frode answered. "Probably a sacred wood where the villagers honor Thor or some other god."

"Why do you stay away from Lundr?" I asked the girl.

She drew in her chin and squinted at me. "Cuz that's where the monsters sleep during the day." If she were a Terran kid she would have ended that sentence with "Duh."

Frode caught my eye and nodded. He was thinking the same thing. We'd found the rift.

CHAPTER

35

ana didn't want to ride on to Lundr.

"How far are you going to pursue this folly?" Only her flashing eyes revealed the extent of her emotion. Was that anger? Fear? "I let you drag me this far, but no more—"

"Be silent!" Sten's voice croaked with fatigue but still held authority. "You are bound by your contract. We will find the source of this scourge before it encroaches further into our land. We will find it or die trying. Are you afraid to die, Valkyrie Dana? Are you afraid to face your gods in Valhalla?"

Dana's lips tightened. She leaped onto her horse and pulled on the reins as the beast danced under her sudden weight.

"You're all fools. We'll search for your nonexistent rift and when we don't find it, I can finally kill the usurper." She wheeled the horse around.

"I think she doth protest too much," Frode whispered as we readied our own mounts to ride. I agreed, but with Nut dead, we had little chance of proving it.

I couldn't leave Raven and Princess behind, so I had no choice but to trust Mason's care to two of Ulf's men, the guard suffering from PTSD and another wounded man who probably wouldn't survive the day.

Mason was bleached white under the noon sun. He still hadn't woken up. I could do nothing for him, but leaving him behind grated on my psyche as much as leaving my screaming sword would have.

We were bound, him and I. Bound by shared memories, by the many times we'd fought back-to-back, and by the love we shared for each other and our family.

Did that mean I had to forgive him? I wasn't sure. But it meant staying mad at him was getting harder and harder.

EVEN BEFORE LUNDR came into sight, I keened the deep, old magic of the place. Liva rode with Frode, perched in the saddle before him, directing him to lead us over a pasture to a knoll topped by a clutch of cedar trees.

We dismounted in the open field and left the horses with a guard to walk the rest of the way. The sun beat down from right overhead, and despite the heat I was glad that it left few shadows for monsters to hide in.

I told Jacoby to keep Raven and Princess with the guard. He agreed, but scowled when Kale followed me. I couldn't stop him. I had no authority over the yggie.

The ground under my feet hummed with energy. Did anyone else keen the immense magic? I searched the faces around me. I'd need an ally if we found the rift. Ulf and his guards walked with measured, if wary, steps. Only Anni seemed nervous. She walked with her shoulders scrunched around her ears and her eyes darting at every shadow. That didn't mean she keened the magic. For all I knew she could be suffering from post-battle trauma too. Dana would see that as a weakness and would show no mercy to her captain.

"That's it." Liva pointed to the grove of cedars looming before us as if we might have missed them.

"And you're sure you saw the draugs coming from there."

"Of course. Old Ravi wanted to burn it down to stop them, but the others refused." She shrugged. "And then the monsters ate Ravi, so I guess it didn't matter."

The child's callousness bothered me, but it could have been a coping mechanism, so I let it slide.

We approached the trees as if they might erupt with ghouls at any moment. The grove was silent. Even the birds seemed to stay away. I stepped from the sunlight of the pasture into the cool shade between the trees and felt the zing of a ward. It wasn't a protective ward meant to keep people out. It was more of a welcome, as if the grove's spirit was saying hello and reaching out to taste my magic. I shivered at the sensation.

The trees were ancient, their bark gray and shaggy like the fur of an old wolf. The uppermost branches were a deep green with the cedar's peculiar fern-like leaf. And in the center of the grove, shimmering in the air like a soap bubble, was the rift.

It was about two feet in diameter, though its edges were ragged as if it had been torn away from the fabric of the universe. Through this door, mist ebbed and flowed, revealing and hiding a dark world lit by the red of flames.

My keening licked the magic coming through the rift. It was alien and spicy in a way I'd never sensed before, but it was also laced with a familiar magic signature.

Sixteen guards, councilors, scribes and hardened warriors stood riveted by the spectacle of a door to another world. Sif's remaining two hounds prowled around it, growling and pawing at the earth. A guard fell to his knees and babbled a prayer to Odin.

Frode wasted no time. He unpacked the kit he'd brought with him and started assembling the siphon that should—in theory—suck all the magic from the rift and close it.

Sten cleared his throat and stepped forward. "Someone opened this rift." His voice snapped like a whip. "Either our enemies from that alien world, or someone from here. Someone we know and trust." He paused and let that thought settle over the witnesses like cold dew. "Nut came on this mission to be an impartial judge, to discover the truth of this rift's origins. Nut would have known instantly who opened it. He knew the magic of every person in Asgard. He gave his life for this mission. And now, I ask, is there any among you with the courage and the magic sensibility to take on his task?"

His eyes scanned the faces in the grove. Some guards bowed their heads. Dana glared back at him. He didn't bother to include me in his request. He knew I had the keening to do it, but my counsel wouldn't be accepted.

"I can." Anni's voice was fragile in the quiet grove.

"You will not!" Dana reached for her captain, but Ulf put himself between them, his face grim. Two hounds prowled at his feet, their black lips drawn back to reveal dripping canines.

"I am tired of your whining, woman." Ulf's tone was a low growl. His hand resting lightly on the dagger at his belt. "You will not interfere."

Dana glanced at Sten and then at Ulf. I knew what she was thinking. She could probably take Ulf, but not the hounds. She stepped back.

Anni squared her shoulders and approached the rift. It took great courage and self-awareness to disobey her Freya. The gods knew I understood that, and I found new admiration for Anni. Her keening was strong enough to tell her something was off here, and she wouldn't let anyone, not even Dana, stop her from finding its source. I just hoped her courage didn't falter when she learned the truth of the rift's origins.

I spied movement in the trees to my right and turned, fearing to find more draugs, but it was only Jacoby riding on Raven's back, with Princess at their side.

I glowered, but Raven wouldn't meet my eye. Couldn't they listen just this once?

Anni approached the rift with her hands in front of her as if warming them on a fire. They shook as she tested the rift's magic. I sensed that her keening wasn't strong or well-honed, but it was enough.

A sob escaped her lips. Then her whole body began to tremble. Sten stood behind her and put his hands on her shoulders.

Anni had discovered what I had known since I stepped into the grove.

The rift reeked of blood magic. Someone had been sacrificed to open it. I didn't recognize the taste of that blood—some poor anonymous soul Dana had found—but I had no doubt Dana's magic had been the blade that had severed that life and sliced through worlds. The zing of her magic still anchored the rift in place. It was as distinctive as a ward and I would know it anywhere.

Sometime in the last fifteen years, Dana had acquired the power and the arcane knowledge to open a rift to another world. I had no idea how she'd done it or why, but the proof was shining right in front of us for anyone with the keening to see it.

Anni knew it too, but I had no idea what her motives were. She wasn't the impartial judge I'd hoped for.

"Tell me what you sense," Sten urged quietly.

Anni's hands had stopped shaking and she balled them into fists.

She whirled around to face Dana.

"You!" The word burst from her. "You did this! You killed Rina! My sister! You told me she died valiantly, battling the ghouls. But her magic is all over this place! And so is yours! Her blood cries out from the ground where you spilled it! And yours clings to that…that abomination!" She pointed straight-armed at the rift.

A draug burst through from the other world and tackled her.

Anni fell face-first into the dirt. The creature sank its teeth into her leg. We were all so shocked by her outburst, no one moved. The hounds weren't so dazed. They pounced on the draug and tore it to pieces. Sif called them off, but the dogs were in a blood frenzy.

In the commotion, no one noticed Dana had pulled her sword.

While Anni lay screaming and clawing the ground, Dana stepped forward and plunged the blade into her back.

CHAPTER

36

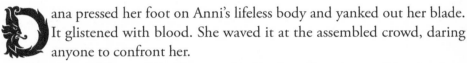ana pressed her foot on Anni's lifeless body and yanked out her blade. It glistened with blood. She waved it at the assembled crowd, daring anyone to confront her.

Sten stepped forward, holding out his hands as if taming a wild animal.

"It won't work, Dana. The council will never ratify your claim to the throne. You don't have Baldyr's approval, and—"

"I haven't had Baldyr's approval since my mongrel sister came home with her mongrel child." Dana's lip curled in a snarl. It was a shocking show of emotion. She pointed her blade at me. "But I don't need Baldyr's approval. I will have something better. I will have the gods' approval." Her snarl turned into a smug smile, and the puzzle pieces clicked into place in my head.

"You're trying to open a door to Valhalla!"

"I will open a door! I just need to find the right location, where the veil opens to the hall of the gods. I thought this was the place." Her gaze lingered on the rift, and I took the moment to shift my weight, putting myself between Dana and Sten. She saw the movement and swung her blade around. Mine came up to meet hers with a clang. I hadn't even meant to do it, but the magic of this place bolstered my sword, and it moved with a will of its own.

Dana bared her teeth over our crossed blades and shoved me. Her hair had come loose from her braid and she wiped it from her sweaty forehead with the back of her wrist.

She was smiling again. This was what she wanted, an excuse to put me in my place—at the end of her blade.

"I thought this grove was finally it. Can't you just feel the magic in the air?"

Of course I could, but I had never shown Dana the extent of my powers, and I wouldn't start now.

"But it's just like the others. Though the rift is more stable."

"Others?" Frode said. His face had gone ashen.

"You opened the rift on Jotunheim," I said. "You almost started a war!"

"We should be at war with the giants! For thousands of years we warred with them! Only Baldyr decided we should let our blood cool. That we should be *civilized*." She spat on the ground. "We are Aesir. Our blood ran in the first Vikings. We are raiders. Warriors. We make war!"

"So you think Odin will sanctify your war?" I was circling her, pulling her attention away from Frode, who was frantically trying to set up the syphon.

"Odin!" She scoffed. "That one-eyed navel gazer. He's probably off composing a new ballad. No. I will have Oor's blessing, and I will rule Asgard with steel!"

I closed my eyes for a moment. Oor, god of rage and frenzy, the one warriors call on to make their blood boil before battle. A much older god than Odin, and one who thrived on chaos.

Frode's syphon flared to life with a roar like distant thunder. Dana whirled.

"Get away from there!" She swung her sword, but before it fell on Frode's neck, it struck my blade. Dana grimaced, pushing down, trying to force me to give way. My arm shook under the strain. I was exhausted from the battles already weighing me down. I'd ridden for weeks, fought ghouls and a life-threatening curse, worried about Mom and Mason and Raven, and all this while pregnant.

It was enough to defeat me without Dana's menacing sword.

Her face, only inches from mine, was red and twisted into a mask of hate. Spittle foamed on her lips as she tried to grind me down. This wasn't the elegant if brutal warfare she'd taught me in the training ring. She wanted to crush me.

And then she'd kill everyone else in the grove. She would leave no witnesses. The rift would remain open and she'd go on making others until she found the door to Valhalla and let the god of war back into the world. Or something worse.

This was how the Flood Wars started on Terra. Arrogance and hate were a fatal combination.

My arms were tiring. I couldn't hold out much longer. I couldn't let go either. She'd take my head off before I could swing my blade around. Dana grinned, seeing my predicament.

"You've always been weak," she said through gritted teeth, "just like Baldyr was weak."

I grinned right back at her.

And I called the trees.

See how weak this is, bitch.

I reached for the clean earthy magic of green growing things and brown burrowing things, but the blood magic hung over the grove like an oil slick and my keening couldn't penetrate it.

I needed more.

I drew deep from my own well. It had to be enough. If I drained my well, I would die, but if I claimed the magic of the land, it would replenish me. If I failed, Dana would kill me anyway, then start a reign of terror in Asgard that would rival the Flood Wars.

I'm sorry, Little Bean. Hold on tight.

I pushed my magic with everything I had. My sword arm dropped an inch. Dana's grin filled my vision. My jaw burned from clenching. The grove went black around the edges.

I…had…nothing…left…

A spark of magic burst inside me, like fire spontaneously lighting in a cold hearth.

And I recognized that flame. I knew it as well as I knew my own magic or Mason's or Jacoby's.

Little Bean.

She understood her Mama was in trouble, and she lent me her fire. More than lent it. She gave it freely.

Our combined magic cut through the dark miasma like morning sun through fog.

And I touched the trees.

Roots exploded from the ground and seized Dana's ankles. She lurched sideways, breaking her crushing hold on me. I fell, landed on my butt, and scrambled away until my back slammed into Frode's syphon.

Dana screamed. She would have fallen but gnarled roots seized her legs and wound around her thighs holding her upright. Smaller roots coiled her wrists, yanking them downward until she was immobilized. Vines wrapped her chest and squeezed. And squeezed.

Her sword tumbled from her grip.

The grove fell silent except for the shrill hum of Frode's contraption. No one spoke. No one moved.

"Release me!" Dana gasped through the crushing grip of the vines.

Ignoring her, I rose on unsteady legs and reclaimed my sword. It was singing for the kill, but it would have to wait. I turned it on the three novice Valkyries who stood frozen like rabbits under a wolf's gaze. None had tried to save Dana. There was hope for them, after all.

"Do you understand what happened here?" I asked. The women looked confused and terrified, but one finally nodded.

"You bested Freya Dana," she said.

"I am not beaten!" Dana shouted.

I nodded to the Valkyries. "I beat her and I can do it again. Any time." They didn't need to know that it had taken everything from me to do it or that I was weak as a lamb until my magic replenished.

"Don't listen to her!" Dana's face was turning red.

"But more importantly," I continued as if she hadn't spoken, "your Freya opened a rift in the veil. She let the draugs into our world. And she sacrificed a Valkyrie to do it. Did you know that?"

The women shook their heads in unison.

"The blood of a Valkyrie was the fuel that opened that rift." I pointed to the shimmering hole in the veil.

One Valkyrie whispered, "Rini!" and clapped a hand to her mouth.

"Rini volunteered to be sacrifice!" Dana shouted. "She believed in our cause!"

I doubted that. Even the Valkyries who followed Dana feared her. That fear was ingrained from years of abuse. Rini might have believed, but she wasn't given a choice. Anni, who now lay face down in the dirt, was the only one who had finally risen above that fear.

"Kill her!" Dana screamed. "Kill her now!"

I pushed the green magic. The vines curled up her throat and gagged her. She thrashed but it did her no good.

I turned back to the Valkyries meeting each one with my gaze.

"Dana's lust for power endangered us all. We were lucky that only draugs came through. The next time she opens a rift, she could call a demon to Asgard." I jabbed the tip of my blade at each Valkyrie. They trembled. Dana's life was forfeit, and they probably believed they would be punished too.

I sighed and lowered my sword. I would not judge them by their proximity to Dana.

I faced my aunt. She watched me in stony silence. I glanced at Sten and he nodded soberly, giving me permission to end this. Beside him, a scribe held up a recording glass. Good. Let the people of Asgard bear witness.

I released the green magic. The vines receded enough to reveal her red face. Dana was panting.

My blade lashed out. Once. Twice. A bloody X bloomed on her cheek. Before she could even flinch, I slashed her other cheek.

The mark of the banished.

"Dana, daughter of Baldyr, I strip you of all your rights. You no longer hold the rank of Freya or Valkyrie. You are no longer a citizen of Asgard. You are dead in the eyes of all Aesir. No one will do commerce with you. No one will speak to you. Until the end of your days, you are a ghost. And when your body finally accepts that you are dead, may the gods have mercy on you."

It was done. Dana could no longer hurt anyone. She would never be let through the gates of Asgard again. She would wander the land, without family and without the Golden Apples to keep her young. She would wither like an autumn leaf and blow away on the wind.

I picked up her sword and handed it to the wide-eyed Valkyries.

I recalled my magic. The roots released her and Dana slumped to her knees. Blood dripped from the cuts on her cheeks. Her hair had come loose and it clung to blood and sweat.

"You can't banish me!" Her eyes had gone manic. Fingers turned into claws as she raked the blood streaming down her cheeks.

No one acknowledged her. She no longer existed. Dana was a ghost.

An animal cry erupted from the ghost and she lunged. Her hunting blade glinted in the sun dappling through the trees as she swung for my neck.

And tripped over something black and furry.

Raven.

Dana fell in a tangle of pony legs. Princess leaped from the shadows and pinned her. Dana had a firm grip on the knife, but she never got the chance to use it.

Princess sank her fangs into Dana's throat and ripped out her life.

"Princess!" I screamed. The hound lifted her head and spat out the hunk of flesh and bone. Her tongue lolled. Her muzzle was coated in dripping gore.

"Arooo?"

Princess wagged her tail.

CHAPTER

37

The shock of witnessing Princess kill so easily froze me to my spot. I'd been treating her like a family pet, but she wasn't. She was a hell hound, bred to guard the gates between worlds and to stop intruders at any cost.

Everyone watching—the guards, the Valkyries, and even the other hounds—watched in horrified silence. Princess whined and gave a playful bow.

I couldn't tell her she was a good dog, though in a dark part of my heart, I knew that she'd just saved us all a lot of pain. She'd done what I couldn't bring myself to do.

I should have ordered Dana's execution for treason. The fact that I'd chosen banishment only proved I was not ready to lead the Aesir, no matter what my grandfather had wanted.

I finally found my voice and said, "Raven, take Princess to the creek to get cleaned up." To his credit, Raven didn't shy away from the hound with blood on her teeth.

The Valkyries were still huddled in a defensive bunch.

"Tell me the truth," I said, "and I'll know if you're lying. Did you know about Dana's plan to open the rift?"

I had no way to spot their lies, but they'd just seen me call up the power of the trees, and I was betting they were wondering what else I could do.

A Valkyrie stood forward. I didn't know her name, which meant she'd been a novice when I left Asgard—still young enough to have worshipped Dana.

"No, Valkyrie Kyra, that is, my lady." She stumbled over her words.

"We knew she had a plan for assuring her claim to the throne, but she only confided the details to Captain Rini."

So maybe Rini had been a willing sacrifice after all. That changed nothing. Dana had been reckless, and she'd endangered the lives of everyone in Asgard and Jotunheim.

"Take her away." I nudged Dana's body with my toe. "Bury her or burn her. Give her what ever rites you see fit. When you go home to Asgard, tell your sister Valkyries what happened here to today. Tell them about Dana's treason. Tell them how Dana's arrogance and stupidity nearly cost us everything. And tell them that I, the mongrel Valkyrie that she so despised, defeated her. If any of your sisters wish to challenge me, I will meet them in the training yard."

I bared my teeth. The Valkyrie swallowed hard and nodded. They scooped up Dana's mangled corpse and left the grove.

I turned to the rest of the group waiting within the trees, and tried to ignore the scribe who stuck his recording device in my face. Sten cleared his throat and the scribe swiveled to catch his words.

"I am satisfied that the criminal responsible for the rift and the draug attacks has been found and punished." He glanced at Ulf, the other senior councillor in the group. Ulf nodded.

Sten motioned to the scribes. "Make copies of those recordings. I want them circulated to all the great houses, in the taverns, in the marketplace, everywhere. Send a copy to King Gillingr in Utgard. I want everyone to see what took place here today."

The scribes nodded and kept filming.

I was a little less enthusiastic about going public. How would the people of Asgard take this news? I had both defeated Dana, and let her go, only to be saved by my hound. Not a particularly heroic ending to our quest.

Sten cleared his throat. "Good. Then Frode, can you close this abomination before more of those beasts come through?"

"Yes. It's all set, and we'd better do it soon. The battery on my syphon won't last."

He crouched before the syphon that looked like a small black granite obelisk set on a tripod. It filled nearly half the rift. Behind it, the air still swirled with red mist, and now I could feel heat coming through from the alien world.

A hellish place populated by hellish creatures.

Frode fiddled with a lever, raising and lowering it. As he did so, I keened magic swell and dip, like the lever was the choke on a mystical engine.

He babbled as he made the final adjustments. "I call it a syphon, but technically, it's an *un*-syphon. That doesn't roll off the tongue though, does it." He tweaked another lever, then tipped the obelisk a touch to the left. "It's working now, getting its bearings so to speak. You see I built in an automatic sensor. It gauges the rift's size and determines just the right amount of energy to pulse into it. This creates a sort of vacuum that collapses on itself and sucks out the magic. Too little pulse and the rift won't close. Too much and…well, that could be catastrophic."

Terrific.

"And you're sure this will work?" I asked.

Frode paused and wiped his filthy face with an even filthier rag. One of his eyes was black and swollen from the fight with the draugs, and the hair on the right side of his head was singed.

"Of course it will work." He shook his head, and I didn't know if I should believe his words or his body language. He smiled ruefully. "In theory it should work."

Theory was all we had.

"Ready?"

I nodded, but inside I was frantically shaking my head.

Frode stood and made a shooing motion with his hands. "You all might want to step away. There could be a backlash."

Raven and Princess had returned from the creek. I put an arm around each one and pulled them behind a tree, beckoning Jacoby and Kale to follow us.

"Here goes!" Frode grabbed the obelisk and spun it. Like a propeller, it started the magical battery, which in turn made the obelisk spin even faster.

Magic surged. I keened its pure, high note. Even the others seemed to sense it. Sif squatted and gathered her hounds. Sten put his hand to his ear as if to block a loud noise. Ulf and several other guards gripped swords at the ready. My hand instinctively went to my belly, but I was starting to realize that Little Bean didn't need my protection from magic.

The obelisk hummed and spun. A light burned in its center and grew until it filled the whole rift.

"Uh-oh," Frode said right before it exploded in a blast of light and granite shards. A full heartbeat later, a sonic boom shook the grove and I hit the dirt.

My ears rang from the explosion and I tasted blood.

When I dared to lift my head again, I saw the rift was still open and now twice its original size. My ears rang. I shouted for Raven and the others to stay down even as I scrambled to my feet,

Frode stared open-mouthed at the ruin of his machine. Small cuts from the shattered syphon scored his face and arms.

"I don't know what happened." He kicked at a red lump of stone that looked unnervingly like a human heart. It pulsed bright orange as his boot knocked it.

"It should have worked. I miscalculated somewhere..." He turned his big, scared eyes on me.

"No time for self pity," I said. "We need another option."

Frode gaped at the swirling red mist through the hole. I grabbed him by both shoulders and shook him.

"Frode focus. How do we fix it?"

"But...what? There's no fixing it." He crouched and cradled the heart stone in his hands. "It's done. I need to start over."

Sten had recovered from the blast and stood beside the rift, armed with a knife "That could take weeks," he said. "And in the mean time...who knows what will come through that gate."

"We'll leave men and hounds to guard it," Ulf said.

But the hounds had scattered. The guards were just coming to their feet, looking shaky. We'd need reinforcements, and soon.

"Frode, how long until you can close it?" I asked.

"I'm not...not sure." Frode's hands were shaking. The blast had done more than break his machine. It had broken his confidence.

Sten and Ulf argued about available resources to guard the rift. I didn't intervene. Even if I was the uncrowned queen, they knew the state of affairs in Asgard better than I did.

Another pulse of light burst from the alien world. Frode grabbed the heart stone and jumped into the rift.

"Frode!" I screamed. "No!"

He stood in the gap, one foot on Asgard soil and one in the alien dimension. He clutched the glowing heart to his chest and mouthed, "Goodbye."

He closed his eyes, and I could feel his magic ramping up. He was going to use his own well as the battery to ignite the syphon. It would kill him, and he knew it.

"Get him out of there!" I shouted, but none of the guards obeyed. No one wanted to go near the rift.

Frode screamed. The hideous face of a draug peeked over his shoulder, its teeth sunk into flesh.

All-father, save us.

Frode hung on. The heart stone pulsed with light between his fingers, then went black. It wasn't going to work. He didn't have enough magic.

"Mistress?" A tiny hand tugged on my shirt. I looked down into the comical yet serious face of Kale. "Will you sing my praises to the great Yggdrasil?"

"What? Why?" I didn't need any more yggie mischief at that moment. But Kale had already slipped away. He glided around the guards, his tiny feet scooting him across the uneven ground until he stood before the rift.

Then he jumped in.

The hundreds of bristles on his body stretched and waved like tentacles. They stretched around Frode's slumped form. Each one latched onto the edge of the rift as if pulling together a tear in fabric.

Frode fell and landed on solid Asgard ground. His shirt was a mess of torn materiel and blood, but no draugs followed him through the rift. Kale held them back. The yggie blossomed until his bushy body filled the hole.

There was no explosion this time. It was a seamless transition. Kale's branches tangled with the rift while his magic weaved a patch over it—like darning the sock on the toe of a god.

At the same time, the little tree-being grew. His feet became roots that burrowed through the ground, anchoring him to the grove. His arms turned into majestic limbs that sprouted more branches. Leaves budded and burst into life. In seconds, the flighty, somewhat annoying Kale that I knew was gone. In his place stood a magnificent ash tree.

The rift was closed.

I lurched forward and put my hands on the ash's trunk. Its bark was rough and warm, and zinging with life. I pushed deeper and keened the faintest whiff of that red, blazing alien world.

"Anything?" Sten asked. He alone among the councillors knew of my keening. Though after today, my secrets would be common knowledge.

"It's a patch, but a solid one."

I patted the tree trunk. Oh, the irony. The yggie's final and greatest good deed had been to become a Life Tree, the one thing he wished for. His spirit would forever rest in the veil between two worlds.

"We should leave a couple of hounds to guard it," Ulf said.

I nodded. That's what hell hounds did. They guarded the doorways between worlds. Somewhere, in my long travels I had forgotten that.

I glanced at Princess, who was rolling in the dirt to dry her wet fur.

Raven saw the speculation in my eyes. "No! You can't have her!" His arms wrapped around the muddy hound. She wasn't just a play thing. She was so much more. What if, one day she hurt someone by mistake in a misguided attempt to protect me? Could I live with that? Maybe I should let her fulfill her destiny just as Kale had.

Raven's hands fisted in her thick mane. Princess cocked her head and licked him up the side of his cheek.

I sighed and turned to Sif.

"Can you round up a pair of hounds to guard the patch?"

CHAPTER

38

ason was awake when we returned to what remained of Toftir Village. The wounded soldier had died during the day. We buried him next to the ashes of the other draug victims. Mason leaned on me heavily as we surveyed the smoking ruins of the village.

Sten approached. His face was pale and dirty under his white beard and his eyes hard.

"I shall have a stone monument erected here," he said. "The story of the foolish Valkyrie who tried to find the gods will be etched onto it, so no one will forget."

And hopefully, no one would ever repeat Dana's folly. But somehow, I doubted it.

Sten nodded thoughtfully and wandered off to prepare the wagons. We were going home.

I held Mason's hand in mine. It was dry as burned paper. A new black spot, like the tattoo of some ancient rune, marked the underside of his wrist. He'd shown it to me but offered no explanation. I needed none. His magic was getting stronger and it was taking a greater toll each time he used it.

We didn't talk about it. Nor did we talk about the other troubles that still separated us. This wasn't the time. Today was a day for mourning the dead and rejoicing in the fact that we were still alive.

Of the two-dozen soldiers and Valkyries who'd ridden out with us, only nine made the trip home. We were dirty, bloody, and heart sore. Frode couldn't stand and rode in a cart with the wounded. So did Mason. He was too weak to stay in the saddle.

Thanks to the scribes, a crowd waited for us at the gates of Asgard. Hundreds of silent faces lined the streets.

We stopped before the gates, unsure of our welcome. Were they angry because of Dana's death? Frightened that more draugs would come?

Someone let out a high pitched whistle. Another voice rose in a cheer. More people took up the call. Then hands were clapping and feet were stomping as we rode by. A child ran up and gave me a flower. The rest of the ride through the city was a blur of smiling faces and cheering voices.

I dismounted in the stable yard next to the castle's main entrance. I wanted nothing more than to check on my mother, have a hot bath and a real meal.

No such luck.

A man dressed in a scribe's uniform rushed up to our group. He conferred with Sten who nodded, glanced my way and beckoned.

I walked over on legs that were still rubbery from so many hours in the saddle.

"Tell me all they want is a good sound bite for the evening news," I said.

Sten scrunched up his face. "I'm not sure what that means, but no, the Council wants to ratify your claim to the throne now."

"Now?" I glanced down at my travel stained clothes. "Can't I get cleaned up first?"

Mason limped up behind me. "She needs rest and food."

Sten held up a hand to stall. "It's not a coronation. Just a promise of a coronation. The people were really stirred up by the images of draugs…"

"And whose fault is that?" Mason growled.

Sten continued as if he hadn't been interrupted, "…and we need to give them something to calm their fears."

"A ratification," I said.

"Yes."

This was it. I had to make the choice whether to stay in Asgard or go home to Montreal.

"Can I at least wash my face first?"

"Of course." Sten waved over a page and gave him instructions to have a room made ready for us, before heading inside.

"And I need to check on my mother!" I shouted after Sten's retreating back. He held up an open hand to signal that he'd heard me, but didn't look back.

By the time I unpacked my horse and patted her velvety nose in thanks for carrying me such a long way, another page arrived and led us to a room near the court where I found water for washing and a simple meal of bread, cheese and fruit laid out.

Princess and Raven were dead on their feet from the long trot back to the city. Princess gobbled down half a wheel of cheese—that would come back to haunt us—and they both curled up in the corner by the hearth. Jacoby joined them and they were soon asleep. For the next few hours at least, all my charges were safe.

I wolfed down a handful of grapes and a piece of bread with cheese, then turned to the wash bowl. A comb had been laid beside it along with a cloth for washing and a towel. I untied my braid, washed my face and combed and re-braided my hair. I could do nothing about my clothes.

Someone had brought in Baldyr's sword, but it didn't feel right to leave mine behind, so I shrugged into my back harness. The smaller blade stuck up a few inches over my shoulder. It was an awkward draw, but I shouldn't need the blade in the council hall.

I glanced in the mirror. I looked every inch the Valkyrie, even if I was on the thin side. The all-day morning sickness had slowed since my visit to Iduna's orchard, but the constant travel had taken its toll. I also looked like myself again. The creases had faded from around my eyes. The line of my jaw had firmed up. I wasn't entirely back to my pre-MMC self, but the disease had finally released its grip on me.

"You know, you have nothing to worry about." Mason stood behind me. His eyes met mine in the mirror. "When you get older, you're still going to be beautiful."

"I guess you must think I'm really vain."

"You?" He scoffed out a laugh. "You're the least vain person I know. But it can be scary to face your mortality all at once."

He was standing so close. I could have leaned back and felt his chest against my back. His hair had grown a little too long and it curled past his ears. His eyes were deep-set and dark. He seemed formidable. Dangerous. The power in his shoulders and his fighter's stance made him seem ready for violence at any moment. It put people off. He knew it, too. Sometimes that was a good impression to cultivate. Other times, I knew it made him feel alone.

But to me, he wasn't fearsome, dark or aloof. He was just Mason. My Mason. And yet, there was still this awful…thing between us.

"I'm going home," he said. "I want you to come with me. But I know you have things to work out first. I won't apologize for what I did, but I am sorry that I hurt you. I'd like to think that we are strong enough together to get past it."

"I…"

I didn't know what to say.

The door opened and Sten rushed in.

"They're waiting. Hurry now."

I stood in front of Baldyr's chair. The elders were arranged in their seats around the great oak table with Yggdrasil carved on its surface. Two chairs were empty—Nut's and my mother's. Asha had sent word. Mom had passed away in the night. I had tucked that news into a small recess in my heart until I could process it.

The elders and all the Aesir who had managed to crowd into the hall were waiting for me to speak, but I just stood there, fiddling with Baldyr's signet ring on my thumb and feeling weighed down by my debt to him.

I thought about Dana and her septic jealousy that went back decades. My mother had been Baldyr's favorite. She reminded him of his beloved third wife, a human woman from Italy that he'd met on one of his few journeys to Terra. His greatest joy had been to welcome my mother and me home to Asgard.

I'd always thought Dana's dislike of me was petty, but maybe she'd had reason. Maybe Baldyr's favoritism blinded him. Would Dana have been a more benevolent leader if he'd shown her the same love as he had to Natalia? Probably not. Dana's bitterness fed a core of spite. Baldyr's affection might have softened her, but it wouldn't have curbed her ambition.

But what if Grandfather's blindspot hid other gems in the family? I glanced at Frode, who sat on the edge of his chair because his back had been flayed by a draug. Despite his wounds, his eyes were lit with joy. He was truly happy for me. How had Baldyr overlooked such a keen asset to the family business? What if the only reason he'd bequeathed me his crown was for love of my mother?

And now she was gone. Baldyr was gone. I had no close family left here.

Mason stood against the wall by the door with his hand on Raven's shoulder. Jacoby and Princess were pressed close to his side. He'd woken them to witness my big moment. Pride shone from his eyes, though I knew what this moment had cost him.

The hushed excitement in the hall faded. The faces of attending Aesir all blurred together. I had eyes only for my family. My true family—the man with the magic of a demon, a pony-boy who might one day be a god, a hell hound and a fire dervish. They stood in a huddle of forced nonchalance. Shoot them in a washed-out sepia tone, and they could be the album cover for some ancient punk band.

Wow. Where had that thought come from? My teen years when I'd favored emo music were a world and nearly a century away.

And that's when it hit me. I'd never fit in with the Aesir or the Valkyries, not because they didn't let me, but because I hadn't wanted to. In my own way, I'd pined for my lost world with its CDs and videos, fast cars and cell phones. I'd always treated my Valkyrie sisters like country bumpkins. I'd never really given the simpler life of Asgard a fair chance. And the irony was that when I finally returned to Montreal, I'd ignored most of those luxuries anyway.

Torsen rose from his chair, impatient for the proceedings to continue.

"Did you hear the question put to you, Valkyrie Kyra?"

"What? Oh. Yes. You asked if Henry Mason and I were married."

"I did. Would you please answer for the council?" The old Speaker of the Council arched his eyebrows. His question had stalled me. It brought up all the other questions that I'd been pushing to the back of my mind for days.

"We are not legally married. But we might as well be. I carry his child."

"I see." Torsen drew out the two words for dramatic effect. He really was a tiresome old man. He sat again and steepled his hands on the table. "It has come to the council's attention that your…ah…partner may be a necromancer. This raises some concerns, as you might imagine. Concerns that we must address before the ratification. We the council feel, ah…"

Oh, just spit it out already.

"…that his…ah…condition warrants further investigation."

Sten sighed with exasperation and rose from his chair.

"If Henry Mason proves to be a necromancer, he cannot be named Consort to the Queen. That's what you mean to say, isn't it?" He glowered at Torsen.

I almost laughed. Consort to the Queen. Mason would love that title.

"In fact, he…ah…would not be allowed to live within the city walls," Torsen said and smiled feebly.

Wow. They'd just made my decision so much easier.

"So, you're saying that my necromantic husband isn't welcome here." I laid my palms on the table and leaned toward the elders, meeting each one with my gaze. "And what about my kelpie son, who might just be a nuckelavee? Is he welcome? And my dervish? You do know that he's made of fire. Is he not welcome either? And while we're at it, do you really want a queen that's more human than Aesir? Or am I just convenient?"

"He's not…that is, ah…you just stated that the necromancer is not technically your husband." Torsen flapped a hand at the corner where Mason stood.

"Oh, please. Just because we don't have an official piece of paper? We're as married as anyone in this room and you know it." The Aesir weren't big on marriage. The most official they got was hand-fasting. But Mason and I were married. I knew it now, just as I knew that Raven was my son and Jacoby was more a little brother than an apprentice. Our family was weak on official ceremony, but strong on love. And no one was going to tell us how or where we could live.

I'd thought I could never trust Mason again, but I did. I trusted him to make the hard decisions for our family, not something I excelled at. And if I looked deep and was truly honest with myself, I had to admit that I would have done the same thing he did. If I could have saved Mason's life, I would have. No matter the cost.

It would take time, but my mother's sacrifice would one day be less like a jagged stone in my heart and more like a soft ember burning with her eternal love.

Mason cleared his throat and leaned in. "If you need that official piece of paper, it's something I plan to rectify as soon as possible." He caught my eye and winked.

"Ah, yes. Well, that still doesn't solve the necromancy problem," Torsen said. "The law states quite clearly that necromancy is forbidden within the walls of Asgard."

"Necromancy, but not necromancers," Frode said.

Torsen shot him a black look. "Semantics not withstanding, this is an issue that needs to be addressed by the council…"

Frode cut him off and started enumerating famous necromancers from Aesir history.

I laid Baldyr's sword on the table. Let them argue the finer points of Asgardian law. The truth was, I could never be Queen of Asgard. It wasn't my crown to take. I pushed the sword across the table to Frode.

"This is for you. It's too big for me anyway."

Frode's one good eye widened. The other was still swollen shut. His mouth hung open in astonishment. I leaned in and gently pushed his chin upward with the tip of my finger.

"Close your mouth," I whispered. "It's not a good look on a king."

I turned my back on the elders and faced the crowd, raising my voice so it could be heard through the hall.

"I renounce my claim on the throne of Asgard." A murmur rose and I rushed on before noise overwhelmed my last words.

"Baldyr chose me because he thought no one else was suited to the task. But he was wrong. My cousin Frode, though young, knows more about the history and law of this land than anyone. And more importantly, he is brave! The scars on his back haven't even healed and here he is doing his duty. He truly has the spirit of a king!"

That was as far as I got before the roar of the crowd overwhelmed me. I turned to leave the dais, but Torsen caught my arm.

"You can't just unilaterally appoint the next monarch like that!" He sputtered and gripped his staff of office like he might like to thump me over the head with it.

I slipped Baldyr's signet ring off my thumb and tucked it into the pocket of his waistcoat with a smile.

"You can try to appoint someone else, but I think you'll find the people of Asgard won't have it. Look."

Frode was already surrounded by a group of well-wishers. He looked bemused as people congratulated him and winced when someone patted his back.

"Have you read any of the stories your scribes sent back? They made him out to be the hero of this epic. And he should be. He listened to a lowly shepherd when no one else would. He found the rift and jumped into it with no thought to his own safety. Without Frode, we'd all have been draug meat within weeks. Make sure the council thinks about that when making their decision."

Torsen's brows drew together as his thoughts played out the possible scenarios for going forward. I left him to it.

Huyn reached Mason's side just as I did.

"Just sailed into town at the right moment, it seems." His smile lit his handsome face, then his expression darkened. "I've seen those scryings. I'll be sure to let Freya Disir know that you took care of things."

"Thank you." I introduced him to Mason. Huyn offered his hand and Mason shook it. They hung on just a little too long, and I could see their knuckles straining as each tried to out-muscle the other.

Oh, no.

"Huyn got us all the way to Utgard," I said, trying to smooth the waters. "We wouldn't have made it without him."

"Thank you for taking care of them," Mason said, though his eyes didn't reflect gratitude.

"You're a lucky man."

"Don't I know it." Mason showed him his teeth.

Huyn gave one more squeeze and untangled his hand from Mason's grip. He faced me and said, "For what it's worth, I think you would have been the best queen this place has seen in a millennium."

"Thank you." I kissed his cheek. He nodded to us both and slipped into the crowd.

"Let's go home," I said. Mason's smile was genuine. He pulled me toward him, and I leaned my forehead on my favorite spot in the middle of his chest.

"It's only a world away. We'll be there in no time." Mason kissed the top of my head.

"Valkyrie Kyra!" The voice boomed like the wrath of gods. I cringed and turned to find Heimdall's big form shoving people out of the way to get to me.

I sucked in a breath.

Mason immediately stepped between me and the looming godling. Heimdall was a direct descendent of the god who created Bifrost. When the gods retired to Valhalla, he took up the mantle of caretaker for the rainbow bridge. Since I'd arrived in Asgard, he'd been trailing me, waiting for his moment to pounce. And I'd run out of places to hide.

CHAPTER

39

Heimdall shoved Mason aside like he was a small unruly child. I keened Mason's magic ramping up. He wasn't the kind of man that would let himself be pushed aside or overlooked. He would protect me at any cost. Princess curled a lip and growled. Her hackles rose like a bristle brush. Jacoby also jumped to my defense with bared teeth.

"All of you stand down!" I said. "Heimdall has every right to punish me."

Heimdall was a full head taller than anyone in the hall and he loomed over me. "Punish you?" His brows furrowed and his ruddy face scrunched up. It was like watching a mountain form. "Why would I want to punish you?"

"Because...because..." I stammered over my words. I was a grown woman, a mother for the gods sake! Yes, he was a big, intimidating guy, but I'd just have to put on my big girl panties and own up.

I stood straighter. "I destroyed Bifrost, and I'm really sorry for it." Those big girl panties were giving me a wedgie. I sniffled and wiped my eyes on my sleeve.

"Aw, come on now. None of that. I hate to see a woman cry." Heimdall fumbled in his pocket for a handkerchief. It was rumpled and dirty, but so was I.

"Come with me," he said. "I've got something to show you. And yes, you can bring your crew with you." He pointed a thumb over his shoulder at Mason and the others. "I can see they won't leave your side anyway."

We left Asgard as we'd come the first time—with little fanfare. Now that

I wasn't being hunted by the Valkyries or sought after by the council, I'd become invisible again. Just the way I liked it.

Outside the city gates, Heimdall led us to the valley where the rainbow bridge had once stood. Along the way, he told me his story.

"I admit I was rather angry when you left."

"No kidding. You chased me for ten kilometers, swearing to take my head off."

Heimdall rubbed his chin. "I might have had too much mead that morning."

When he'd tired of chasing me, he'd slept off the drink and woken to find himself in Terra with no way home.

"Took me five years to find a giant who'd bring me back. I thought about finding you instead, but I knew my beloved Bifrost needed me more."

"I don't understand," I said. "Bifrost is gone."

"Is it? You don't think this is the first time Bifrost has been destroyed, do you?"

We'd come to the cliff where once the elegant bridge had clung to the edge of Asgard. Wind snugged my shirt against me and tore tears from my eyes. Heimdall stood like a boulder against the air currents. His face turned toward the mist that hid Terra from view.

"No, Bifrost has seen many wars. It's been broken and burned before but it always comes back. Look."

He pointed to a ledge about a meter below the lip of the cliff where the rock face fell away into dizzying blackness. I couldn't see the ground. It was a long way down. But there, on the ledge, shimmering like an opal in the sun was a small crystalline structure, little more than a block with two rainbow-hued arms reaching for the sky.

A baby Bifrost.

I crouched to get a better look and Heimdall knelt beside me.

"It took these fifteen years to grow just that much." His face wore a silly grin, like a proud papa. Then he frowned. "But you can make it grow faster. There's a rite. Only the one who destroyed the bridge can reforge it."

I sank back on my ankles.

"My blood, right? You need my blood for the rite." Why was it always about blood?

Heimdall's massive hand covered my knee and he squeezed. "Not blood, Valkyrie. Tears."

I laughed and sniffled. "I have enough of those to spare."

Heimdall grinned and nodded toward the tiny bridge clinging to the cliff.

I lay on my stomach with my head hanging over the edge. Mason's grip on my legs anchored me. I thought of my grandfather and how I wished I'd come home sooner to hug him one last time. I thought of nearly losing Mason to my own stupidity.

I thought of my mother who would never get to hold her granddaughter.

My tears flowed freely and watered the seedling Bifrost.

"This is for you Mom, the bridge between two worlds."

RATATOSK—MESSENGER OF THE GODS

November 5, 2081

I've been away visiting family in Asgard, so please forgive the interruption of the blog. I won't go into details of my trip, only to say that it was more successful than I could have hoped and also more devastating.

One good thing that came out of it was that I met a new friend. His name is Raol, and he's a ratatosk, the only one on Terra as far as I know.

Ratatosks are descendants of the creature known as Ratatoskr.

The old Norse tales don't have much good to say about him. He was a large squirrel who ferried messages between the great eagle atop the world tree, Yggdrasil, and the monster Niohoggr that gnawed on the tree's roots. He was a creature who delighted in malicious gossip and fomenting discord.

If you've ever been scolded by a red squirrel for invading its territory, you can imagine that it's not a big leap to make from squirrel to hateful gossipmonger.

I can't attest to the truth of Ratatoskr's role in the drama that surrounded the world tree. By the time I went to live with the Aesir, the gods had long since retired to Valhalla, leaving Asgard in the hands of godlings. The pathways to Yggdrasil with its sacred wells and fantastic creatures faded into the mists of memory.

I know one thing to be true about Ratatoskr, however. He was a horny bugger. He spawned dozens if not hundreds of children from regular squirrel stock. These children became the ratatosks. They were one rung up from regular squirrels on the ladder of sentience. And like their sire, they made their place in Aesir society as pages, messengers and servants. Today, the city of Asgard would come to a standstill if the ratatosk workforce decided to go on strike.

I had the pleasure recently of making the acquaintance of an unusual ratatosk who was neither courier nor servant. He is a guide. There isn't one forest on Asgard or Jotunheim that he doesn't know intimately.

Unfortunately, in Asgard, few ratatosks seek out other roles in society. The Aesir have no problem accepting a message carried by a squirrel, but not a loaf of bread baked by one. Likewise, the ratatosks are banned from farming or being merchants. Under Aesir law, they cannot own land or businesses.

Though the ratatosks seem content with their lot, I can't help feeling that they deserve more. After spending time with our ratatosk guide, I can attest that these beings are intelligent, creative and nimble. They could be a much more valuable asset to any society, given the chance.

Our guide returned with me to Montreal. I hope he'll find a warm welcome here. And now that he's made his home on Terra, I'm sure he'll become intimately acquainted with the paths of the Inbetween.

That's my two cents on the topic. I hesitate to open comments because I know I'll be blasted with the usual hate, drivel and racism. But, what the heck. Bring it on.

COMMENTS (8)

Don't we have enough trouble with the godling uprising? You want to introduce another new species to the mix? Forget it. Go back where you came from and take your vermin with you.
FromTheForge333 (November 5, 2081)

———•———

That's a big nope. Squirrels are just rats with fluffy tales. You can keep them.
SunnyG45 (November 5, 2081)

———•———

I applaud your concern for an overlooked species. I hope your ratatosk friend finds a warm welcome in his new home, but I fear humans won't be much more open-minded than the Aesir.

cchedgewitch (November 6, 2081)

* • *

What is this? Story hour? You want us to believe that you were on another world. Fake news!

HoaxFinder455 (November 6, 2081)

> Other worlds exist! I've been to Mars, Neverland and Lilliput. The truth is out there.
>
> *Foxyfox27 (November 6, 2081)*

> > Loser
> >
> > *HoaxFinder455 (November 6, 2081)*

> > Ignoramus.
> >
> > *Foxyfox27 (November 6, 2081)*

* • *

Thanks guys, but I'm cutting you off. Comments are closed.

Valkyrie367 (November 6, 2081)

Dear Reader,

Every time I publish a new Valkyrie Bestiary book, I inevitably get emails and social media comments to the effect of "I wish this wasn't the last book in the series!"

I'm here to say that there will be more Valkyrie Bestiary books to come! *Ghouls Don't Scamper* wraps up a 3-book story arc about Kyra's extended family that began with *Grimalkins Don't Purr*. However, from the very beginning, I planned 9 books in this series. So there's more Inbetween fun to come.

The next books will bring the focus back to Montreal where Kyra and Mason get caught up in the godling uprising and face off against other, darker villains. Don't miss out on Valkyrie Bestiary news. Be sure to join the reader's group at https://kimmcdougall.com.

In the mean time, check out the new Valkyrie Bestiary holiday novella, *Oh, Come All Ye Dragons*, where Kyra's holiday is interrupted by some old friends (hint, hint: take a look at the blue dragon on the cover).

I want to thank all the readers who have taken the time to send me emails or post reviews of the Valkyrie Bestiary books. When I started my adventure in this series, I knew I had a character I could love in Kyra and that the critters were going to steal the show. Your outpouring of support have been amazing and heartwarming. I'm so glad readers love Kyra, Jacoby, Hunter and all the rest as much as I do.

You probably know that authors love reviews, but do you know why? Reviews are important because they help other readers know what to expect from the book, they let me know how my books are received by readers, and they help booksellers decide which books to show to new readers.

If you enjoyed this book I would be grateful for your honest review. It can be as short as you like. Even a few positive words will go a long way. And I'll try to make it as painless as possible. Visit the review page on my site at https://kimmcdougall.com/review-ghouls-dont-scamper to leave a review on Amazon or your favorite review site.

Thank you for reading *Ghouls Don't Scamper* and I hope to see you in the Inbetween again soon!

Kim McDougall

There's more Valkyrie Bestiary to come!

This story may be over, but Valkyrie Bestiary isn't done yet! Don't miss out on the latest new releases and other writing news. Join the VB Reader's Group at https://kimmcdougall.com/contact.

Want to find out more about Kyra's world?

- Learn more about the Valkyrie Bestiary series and other books by Kim McDougall at https://kimmcdougall.com.

- Poke around at Kyra's blog at http://valkyriebestiary.com.

- Find all the Valkyrie Bestiary books (including prequels and novellas) along with deleted scenes and series FAQ at https://kimmcdougall.com/valkyrie-bestiary.

- Buy Valkyrie Bestiary merchandize on Redbubble.com.

Other places you can follow Kim McDougall Books:

- Facebook: https://www.facebook.com/KimMcDougallBooks

- Twitter: @KimMcDBooks

- Instagram: https://www.instagram.com/kimmcdougallbook

- Amazon: https://www.amazon.com/-/e/B002C7CI2M

- Bookbub: https://www.bookbub.com/authors/kim-mcdougall

- Goodreads: https://www.goodreads.com/author/show/1432797.Kim_McDougall

Oh, Come All Ye Dragons

A Valkyrie Bestiary Holiday Tale

The Inbetween is full of magic, monsters and marauders. But it's also full of booty, if you know where to look. And Between the Green Reclamation Services knows just where to find those resources that are so scarce and valuable in the post-Flood-War era.

But when dragons nest on a valuable copper reclamation site, who do they call? Kyra Greene. No pest too large or too small.

Now Kyra must leave home days before her baby's first Christmas, for a three-day trek into the wilds. Can she convince a stubborn dragon queen to move her nest before BG Reclamation brings in the guns?

Kyra Greene's new adventure into the Inbetween turns into a rollicking girls' weekend away and brings her face to face with some old friends even as she comes out of her comfort zone to make new ones.

Excerpt from Oh, Come All Ye Dragons:

December 2082

I was thumbing through recipes for gingerbread cookies, pumping milk, cooking sweet potato mash for the baby, and thinking of a dozen other tasks that needed doing, when out on the lawn there arose such a clatter. I dropped my widget on the table, tore open the shutters and threw up the sash. The moon on the breast of the new-fallen snow…

Oh, screw it. My new ward was fighting with the goblin twins.

Again.

There was no moon. Only blood on the mangled snow along with hats, gloves and boots flung off by three tussling boys.

I sucked in a deep breath to yell at them, and the milk bottles harnessed to my chest by the pumping machine clanged together. I wasn't dressed for outside eyes. My nursing blouse barely covered me.

I leaned my forehead against the cool window. My head hurt. My boobs hurt. I hadn't showered in days. Christmas seemed more like work-work-work, than ho-ho-ho this year.

I knew I had only myself to blame, but that didn't make things easier. I wanted everything to be perfect. Baby's first Christmas only came once. At six months old, Holly wouldn't remember it, but I would.

I threw a sweatshirt over myself, harness and all, then flung open the back door.

"Raven! Get inside and finish your homework! " I yelled in my best mom voice.

Three startled faces looked up. They were red from the cold. Tums's nose was bleeding. "Tums, Tad, get cleaned up and find your sister. She'll expect a good reason for fighting. Again!"

I slammed the door making sleigh bells on the wreath jingle. Oh, what fun it is.

Oh, Come All Ye Dragons is now available at https://kimmcdougall.com/oh-come-all-ye-dragons.

About the Author

If Kim McDougall could have one magical superpower, it would be to talk to animals. Or maybe to shift into animal form. Definitely, fantastical critters and magic often feature in her stories. So until she can change into a griffin and fly away, she writes dark paranormal action and romance tales, from her home in Central Ontario.

Visit Kim Online at KimMcDougall.com.

Made in United States
Orlando, FL
12 March 2023

30968991R00168